A. J.

the INNER LANDS
LANDS
SOMETHING STIRS

 SELF-PUBLISHING

@iamselfpub
www.iamselfpublishing.com

Speak up, love, please don't fear to
Speak up, I cannot hear you
Cry out with all your voices
Loud enough to wake the dead
Loud enough for all to finally hear

FOREWORD BY THE AUTHOR

If I could tell you what a struggle this first book has been to write. If I could put into words some of the periods of my life. The heartache, the frustration, the suffering. The perseverance.

But I can't. And that's why I write. I express myself through plot and characters, through their bravery and love. Perseverance is the key. I always knew I would do it, because I never gave up. Not when illness struck. Not when jobs were lost. Not when other people lost faith in me. Never.

The exciting thing is, this is just the start. I have bigger, better plans on the horizon and I look forward to sharing some of them with you in the future.

My sincere thanks to all those who were patient enough to read early excerpts and drafts for me (and provide crucial feedback!), and to fellow authors Marissa Farrar and Edward Nield who were so forthcoming with advice. Special thanks go to my mother, who has always supported my decisions, and must surely be responsible for empowering me with this unwavering sense of self-belief.

I would like to dedicate this book to anyone who has gone through difficulties in life, and with this story remind you that you are not alone, even though it feels like it sometimes. I also dedicate it to Bridget Morgan, a true lover of fantasy fiction, who introduced me to some of the greats and whose generosity has, in part, made this book possible. I wish you could be here to read it.

To all those with a dream, big or small: never give up, no matter how hard life tries to make you. Never give up.

A.J. Austin

CHAPTER 1

Sill cursed quietly as she pricked her finger on the needle she had been using to sew the quilt. Then she glanced over her shoulder, fearful that her father had heard. She knew he was lurking about out there somewhere, waiting for her to make a mistake, waiting for her to fail so he could justify another beating. *I won't fail. Not this time. I'm going to make the best quilt they've ever seen.* To her relief, there was no sound from outside, no heavy footsteps nearing, so she turned back to her work.

The material was old and tough, and in truth well past its prime for sewing. Sill, however, had little choice in the matter as the quilt was intended to celebrate the birth-sun of Fallor, Hillock's wisest Elder and village Leader. Nobody was sure exactly how many winters Fallor had seen – and nobody dared ask – but although it was never very cold in the village of Hillock, Fallor's bones were beginning to feel the chill of old age. Now, with the winter sun once again looming, a warm quilt seemed the ideal gift. Ideal in gesture at least; production was another matter, as Sill had the misfortune of finding out.

The idea had not been Sill's. She was only to make the damned thing. But the various furs of growler, grunter, bear and the occasional feathered patch of phail she had been given were proving an awkward combination.

Sill resented this task. She knew her father had only volunteered her for the job because he thought it would keep her out of trouble. That was typical of him. She couldn't remember the last time she had done anything to warrant being labelled *trouble*. But how he saw her and who she really was were two different things. *Nobody really knows me, not even Raffin. I don't belong here. I want to see things.* There was a whole world out there to see and, right now, Sill wasn't even able to leave the hut. *I have to get away. I just have to.* But in truth, the thought scared her almost more than her father did. She was too young for such a journey and she didn't know the first thing about looking after herself. What she did know was that these were not the thoughts of a normal twelve-year-old, but nothing about Sill was normal.

Two suns had come and gone since she began her current task, and yet it was far from completion. Her back ached from leaning over the quilt, and her buttocks were so numb it was as though they had become a part of the wooden floor. Her fingers and forearms hurt, too, from trying to force the needle through the tough growler-hide. Even more aggravating was that Sill knew this particular fur was only being used due to its worth and rarity, rather than practicality. Growlers seldom intruded upon Hillock's borders these days and Sill suspected this growler had met its end some time ago. *At least it'll be strong*, she mused, and she urged herself to concentrate harder on the task in hand.

The room she was in – her room – was hot. Swelteringly hot. A bead of sweat dripped from her long, brown hair and slid slowly down her forehead, threatening to sting her eyes. Sill sighed and wiped a slim wrist across her brow, mopping up some of the moisture. She closed her eyes for a moment and focussed her mind. Gradually the air around her began to stir. Particles buzzed excitedly as they grew in speed, gently accelerating until the air became a light breeze. Sill concentrated on the breeze, forcing it to swirl around the room until she had dispelled some of the hot air and reduced the room's humidity. This was a trick she usually refrained from doing around the village but in this instance there was really no choice. Besides, she was all alone and her father had told her she was not allowed to leave the hut until she had finished her work, and she could not finish her work in such stifling conditions. *I'm so bored,* she thought and she sighed again and set her mind upon *not* calculating how much longer it would take to complete this tiresome chore.

The village did not own enough growler skin for a whole quilt and could not spare enough grunters – whose texture would have provided a far more suitable fabric – to finish the job. Instead, Sill was faced with the tedious task of sewing all the various parts together in a manner that alluded to intentional design, and not mere extravagance. As fatigue and dizziness began to cloud her young mind, she felt as though the quilt was getting further and further from completion. There was no arrangement of furs that would avoid making the phail-feathers stand out horrifically against the other fabrics, and the thread she had been given kept falling apart as she tried to work it through the thick growler-hide. When the needle once again slipped, scratching painfully along her finger, she cursed and dropped both fabric and needle as the scratch turned from white to red. Frustrated tears began to well in her eyes but she forced them back. Crying would only blur her vision and make the task harder. She did not want to give her father the satisfaction of failure. Nor would she give him another reason to beat her.

Sill froze as the room suddenly darkened. She turned her head just enough to make out her father's thin, tense frame silhouetted in the doorway. She turned quickly back to her work, clenching her teeth against tears and pain, and sewing with feigned enthusiasm until light once again spilled into the room, and she knew he was gone. At his departure, she paused briefly to let a single tear slide down her young cheek and hang from her chin. She watched it fall. Then, as quick as the tear blotched the wooden floor, she regained her self-control, working with renewed vigour as though that single release was enough to heal the bruises of today's pain.

Sill's father was the village cook. Hillock may have been a comparatively small settlement compared to some, but the workload was still too much for him and his poor helpers. The recent shortage of food in the village meant that her father often had to improvise with the meals in order to make the food stretch. This in turn meant that meals were often plain and with little substance. It also meant that Sill's father was almost always angry. The disappointed looks that greeted most of his meals left the man vexed and frustrated. If Sill's mother had been alive she may still have been able to soothe his volatile temper, but since she had died giving birth to Sill some twelve winters ago, Sill would find, more often than not, that she would bear the brunt of her father's bad moods.

Food shortages aside, the men of Hillock were naturally strong and hardy. They had come to be this way through generations working with wood, the main resource supplied by Hillock's forest and also the village's major source of trade. The *serethen* wood was of a quality not found anywhere else in the Inner Lands. It was both light in weight and dense in grain, making it ideal for building homes, furniture, canoes and other such structures. *Serethen* sap was also of value as it cast a bright, long-lasting glow when burned. The villagers used it to create light in the evenings when the sun had exhausted its own daily supply and dropped below the shoulders of the high, neighbouring mountains. Due to the tree's many uses, traders would come from relatively far afield, and in this way the village kept abreast of news from other quarters of the Inner Lands. Sill remembered hearing that a large proportion of Rydan Fort, the Inner Lands's one defensive stronghold, was made up of *serethen* wood, shipped down centuries ago when their ancestors had fled the Grinth to finally establish a home here. Nobody from Rydan had visited for many seasons, though, since the Inner Lands had proved itself to be the sanctity their ancestors had hoped for.

As much as it was a virtue, the forest was also the reason the villagers were reluctant to leave Hillock, and hence they tolerated their plain diet. But the recent shortage of wildlife was beginning to cause great tension, even if nobody wished to speak of it. This tension was compounded when men like Kallem refused to aid the rest of the villagers in their daily duties.

Kallem had been pitied at first. He was only a child when his father and younger sister had been horribly slain by a bear. Kallem had witnessed the event and apparently convinced himself it was the work of a Grinth, the very race that humans fled to the Inner Lands to be rid of. But everybody knew that the Grinth were not built to scale the protective heights of the mountains and none had ever been seen in all the history of the Inner Lands. So, with many winters passed, people had lost patience with Kallem's solitary wanderings in the forest and his cold, detached manner. Most believed him deranged and only now tolerated him as his mother, Artell, was a respected member of Hillock's council of Elders. She rarely spoke of her son and seeing as she had already lost a husband and daughter, nobody had the heart to ask her about her remaining child's unsettling behaviour or lack of responsibility.

Sill's current task, however, could not be shirked. As the quilt was intended for Fallor, Leader of the council of Elders, Sill knew that the eyes of the village would be on her until it was completed. Her father knew this, too. It was not the first time he had set her up to fail. *Except*

I won't fail this time. Savouring this thought, she took a deep breath and once again set herself to the task at hand with renewed and stubborn vigour.

Over the next few days, Sill did little but sew. At one time, when she was giddy from heat and concentration, she finally risked stepping outside for a break only to receive a whack from her father for shirking off which sent her running back to the hut, angry and hurt.

She felt like tearing the quilt up and running away, but she knew that would only lead to a more severe punishment. So, instead, she worked harder to get it finished, even turning away her only friend, Raffin, when he came to share his latest stories. Other children visited, too, but only to tease and call her names from the doorway. Sill had never understood why they hated her so much; at least her father had a reason. Once, one of the Elders had said she was smart for her age, which seemed to annoy them, but Sill suspected the bullying arose more from the fact she often looked a bit scruffy and unclean. *The other girls have mothers to brush their hair*, she thought glumly. *I don't even have a comb.*

At last, by the fall of the fifth sun, the quilt was finished.

Pale with fatigue, Sill sat and stared dumbly at it for a while, too tired to trouble herself to tell anybody.

Eventually, she stood and wobbled to her bed where she collapsed messily on the leaf-filled mattress. The leaves had recently been changed and the mattress felt satisfyingly soft and comfortable under Sill's light body. Outside, the sun had long since withdrawn its aid, dropping earlier each day as though it, too, were suffering a sense of overwhelming tiredness.

Earlier, whilst the sun slowly fell towards its bed behind the mountains, Sill had been forced to work in the saplight. The three small, bright glows, which sat in three corners of the room – the fourth corner being occupied by Sill's bed – now burned quietly towards their own ends, and Sill did not bother rising to put them out. Instead she lay still, gently massaging her aching wrists and wondering what the villagers would make of the quilt. She knew she had done a good job. In fact, she had far exceeded her own expectations. Before she began, she had not thought it possible to sew the different materials together firmly enough to stop them falling to pieces again a few days later. But she had tested and tugged at the quilt upon completion and knew the bonds to be good. She had spread out the skins so that the various browns, blacks, whites and greys mixed successfully and no part stood out too much against another. She'd used the phail-feathers for the rim, which now appeared elegant and decorative alongside the other fabrics, and she had even managed to hide the stitch fairly well within the natural hairs of the different materials.

'Sill.' Her father's gruff voice startled her awake and she automatically sat up and swung her legs around until they dangled freely from the side of the bed. 'Is it finished yet?'

'I think so,' she said, tiredness making her voice weaker and quieter than she had intended.

'What?' he asked angrily. 'Speak up girl for peaks sake!'

Sill cleared her throat. 'I think so,' she said again, louder.

'You think so?' She could already tell by his tone that she'd said the wrong thing. 'You do realise that this quilt is going to be the main gift for Fallor's birth-sun, don't you? And you do know who Fallor is?'

'Yes,' Sill said. *And everyone's going to know I made it. And after that I won't need you anymore.*

'Yes, to which?'

'Both,' she said quickly. Her fatigue must have made her bold because, as she met with her father's cruel eyes, she failed to mask the anger that was lurking deep in the pit of her stomach.

He must have seen it, too, as his teeth suddenly clenched.

Sill swiftly shifted her gaze to the floor instead.

Too late. He marched straight forward and, before she could react, delivered a quick slap across her nearest, exposed thigh.

Sill shrank backwards on the bed, flattening herself against the wall and hugging her legs to her chest. 'What did I do?' she asked, panicking, even though she already knew the answer.

He leaned over her, his muscles tensing, and raised his hand as though to strike her again. 'You know what!' he rasped, his hand curling into a fist. But instead of hitting her he grabbed her wrist and dragged her to the floor, taking care to avoid the space occupied by the quilt.

Struggling against him in fear, Sill failed to control her landing and her right-knee hit painfully into the wood. Rolling over and curling into a defensive ball, she bit her tongue and refused to acknowledge the pain, not wanting him to see she was hurt. It would only make him madder.

He growled and she heard him take a step backwards. 'Why do you make me act like this?' he asked. He always sounded guilty straight after.

I don't know, she thought, hiding her face and the tears streaming down it. *You're my father. We should love each other, shouldn't we?* She missed her mother most at times like this, even though she had never met her. *I know you miss her too.*

'That anger of yours,' he said. 'There's evil in you girl.'

Maybe he was right. What she could do with the wind wasn't normal, she knew that. *I know I killed her. Somehow.*

She heard him leave and finally let herself cry properly, sobbing softly into the tangled hair that lay between her face and the cracks in the floor. Every now and then her body twitched slightly, and she lay there, staring pointlessly at her reddened knee, until the twitching stopped. As soon as she felt able, Sill picked herself up and moved back to the bed. She lay down and let tiredness engulf her.

As she drifted into sleep, various animals began to take shape in her mind. They scuttled this way and that, playing games with her amongst the trees and undergrowth of the forest. Then a great bear appeared and the animals fled, slipping into bushes and through hollowed tree trunks, until they were gone. The bear raised itself tall, standing huge on its hindquarters, and roared out its authority over the quiet forest.

CHAPTER 2

Sill awoke with a jolt. Rolling quickly over, she peered over the side of the bed.

The quilt was still there.

Relieved, she shook herself awake and hopped gingerly out of bed to gaze down at her masterpiece. It lay square in the middle of the wooden floor, just as she had left it. It was morning now, and natural light poured in to illuminate the full glory of the quilt's beauty. *I can't believe I made this.*

She allowed herself a faint smile as she admired her handiwork. It was easily the greatest achievement of her life so far. Fleetingly, she wondered if her father would think so. Then, just as quickly, she dismissed the idea. *I can't afford to think like that.* He had never been impressed by anything she did. As far as she was aware, he hated her, and this was unlikely to change over one quilt. She smiled. *It is a fine quilt, though, and the whole village will know I made it.* Fallor himself was to be the beneficiary. If she could impress Hillock's Leader, that would be gratitude enough. It may even improve her standing in the village.

Sill jumped, as a boy, a little less her own age, burst excitably into the room. She rushed to block his way, fearful his momentum would propel him right onto the finished quilt.

"Sill!" The boy stopped short, caught by surprise, and tipped forwards, arms flailing for support as he struggled to remain upright.

Politely as she could, Sill gave him a small but firm shove in the chest until he regained his balance. He did so and then collapsed theatrically against the door frame, breathing heavily.

'What did you do that for?' Raffin panted, clutching his chest dramatically as he fought for air. Then he saw the quilt and his performance abruptly ended. 'Is that it, then?' He scrambled back to his feet, trying to get a better view.

Sill tried again to block his way but this time he brushed her hand aside.

'Wow, you sure have done a good job,' he said after some scrutiny, although a slight frown still knotted his brow.

Sill smiled, enjoying another small sense of triumph. 'It's strong, too, Raff,' she told her friend.

To her dismay, he bent and started gently tugging at it. Then he stopped and stood up straight, hands on hips.

'You sure have done a good job,' he repeated, distantly. He couldn't seem to take his eyes off the thing.

Sill smiled at her friend's reaction. Raffin had a competitiveness that often made him critical. On this occasion, however, it seemed he really couldn't find anything worth criticising.

'So,' Raffin said, 'you free to come out, then?' He continued to survey the quilt as though it may contain some hidden secret he had not yet discovered.

'Come out where?' Sill asked, hesitantly. *Will he mind if I go outside, now that I've finshed?* 'I should probably go ask,' she said, more to herself than her friend, although at her words Raffin's face miraculously changed to a portrait of pure disappointment.

'There's traders coming from Anell!' he said, immediately perking up again as he remembered the purpose of his visit. 'I bugged Telfor until he said we could go along. There's talk they may have some bear meat! There'll be a feast tonight if it's true. Maybe they'll give old Fallor your quilt? You wanna come?'

Typical, Sill thought. She could have done with a fresh bear hide several days ago. Rather than dampen Raffin's mood, she asked, 'It's not his birth-sun yet? Is it?'

'I heard no one knows when it is, exactly,' Raffin said, 'not even Fallor!'

Sill couldn't help but laugh. Raffin's company always cheered her up.

Eventually, she decided, with some scarcely needed encouragement from her friend, that she'd best not ask her father's permission if she were to accompany him on the trade. As Raffin pointed out, it was probably safer to assume one of the other villagers would tell him; there were several around, and that way he would most likely pretend it was his idea to let her go. *Either way, he'll find a reason to hit me. May as well enjoy myself while I can.*

As the two friends began the shallow descent from Hillock's north side, Sill laughed as Raffin perfectly mimicked the slightly nervous voice her father assumed when he was forced to talk about her. She nudged him with her elbow and began to run happily towards the bottom of the slope where a small group of people were gathered, evidently preparing to leave for the trade.

'Hey, wait up!' Raffin called after her as he joined in the race.

Sill sensed he would gain on her, but resisted using the wind to slow him. Even Raffin could not know about her power. *No one can ever know, or they'll know what I did to my mother.*

She heard a voice comment from somewhere that they should behave themselves if they were going on the trade or they would embarrass the village. Involuntarily, she dismissed her negative thoughts and giggled, then turned to see that Raffin was also suppressing a smile as he struggled to catch her. He overtook her as they reached the bottom of the hill, and they both collapsed to the ground, striving to catch their breath between small fits of laughter.

A tall, unimpressed man strode over and promptly instructed them to get up and start acting sensibly.

Raffin got to his feet, his face instantly blending into seriousness. 'Sorry, Telfor.' Her friend clearly knew how to handle this villager. 'Just excited by the trade is all,' he said, dusting himself down. Sill stood and did her best to look suitably ashamed, which wasn't hard, given the circumstances. The other villagers were not like her father. Most of the adults were kind and light-hearted, so she did not feel afraid, despite Telfor's grumpy demeanour.

Telfor's eyes narrowed slightly as he regarded the pair. 'So I see, young Raffin,' he replied, no more impressed. 'Well, as long as you behave yourselves once we're there?'

'Oh of course!' Raffin mustered all the sincerity he could manage. 'We don't want to embarrass the village or anything, Telfor.'

The tall man's brow tightened further as he searched Raffin's face. After a moment he tutted and walked away, returning to help the others with their preparations.

Raffin let out a quiet breath and then flashed a sly smile in Sill's direction. 'Don't worry,' he whispered. 'He's harmless really.'

As they moved to join the others, Sill wondered how it was that Raffin seemed to know all of Hillock's villagers by name and she didn't. *Father doesn't like me mixing with other people. He won't like this at all.* But it was too late to change her mind now. Raffin deserved better from her.

Besides themselves there were only four others embarking on the trade. This included the moody-looking man Raffin had addressed as Telfor; a huge

– both in height and shoulder-width – bulk of a man named Brorn, whom Sill did at least know by sight (you could hardly miss him); and two others, Trew and Hiddelle, whom Sill assumed were a couple by the way they joked and flirted together as they went about their business. Hiddelle was the most impressive female Sill had ever seen. She was tall and muscular for a woman and appeared to have a man's strength, judging by the way she effortlessly eased up her bundle of goods. She was attractive too. Trew looked full of good humour, grinning at Hiddelle as he made a show of lifting his own, larger bundle. The two evidently had a playful rivalry where hard work was concerned.

The giant Brorn, on the other hand, made nothing of the fact that he carried an equally stacked load in the crook of one arm whilst simultaneously balancing several long *serethen* logs on his opposite shoulder. Only Telfor had nothing to carry.

Raffin said that was because his job was overseeing the trade.

Sill wondered, and was surprised at her sudden pride, if the village couldn't have chosen someone friendlier to represent them. *I wonder if Raffin will be a trader when he's older?* She couldn't even begin to imagine a future for herself. *Not here, in Hillock.* Not with her father around.

The Soulslide River where they were to meet the Anell traders was not a long walk, which was fortunate for the village as the river was their only source of both drinking and bathing water. Sill was glad, too, since her knee was still sore from the night before, although she was doing her best to ignore the discomfort.

Hillock itself was named thus for the very reason that the village sat upon a shallow hill. It was situated in the north-west corner of the Inner Lands and was famous for being the first established settlement.

To the west of the village, just before the ascent of the mountains, was the forest with which Hillock's way of life was founded; the *serethen* wood being a source of trade as much as it was the material they used to build their homes and furniture.

To the south were the Barren Plains, thus named, in more recent history, because animal life was scarce where it had once been plentiful. This was one of the reasons, the Elders said, why the village produced less food than it used to.

The east led towards Anell Village, following the path of the Soulslide River; and to the north was the river itself, where Sill and her companions were now headed.

In all directions: beyond the river, the forest, east of Anell and much further south, mountains rose to form a lofty perimeter around the entirety of the Inner Lands. On a clear day they were visible in all directions. Their presence brought comfort and safety to most of the inhabitants of the Inner Lands. To others, they were a constant reminder of their ancestors' plight to flee the human-hating Grinth. Irrespective of one's stance, Hillock itself was thought to be the perfect place to call home, with the exception of the current shortfall in animal life and some of its more colourful characters.

To Sill, it was less a paradise and more a daily hell in which her father beat her and forever blamed her for her mother's death, but that kind of thing seemed to go unnoticed.

As they walked, and as Raffin amused her with tales of his latest shenanigans, Sill took the time to register her surroundings. There was much beauty to behold in and around the village. Here, the land was lush and open. If she looked behind her, she could see the edge of the forest, with its giant trees rising up towards a ceiling of dark green, capped by a light blue sky, smudged by airy, white clouds. Before her the land was almost flat until it rose suddenly and dramatically up into the grey tips of the adjoining Northern Range and Western Range. Sill wondered briefly how different it might be in the Outer Lands, beyond the refuge of the mountains, but she quickly banished the thought from her head. *I shouldn't think about it.* At least that's what Raffin had told her. Legend had it that the Grinth had slaughtered all but those few who had escaped here. Sill knew the thought should terrify her, but in truth it was too far removed. Nobody in her lifetime had even seen one of the creatures and she, like everybody else, preferred to believe that the Grinth had long since died out and perhaps now, beyond the mountains, was a lush paradise just waiting to be rediscovered. She wondered if anybody had even tried to find out what was out there. It seemed to her that people didn't much care, or would rather not know.

As the group drew nearer to the trading point, Sill gazed up at the mountains to her left. She knew one of them, Springwell Peak, was the source of the Soulslide that channelled fresh water down from the summit, right across to Soul's Rest Lake in the east, but she could not recall the names of the others. The solidity of the mountains both reassured and daunted her. She wondered how people had ever managed to scale their enormous heights to reach the sanctity in which they now lived. They looked cold and dangerous with their snowy tips and jagged edges. *I'll never know anyway.*

'What's up with you today?' Raffin's interruption shocked her back to reality.

'Nothing,' she answered, a little unconvincingly.

'What do you mean?'

'You're all...quiet.' Raffin emphasised the word as though disgusted at its very meaning.

'Am I?' she said, still recovering from her daydream.

'Yes. You are.' Raffin confirmed. 'Have you been listening to me at all?'

'I think so,' she faltered, 'I mean, of course!' She didn't share Raffin's knack for pretence.

'Too much time trapped indoors is what it is,' Raffin deduced, looking suitably smug for having done so.

Yes, he's right, she thought. She had spent too many suns inside lately: it was no wonder her mind had learned to drift elsewhere.

'So what do you reckon a rug like yours would fetch at a trade, then?' Raffin asked, changing the subject as casually as he had begun it.

'I don't know,' Sill wondered what grand ideas he was dreaming up now.

'I bet you could get loads for that, considering its worth and all,' he continued, unabashed by her neutral response. 'Not to mention how difficult it must have been to make, huh, Sill?'

The question felt somewhat rhetorical. 'I guess,' she said. Then she added quickly, 'I'm not making another one.' But Raffin was already too preoccupied with his own imagination to pay any attention.

'Maybe we could trade it for a sword!' he exclaimed, suddenly grabbing up a stick from the ground and waving it about as though he were fending off a growler.

Sill couldn't help but laugh at his stupid behaviour and was about to join in until Telfor commented, somewhat tactlessly, that the traders would be very tired after paddling against the current of the Soulslide, and would be in no mood for 'childish games'. At which point Raffin dropped his stick and looked suitably disappointed in himself until Telfor, once again, tutted and walked on ahead.

When the group reached the Soulslide, Sill was amazed to find that a whole host of canoes were lined up along the shore. Only a few looked as though they had seen the water; the rest looked too new, and a large number were unfinished. Some had not yet even begun to take proper shape and still resembled the trees they were crafted from. She wondered why the village needed so many boats when only a handful of people ever travelled to Anell. *Have we started trading something else?* She looked at Raffin but he merely shrugged, presumably uninterested.

Besides the canoes, two men were waiting for them at the river's edge.

The Anell men sat facing the party, their backs resting against the long, slim raft on which they had travelled. One looked very relaxed, his arms draped leisurely over the upturned hull and his legs stretched out before him, evidently enjoying the sun's rays on his tanned, slender body. The other was a stark contrast to his companion. He hugged his knees and sat motionless as a rock, his short, stocky frame condensed further by his posture and giving the impression that upon coming to shore he had simply curled up and turned to stone.

The relaxed man spotted the party and a broad, infectious grin spread across his face. He jumped to his feet and bobbed up and down excitedly on his toes as he waited for the group to come into earshot.

Without using his hands, the rock rose slowly and easily, morphing out of the earth to again become human. He folded his arms as he reached his full, albeit short, height.

'Greetings!' the excited man called cheerfully when the party were near enough to hear.

'Arnak. Broll.' Telfor's demeanour remained as rigid as ever as he nodded first to the cheerful man and then to his stolid companion. 'I trust you have not been waiting long?'

'No, but we would not mind if we had.' The man named Arnak grinned. 'Paddling against the Soulslide is tough work on a hot day, even under a low sun,' he remarked, 'and Broll here badly needs a rest.' He elbowed

Broll playfully in the ribs who did nothing more than raise an unimpressed eyebrow.

His lack of reaction only made Arnak's grin widen as though they had shared some sort of private joke. Arnak swiftly returned his attention to Telfor. 'I see you have some extra help today?' He jerked his head enquiringly towards Sill and Raffin who had remained a respectable distance from the adults.

'Oh, er,' Telfor stammered – he may have hoped the pair would go unnoticed – 'these two wanted to come along.' He waved a dismissive hand in their direction. 'I thought there was no harm in it. They may find the experience useful.'

'Yes, of course.' Arnak's smile suggested that he may have resisted a wittier response.

'Right then,' Telfor said, clapping his hands together assertively and clearly keen to change the subject. 'Shall we begin?'

'Ha!' Arnak pointed at him as though he had been found guilty of a crime. 'Your haste betrays you, Telfor! You wish to know whether or not we bring a bear with us, am I right?'

Telfor's face showed he was not fond of being teased. 'I will not deny there have been hopes among the village,' he said plainly.

Arnak's grin faded for a second as he must have realised the folly of his words.

'Anyway,' Telfor continued, waving away Arnak's apology before he could make it. 'I'm afraid it is you who are betrayed.' He nodded towards the Anell men's canoe. 'Unless my nostrils deceive me, I can smell the beast from here.'

'Ha!' Arnak exclaimed again, this time delighted at the quick comeback. 'Well said, my friend! Indeed you are not deceived.' He motioned to the silent Broll to reveal their goods.

The group watched as Broll almost leisurely turned and slid the long, heavy raft aside, revealing a mighty bear carcass wrapped in cloth. Broll flung open the top covering of the cloth so that all could see the dead bear in its full glory.

Standing next to Sill, Raffin gasped audibly as the bear was revealed.

The others openly voiced their approvals as they moved to take a closer look.

Sill was abhorred – to think that part of her quilt had once belonged to such a beast! It was not the first time she had seen a bear carcass but it was the first time she had seen one so recently killed. She knew growlers were supposed to be more dangerous but she was certain she would rather meet a growler in the wild than one of these. *I wouldn't want to meet any of them,* she thought, losing further faith in her ability to ever leave.

'There were two of them,' Arnak was explaining as he and Broll heaved the carcass up and began to bring it closer to Hillock's own offerings. The large stretcher they had brought to transport the bear had been abandoned, and Hiddelle, Trew and Brorn now swiftly returned to their senses and moved to shift the *serethen* from the stretcher to the Anell men's canoe.

'Don't know where they came from,' Arnak said in a strained voice as they lowered the bear carcass onto the stretcher, '...or where they were going. Must have wandered down from the north, we reckon. Some of the women spotted them whilst washing in the lake.' He laughed. 'Gave them quite a scare, I can tell you. It took all of our hunters to finally corner the pair. They didn't like that.' He raised his eyebrows at Broll and the stocky man nodded his concurrence. 'Anyway,' Arnak concluded. 'We're looking at it as a good omen. Thought it was only right to share it with our neighbours. Looks as though we may be sharing more than just food soon?' he added with a wink.

At this, Telfor seemed to shoot him a warning glance and flicked his head in the direction of the children.

Sill looked at Raffin but he appeared oblivious to the discussion, still staring at the bear. *How does he ever manage to find out so much gossip?* she wondered.

'It is indeed a fine beast,' Telfor said, returning conversation to the matter in hand. 'We thank you for your kindness.' He nodded to both Arnak and Broll.

Sill thought that, despite his words, Telfor did not appear as joyous as the other men about the bear, nor anything else for that matter. Not for the first time, she wondered why the village hadn't sent someone nicer to do their trade.

Luckily, Arnak didn't seem to mind. He smiled in response to Telfor's thanks and nodded towards the stacks of *serethen*. 'And I assume that is Hillock *serethen*?' he asked keenly.

'No less,' Telfor responded, with obvious pride.

'Well, then, we are equally grateful.' Arnak exclaimed. 'I could make a fine raft with this wood.' He strolled over to the stack and stroked a hand along the smooth surface of one of the logs. 'If Anell would allow it,' he added with a sigh.

'We also bring bamboo,' Telfor said, as if to consolidate Arnak. He signalled to Hiddelle who unravelled one of the bundles she had placed down, displaying a pile of bright green bamboo from the forest.

'Aha!' Arnak cried in delight. 'Yes! A good trade indeed.' He beamed his approval at the Hillock group and gestured to Broll to begin moving the goods closer to the canoe.

Sill did not think the things Hillock had traded really matched the bear meat that Anell's traders had given them, but then she remembered that *serethen* wood could not be found anywhere outside of Hillock's forest.

'Well.' Telfor's tone suggested the trade was over. 'We must make haste if we are to keep this fresh,' he said, indicating the bear. 'We will celebrate tonight,' he added.

'As will we, my friend,' Arnak said, approaching him. The tall Anell man grasped Telfor's shoulder firmly. 'I hope this does indeed signify a good omen,' he said softly, levelling his eyes with the Hillock man's.

Telfor straightened himself and returned Arnak's gaze and grasp. 'Yes. And we thank you again for your kindness.'

'Pah!' Arnak exclaimed, releasing Telfor's shoulder and sweeping the air broadly. 'Trade is trade!' He turned on his heels, signalling to Broll that it was time to leave.

Hiddelle quickly gave Broll and Arnak a hand loading their canoe before the three tugged the long vessel down a short slope and into the Soulslide River. The raft slipped smoothly into the flowing water and sat firmly with the new load as Broll held it still for Arnak to hop athletically aboard. Sill noticed that the men talked freely with each other now that the trade was over. They joked and laughed as Broll scrambled up to join Arnak on the raft.

Trew and Brorn meanwhile were testing the weight of the bear in preparation for the walk home. Together, they each gripped an end of the cloth and then hauled the carcass onto the stretcher before hoisting it up between them.

Sill and Raffin, unsure of their place, remained close to Telfor who watched the activities of the other men with an air of silent supervision.

'Well, you two,' he said abruptly to Sill and Raffin, 'I suppose you are now free to behave as you will. May I suggest a wash?'

Sill was mortified when he looked straight at her, even though she knew he was right. After days alone in her humid home, she must smell terrible.

'Come on, Sill!' Raffin yelled, running and then launching himself into the river.

She copied him, hoping the action would spare her any further embarrassment. She gasped as the cold water swallowed her up and then revelled in the silence as she found herself beneath the surface and everything went still. She opened her eyes and found Raffin grinning at her under the water. The sight made her grin too and she forgot to hold her breath, forcing her to erupt quickly back up into the world.

'Refreshing, isn't it?' Arnak grinned from the canoe as she spat out water. He held his hand up, signalling his departure, and then grabbed up an oar and began to paddle away.

Telfor loomed over them from the riverbank. 'Quickly, please,' he said and with that he strode purposefully off, back in the direction of Hillock.

Sill washed as best she could before dragging herself back to land, leaving Raffin to follow. Her clothes were soaked but would soon dry off in the searing sun. *They needed cleaning as much I as did*. She just hoped nobody could see the bruises through the wet fabric.

As they followed Telfor, Hiddelle sprang gleefully past them. She turned to face Sill and Raffin, smiling. 'Will you walk with us, young ones?' she asked cheerfully. 'I think Trew could do with some distraction if he's going to manage this load all the way back to Hillock!'

'You could always take my place,' Trew suggested as he wrestled with the weight of the bear.

Hiddelle gave him an amused grin. 'I wouldn't want to show you up,' she teased, 'besides, Brorn's having no trouble.' She kissed him on the cheek and leapt playfully away before he could retaliate. Trew frowned and then shook his head, perplexed, as the massive Brorn removed one hand briefly from the stretcher to show his strength.

'At least I'm better-looking,' Trew said and the big man rewarded him with a flash of teeth.

Sill and Raffin gladly walked with them as the three continued to taunt each other throughout the journey home. Raffin, as usual, was able to join in, entertaining them with various stories, of various truthfulness, involving some of Hillock's other inhabitants.

Telfor walked alone ahead of the group, forever upright and authoritative.

As they moved, Sill struggled to keep her eyes from the sheer size of the bear and was glad that it remained mostly hidden beneath the cloth. *There really will be a feast tonight,* she thought gladly.

CHAPTER 3

Kallem wandered through the trees. The air was clean and fresh, the bark of the tall *serethen* sweet and fragrant. Birds chattered amongst the treetops, so high up that Kallem rarely saw them, unless they visited to stare at him from exposed roots, or branches of smaller saplings. *Like everybody stares,* Kallem thought, as he gazed up towards the dark-green canopy, looking for movement above. Shafts of light revealed dust, drifting lazily through the air as he drifted through the forest. *Drifting, that's all they think I do. Fools.*

They know nothing. You are the only one who understands. Forget about them, they don't deserve your protection.

I don't care about them.

You don't care about anything, that's what makes you special.

The forest offered him shade from the vicious sun above but that was not why he spent all his time here.

He reached the spot he'd been heading for. *This is where it happened.* There were smaller trees here but no birds dared perch on these branches, like they, too, hadn't forgotten the horror that occurred here, all those years ago. Despite the memories, nothing stirred in him. The villagers treated him like a freak. An unfeeling, uncaring shell of a human, and that's what he'd become. *I am ready, that's all that matters.*

You have been ready for a long time.

Kallem bent to the ground, picked up a handful of earth and smelled it. *Nothing.* The change had been gradual at first, hardly noticeable, but he could not ignore it anymore. *The animals are leaving.*

They can sense it, too, as you can. It won't be long now.

He let the earth fall through his fingers and then paused as he noticed the hawk. The bird was standing in front of him, only ten paces or so from where he knelt. *How long have you been there?*

The hawk's feathers were a speckled brown and blended in well with the dry dirt and dead leaves scattered across the forest floor. He stared at Kallem through bright, yellow eyes.

Kallem stared back. Then he turned his head as he heard a noise coming from behind him. It was the distinctive sound of clumsy footsteps, crushing twigs and leaves without a thought for the stupidity of the approach.

Nobody would hear you coming.

The hawk took off in a brief flurry of wings and then was gone, silently slipping back into whatever part of the forest it had come from.

Kallem stood and turned to see what visitor had dared intrude on his part of the land. His right hand moved instinctively to the red sword at his side, even though he feared nobody.

'I knew I'd find you here,' Marn said as he approached, far too confidently for Kallem's liking. He sounded annoyed, as though he blamed Kallem somehow for his decision to come here. 'What are you doing?' He asked.

Kallem didn't answer. Marn had a stout frame, like many of Hillock's people, but Kallem did not feel threatened by his physique.

'Fine,' Marn growled to his silence. 'Well I'm sure you can guess what I'm doing here. I came to see you, to try to talk some sense into you, although I don't know why I bother.'

Neither do I.

'You know what the village thinks about you, I don't need to tell you that,' Marn continued. 'But this has gone on long enough Kallem, it's time for you to come back, contribute something.'

Kallem looked at him curiously.

This one is persistant. He should mind his own business. You don't owe him anything. You don't owe anyone. He should not be here.

'Well?' Marn said, clearly growing angrier. 'Haven't you got anything to say for yourself?'

'You should go,' Kallem told him.

Marn put his hands to his hips and pursed his lips for a second. He turned as if to leave but then seemed to change his mind. 'Look, Kallem,' he said, as softly as he was able in his gruff voice. 'I still don't understand exactly what happened to you but your father and sister; it was a tragedy, we were all hurt by it.'

Do not mention them.

'But you can't hide forever, you can't keep punishing yourself, it was years ago!'

'Punishing myself? You think that's what I've been doing?' Kallem asked. *I was weak, helpless. All I could do was watch.*

'You were just a boy, Kallem, a child,' Marn was saying, 'but you are not a child anymore. You are a grown man.'

You are not weak anymore, either. You should remind him of that.

'You should go,' Kallem told him again. 'Do not come back here.'

'Don't you dare threaten me!' The warning had only served to make Marn madder. 'Have you forgotton that I was the one who found you? I was the one who brought you back. I've only been trying to help you, but you don't want any help, do you? You just want to hide out here in your little fantasy, instead of facing up to what happened.'

How could I forget? I haven't forgotten anything, Kallem thought, but Marn's words had caused a faint flicker of doubt to pass through his mind. *I was just a child; do I really remember?*

Did you not listen to what he said? This one found you, so he must know the truth. That means he lied. He lied to everyone. Kill him, it's what he deserves. It's what they all deserve.

'Go,' Kallem said, before he acted on the impulse. 'Now.'

'Oh, don't worry,' Marn sneered. 'I'm done with you. But heed my words, Kallem, people *are* running out of patience.' He raised his hands in the air. 'Peaks, they ran out of patience years ago. It's time to start acting like you're one of us, and that is a threat.' With that, he turned and strode loudly away.

Like one of them? I will never be one of them, not after what happened.

This one will cause trouble for you. You know what you have to do.

Kill him? Wouldn't that make me just as bad? Make me what they already think I am?

He lied. About everything. He's the reason they think that way.

I will not kill my own kind.

Are you sure?

The sun shifted in the sky. A passage of time passed without consequence. Kallem wandered again through the trees but, now, everything had changed. The air was stagnant and stale, and a bitter scent filled his nostrils, making him wary of his surroundings. The birds clamoured above, screeching at each other about the onset of dusk. Finally, the sun abandoned him entirely and the moon took its place, taunting him through small gaps in the shadowy *serethen* leaves.

I am not a killer.

A breeze whistled through the forest, lifting leaves from their open graves to brush past Kallem's legs, rousing him from his restless thoughts. He followed the leaves, sensing something in the air. *This isn't natural.* He kept going until the wind died down and the leaves were again allowed to settle, falling silently to land in their new resting places. *I am nearing Hillock,* he knew. The village was the last place he wanted to be but he pressed on regardless, other instincts urging him on. Then, finally, something caught his eye and he understood what was wrong.

A young girl lay curled up in a nest of leaves at the wide base of a *serethen.*

Silently, Kallem slipped into the shadows and watched her, wondering what she could be doing in the forest, alone, at night. *It is not safe here,* he thought.

What will you do with her?

CHAPTER 4

On the evening of the trade, the people of Hillock engaged in lively celebration. The bear they had acquired from Anell seemed the perfect excuse to host Fallor's "surprise" birth-sun that night. Seeing as Sill had finished the quilt (it was to be presented at the end of the feast) and nobody truly knew when Fallor's birth-sun actually was, it seemed apt to presume it was today and had been planned for some time.

And, so, the preparations had begun as soon as the traders returned. The other Elders, most of them slightly younger than their Leader, Fallor, had issued clear and quick instructions to be followed immediately. Phails were to be caught and cooked in order to add to the main bulk of the meal. Women had been sent to raid the herb and vegetable stores, taking care to leave enough in reserve for the winter months that lay ahead. Some of the children had been instructed to keep Fallor occupied, barricading him in his hut and demanding stories until the miffed Elder eventually threw them all out, much to their amusement. And finally, a great cooking fire was built to begin roasting the bear. Apparently it would take some time to cook the beast and would likely need to be cut into much smaller chunks in order to do so quickly enough for the celebrations. That job had inevitably fallen into the strained hands of Sill's father who had wasted more time, cursing and quarrelling, before finally going to work on the bear.

Sill herself had spent the afternoon ensuring she was as far away as possible from the heart of the preparations, and subsequently her father's bad mood. Raffin had aided her in that task by suggesting to the Elder, Malfur, that the two of them help collect *serethen* sap from the forest to ensure there would be an ample supply of candles to last the duration of the feast. Malfur had at first seemed to think that enough people were already collecting sap and actually the firelight might suffice until Raffin had contrived to convince her otherwise.

Now that the main feast was underway, the pair had returned to the heights of their small village, dotting the camp with the saplights they and others had collected and assembled on their way home. The ground now mirrored the sky above, the little lights twinkling like bright orange stars while the roaring fire competed for rank against the glowing white moon.

Raffin had grown eager for a share of the cooked bear, which had sent enticing, meaty aromas wafting down Hillock's western slope for some time.

Sill had settled a safe distance from the fire (and her father) and was glad when Raffin – initially too engrossed by the beast's huge, blackening body – had finally offered to go and fetch some meat for the both of them.

As Sill sat gazing at the twisting plumes of smoke, gently rising and drifting to become one with the black night, she was mildly startled when a woman suddenly sat down beside her.

'Sorry.' The woman's soft voice carried a calming tone. 'I didn't mean to startle you.'

'That's ok,' Sill said politely. She felt slightly embarrassed that her reaction had showed. *Why would anyone want to sit next to me?* Then, she remembered she was responsible for the quilt.

The woman was Artell, one of the Elders, and somebody even Sill knew by name. Artell was easily recognisable by the streak of white that corrupted her otherwise radiant black hair and by her thoughtful, greyish-blue eyes that mirrored the colour, if not the nature, of her son Kallem's. The strands of white belied the true years of her age as Artell was not as old as the other Elders – the youngest in fact – but she emanated a sense of empathy and wisdom that others quickly warmed to and that had ultimately led to her early calling. Although the Elder often carried a saddened look, Sill thought Artell to be kind and considerate and someone who was much liked within the village. She was also pitied by the other villagers, due to the loss of her husband and daughter and the fact that Kallem, her only surviving kin, had lost his mind.

Still, despite Artell's pleasant demeanour, Sill was nervous of the fact that the Elder had chosen to sit by her. She usually tried to be inconspicuous at these events and had grown quite adept at it. Her father did not stand for her talking to others and he would make it known in private, sometimes with his fists. Raffin was the only one who somehow managed to escape his notice. *This is going to be harder than I thought,* Sill worried. Making the quilt had been difficult enough. But sharing it with other people...*Maybe it's me who needs to change?* she thought. *Or my life never will.* She shifted her weight uneasily and then realised what she was doing and tried to remain still. Being the creator of Fallor's main gift was bound to draw more attention than usual. *So, I'd better get used to it. Isn't this what I wanted?* Suddenly, she felt unsure that she wanted to be connected with the quilt at all. Nobody had even seen it yet, besides Raffin. Malfur had told them to wait until the bear had been eaten before collecting it; it would not do for the quilt to forever smell of meat.

Whatever her motives, for the moment at least, Artell opted not to speak. Instead, she sat staring at the fire and the bear as though she were either waiting for Sill to say something, or she was thinking carefully about what she wanted to say.

The silence made Sill even more uncomfortable, so she was relieved when Raffin returned with the food.

'Here you go,' he said, dumping a platter of steaming meat and vegetables unceremoniously onto Sill's lap. He scrunched his brow quizzically over Artell's presence.

Sill shrugged slightly and then hoped that Artell hadn't seen that, too.

'Sorry. I would have got more if I'd known,' Raffin said, addressing the Elder as politely as he knew how.

Artell smiled warmly. 'That's fine,' she said in her calming tone, 'I've already eaten.'

'You're Kallem's mum, aren't you?' Raffin asked, casually seating himself.

Sill stared a warning at him, not liking where this questioning might lead.

If Raffin noticed her he pretended not to. He sat facing them, his back to the fire, scoffing his meat greedily.

'I am,' Artell acknowledged.

'Is it true Kallem lives in the forest?' Raffin asked.

Sill tried to give him another *look* but he continued to ignore her.

'It's true that he spends most of his time there,' Artell responded evenly. 'But it hasn't always been so.' If she was offended by his line of questioning, she did well not to show it. She smiled thoughtfully into the mid-distance, occasionally switching her gaze to the ground before her and only turning her attention back to Raffin when addressed.

Raffin's curiosity was not easily satisfied. 'Why doesn't he work like the other men?' He asked tactlessly.

Sill could have kicked him. She blushed, both ashamed of him and for him. Sometimes he knew exactly what to say in a situation but at other times he appeared to have no concept at all of what was and what certainly wasn't acceptable conversation. *Raffin, please!* Knowing her friend, Sill imagined he knew precisely what he was doing; he was just too curious to resist.

Raffin fingered his plate of food casually as though he thought the act might conceal his darker purpose.

Artell's smile faded for a second and Sill held her breath, not daring to move. She waited awkwardly for Artell to respond, wondering if Raffin was about to get the scolding he deserved or if Artell would simply get up and leave. Fortunately, neither happened and instead Artell's smile returned, although when she spoke, a hint of sadness now laced her mellow voice. 'Kallem has had a difficult life,' she explained steadily, 'and now he is different from other people. I believe he will help us when he is ready but perhaps not in the ways people might expect.' She turned her head slightly and looked at Sill. 'Sometimes people are not always what they seem to be,' she said and she winked.

Sill averted her eyes instantly and, eating her food, tried to appear ignorant. *Why did she wink at me? What does she mean, some people are not always what they seem to be? Does she know about my power? How could she?*

Her heart began to pound in her chest. As inconspicuously as she could, she took a deep breath through her nose, trying to calm her nerves and slow her breathing. *So what if she knows? Nobody would believe her anyway.*

Except perhaps her father. He already blamed Sill for her mother's death. He had told her that there had been a huge storm that night – the night Sill was born – and her mother had died giving birth to her. Maybe it *was* her fault. *Maybe I did kill my mother?*

She hated her power at that moment as she hated herself. *Why can't I just be normal? Or strong and pretty like Hiddelle? Or even kind like Artell?* What use was an ability to move the air anyway? *No use at all. I shouldn't be like this, it's not right. I'm not right.*

But wait, Artell had been talking about Kallem. *Does that mean he's different, too?* His father and sister had also died. Perhaps Kallem had killed them himself. That's what the villagers thought. *Are you cursed, too, like me? Is that how I'm going to end up?* It was a small relief when Artell suddenly rose and, with a final smile and nod to the pair, faded elegantly back into the night. The relief was scant, however, as Sill continued to fret about what Artell had meant by the wink. *Perhaps it meant nothing at all. She was just being friendly. But she didn't ask me anything about the quilt.* So why had Artell sat by her?

Beyond Raffin, the busy fire threw up cruel shapes in odd directions. The flames flickered and flashed, groping at the dark with long, yellow fingers and casting eerie shadows around the camp. Sill glanced at her friend who appeared as unfazed as ever by the current events. He was likely dreaming up various scenarios involving Kallem in the forest. The thought annoyed her.

'What did you ask her that for?' she said moodily.

'Ask her what?' Raffin shifted himself slightly before meeting her gaze. He looked distracted, either by the question or from his daydreaming, she couldn't tell which. 'What'd she want anyway?'

'I'm not sure.' Sill shrugged, her anger fading as quickly as it began. She was too tired for it and she could not say what she really wanted without talking about her power. *I can never stay angry at you. You're my only friend.* None of it was really his fault anyway. 'Maybe she was just lonely,' she said.

She avoided the look he gave her and chose instead to focus on finishing the meat he had generously fetched – perhaps, she now realised, because he knew that she did not want to come into contact with her father. She did not know how much Raffin knew about her father and they never spoke of it, but sometimes she got the impression he understood more than he would have people believe. *He does look out for me, in his own way.* She hated having to keep secrets from him, but as far as her gift was concerned she just wasn't sure how he, or anyone else for that matter, would react to it. She couldn't bear have him look at her the way her father did. Or the way the villagers looked at Kallem.

Suddenly, Sill felt very alone. It made her wonder where Kallem would be on a night like this. Surely even he should be present at Fallor's birth-sun? *Perhaps he isn't allowed?* Mad or not, she felt strangely sorry for him.

She looked again at Raffin who had already slipped back into daydreams. The other kids were too afraid of her father to talk to her. Raffin didn't seem to be afraid of anyone. She couldn't tell him about her secret, not now at least. *You're too important.*

She stood up decisively, took a step in his direction, and then dropped herself down beside him, poking him in the ribs playfully to get his attention.

'Ouch! What'd you do that for?' he moaned, rubbing his side.

'No reason,' Sill said. She smiled at him.

Raffin pulled a face.

'Hey,' Sill said. 'How would you like to help me fetch the quilt for Fallor?' She kept her voice low, mindful that the gift was supposed to be a surprise.

'The quilt!' Raffin quickly perked up at the idea.

'Ssh!' Sill hissed, reminding him to be quiet.

'Your quilt?' Raffin repeated more softly but with equal enthusiasm. 'Yeah, let's go get it now, the bear's pretty much gone anyway. I mean, if you really want my help?' He turned his head this way and that, as though scanning for unwelcome listeners.

'Well, I can't really carry it on my own,' she said. That wasn't strictly true, although when she'd lifted it onto her mattress earlier in the day, it had weighed more than she expected.

'Well, if you're sure, then,' Raffin said. 'I'd be glad to help.'

'Thanks,' she said, cheerfully, 'let's check with Malfur if it's time.'

Once the rather flustered Malfur had reluctantly awarded them leave to both fetch and, to Sill's mixed excitement and horror, present the quilt, the duo ran straight to Sill's hut, where she had laid the quilt down safely across her bed earlier that day.

Since she had assumed everybody was busy enjoying the feast, Sill's shock was amplified when she burst through the doorway to find her father standing right there in her room. She gasped and took a step back, bumping into Raffin as he entered behind her.

Her father's angular frame loomed menacingly over the quilt, a bottle of liquor swaying loosely in his right hand. In his left, a saplight cast a crude glow over his lined face as he fought, absently, to retain his balance.

Sill squirmed against Raffin, trying to sink back into the shadows, but Raffin wouldn't budge and in any case it was already too late.

'Come here, girl!' her father rasped as his head turned sharply toward her. The wooden walls added an eerie echo to his already sinister, drink-slurred voice. He waggled a long finger at her, beckoning her closer.

'It's ok, Sill,' Raffin said sternly, behind her. 'I'm not afraid of him.'

You should be. Near-paralysed by fear, Sill helplessly conceded to Raffin's gentle touch and let him guide her slowly into the room. Reflexively, her eyes went to the quilt, which to her relief lay, as yet, untouched.

'Who did this?' Wobbling slightly as he tilted his body, her father jerked the bottle in the direction of the mattress, indicating the completed quilt.

Sill tensed, hoping that he would not spill any of the contents on it.

His eyes were red and unfocussed as he tried to stare in her direction. 'Who did this?' he rasped again.

'I did. Is something wrong?' Sill's voice was barely a whisper. Confusion intensified her fear. *You know I made it.* Was that what he meant?

Her father's bobbing head swayed lazily to the quilt and then back to Sill and Raffin, creases of puzzlement and anger adding extra folds to his customary scowl.

'That's right,' Raffin put in boldly behind her, 'Sill finished it. And a real good job she did, too –'

'Quiet!' Her father's voice was more of a squeak than a shout. His shoulders hunched as every muscle in his body seemed to tighten. His knuckles whitened around the bottle of liquor. 'You dare lie to me, boy?' Now his voice shook, too.

Raffin looked perplexed. 'What's wrong with him?' he asked her quietly. 'Why's he acting like this?'

Then Sill understood. 'Because today is my birth-sun,' she said sadly. *I'm thirteen.* She had never known exactly when it was, only that it was around the same time as Fallor's. She had hoped this year that her father would be too distracted to remember, but he never forgot. *You never let me forget.* He was always most angry on this day, and it didn't help that he was clearly very drunk. *You're even worse when you drink.*

'Who did you get to do this, Sill?' He pointed an accusing finger at her, daring her to counter him.

'No one,' Sill pleaded, despite the fact that she knew it was futile to argue her cause. As tears began to well in her eyes, an anger of her own began to grow somewhere inside her. Perhaps Raffin's presence made her unusually brave but she decided she was not going to play this game with him today. *I'm going to take the quilt and present it to Fallor in front of the whole village, so everyone can see, and you're not going to stop me!* 'I did it,' she said more boldly, 'I did it all on my own.'

Her father's face turned so red that for a second it looked like his head might explode. At first he was speechless, taken by surprise. His jaw throbbed rhythmically as he clenched and unclenched his teeth; his mouth twisted into an ugly grimace. Then, ever so slowly, the grimace moulded into a grin so full of malice that Sill took a step back, again bumping into Raffin. *Please don't, not in front of Raffin.*

Making a show of stretching out his arm, her father dangled the bottle of liquor warningly above the quilt. 'So,' he began, the ugly grin broadening as he spoke, 'you did this all on your own, did you? The whole thing, with no help from anybody?'

'I did it on my own,' Sill repeated, a little more tamely. The implied threat was enough to suck the courage out of her and now the tears began to flow freely down her face. *Please, not my quilt!*

She had put so much of herself into it. And perhaps, she now realised, a little too much hope. Bruises would heal but this she could never replicate. Surely, he wouldn't dare? *It's for our Leader!*

'That's right!' Raffin blurted as he suddenly stepped around and in front of her. Sill had never seen him so angry. His hands tightened into fists as he bravely faced up to her father. 'Sill made it!' he shouted. 'And *she's* going to take it. So why don't you just leave her alone and get out of our way, or I'll tell Fallor what you've done!'

Sill's father hesitated for a moment, most likely in shock. Then he started to shake.

'Fine,' he hissed, his eyes full of threats. He clasped the bottle of liquor so tightly now that the veins in his arm stood out like angry snakes, poised to strike. 'I'll leave *her* alone.' Suddenly he laughed, and as he threw back his head, the saplight's glow exaggerated his gaunt features and cast a horrifying shadow on the wall behind. When he moved, it was an act of pure rage.

Raffin stood, dumbfounded, as the drunk man swung at him, bottle in hand.

But his swing never hit.

The mass of air that rushed into the room swept Raffin aside, and slammed Sill's father against the far wall. As his arms swung out beside him, the bottle of liquor shattered, spraying the contents out and down towards the floor. The saplight also fell and as it met with the liquid a section of the floor instantly burst into flames.

Sill gasped as she felt the heat hit her face. The *serethen* wood of the hut was practically impervious to fire, but the leaves in her mattress were not.

The quilt! Sill was about to reach for it when she saw Raffin on the ground in front of her. He was bleeding from a gash on his head and struggling weakly to lift himself.

Already the liquor had spread and now smoke was beginning to rise from the far corner of her mattress. In seconds the leaves inside would catch and the whole thing would go up in flames.

Panicking, she tried to redirect the flow of air to the mattress, but only succeeded in feeding the fire. Blinking against the heat, she grabbed Raffin's arm and tugged at him to move towards her – away from the growing blaze. In the corner of her eye she was aware of her father's crumpled form beyond the wall of flames. Raffin started to move towards her and she backed away from the hut, allowing him to scramble out after.

As they reached safety, clouds of smoke began to bellow from inside the burning hut.

Father! Sill nearly ran back in but the heat and fumes stopped her. *What have I done?*

Raffin continued to back away as she stared dumbly at the hut's smoke-filled entrance. She could no longer see her father behind the wall of grey. She remembered Raffin's head and turned to see if he was ok. He was still bleeding.

He glanced up at her, a glazed expression coating his usually playful eyes. 'What...?' he stammered. 'What did you do?'

People were beginning to appear through the dark and now Sill became aware of the sound of shouting and running feet.

Raffin stared up at her, bewildered and afraid. She turned away from him, unable to watch the red pouring from his brow. *I did that*, she thought. *My best friend, my father, the quilt. It's all my fault!*

She began to back slowly from the scene. The running feet were getting closer. How could she explain what had happened? She looked up at the hut one last time. Great plumes of smoke filed endlessly through the doorway and rose steadily up, staining the night sky.

Sill turned and ran.

She ran west, past confused and angry faces, down towards the forest. She ran so fast that she stumbled but managed to stay upright. She kept going, desperate to get as far away as possible from the destruction behind her; away from the village, away from the burning hut and her father's limp body, and away from Raffin's frightful stare.

As she neared the first line of trees a terrible voice cried out from somewhere up on the hill.

'Sill!' Her father's cry howled for blood. 'Get back here you demon!' The sound held up horribly in the wind for a second until Sill urged it away.

Then she was in amongst the trees, skipping roots and dodging trunks as she plunged deeper and deeper into the beckoning forest. She ran and ran until her heart thumped angrily against her chest and her head throbbed, echoing her body's distress. Eventually, when she could run no longer, she collapsed into thick moss and soft leaves that must have only recently fallen from the large *serethen* above. She lay there a while, panting heavily. Then she sat up, shifting her body so her back rested against the bark of the tree's huge trunk. She remained like that, numb and shaken, until her lungs began to settle and her heart finally stopped pounding. Then, heedless of her surroundings, she lay down on her side and curled herself up into a ball. Her small hands clutched at the leaves beneath her as she sobbed into the earth, alone.

CHAPTER 5

Sill awoke to the warm aroma of what smelled like some kind of phail-stew. At first she didn't open her eyes, enjoying the sensation in her nostrils and the comfort of the mattress beneath her. Then her brain caught up with her body and her eyelids quickly opened, taking in the unexpected surroundings. *Where am I?*

The Elder, Artell, sat cross-legged on the floor. A bowl of steaming stew lay untouched a short distance before her like an offering to the gods.

Sill sat up and shuffled backwards until her back met the wall.

'Where am I?' she said, afraid. Am I still in the forest? Thin beams of light splintered down and out from cracks in the wooden ceiling, indicating that the sun was somewhere up above. In patches, the floorboards were damp where rain must have leaked through the gaps.

'Don't be alarmed.' Artell raised the palms of her hands as though the gesture signified that Sill had nothing to fear. 'You are back in the village. This is my home,' she explained. Her hair was tied back today, but the streak of white was still a visible line amongst the dark, stubborn black.

'How...how did I get here?' Sill asked, not yet relaxing her position against the wall. The last thing she remembered was falling asleep on the forest floor.

'Kallem brought you here,' Artell said gently. 'He found you sleeping in the forest,' she added with her familiar, warm smile. 'You have slept for half the day,

Sill, it is lunchtime now.' She nodded towards the bowl in front of her. 'I made this for you.'

'Kallem?' Sill struggled to comprehend Artell's words. Had she really been so deeply asleep? Perhaps the previous night's events had taken more out of her than she realised. *Kallem found me? And brought me here?* She shuddered at the thought of his hands on her and began to systematically check her skin for new marks or bruises. None were visible.

'Yes,' Artell was saying, 'this is his bed, or it used to be.' Her smile waned as though the thought brought back unwanted memories. 'He doesn't have much use for it anymore.'

'What happened?' Sill asked. But what she meant was: what had happened to her own home? *And Raffin? And my father? Peaks, what did I do?* She was not even sure she really wanted to know.

Artell seemed to understand. 'It's ok,' she said promptly. 'Your room was damaged by the fire and may take a while to repair – you'll need a new bed for a start – but you're welcome to stay here in the meantime. Your friend, Raffin, hurt his head but he's fine. He spent most of the morning waiting for you to wake up and when you didn't he left to find out what's going on outside – Fallor has called a village meeting, for everybody. It is starting shortly, I must attend, too.' Her eyes went to the floor as though there was something more she wanted to say but couldn't.

A village meeting? About what? Me? Sill still had too many questions to ask but Artell was not yet finished explaining.

'Your father will not harm you,' she said, perhaps answering what she thought was the most pressing question first. 'The role he played in destroying the quilt you made for Fallor will not go unpunished, not to mention the harm he did to Raffin. And the harm he has done to you, Sill.' A single tear slid down Artell's face and she let it fall, undisguised.

Sill hugged her knees and averted her eyes, taken aback by the unexpected display of sympathy as much as the fact that Artell must now know of her father's "scoldings". *Did Raffin tell you? Or did you already know?* Sill had never seen the point in telling anybody and in any case she was too afraid of the consequences. *Who cares what happens to me anyway? Nobody cared before. I'm just a girl.* She knew full well she was insignificant compared to the fate of the village. Despite what Artell said, she was sure her father would kill her for this betrayal. *I have to leave. I have to get away from the village.*

Once again, Artell seemed to sense her thoughts. She looked Sill over before saying, 'Your father's future will be decided at the meeting, but there is more, Sill.' The Elder's voice held an unusual anguish, forcing Sill to meet her gaze. 'It seems after Kallem brought you back, he got into a fight with one of the villagers.' She shifted herself uncomfortably on the wooden floorboards before continuing. 'The man was displeased with Kallem and he drew a weapon.' Another tear trickled down her cheek and this time she wiped it away. 'Kallem killed him. His fate will be decided, too.'

Kallem killed someone? If all the stories about him were true, she was lucky that he had spared her the same fate. And yet... *Why did you help me? Am I the reason you got into trouble?* She hoped not. *I have enough guilt of my own.*

Artell rose just as Raffin arrived at the door. She smiled and moved towards him, evidently preparing to leave, but before she did she turned to Sill one last time. 'Kallem is not what people make him out to be,' she said, 'remember that he was kind to you.' She walked out, allowing a bandaged and bemused Raffin to take her place as Sill's ward.

Raffin plonked himself down by the bed, eyeing up the enticing bowl of stew. He surprised her when he lifted the bowl and handed it up to her.

'Eat,' he said. 'You must be starving. You've been sleeping for *ages*.' The way he emphasised the last word left no need to express how bored he had been waiting for her to wake up. To get Raffin to sit still for any reason other than food could be deemed a success.

He spent most of the morning waiting for you, Artell had said.

'So where'd you go then?' he asked, watching her eat with perhaps a hint of envy. The grimy bandage concealing the wound pushed his hair up, making him appear even more troublesome than usual. Sill looked at it guiltily, wondering how her friend had forgiven her so easily. *Maybe he doesn't remember?* She thought, half-hoping that was true. Then she felt guilty again for thinking such a thing.

'I just ran,' she said, aloud. A lump in her throat made her want to cry but she managed to resist it. When he didn't answer, she added, 'To the forest.' Artell's stew was delicious. She hadn't realised how hungry she was.

'I can think of smarter places to go, Sill,' Raffin said, grinning. 'I'm just glad you're ok.'

Glad I'm *ok?* This time she couldn't hold back the tears. Her small frame began to shake as she sobbed and she had to pass the bowl of stew back to Raffin whilst she worked to control herself. For a moment she couldn't. She cried because of her father and Raffin's bandaged head. She cried for the ruined quilt and for spoiling Fallor's birth-sun and, lastly, she cried because of Raffin's kindness and acceptance of her, and because she knew she didn't deserve it.

Raffin looked mortified. He had not spoken a word whilst Sill wept, nor had he turned away. When she composed herself enough to finally look at him, she couldn't help but smile. She might have laughed were she not so embarrassed herself. The poor boy sat completely still, delicately balancing the bowl she had given him on fingertips. His mouth opened and closed silently like a fish, as though the untrained effort of choosing the right words of consolation had thrown him into a state of temporary paralysis.

'I'm sorry,' Sill managed, wiping away remnants of tears, 'I'm sorry I hurt you.'

Raffin grinned, his relief palpable. His rigid shoulders swiftly sank back into a relaxed state and he lowered the bowl as though its physical weight had just lightened considerably. He reached out and handed it back to her.

'Thanks,' Sill said, accepting his offer. She, too, felt like a huge weight had been lifted from her.

Raffin laughed, the familiar mischief returning to his eyes. 'That's ok,' he said playfully, 'I wouldn't want to upset you, especially after last night.'

So you do remember? Sill thought. And yet he had still come back to her.

Her gratitude was such that she might have cried again if there had been any tears left to fall. *I'm done with crying now*, she told herself sternly. It was time for change. *I need to be stronger. I have to be stronger, to face the village; to face my father*. She decided then and there not to weep again, just as she would not use her power again. Despite the relief she felt in sharing her secret with Raffin, she didn't want anyone else to know. She was almost certain Artell knew, and possibly her father; he already thought she was evil. *Get back here, you demon!* his abhorred voice still screamed inside her head.

I need to know what my power means, she thought. *Am I really evil?* Despite everything, she didn't *feel* evil but when she had brought the wind to her aid it had been uncontrollable, as though the power emanated from somewhere deeper within her and not, for once, from simply choosing to manipulate the air. She had never experienced that before and she did not care to go through it again. Maybe she could speak to Artell? Artell had said that Kallem was different from other people. *Different like me?* No, Kallem had killed somebody. He wasn't like her at all. Then she remembered how close she had come to doing the same thing. *I shouldn't judge him so quickly, I don't even know him.*

Remember he was kind to you.

'Please don't tell anyone,' she said to Raffin, 'I mean, about me.'

'Who would believe me anyway?' Raffin said and he was probably right. 'Just next time you decide to do *that*, warn me first, will you?' He touched a finger to his bandaged head.

'I won't use it anymore,' Sill said urgently, 'I can't anyway.' *I can't risk it. I have to be stronger.*

Raffin's eyes narrowed as though he could see straight through her.

'What's happening outside?' Sill asked, thinking it best to move on quickly from the subject. 'Should we be going to the meeting?'

Raffin took the bait and his eyes widened in apparent excitement. 'Something big!' he said, jumping to his feet. 'Fallor isn't happy – it's not your fault, Sill,' he added considerately. 'Everything's been cleaned away from last night and the Elders were just getting seated so everyone else will be going there now. We should go, too.'

The last thing Sill wanted right now was to be amongst the entire population of Hillock's village but she had made a promise to herself and she intended to keep it. Plus, she needed to see what happened to her father. *I have to see for myself.* She just hoped he didn't see her first.

'Ok,' she said to Raffin, 'let's go.'

He looked her over for a second as though judging her condition, but when she skipped lightly from the bed he shrugged and let her follow him from the room.

As they made their way to the meeting, Raffin remained her protector, guiding her through gaps in the throngs of villagers, moving ever closer to the heart of all the excitement.

Sill didn't mind his added attention. In spite of her show of energy, she was still too weak to look out for herself and, without his help, she may not have got close enough to witness the results of her father's punishment.

As they squirmed their way forward, she began to take note of the atmosphere building around her. Hillock was alive with voices and bustling movement. Sill could not remember a time like it. Whereas the previous evening had been a relaxed and celebratory affair, this felt very different. There was an air of restlessness to the crowd, a hostility even, that was not common to Hillock's people. The last time they had held a full village meeting, Sill remembered vaguely, she had been much younger and the younger children were not normally required to attend such events. But Raffin had made it clear on their way that Fallor expected *everybody* to be there: male and female, young and old, hunters and traders, woodcutters and ironmongers, growers and gatherers – everybody.

As the pair squeezed nearer to the inner ring, which held space enough for the seated Elders, Raffin stopped just short of the front row, presumably allowing them to see and hear what was happening without being spotted too easily. Once again, Sill couldn't help but appreciate Raffin's natural art for cunning.

The open circle containing Hillock's wisest (in some cases *wisest* really meant *oldest*) men and women was protected by a ring of stern-faced hunters who kept the crowd from encroaching any further on the open space. Each hunter possessed the deterrent of an upright spear, clenched tightly in one hand. Their rigid frames suggested a warning not to get too close. Sill had never seen anything like it before. Hillock was a peaceful village and, generally speaking, nobody ever had need of protection from anybody else. Then Sill remembered that not only had Raffin supposedly been injured by another villager, but a man had been killed, too. It seemed a lot of things were changing around her. Despite the steadfast appearance of the hunters, Sill wondered how effective they could really be against the growing animosity of this crowd. She did not need to see the faces to discern their discontentment; the mood was palpable.

While they waited for the meeting to start, Raffin updated Sill on all that had happened since the previous night. Sill learned how he had convinced the villagers that his head wound had been caused by her father hitting him with the liquor bottle – he justified the lie by shrugging and commenting that that's what would have happened anyway, had Sill not intervened. Upon finding the broken shards and witnessing the drunken ravings of her father, they had no choice but to believe him. Sill had fled, of course, fearing an attack on herself and the spilled liquor had then caused the fire, burning Sill's bed and Fallor's quilt to ashes as a brave, injured Raffin somehow crawled to safety. Raffin was particularly proud of this detail, as several of the villagers had reportedly commented on his courage and fortitude in the face of danger. Finally, he told Sill truly that his injury was only a minor wound and he'd so far managed to use it to his benefit, escaping any chores that morning and allowing him the time to monitor her recovery.

Sill listened to it all with a growing admiration for her friend. She could not blame him for his small lie on account of her father; her father had certainly intended to hurt Raffin and she was convinced that he would have done, had she not inadvertently done so instead. Also, the lie had been told to protect her and her secret, and she could not fault him for that. Regardless of his flaws, Raffin was a true and loyal friend and, Sill knew, he was indeed brave, although she could never tell him that. It shamed her to think she had doubted him. She had been too enveloped in her own fears, too afraid of her past, of abuse and of abandonment, to trust in anyone else; and so she had fled, whilst Raffin had remained to face the consequences alone.

There was no running right now, even if she wanted to. As the congregation closed in around the guarded circle, bodies hemmed Sill in on all sides, making her feel both trapped and somehow safe at the same time – her father would certainly not be able to get to her through this crowd, and the crowd was in no mood to compromise.

Villagers shouted and complained above the heads of the hunters who boldly stood their ground, confronted as they were by the people who were likely also their families and friends. The focus of the displeasure was obvious. As Raffin grabbed Sill's arm, pulling her nearer to him, she watched as Kallem's slim but strong form was led towards the semicircle of Elders and then roughly thrown to the ground before them. His hands were roped behind him, but he had no trouble rising to his knees before shifting to a more comfortable cross-legged position. He straightened his back as he faced the arbitrators of his sentencing.

Next her father was brought out. Unlike Kallem, his hands were not tied and he was treated less roughly by the huge Brorn who gently steered him to his place before the Elders, a large hand guiding his taut frame to where he ought to sit. Her father shrugged off Brorn's hand before grumpily dumping himself to the ground. Seated close to Kallem, the two could not have looked more different.

Kallem's manner and comparative youth lent his posture a natural grace as he sat tall and seemingly relaxed, despite the fact his bound hands were forced to rest uncomfortably behind his lower back. His head was slightly bowed as though he were deep in thought or simply resting. He looked almost as though there was nothing special about the occasion or the people before him.

Sill's father, on the other hand, sat with his hands squeezed tightly under his armpits, his shoulders hunched and his muscles contracted as though he were trying to compress himself into a ball and roll away. He even appeared to rock back and forth very slightly on the spot. His face still wore smoke stains from the night before, his clothes were just as filthy, and he glowered at the Elders opposite as though daring them to judge him. If their crimes were not already known, Sill thought it would be a hard task to pick Kallem out as the murderer.

As the din around her grew, Sill watched as Fallor levered his weight on a wooden staff and then used it to stand quietly in the centre of the curved row of Elders. His aged, bony legs made the process a slow one. When he finally reached his full, bent height he closed his eyes and held up a hand for silence.

Nothing happened.

Wearily, he raised his wooden staff slowly above his head. Then, with unexpected force, he swung the staff back down sharply against the base of a tree. A deafening *thwack*, closely followed by a loud *crack*, shocked the crowd into a stunned silence. People stared, some in surprise, others shamed, as Fallor crossly discarded the two broken halves of his staff. The villagers averted their eyes like scolded children as he shot fierce looks around the ring of onlookers. His old bones shook with rage – or perhaps it was the impact of the staff on the tree trunk – but he somehow managed to remain upright without further aid.

Upon witnessing the impact, Sill's father had shuffled backwards cowardly, she noticed, a protective arm shielding his face from danger. When he realised he was unharmed, he quickly readjusted his position and resumed sulking as though nothing had happened.

Kallem remained unmoved.

The other Elders wore a mix of perplexed approval and abashed awe.

'Silence!' Fallor squeaked, his voice shaking as much as the rest of his body had. 'I *will* have silence!' His aging head bobbed on its neck as he continued to throw accusing looks at the now subdued audience. Assured that he had at last gained their attention, the Elder steadily calmed. Sighing deeply, he descended slowly back into a seated position, sparing one last shake of his head for the broken staff.

The mood of the crowd remained disgruntled but for now at least they retained enough respect to wait for their Leader to speak.

Fallor took a deep breath. 'This kind of matter,' he huffed, the slowness of his voice enforcing a kind of calm amongst the crowd, 'should not be decided through anger and impatience.'

'It won't be decided at all if *he* won't speak!' The interrupting Elder was a male with bushy, black eyebrows and a pointy, grey beard, named Soffus. Although he directed his words at Fallor, his hand gestured towards Kallem.

Fallor shot Soffus a fierce look and held it until the flinty-faced Elder tutted and looked away. He shifted his body weight irritably but refrained from further argument.

'The greater importance...a decision holds,' Fallor continued, perhaps intentionally slowly. 'The more we must distance ourselves...from that decision.' He gave a regretful glance towards Artell who sat sullen-faced amongst the ring of Elders.

Next he turned to Kallem. 'Kallem,' he said softly, 'you know as well as I do that your silence will not aid you in this matter. Marn was a much liked and much... respected man.'

Raffin had told Sill that Marn was a show-off and a bully. But that hardly justified his death.

'His death deserves explanation.' Fallor finished with just a hint of ire. He waited for Kallem to respond.

Kallem remained silent.

'I know,' Fallor continued, patiently, with another glance in Artell's direction, 'that you and he had your... differences.' This remark stirred more irritation in the crowd, including a grunt from Soffus. Hillock's Leader swiftly silenced each perpetrator with a customary glare before returning softer eyes to Kallem.

'Perhaps,' he waved a hand in the air as he sought the right words, 'a...disagreement...was what led you to this?'

Kallem appeared to shift his head slightly but Sill could not make out whether or not the movement was intended as a nod.

'His silence betrays his guilt,' Soffus blurted out impatiently.

'You will have your chance, Soffus!' Fallor snapped at his fellow Elder. He rolled his eyes to the sky momentarily as though pleading the heavens for assistance. 'Very well,' he continued in a more solemn tone. 'Artell, have you anything to say in your son's defence?'

All heads turned to Artell who cut an emotional figure amongst her aging peers. Her typically calm, blue-grey eyes today made no effort to hide their distress. They searched her son's face anxiously as though the act might unveil his hidden motives. 'Why will you not tell them?' she urged him, her dismay plain to hear. 'You are not a murderer!'

Roars of derision greeted Artell's words but she did not take her eyes from her son. Finally, Kallem raised his head to look at her, but Sill could not make out his expression. He turned to Fallor.

'It is true,' he responded plainly. 'Marn attacked me. I was just defending myself.' But even he didn't sound very convinced by his own words.

Shouts of contempt rang through the crowd and even from some of the Elders. Fallor seemed to grope for a staff that wasn't there before waving his arms to shush them.

Kallem had not finished and the crowd quietened briefly to hear his words. 'I did not want to kill him, but neither will I mourn his death.'

That didn't please them. Again, the village broke into chaos and disorder. Sill heard numerous shouts of 'liar!' and 'murderer!' before Soffus spoke up through the commotion.

'Preposterous!' he fumed at Fallor. 'How could he even defeat a man like Marn? He would have had to sneak up and run him through! The wound showed as much.' Shouts of accord echoed through the onlookers and Soffus folded his arms arrogantly as though he needed no reply.

Again, Fallor battled to keep order without the aid of his staff. When the noise eventually died down he asked, 'Kallem, what say you to that? You must say that they.... have...a point. You have not trained as a hunter. Neither have you partaken in any of the swordfighting lessons for many a year.' Fallor ticked off the points of his argument methodically on his fingers as he went. 'Lessons, I might add....that....Marn, on occasion, instructed.'

At that, Kallem's body seemed to tense. 'I have been prepared,' he said, his voice low, 'for a long time. More prepared than the rest of you. How do you think I eat if I cannot hunt?' He spoke as though the very action pained or disgusted him. 'When they return, I will be ready. Will you?'

'When who return?' Fallor said, as confused as everybody else.

Kallem hesitated as though debating another silence. 'The Grinth,' he said finally.

A barrage of angry voices broke out all around them and from some quarters Sill even heard laughter. Artell hung her head, apparently defeated.

'Enough!' Fallor screeched as cries of 'Madness!' and 'Liar!' erupted around him.

'I have heard enough.' His eyes shot daggers at Kallem as well as the surrounding crowd. 'I will make my judgement.'

The Elders began to argue amongst themselves, whilst Sill's father's scowl conveyed his displeasure at having been forgotten about. Artell was now mouthing and gesticulating frantically at Fallor as well as Soffus, but her words were inaudible to Sill, lost in the din of the crowd. Perhaps she was pleading for mercy? *Remember he was kind to you,* Artell had told Sill but that hardly seemed to matter now. *I don't even know him. There's no excuse for killing someone.*

Soffus was ignoring Artell and now sat looking smugly satisfied, evidently pleased by the day's events. 'Our Leader has spoken,' he called out above the noise, his gruff voice carrying like thunder reverberating from the mountains. 'We must hear his verdict!'

The mob quietened and for once Fallor did not hesitate. Fuming, he grabbed up one of the broken halves of his staff and smashed it again into the tree trunk. Although the sound was not as loud this time, it had the desired effect. Without pausing, he addressed his audience with a voice full of resentment. 'Enough!' he repeated. 'It is clear I have been too soft in my time. We have grown weak as a people.' His glare dared anyone to contradict his words. 'Our ancestors would be ashamed! There are many issues that need addressing and we will waste no more time. Kallem, you are banished from our lands and think yourself lucky to escape with your life. In respect of your mother's commitment to your cause, and to this village, I will tell you that there is man, a shaman, in the south who still believes in magic and myths as you appear to. Who knows? Maybe he will find some use for you!' His words rasped at Kallem who merely bowed his head as though accepting his fate. Immediately Fallor turned his scorn on Sill's father. 'You are banished, too,' he waved dismissively at the man who could only gawp back, open-mouthed, as though he had seen a real-life Grinth. 'I want you gone before the new sun rises. I don't care where you go so long as you don't come back here.' Sill exchanged a glance with Raffin who looked as astonished as everybody else at Fallor's sudden and uncharacteristic turn. 'We have cowered too long under the safety of these mountains,' Fallor said, raising his arms and voice as though addressing the peaks themselves, 'and whilst they have stayed true, many things are changing. For one, food here is no longer abundant and we must adapt.' He seemed to grow weary all of a sudden, age creeping back into a voice short on time. He sighed dejectedly and lowered his arms. 'Which is why we will be leaving Hillock to join our cousins in Anell.' Gasps swept round the villagers but Fallor had another announcement. 'For tough times, one needs a tough Leader,' he said despondently, 'so from this moment on, I renounce my title as Leader of the Elders. Soffus will take my place.' His body seemed to sink into the ground as he announced his final decision. He sat silently and sullenly, ignoring the arguments breaking out amongst his colleagues, friends and family, both inside and outside of the circle of Elders.

Besides Fallor, only Soffus and Artell remained silent. Soffus eyed Fallor quizzically as though he could not quite trust what he heard. The fingers of one hand stroked repeatedly down through his pointy beard. Artell's head hung low in an act of defeat that saddened Sill to watch. *She will be all alone,* she thought. *And so will I.*

A rumble of thunder forced her eyes away, and when she looked up she found that thick, black clouds had blotted the sky above as though the weather had changed to reflect the mood below. A drop of water hit her face and she ducked her head away from the oncoming rain. It fell heavily, sucking water from the brooding skies and hurling it down in torrents on the people below, forcing the crowd to split and disperse. Another drum roll echoed from the mountains and people began to scatter, fleeing from the rain. Raffin grabbed Sill's arm and together they ran for shelter as the storm erupted above. They reached Artell's hut – the nearest sensible place of refuge – and threw themselves through the door, gasping and shivering as they shook off the weight of the rain.

Outside, the storm raged on. Thunder boiled and cracked the skies as lightning licked at the earth with a savage tongue. Water had begun to spill into the hut through the cracks in Artell's roof and drip heavily into the two pots she must have placed intentionally for that purpose.

Sill wondered why Artell had not bothered to have the roof fixed. Rain hammered down from above, forcing the two children into silence as they waited for the storm to pass.

Sill watched the event with a deep sadness. Not because of her father – she no longer cared what happened to him – but because it reminded her of the story of her birth: the day her mother had died. Storms were a bad omen. *Even so*, she thought, watching the rain pour down, *I know what I have to do now*. The thought of it pained and terrified her, but she knew it was her only choice. The only way she may ever find out who she really was.

I have to leave, she told herself resolutely. *I have to find the shaman.*

CHAPTER 6

Sill sat on the bed – Kallem's bed – drying her hair as she watched Artell place saplights in each corner of the room. The light and warmth were a comfort after the dark and wet of before, and yet her mood was still sullen. Her decision to leave was the right thing to do, the *only* thing to do, if she were to uncover the meaning of her power; of her birth. But she was sad for Raffin and Artell and did not relish the prospect of telling either of them about her plans. Raffin had been devastated by Fallor's news. Hillock was and always had been his home, and Sill knew better than anyone how much he loved living here, it was all he knew, all he was. As soon as Artell came back, he had returned to his parents, unerringly quiet, and not even waiting for the rain to stop falling as though he felt the need to punish himself somehow.

Artell had not spoken a word. She moved slowly around the room as though she had aged several years in just a matter of hours. She hadn't even changed her clothes yet and her usual elegance was somewhat tarnished by her sodden garments and dripping hair. She laid the final candle down, lowered herself to the floor, and then slumped against the wall. After a moment she sat up straight and began to untie her hair.

Sill wondered whether now was the right time to tell her. Whether she should tell her at all. The Elder looked hurt and vulnerable in a way that Sill would never have imagined from seeing her around the village. Artell had treated her kindly and tenderly, something she was unaccustomed to and had no right to expect. But she was done letting other people make her decisions for her.

I have to be stronger. I didn't ask for her help. She used that thought to muster the courage to speak.

'What will Kallem do?' she asked Artell. After all, she did not know how to find the shaman on her own. She would need to follow Kallem if that was even his plan, or go with him if he would let her. She knew it was dangerous, that she should be afraid of him, but it was a risk she was willing to take. A risk she had to take. If Kallem had wanted to harm her he would have done so when he found her asleep in the forest.

Remember he was kind to you.

Artell inhaled deeply before responding. 'He will go to the shaman,' she said simply, staring ahead into nothingness. 'I wanted to go with him, but he would not let me,' she added.

'I could go,' Sill blurted. The words had barely escaped her mouth and she already knew how ridiculous they sounded. If Kallem didn't want the company of his own mother then he would hardly allow a useless young girl to tag along. She waited for Artell to laugh and tell her not to be silly.

But Artell did not laugh. In fact, she didn't say anything. Instead she glared at Sill as though her words had been the final betrayal in Artell's long, cruel life. The Elder pulled herself to her feet and walked from the room.

Sill's heart sank like the evening sun, drowning in darkness, and at that moment she did not know if she had the strength to see her plan through. *Is this how it has to be, then? Must I go alone?* Somehow she had so far managed to lock away the reality of leaving, of actually going out into the wild, scared, useless and alone. *Then again, I've always been alone anyway. Did I really think it would be so easy to leave? That everybody*

would bring me gifts and wish me well on my journey?
No, that was not reality. Reality was harsh and dark,
and painful.

Just as Sill was about to get up and leave, Artell
returned holding a satchel and began filling it hurriedly
with some of Sill's clothes.

Fine, she thought. *I don't need your help anyway.*
She was not going to cry this time either. *I have to be
stronger.*

'You will need to leave first thing,' Artell said as she
shoved some food and a flask of water into the satchel.

Sill stared dumbly at the bag for a moment as though
the key to her future was hidden somewhere inside. Then
she began to realise what Artell was saying.

'Kallem has gone to pay his final respects to the forest
and then he means to head south. If you leave at first
light, after the rain, you should soon catch up with him.
The barren plains are scarce of animal life so you should
be safe...'

Sill looked at Artell, amazed that any adult would
ever support her in such a rash decision. 'So you...you
don't mind?' she asked, still a little dumbstruck.

'No, Sill.' Artell stopped what she was doing for a
moment and looked at her kindly. 'I just can't believe
I didn't think of it myself. And they call me wise!' She
allowed herself a wry smile. 'Don't misunderstand me,
Sill, I will be sad to see you go and I will worry about
you. But I believe this is fate. Going with Kallem is
what you are supposed to do, what you must do.' She
continued to hurriedly pack the satchel.

Sill was not so sure about fate. All she knew was that
she needed to learn about herself – about her power –
and this shaman sounded like the only person in the
Inner Lands who may be able to help.

'What about Raffin?' She suddenly remembered
her friend. The thought of leaving him without saying

goodbye made her heart wrench. 'Do you think he would come with me?' she asked but really the question was rhetorical; she already knew the answer. *He would talk me out of it.*

Again, Artell stopped what she was doing. 'I will tell Raffin,' she said firmly. 'Don't worry. Now get some sleep.'

Sill curled up on the bed, a fusion of fear, sadness and excitement muddling her bedtime thoughts. She watched a saplight, gently dwindling, in the corner of the room and as it slowly melted away, she took Artell's advice and went to sleep.

Artell woke her early.

The birds had not yet begun their morning chorus as Sill was urged to clamber weakly out of bed. She sat for a moment with her legs dangling over the side of the mattress as she waited for her mind to transition from dreams back into reality. Then she almost wished it hadn't. Groggily, she stretched out her thin arms and yawned deeply as her body trembled, shaking off some of the weightiness of sleep. She was surprised she had slept so soundly, in light of what lay ahead.

Artell was unjustifiably cheerful as she encouraged Sill to wash and eat before marching her down Hillock's southern slope just as the sun poked its fiery head up from behind the mountains to the north. Sill was thankful to be half-asleep or she may have had time to reflect on just how afraid she was. *I'm about to chase after a man who has recently killed another man, to find a man who apparently lives in a mountain and is probably crazier than Kallem is,* she thought. Despite Artell's assurances to the contrary, it was not a subject Sill wished to dwell on, and so she decided not to think about it any further. *Sometimes I'd be better not to think at all.*

'Promise me you will come back when you've found what you're looking for,' Artell said as she crouched to

Sill's level. 'And trust in my son. He will not harm you. Perhaps you will return together.' She handed Sill the satchel she had packed the night before and gave her a brief, tight hug.

Sill let her and then turned and started to walk. She did not have the words for a fitting goodbye, nor the heart to remind Artell that Kallem had been banished and was not allowed to return, ever. She, on the other hand, fully intended to, as soon as she had spoken to the shaman.

Kallem felt no pity. No remorse. That's what his thoughts told him. He had expelled such feelings long ago into the darker depths of his inner self; buried them deep down in the dungeons of his mind. *I locked the door and threw away the key,* he thought, *and now I can't remember where I left it, where I left the key. That part of me died.*

Fear was dead to him, too. Dead as his father and sister, ripped to shreds by one of the monsters known as a Grinth. Dead as the innocent boy who witnessed the nightmare, the horror, all those suns ago. *Dead as Marn.*

His mother had told him that she loved him, but Kallem could no longer comprehend such things. Besides, it was a weakness he could do without. Even hate had abandoned him now. He hated the Grinth no more than he hated himself. *I'm just a husk, filled only with something I can't explain.* Something that told him the Grinth were coming. Something that urged action over inaction. When Marn had again returned to him, this time armed, he had acted without care, without consequence. His sword had flashed, Marn had died; Kallem lived. It could have been the other way around, and it mattered not one bit.

You did the right thing, the smart thing. He brought trouble.

I know. Marn was the final piece in the puzzle, the one who had sealed Kallem's fate. Marn had made him into what they already thought he was, what *he* sometimes thought he was: a killer. The Grinth had laid the foundations. Witnessing their hideous crime had set him on the path. *It was always going to turn out like this.*

But then there was the girl. The girl had muddled things. *I could have left her in the forest, left her to her own grief, her own consequence. But I didn't.*

Instead, he had taken her to his mother where she would be cared for, protected. *What was this kindness? I thought you felt no pity?*

I don't. It was cruelty. There will be more pain to come, more suffering, for all of them. He was sure of that. He had merely prolonged the inevitable.

He laid the last of the earth on Marn's grave, discarded the spade, and turned from the scene, unmoved.

As he passed through the trees he paid his respects to the place that had been his home since childhood. The place that had been his escape, his haven. *The place where my nightmares came true.* If there was anything that Kallem still cared about, it was the forest, though he was not sure why.

The sun's heat hurt his eyes but he welcomed the discomfort; embracing its strength, relishing its power as though it could burn away his sins. The sun was the one constant in this place. The one thing that never changed. Even the forest would not last forever.

Pain was the real truth. The truth the people of Hillock hid from – perhaps not for much longer. Pain was another constant. Pain was what he deserved.

Is that guilt talking? You have no guilt, remember how they treated you. Remember what happened to you.

Yes, that's right. I am exactly who they think I am, who they created.

He emerged from the trees, heading south. Burying Marn was to be the last act before he left, maybe for good. Kallem was surprised the Elders had not sent somebody, Brorn perhaps, to ensure he left as instructed. *Aren't I supposed to be dangerous?* Maybe they figured he had nothing to stay for? Maybe they thought he was just unlikely enough to care, too impassive to oppose the decision? *Maybe they're right.* Either way, he was still surprised. Had they known the real threat he posed, perhaps they would have treated him more cautiously.

Countless suns had risen and fallen as he trained his sword beneath the leaves and, as untried as he was in combat, he knew he had long since mastered the art of the sword. Marn had been the final proof of that fact.

He could not explain why it was he practised. Perhaps the same urge that forced action over inaction demanded it so, and the exertion seemed to soothe him somehow.

At times he felt at one with the forest. The speed of the wind, the gentle sway of a falling leaf, the ferocity of a bear, and the endurance of a growler. The forest was his inspiration and its inhabitants his teachers. Perhaps the Grinth were his Master. If so, they had taught him savagery, taught him how to kill. But where had the Grinth gone? No one had ever seen his kin's attacker. *No one but me.* Hunters had tracked down a bear and named it the perpetrator. But he had seen the Grinth with his own eyes. Seen its claws and its teeth, its purple-black skin, seen everything.

They were the eyes of a scared child. How can I trust what they saw?

Do not doubt yourself. It is weakness.

Perhaps the villagers were right. Perhaps he was mad after all. *The truth still matters. And revenge.*

How can you seek revenge without hate? You are lying to yourself, as well as everybody else.

Why would I lie? I have no need for lies.

Kallem finally emerged from the leaves, the forest coming to an abrupt end and morphing into a scene of dusty soil, shrubs and scattered rocks. Here and there the odd gnarled, old tree clung stubbornly to the land as though staking its claim where the forest had long since retreated.

Without any shade, the sun was unmerciful. Its dry heat stung Kallem's skin, sucking at his energy as if to feed its own voracious appetite. *At least I'm travelling light*, he thought. Other than the clothes he wore and the sword at his belt, his pack contained only food, water and a blanket. As hot as it was here, Kallem knew it would be cooler further south and his destination would be colder still, especially at night. He had never felt snow before but its image was ever-present, resting as it did on the shoulders of the mountains to his right: the western border of the Inner Lands. Collectively, these mountains were known simply as the Western Range, but Kallem knew each peak also had its own name and its own story, often derived from some ancient warrior of the Outer Lands, famed forever for their battles against the Grinth.

Kallem cursed himself for not knowing the individual names. Vorathius was the highest, he thought. Luthur another. Stories were all they had left of the past. Much had been lost over years gone by, and even more forgotten. *We are so unprepared.*

Luthur, Kallem now remembered, was said to have wielded a great hammer, forged of metal and stone, somehow smelted and fused together – another skill long lost to the people of Hillock. With his hammer, he had fought off wave after wave of Grinth to protect his village and his wife. But the Grinth had a way of knowing people, a way of learning. They had snatched Luthur's wife and held her before him, claws twisting inside of her, taunting Luthur with their barks and grunts whilst his wife moaned before him in agony. They had thought Luthur would throw down his hammer and submit but in this they were wrong. Luthur screamed, mad with rage, and rushed the Grinth, scattering bodies and limbs in all directions until he had smashed a path to his wife's side. But when he held her in his arms she was already dead. Luthur dropped his hammer there and then and embraced his wife in silence as the Grinth closed in and finished the job. The village fell after that but somehow Luthur's plight remained in the stories of men.

Over the next few suns, such thoughts weighed heavily on Kallem's conflicted mind. He pressed on quickly, always conscious of dwindling supplies. Water was scarce in these parts so he drank rarely, allowing himself but a few scant sips and usually only when the sun was at its highest. A couple of days gone, he had been lucky enough to come across a small brook whose measly trickle has sufficed at least to refill his flask. Since then, dehydration had set in and the going had been tough.

Water was all he could think about now. He passed through shade as often as possible and never rested in the sun's heat. When he slept, he did not risk the blanket for fear of sweating more moisture than he could replace. It was less muggy here than he was used to, but it also lacked the forest's natural blanket of shade and, although his skin wore the same deep tan of the rest of his people, his face and arms now ached with a burn he'd never experienced and was wholly unprepared for. Already he missed the comfort and familiarity of the branches above him, the sound of the birds, the smooth feel of *serethen* bark. He also sorely missed the Soulslide River, which he bathed in and drank from on a daily basis. Right now its image was inviting him to jump in and drink his fill, relish in its refreshment, feed from its vitality, and soothe his skin in its cool, fresh waters.

Thirst is making me weak, he thought. Bitterly, he turned his mind from such thoughts and tried instead to be glad of the sight before him. The area he now walked was known as the Barren Plains, named thus because wildlife had grown scarce in recent history, but in truth the land was far from barren. Although open on the most part, the plains were filled with many different plants of all shapes and sizes. Their flowers splashed the ground in vibrant colour: bright pinks and dazzling blues melting into deep purples and fiery reds. In some places slim, fragile yellows and whites caught the breeze, sending gentle waves like ripples across their humble bloomage whilst in others, long, tubular orange shafts, flecked with gold, competed starkly with broad jet-blacks, bordered in shiny, silver-blue. Jagged, tall, grey rocks jutted out here and there, offering mossy tips as sacrifice to the sun's rays, and casting pockets of shade over small patches of lush grass and wild shrub. The few dotted trees were low in height and their trunks bent and twisted at odd angles, throwing eerie, human-like shadows onto dry earth. No plants grew within several strides of their bases as though the trees needed every bit of strength they could suck from the starved soils. Pinkish-white blossom lined their branches like a silent display of the life still held within. *The trees here are thirsty too,* Kallem thought, *and yet they are still strong. As am I.*

That's right, you are strong. Always, you are strong.

The land was hilly here – not to the extent of home or compared to further west where Kallem gazed upon brown slopes rising ever steeper towards an azure sky – yet hilly enough that he could not yet see his destination south.

The journey was thought to last only several suns on horseback, but since the people of Hillock owned no horses and nobody from the village had actually ever travelled the distance, Kallem really had no idea how far it would be. The thought only served to remind him how cut off the village seemed from the rest of humanity. *Fools. They have all grown weak.* At least Fallor had acknowledged that truth. Besides their friendship with Anell Village, a conveniently short trip east along the Soulslide, they had little contact with the south. On rare occasions nomads would visit, bringing tales of afar in exchange for food and shelter. Although always hospitable, Kallem knew from his mother that Hillock did not greet these strangers with much trust. The thought of abandoning one's home was deeply frowned upon, and such visitors always ensured they did not outstay their welcome. The only other contact they had was with Rydan Fort, the one human stronghold of the Inner Lands. Even when Kallem was a boy, riders had come almost every year to take *serethen* wood back to the south to restrengthen the Fort. But they never brought anything in return, and since the vast majority of Hillock's residents did not see the need for a stronghold, relationships had grown strained to the point where the riders no longer came. Kallem wondered what shape the Fort would be in now. *Perhaps I will get to see for myself.*

As he reached the next hilltop he stopped to rest. There was *ether* here – an edible plant people chewed to keep their strength up during hard labour. *Ether* was one thing the lands surrounding Hillock had in abundance and was one of the reasons the people remained strong, despite the dwindling wildlife.

The plant was green and tough and never flowered but was present all year round and always regrew what was taken from it.

Kallem snapped off a short leaf from one plant and chewed on it whilst taking pickings from other plants to add to his pack. Then he chose a shaded spot to sit in, resting his back against one of the moss-tipped rocks and fumbled through the pack for his flask.

He shuddered as the water touched his throat for the first time that day, then sagged gratefully against the rock and licked the sweet moisture from his parched lips. He allowed himself one further sip before returning the cap and then thrusting the flask forcibly back down into the pack. He didn't know how long it would be before he could replenish the water. *I must be sparing*.

Still missing the forest, he wondered why people had formed the first village of the Inner Lands atop a hill when there was such natural comfort and shelter in the trees below. A rueful smile curved his lips as the answer struck him with bitter blatancy. *They wanted to see what was coming*. If anything, the forest was probably a blight on their safety, but they needed the wood to build and trade.

Thirst is making me slow, he thought.

He chewed on a second *ether* leaf and gazed out over the land he had just covered. The forest was now completely out of sight, as was Hillock, long since obscured by the taller hills he had climbed on his journey thus far. If he reached a higher point he may still be able to see the village, but from this rest place, the bulging landscape now obscured the view between himself and his former home.

Something moved in the distance.

Kallem raised himself upright against the rock, suddenly more attentive.

There it was again: movement.

Sunlight reflected brightly from the hillside across from him, making it hard to discern much detail. Rocks, trees and thick ferns offered cover enough for smaller creatures to remain hidden, should they so wish.

Kallem wiped the sweat from his eyes and strained harder. *Am I seeing things now?*

No. The shape, more of a speck at this distance, moved again. Emerging from a blunt rock, it soon vanished behind another. A part of it caught the sun, glinting brightly.

Kallem stood slowly, taking care to keep his body confined to the shadow of the rock behind him.

He watched as the dot moved again, flitting quickly from one cover to the next. *Was that the same shape, or another?*

It was not so much the deliberateness of the movement that intrigued him, but rather the fact that whatever it was had chosen an identical path to the one he had taken. There was no doubt about it. *I am being followed.* Choosing his moment carefully, Kallem snaked around the rock, drew the red iron sword at his waist, and waited. *Thirst will make me dangerous.*

Sill was worried. Initially, it had not taken long to pick up Kallem's trail. Tracking was one of the more useful skills she had learned from Raffin in his quest to know every*thing* about every*body*. On a few occasions, he had made a game of following villagers about their daily lives, but that had ended rather abruptly when he had supposedly seen something he didn't want to see and, for once, didn't want to talk about either.

Besides the infrequent physical clues of Kallem's presence – flattened grass and the odd broken fern – logic dictated that their paths would be more or less the same, and on that basis Sill had assumed following him would be easy. Once, during the first sun of her journey, she had watched him steadily zigzag his way up and over a steep rise as she descended on the opposite side, barely any distance between them. Why she had not called out to him, she couldn't say. Perhaps she thought he had been too far away to hear, or perhaps she had just been too scared to do so. *I'm not sure I've ever even shouted before*. And she still did not know how Kallem would react to her following him. Artell had said he would not harm her – *remember he was kind to you* – so she had to trust in that. Having not seen Kallem again since that first day, Sill now regretted the missed opportunity.

I have to be smarter, too, not just stronger.

Had she called out to him then, perhaps they would be walking the land together now. *Sharing food and drink, and safety.*

As it was, she was all alone, out of water and growing more concerned with each footstep. There had been no sign of Kallem at all under this sun, and she had walked all morning. What if he'd changed direction suddenly? What if he never intended on seeing the shaman at all? *I suppose it shouldn't matter*, she told herself, *it's the shaman I need, not Kallem.* But then who knew if the shaman really lived where people said he did? *Who knows if he's even still alive?*

For the first time since she set off, Sill considered turning back. *Would I even make it home with no water?* And what would she say to Artell, to Raffin, when she got there? How would she be any better off than she was now? *At least I'd be safe.* She was used to spending time alone but this was different. Nights beneath the stars left her feeling exposed and vulnerable. When she did manage to sleep she would dream that her father was following her, and wake in fear and sweat beneath the blanket Artell had packed for her. When she had drained the last of her water she soon realised what being alone truly meant. Kallem lived alone in the forest so he must know how to survive. Whether she liked it or not, he was now her best hope. *I'd better find him soon. Stronger or not, I still need other people.*

So despite the constant nagging of her conscience, Sill refused to give up. *Otherwise I may as well go back to my father. And who knows where he is now anyway?*

She started to run. Slowly at first but as the decline deepened, her legs moved more quickly and she let the hill take her, guiding her down as she skipped over ferns and hopped from one animal track to another. Giant rocks stopped her from picking up too much pace and allowed her to restore balance, bracing her hands against their rough granite edges as she slowed before bouncing off and picking up speed again as she snaked her way ever downwards. When she reached the bottom of the hill, the slope levelled off before quickly rising again, and she matched her speed to the gradient, slowing her run into a purposeful march as she began the next ascent. Her slim legs already ached from days of unaccustomed travel, but the discomfort did not bother her. That was something she was used to at least. Aches, pains and bruises were just part of everyday life for Sill. It was a new kind of ache, but for some reason she found it more bearable. *Because I chose this.* She pushed her hands against her knees, forcing her sore feet down as she climbed ever higher. The heat of the sun was less punishing on the upward slopes, but that felt like scant consolation. Her chest laboured hard as she reached the top of the hill and finally she was forced to stop and catch her breath. Her lungs burned from the exertion and felt unusually tight, as though her ribcage was closing in around them, crushing her on the inside. Her head throbbed as though a fog shrouded her brain, clouding her thoughts. But the discomfort was only brief and soon enough the fog cleared and her breathing gradually returned to normal. Now she was even more thirsty, but there wasn't much she could do about it so she just kept going. As her senses rallied and her focus sharpened, Sill realised to her delight that she was surrounded by *ether* plants. *Some bits have already been broken off,* she saw. *Kallem must have come this way!* Snapping off leaves as she walked, she stuffed as much *ether* in her pack as she could and then did the same with her mouth.

Chewing greedily and gratefully, Sill again began to run. Urgency was crucial now. Either she would find Kallem, or she would find water, and she dared not rest again until she had achieved at least one of these objectives. She had been too complacent before, too distracted by doubts and fear, but thirst and survival had shaken her awake. *I can't remember ever feeling this alive!* Sill thought, elated. She hoped she would remain alive to enjoy the sensation.

The next downward slope looked much like all the others, and as she ran she planned her route, judging each step so as not to land awkwardly and twist an ankle or find herself trapped in vegetation and have to wade through dense fern or crunch through bracken. The flowers of these lands were a beauty to behold and she used their colours to plot her course. Natural grassy pathways seemed to form slim barriers between the contrasting plant types as though a silent war was being waged between the harsh browns and enduring greens of the ferns and the radiant spectrum of the elegant flowers. Rocks and trees proved good waypoints, helping to control her pace and provide welcome breaks from the merciless sun.

As Sill pressed off another rock and skipped around it, a man barred her path. His hands closed painfully around her upper arms as he steadied her and she kicked out at him in a panic and then fell backwards as he released her. Sill shuffled back a few yards on her hands and buttocks, struggling to catch her breath as she tried to move beyond his reach.

'Get up,' Kallem said without inflection. His eyes were empty and strange as though he was unsure whether to be cruel or kind but was capable of neither.

I won't cry, Sill told herself. *I have to be stronger.*

She glared back at him. 'You can hit me if you want, I'm still coming with you.'

Kallem gave her a puzzled look and then reached a hand into his pack and brought out a flask.

'Drink,' he said and threw the flask at her feet. 'Quickly.'

Not taking her eyes off him she reached down and picked up the flask of water. It was not full. Sparingly, she took a few small sips, trying not to show her desperation, whilst Kallem continued to watch her.

'Why are you following me?' he asked.

Sill barely knew where to begin. If she told him the truth, would he believe her? *Would he care either way?* If only Raffin were here to stick up for her. *But he isn't, I made sure of that.* It was just her and Kallem.

'Your mother,' she said, deciding a half-truth was better than none at all. Involuntary tears started to well but she fought them back. *I'm just tired*, she told herself, *there's no reason to cry. My father is much worse than you are. My father didn't kill anyone…*

The water Kallem had given her barely touched her thirst and her head had started to throb. She didn't really know what she had expected from Kallem, but whatever image she might have had, this was not it. *Remember he was kind to you,* Artell had said, but besides the blue-grey colour, Sill saw nothing in his eyes that resembled Artell's. No warmth, no compassion. Nothing.

'Get up,' Kallem said again. He turned and began to walk away.

Whether it was his manner, fatigue, or just her own disappointment, Sill could not say, but the anger she felt stirred the air around her as she rose to her feet. Images of Raffin's bleeding head and thick smoke billowing from the doorway quickly filled her mind. *I can't use it again*, she thought. *I mustn't.* Instead, and without thinking, she flung the flask at his back.

The speed with which he turned and drew his weapon startled any remaining anger from her. Kallem stared at her and Sill could have sworn a flash of hatred brightened his eyes, just for a moment. As quickly as it had changed, his expression went blank. He bent to pick up the flask and tucked it back into his pack. What he said next frightened her even more than his sword. 'We need to keep moving,' he said plainly, sheathing the weapon that he'd probably used to kill Marn. 'Something is following us.'

CHAPTER 7

To the west, a bold wind swept across the mountains, brushing snow from their dusty peaks as it made its way over and down the vast, treacherous slopes. The wind slowed as it slipped beneath the warmer air of the lower hills, eventually arriving to blow a cool, welcome breeze over Sill's tired face.

The pace Kallem set had been as uncompromising as his character. He spoke little and when he did it was usually to issue an order, such as 'hurry', 'quickly' or 'keep moving'.

Sill was exhausted. At first the pain had resided mainly in her feet, a dull, irritating throb that was present when she walked, when she sat, when she went to sleep, and when she awoke again. Then the pain had spread through to her calves and thighs and eventually up into her lower back, accentuating every climb and every descent, and fatiguing her more and more with each passing sun.

Her whole body was now a conduit of stiff pain and with each step she felt more weak, more tired, and more desperate to reach their destination. If she were a different girl she might have complained, might have whinged and whined and sulked, or simply refused to go on, but she was from Hillock and her people were strong. *I am strong.*

As she walked she thought about the recent days spent in her hut, stitching together the unsuited furs she had somehow managed to combine to create Fallor's quilt; the quilt that was now ashes. In a way, that discomfort had been worse: she had been given no choice in making the quilt. Now she had a choice. *I can keep moving or I can give up*. It wasn't a great choice but it was hers to make. She still wasn't sure if Kallem cared either way, if he did he didn't show it, but whoever, or whatever, trailed them had him anxious enough to maintain this gruelling pace and that worried her, so she kept moving.

As she walked, she tried not to think about what might await them when they reached the mountain, just as she tried not to think about Raffin – whom she had abandoned without so much as a goodbye – or about how inexplicably tired she was. She also didn't think about who or what was following them. Any effort to glean information from Kallem had earned her either a disobliging one-word response or simply silence. Eventually she had grown too weary to waste any more energy and had thus abandoned her attempts to yield further knowledge. But that single word had stuck with her, gnawing at her self-resolve, and it was proving hard to shake. Some*thing*, he had said. Not some*one,* some*thing*.

In some ways, she found Kallem's silence to be oddly comforting. He did not ask anything specific of her, other than to keep pressing forward, and at times he would think to offer her water or a piece of *ether*. When she needed to relieve herself, he was respectful enough to slip out of sight and on the few occasions he had allowed her to sleep, he would choose a tall rock to sit on and keep watch. Sill wondered if he even slept at all. If he did, she had not witnessed it. That was one of his more disconcerting traits. Another was the way he continued to look behind him every few strides as though every rock or shrub posed some kind of hidden threat. Sill dared not look back too often just as she dared not think too much. On the few occasions she had chanced a look, she had seen nothing to cause alarm, and after a while Raffin's stories of Kallem's alleged insanity had begun to resurface from the previously dormant depths of her memory.

Fortunately, hunger, fatigue and dehydration were enough of a distraction to keep her mind largely in the present. She had found that *ether* could sustain her energy levels for a surprisingly long time, but it felt absent of any real nourishment and her stomach was now begging to be filled with a warm meal. Her mouth was so dry she could not refrain from frequently licking her lips, even though the salty taste of sweat only served to worsen her thirst. Her back and shoulders ached almost as much as her legs did, and painful blisters had formed on the soles of her feet, making walking even more of an ordeal.

Two suns ago, the land had begun to level off, insomuch as it was now a more steady, gentler climb. Still, Sill saw this as a blessing after the giddying rise and fall of the previous day's work, and at least now they could see their objective plainly in sight. Moonmirror Peak loomed tall and obstinate in the near distance, another stalwart defender of the Inner Lands.

At night, they had witnessed the reason for its name. The mountain's black, ice-coated rock glistened in the moonlight like a shining beacon of hope, guiding them through the dark. The sight spurred them on, almost as though the mountain was imploring them to seek safety and refuge within its effervescent walls.

In the daylight, it was less spectacular. The surrounding mountains were all tall and broad, growing into sharper, spikier shapes the higher they rose. All that separated the Moonmirror from its brothers was that it was slightly smaller and less jagged, sat more inland, and had a duller complexion, due to the darkness of its rock. Sill thought it looked a sad and lonely peak, isolated as it was. It was as though the mountain had been cast out from the rest, due to its differences. *A bit like Kallem.*

Being in sight of the Moonmirror had made the mountain seem frustratingly close and yet it had taken another two suns to even reach the mountain's base. Grass and plants had since given way to dirt and leafless trees, and now a light smattering of snow slicked the ground, threatening to slow the final climb. Sill had never seen snow up close before, and had she been less tired, she may have found more to express about it than simply observing it was wetter than she'd expected.

The murmur of a distant waterfall marked their nearness to the mountain's open base. Sill could not yet see the source of the noise, obscured as it was by the increasingly tall, white-tipped rocks that sat dotted here and there as though they had fallen from the sky, but she knew the sound of the falling water could be heard from some distance. The Frosty Falls, as the waterfall was known, fell some three hundred feet from further up inside the Moonmirror's heart and was one of the natural marvels of the Inner Lands, as Sill had often heard about in Fallor's stories when she was younger. Now she wondered how much else in those stories could be real. As far as the Moonmirror was concerned, she would find out soon enough for herself. She hoped bitterly that Draneth, the shaman, was real, too – and alive – or this could all turn out to be just a huge, painful, waste of time. *And then what will I do? I don't even have a home anymore.*

The sun sat low now in the sky before her, painting the clouds red and casting an orangey glow over the snow-flecked landscape. In a while the Moonmirror would glow again, too, sparkling against the moonlight. Sill hoped they would find somewhere sheltered to rest before then. Kallem seemed at his most vigilant during the night and his watchful gaze was beginning to concern her.

As she trudged wearily onward, watching each footstep leave a sludgy imprint in the snow, she was vaguely aware when Kallem stopped and turned suddenly ahead of her.

'Move,' she heard him say.

Sill sighed. 'I am moving.' In fact, she hadn't *stopped* moving all day, despite the fact that she hurt all over, was hungry, thirsty, and desperately needed rest.

Kallem drew his sword and the red iron gleamed like blood against the white-orange backdrop. 'Sill,' he said more coldly. It may have been the first time he had used her name.

Her eyes widened as they tried, wearily, to focus on the sharp, red metal. She dropped to her knees, finally defeated. *What do you want from me?* Then it dawned on her. What if they were never really being followed at all? What if Kallem had just been checking to make sure that they *weren't* being followed? She looked up at the red sword, at his dark, yellow-pupilled eyes. Eyes as cold as the snow at her feet. *Your eyes?* But his eyes weren't looking at her, they were looking past her.

As she turned her body to look behind her, she heard a deep noise, like a loud grunting or coughing. Then she saw them, and any fleeting fragments of fight that she may have had left seeped swiftly out of her. Her fear of Kallem was replaced by something far deeper. A fear that even her father could never equal. It crept through Sill's fragile body like an aggressive frost, numbing her thoughts and rendering her limbs useless. She had never felt anything like it and it crippled her right to the core. She stared, speechless, as the two creatures bounded towards her at a frightening pace. Even at a distance the way they moved struck terror into her heart, her very being, in a way she hadn't known possible. Their legs resembled the hind legs of some animals, hoofed and bent at the knee but their thighs were thick and muscular and they moved on two legs, their upper bodies bent forward as they narrowed the distance. The creature's heads stretched forward from their necks, longer and lower-set than a human's, accentuating the forward motion of their momentum. Lipless mouths were lined with sets of short, sharp teeth that stretched all the way back along a deep-set jaw. Dark, narrow eyes sat either side of their heads, centred with two bright yellow pupils that seemed to glow in the fading light of dusk. At first Sill thought they carried knives, but then she saw that instead of fingers, their hands merged into two long, sharp claws, evidently made for tearing through flesh. A deep, dark purple skin coloured their whole, hairless bodies like nothing she had seen on any animal. The stories of the Grinth hadn't lied but neither had her imagination accepted the whole truth, for nothing could have prepared her for this.

Suddenly, she was yanked up, turned and dragged forward. Instinctively, her blistered feet began to grope for grip on the soft ground, and she soon found herself running as though she had never walked the vast expanse of the journey before. But her body knew otherwise and after what felt like just a short distance her legs gave way, sending her sprawling painfully to the ground. She managed to twist around so that she could see the beasts coming but as she tried to stand, her feet kept slipping in the snow and her numb arms and legs lacked the strength to lift her back up.

Kallem leapt over her and faced the onrushing Grinth. Firmly planting his feet, he held the red blade out before him in both hands. The two creatures skidded to a controlled halt just out of range, their breath steaming the cool mountain air through barely visible nostrils – just small slits above those spiky, fearsome teeth. One stomped a hoof, raised its head and gave another of the awful coughing sounds: a deep, guttural noise that seemed to emanate more from the creature's stomach than its throat or lungs. The other began to circle to Kallem's left, hissing threats.

Kallem traced its movement with his sword whilst keeping his eyes on the beast ahead.

Despite the paralysing fear she felt, Sill's eyes and instincts told her that these Grinth were in poor health. Both bore several scars across their bodies, and one had such a badly damaged arm that it could barely lift it. Whilst muscles were visible throughout their bodies, they seemed almost malnourished as opposed to strong, and in places their purple colouring had faded to a pallid pink, giving the impression they were old or sickly. The knowledge hardly eased the dread they inspired but for now at least the threat of Kallem's sword appeared to keep them at bay. *He thinks the Grinth killed his family,* Raffin had once told her. She just hoped his hatred of them outweighed his indifference towards her. *Please don't leave me!*

The Grinth on the left continued to circle around, drawing closer to her.

Kallem took a couple of steps back, cutting off the angle.

Sill scooted back a little, trying to give him more room to work, but only succeeded in drawing the attention of the nearest Grinth. Its head flicked towards her and for a moment she met its dark, deadly eyes. The bright pupils burned like two saplights in the blackest of nights. They held no emotion, no anger, no fear. Nothing but intent. They were the eyes of a predator. *Don't look at them, just keep moving.* Again, she shifted herself backwards on the ground, trying to resist her body's urge for paralysis. With every move, she could feel the creature's eyes boring into her, watching, waiting for an opening.

'Keep still,' Kallem said, his voice as dispassionate as the Grinth's empty eyes. He slashed his sword quickly to the left and the Grinth shuffled back a step, then bent forward and hissed at him in frustration.

The Grinth with the damaged arm – the one closest to Sill – widened its arc and continued to circle, keeping just out of range of the red blade. *It's trying to get behind me*, Sill realised and she froze as Kallem had instructed.

Kallem was also aware of the Grinth's movement, and he stepped slowly backwards until he was all but standing over her. He shifted his sword into one hand and widened his footing, doing his best to maintain a view of both creatures. Then suddenly he seemed to stop. Without warning, he brought the sword in close towards his chest and held it upright, gripping the hilt tightly with both hands. He closed his eyes.

Both Grinth hissed uncertainly and then began to move in.

No! What are you doing? Sill tried to shout but when she opened her mouth no words came out.

Kallem did not move.

I have to be stronger, I have to be stronger, she repeated in her head. That's what she had told herself before she left Hillock. A lot of good that was now. In desperation she tried to call on the wind, but the air was still and remained so. *No, not now!* She was still too weak, too afraid. The Grinth with the damaged arm was so close she could smell its foul breath defiling the air. She found herself staring into its eyes and now she could not pull her head away. The bright, yellow pupils fixated on her, but there was no seeing through the dark that surrounded them. *I have to be stronger*, Sill repeated uselessly in her head.

As the Grinth lunged, Kallem sprang to life. In the blink of an eye, he crouched and slashed in a wide arc, so fast that Sill's brain barely registered that he'd moved. His blade caught the beast before him across the chest, opening a gash that spewed black liquid across the wintry scene, ruining the purity of the white snow. The Grinth screamed in a last defiant squeal and then fell dead. The other Grinth buckled as the sword's tip clipped its thighs but the contact only succeeded in wounding and angering it.

Sill could only stare, terror-stricken, as the knife-like claws of the creature's good arm swiped towards her, aiming straight for her throat. She closed her eyes and waited for pain and death.

A thud ended the wait.

She opened her eyes.

The Grinth lay dead at her feet. Black liquid oozed from the crushed side of its lifeless head. Above its body a bald man stood clutching a wooden staff in his right hand. The top end of the staff had been sculpted into a skull and was made more fearful by the black blood that now dripped from it.

A shrill *keeeeeeee* rang out across the sky as a brown hawk swooped down to land on the stained skull. It flapped its wings for balance and then craned its neck forward to peck at the black blood with an air of quizzical interest. The bald man ignored the hawk and continued to scowl down at the dead creature before him with his fierce, bright blue eyes. The eyes turned to Kallem and the bald man's scowl deepened.

Sill looked up and was relieved to see that Kallem was unharmed. His eyes were still the black she thought she had imagined, mirroring that of the Grinth's, but as she watched them they slowly returned to the familiar blue-grey of Artell's and she was left to doubt that they had changed at all. 'Are you ok?' she asked in a daze and he looked at her with the same empty expression that greeted everything she said.

The brown hawk squawked and she turned again to look at the bald man with the staff. Behind his weathered face, the sun burned low and red in the darkened skies, descending upon the horizon like an avatar of death.

Kallem felt infinitely strong. The twisting stairway leading up towards Draneth's cave had been carved straight into the rock and was covered in a thick layer of ice. As they wound their way up into the mountain each step took them higher, increasing the chances of a fatal slip or fall; yet Sill felt safe, cradled as she was in his arms. *You protected me.* She was so exhausted, from journey and danger, that her mind barely recognised what was happening and in any case the roar of the Frosty Falls was such that it drowned out any hope of reflection or contemplation. The sound was so overwhelming, her fatigue so absolute that she scarcely noticed the cold spray that wetted her face or the large sheets of ice that passed her by, tumbling with the waterfall to crash heavily into the lake below. The ice pounded the lake in a constant barrage of noise, which then reverberated off the surrounding rock faces, causing the legendary, thunderous sound of the Frosty Falls.

Sill was vaguely aware that she was shaking. Perhaps it was from the cold or shock, or simple exhaustion; more likely a combination of all three. In any case, the sensation was distracting enough that she still could not sleep. Her mind flitted from one thought to the next, never settling on anything cohesive; as slippery as the icy steps on which Kallem unflinchingly trod. She had not asked him to carry her, but she was grateful for it. She doubted she would have had strength to make the climb on her own.

Draneth remained a couple of yards ahead, the light thud of his staff against the ice the only sound audible beyond the perpetual clamour of the waterfall. The shaman seemed a dour man and had barely spoken a word to them since they left the two dead Grinth behind.

'Follow me,' was all he'd said and Kallem had obeyed. He had lifted Sill from the ground and, with her in his arms, they had followed the bald man beyond the white and black of the Moonmirror's outer shell and headed deeper into the mountain. They passed through a narrow tunnel that smelled of damp and dirt and eventually emerged into a huge, moss-walled cave with a lake in the middle. The water in the lake churned and bubbled and spat with the endless torrent of the Frosty Falls. Light leaked in from cracks far above, illuminating the cave and creating odd panels of floating dust. The shaman had pointed his staff at a gap resembling the mouth of another tunnel, higher up and to the left of the waterfall. The steps began to their right, which meant they had to pass behind the Falls during their ascent, although fortunately they never came too close to its main body since it fell more or less precisely in the centre of the churning lake. The waterfall itself stemmed from a vast, rocky outcrop, stretching out like an arm far above, but it was barely visible through all the spray and misty vapour thrown up from the force of the fall.

The brown hawk still clasped its claws around the skull of the shaman's staff and every now and then it would turn its head right around to peer at Sill, a habit she found vaguely disconcerting, not least because the hawk's eyes closely resembled those of the Grinth. *The eyes of a predator.*

After a time, Sill's subconscious registered that they had stopped climbing and her ears noticed that the roar of the waterfall had subsided. Her eyes took in new surroundings as she was lowered gently to the floor and her hands gripped the blanket that Kallem had wrapped around her shoulders and pulled it in tight. Soon, her face felt the warmth of a fire and her nose smelled the rich aroma of food cooking for the first time in too many long suns. The promise of food helped to meld her scattered thoughts and after a while she found she was able to concentrate enough to take note of what was happening around her.

The new tunnel they had entered was not a tunnel at all, but rather the mouth to a small cave with clean, smooth walls that Draneth had somehow managed to make *homely*. In here the Frosty Falls was muffled to a more bearable background hum that whispered lullabies of sleep into Sill's weary ears.

But she could not sleep yet. *Not until I've eaten.*

The smell emanating from the cooking pot, which hung from a metal rod fixed above the fire, seemed to call out to her as though begging to be devoured. Kallem must have felt it, too. He sat close to her, cross-legged, his eyes fixed on the steaming, sizzling pot.

Draneth sat across from the fire, the flames throwing eerie shapes onto the wall behind him. The firelight flickered across his form, accentuating the angled features of his face and the harsh lines of his seemingly permanent scowl. His bright blue eyes, more orange in the light of the fire, remained on Kallem as though he were reading his thoughts, just by staring at him. The muscles in the shaman's jaw twitched every now and then, perhaps involuntarily.

Kallem did not seem to notice but the hawk must have sensed the tension as it squawked audibly, and with a brief flutter of wings, took off and flew low and gracefully back out through the cave entrance.

'Your eyes.' The shaman broke the silence in a rough, low voice. 'They were yellow,' he said, looking at Kallem accusingly.

Kallem gazed at the bubbling pot in a trance-like state. He seemed tired for the first time since Sill had caught up with him. Or rather, he had caught her following him.

The shaman broke his glare momentarily to wrap some cloth around a hand and then used it to remove the pot from its metal structure above the fire. The air hissed out as he lifted the lid and eyed the steaming contents. 'They used to speak,' he said as he began to dish out the bubbling broth into two small bowls, 'of yellow-eyed men that walked with the Grinth, defying their own kind to do the creatures' bidding.'

Sill eagerly watched the bowls being filled. Her body had shed the cold, thanks to the fire, but hunger still nagged at her from within.

'Who did?' Kallem said, sounding drowsy.

'People. Stories. Others, too.' The shaman handed Kallem one of the bowls and beckoned for him to pass it on to Sill.

Sill wondered who the shaman meant by *others*? If she were less tired and hungry she may have had doubts about this man. Draneth's actions were hospitable enough, but his manner was as frosty as the place he had made his home and he was far from welcoming. But it was he who she had come to find, so at least now she knew he was real and Kallem had already taught her that not everybody was what they seemed. He was a murderer, yet he had carried her safely from the forest that night, and now he had risked his own life to save hers. *Remember he was kind to you,* Artell had said. *I'll try,* Sill thought. Perhaps she should not judge the shaman too quickly either. Besides, the food he had prepared smelled *so* inviting that she could almost taste it through the scent.

'They speak about a lot of things,' Kallem replied to Draneth as he accepted the bowl and set it down in front of Sill before taking the second bowl for himself. 'Not all of it is true.'

'No, not all is true,' the shaman snapped as he motioned for them to begin eating, 'but do you doubt all of our past? Do you doubt what exists beyond our borders, or the fate of our ancestors?'

'No,' Kallem said as he began to tuck keenly into the food before him. 'No, I don't.'

Sill blew on the contents of her bowl to cool it and then sipped at the liquid broth that accompanied the bulkier contents of the stew.

'Good,' the shaman said sharply, 'so let's not waste any more time. If you haven't yet realised we just witnessed the first Grinth who have ever been sighted in the Inner Lands – coincidentally, just as you two appeared here, at my home. I assume it's me you were looking for?'

The rasp of the shaman's voice echoed around the cave but Kallem barely seemed to notice, preoccupied as he was with wolfing down the hot stew. A curt nod was all the shaman received in response.

Draneth's scowl grew deeper. 'Where did you come from?' he asked, more forcefully.

'Hillock,' Sill said hurriedly, to fill the gap. 'We came from Hillock.'

'And what about them?' Draneth said, his eyes boring into her. 'Where did they come from?'

'I, I don't know,' Sill realised as she said the words. She had not even thought about where the Grinth might have come from. *How did they get here?* 'They were following us,' she told the shaman.

But from where? As far back as Hillock? Oh no! Now she understood what the shaman was getting at. *What if there are more of them? Raffin!* she thought. *The village! I have to go back. I have to warn them.* But for some reason she said nothing and made no motion to leave.

Meanwhile, Draneth had resumed his questioning of Kallem. 'Don't you understand what this means?' He pushed himself up on his staff and began pacing back and forth beyond the fire. 'It means the Inner Lands are no longer safe!' He glared at Kallem from across the fire and for the briefest of moments reminded Sill of her father in the hut. 'Where there are two there will be more. Many more! Now tell me,' he hissed as he squatted down to peer at Kallem through the flames. 'Your eyes, why were they yellow?'

'*Yellow*?' Kallem said lazily. 'I didn't know. But I felt something when they were near.' The bowl of food lay empty before him and his head nodded gently as though he could fall asleep at any moment.

Sill tried to focus but her eyelids felt so heavy she could barely keep them open. She set her bowl down clumsily before she dropped it. 'The village,' she tried to warn Kallem but her words were a slur, 'we have to...' But first she had to sleep. *I'm so drowsy.*

'Yes,' Draneth had abandoned Kallem and resumed prowling the cave. 'We have to risk it, Tamarellin.'

Sill no longer knew or cared what he was talking about. *I must sleep*, was all she could think.

'If these were the first, they were not the strongest.' The blur across the fire moved from left to right, muttering to itself. 'They looked like they had travelled far. Perhaps they found some way to slip through? Yes, many will die.'

Sill knew she needed to wake, needed to rouse herself enough to stir Kallem but her limbs felt loose and unresponsive; and she was so very tired. *The food,* she thought fleetingly. *There was something wrong with the food.* The smell had been too enticing, too intoxicating. They had been so hungry from their journey. *We couldn't resist it...*

The blur across the fire was still talking to itself but Sill could no longer make out the words. *I have to wake Kallem*, she thought, *have to tell him...something*. But she also needed to sleep. *Yes, I must sleep.*

'Not the first,' Kallem mumbled beside her. 'Not the first.'

CHAPTER 8

Artell set down the comb for a second and ran her fingers through the long, black hair, checking for tangles. The white streak fell down in front of her face, as it always did, and she stroked it back, holding it there whilst her spare hand groped again for the comb. *It won't be long*, she thought gladly, *before the rest of my hair matches the streak*. Lately she had noticed the odd white stray in the comb after brushing and she was certain it was not only coming from the front of her head.

Unlike most people, she would welcome the change when it came. The streak had always been a cruel reminder of the past, the physical part of her that had died along with her beloved husband and beautiful daughter. The rest of the harm ran deeper but that she did not show. That part she suffered alone.

The damage to her son was plainer to see. Kallem had been a bright and empathic child, a sweet, quiet boy with playful eyes and a ready smile. She remembered how he used to help her at the vegetable patch, laying the earth and patting it so gently before smiling up at her, waiting for her approval. But just like her hair, Kallem had changed, and that sweet boy was gone; hidden somewhere deep inside where a young boy had witnessed an unimaginable horror. Why he had told them it was the Grinth, Artell didn't know. From that day on, she could no longer read him as she used to and he barely spoke a word. Instead, he used to get up in the middle of the night and wander out into the forest, alone, until the villagers found him and brought him back. That had terrified her almost as much as her loss. She watched him day and night, would sit awake by his bed when he slept. She cried and held him, begged and pleaded with him, screamed and shouted at him, but it made no difference. He would always find a time, a chance, to slip away again. Why he did it nobody knew. Perhaps he was searching for his own death. Whatever his motives, eventually she gave up on him and let him go. It was too much for one person to take and she was too tired, too weak, too filled with her own grief to cope. The villagers had given up on him, too, and stopped bringing him back.

Instead, Artell had preoccupied herself by focussing on her plants: her vegetables and her herbs. But she knew deep down that no matter how much life she created, it would never replace that which she had lost. They had found the bear, she remembered. Marn had reported it, not far from the incident, its claws and teeth bloodied with the evidence of its crime.

The sound of knocking interrupted her thoughts and brought her back into the present.

Hillock's new Leader strode in without further warning and hovered in the doorway to Artell's room.

Artell was so taken aback, she hesitated before beginning to rise, as was custom, but Soffus dismissed the gesture anyway with a raised hand.

Artell lowered back onto the stool and resumed brushing her hair. 'You need to see me, Soffus?' she asked courteously. There was something about the man she had never liked or trusted. Brash and outspoken as he might be, Artell always had the impression that there was something more sinister, more calculating, lying beneath the surface, concealed behind those dark, bushy eyebrows and pointy grey beard. For now, the contents of her room seemed to occupy his attention and that unsettled her to the point that she stopped what she was doing and searched out his eyes with hers, imploring him to look directly at her.

Soffus found his voice but little in the way of manners. 'So,' he said gruffly, 'your son's left then.' It was more matter-of-fact than question but Artell treated it as one all the same.

'Yes. A while ago now,' she said, striving for her usual calm.

'Hmmf,' he grunted. His eyes went back to scanning her room and she resumed her combing, trying not to show her irritation. 'You know Malfur and Purdock have gotten together?' Soffus said.

She did know. The two council members had formed a close bond over the years. Artell was pleased to see them as one at last. She nodded silently, allowing him a faint smile. *But you didn't come here just for chit-chat.*

'Malfur hopes to be with child,' he snorted, apparently amused.

She wondered how he had gotten that information, unless it was just hearsay. There was a lot of that in Hillock and she tried her best to ignore it and only hear the truths, although sometimes the gaps in-between were admittedly more honest.

'It seems you're all alone now,' Soffus was saying, 'but I suppose you're used to that.'

'I suppose so,' she answered plainly. If Soffus was aware of tact, he clearly had no patience for it.

'Perhaps it's time *you* found somebody else, too,' he said, clearly trying his best to sound casual, which only served to make his intention more transparent. 'I mean, besides those damn plants you seem so fond of.' He chuckled to himself as he strolled further into the room, until his hands rested on the side of the table she sat at. He leaned towards her. 'You know,' he said quietly, 'you're not too old to be with child again either.'

She set the comb down loudly enough to ensure she had his full attention.

'I have a child,' she said firmly.

That seemed to anger him. 'Do you?' he said, rising and beginning to pace the room, *her* room. 'Kallem is banished, you know, he's not coming back,' he let that linger a moment as though to be sure she heard the threat. 'And we both know he has not been *your son* for a long time.'

'That doesn't mean I would want another!' Artell said, her own temper flaring. *Insufferable man! Who do you think you are that you can just walk into my home and talk to me like this!* She had also not forgotten his part in her son's sentencing. If he had been given the decision, she wondered if Kallem's punishment would not have been more severe.

She tried to calm herself, not wanting to provoke his ire, or risk too much of her own. He was Hillock's Leader now. She would have to get used to that, or leave, along with her son. *Perhaps I should have left with Sill?* She had been so eager for the girl to catch up with Kallem that the only thoughts she had spared for herself were of slowing Sill down. *Perhaps my sense is fading, along with my hair?*

'Hmmf,' Soffus grunted. He sighed audibly, evidently trying to suppress his own temper, albeit with greater difficulty. 'I was just saying, isn't it about time you moved on?' he continued. 'The world's seen many suns and seasons since your husband died.'

'And my daughter,' Artell reminded him. *You're not the only one who can do tactless.*

' 'What?'

'My daughter was killed, too.'

'Oh, yes.' Soffus waved a hand dismissively, as though that fact was insignificant. 'That wasn't my point,' he said, quickly angering again – she cut him off before he could make it.

'Did you come here for a reason, Soffus, or just to bring up the past?' She held his answering glower coolly for a few moments before he, mercifully, turned away.

'Hmmf,' he grunted, as he strolled slowly back towards the doorway. He stopped there and chuckled as he turned to face her again, stroking the pointy grey beard thoughtfully – another mannerism Artell detested. 'We're having a meeting,' he said, eventually. 'The Council. To discuss plans to join Anell Village. Make sure you're there.' And without another word he turned and strode purposefully out.

Artell reached quickly for her comb and resumed brushing her hair. When the white lock fell in front of her eyes again she cursed and threw the comb against the wall before her, then thumped her fist violently into the wooden table. She sat up straight, head facing the ceiling, and with her eyes closed, took a deep breath and held it for a moment. Then she exhaled and relaxed.

Ignoring the pain in her hand, she took a piece of string – died an earthy-brown – and tied her hair back in the usual way. *Soffus is right*, she thought ruefully, *I am all alone*.

Later that day, Artell made her way over to the *Palakhar* where Hillock's eldest (and allegedly wisest) met to discuss and resolve the crucial decisions affecting their people's daily lives. Often these decisions were of minor consequence in the grand scheme of things; a trade taking place, the winter harvest, a dispute between two villagers; but today's meeting was to reshape their very way of life. If they were really abandoning Hillock, what was to become of them? Would they truly be welcomed in Anell with open arms? What would happen if the food was not enough to sustain them all? Would they get a say in the major decisions that concerned Anell's leadership? She wondered if Sill would return before the whole village packed up and left. Would she even know her way back? Artell grimaced as she realised what a fool she was, sending a young girl out alone on such a reckless errand when there were far greater things at stake than her own selfishness. *But that's just it.* There were greater things going on and she was certain Sill was to play an important role in whatever was to come. *There's something different about her, something special. Just like Kallem.*

Those thoughts and others weighed heavily upon her as she crossed the short distance to where the *Palakhar* rested, at the top of the hill the village had been named after. She had always thought the name hardly did the village justice; with its view of the forest and the mountains, it really deserved something grander. *Something in the old language.* But who knew what the people who came here had gone through. *Naming this place was probably the last thing that mattered to them.*

As she walked, people smiled and nodded at her respectfully whilst they went about their daily chores. The kind faces of her fellow villagers went some way to easing her burden and Artell mirrored their smiles, feeling grateful for, and proud of, her people's resilience. *Perhaps we will be ok.*

Meggum was waiting for her by the entrance to the *Palakhar*. Since Soffus had not thought to tell her what time they were meeting, she had paid a visit to her friend as soon as he'd departed and her calm had returned. She had not told Meggum the full story of Soffus' visit. He was, after all, Hillock's Leader now and it would not serve the village well to stir up any more trouble at such a vital time.

Meggum greeted her with the adolescent grin she had worn since her youth. Artell liked that about her. She was much older now, but not much else about Meggum had changed. She was a gentle and benevolent woman, with a warm nature and youthful laugh. When she was younger she had been the older girl that all Artell's friends both admired and envied. With her green, sparkling eyes, shiny brown hair, slim body and full breasts, all the men had lusted over her, until Fallor had finally won her for his own. He had been notably older than her, but at that age he had always seemed destined for great things and so her father had approved of the match. Artell knew that Meggum had not always been faithful to him in her youth, but as the brown hair made way for grey and her body and mind matured, that part of her at least had moved on, and what was left, Artell liked well enough. Meggum was not brave and rarely spoke up in the meetings, but she was easy company and loyal at least to her village.

As Artell reached Meggum, they clasped each other's wrists briefly before passing through the doorway and emerging in the small, round, open hall that would house the outcome of Hillock's fate. *Palakhar* meant 'speak to the gods' in the old language but as most did not believe in the gods anymore it was generally understood simply as 'the place where decisions are made'.

The other ten Elders were already seated in a circle, with Soffus heading them at the farthest side, opposite the entrance. Meggum sat down beside her husband and Artell joined her, sitting herself next to the usually cheery Bodin who, today, cut a graver figure.

Malfur and Purdock sat closely together, across from her, and appeared relaxed and contented in their newly shared fondness. The rest of the council – Bodin, Sethum, Karth, Mynnelle, Toldir and Kessan – were all suitably sombre.

Soffus began in typically direct fashion. 'We're all here,' he stated, 'so let's begin.'

Kessan immediately interrupted. 'I still don't see why we are being so hasty,' he said. 'Are we in that much peril that we really need to flee our own village? If so, I don't see it.' He folded his arms stubbornly.

Kessan had been against the move from the start, not that it had ever been much of a discussion. To Artell, it had seemed Soffus, Karth and Toldir had been the main drivers, and Fallor had eventually seceded to them during his unaccustomed outburst at the all-village meeting. It was strange to her that Soffus would be so keen on a move when he had finally got the position he craved, as Hillock's Leader. On the other hand, her dislike of him aside, perhaps he really did just have the village's best interests at heart.

Soffus waited tensely for Kessan to finish, before replying.

He's trying to show us he has patience, Artell thought, knowing better.

'We all know that our wildlife has been depleting,' Soffus began.

'Then let us live off vegetables.' This time it was Bodin who interrupted. 'Do we need meat to survive? Perhaps if we give the animals a chance to recover their numbers?'

'And what happens when we have a bad crop?' Soffus asked him. 'And another? It's happened before?'

'What about the forest?' Kessan said. 'It's our best source of trade.'

Kessan would say anything to contest the move. He had always been afraid of any sort of change, as most of them were.

'We will still travel back and forth to the forest,' Soffus answered in an assured tone. 'We have built many canoes, we *are* ready.'

'Well then what's the harm in waiting until we *have* a bad crop?' Kessan said. 'Why move based on what *could* happen when it has not happened yet? And what about our homes?'

Kessan had clearly come prepared, Artell thought. She would wait to hear both arguments before she shared her thoughts.

'Do we plant our vegetables in the hope that they might grow?' Karth said evenly. Karth was generally known to possess a logical thought-process. 'No,' he continued, 'we plant them in places where we *know* they *will* grow. We have strong bonds in Anell, many of us have relatives living there. They have the space, they have the lake, and they are willing to accept us.'

Soffus nodded in concurrence and then held up a hand, this time not giving Kessan the chance to counter. Kessan grimaced but held his tongue.

'We have had these discussions before,' Soffus said in a manner that made clear he thought this a waste of time. 'The decision has been made.'

'Has it?' Kessan snorted. 'I don't recall being present for that discussion. I still think we are being far too hasty.'

'Really?' Soffus shot back at him. 'And what if the Grinth ever did invade? Our village was the first place people came to when our ancestors fled here. Likely, we'd be the first place to be attacked, too, if they ever broke through.'

'Have we any reason to believe the Grinth could break through?' Artell asked, mildly alarmed. 'They haven't breeched the Inner Lands so far.'

'That's beside the point,' Soffus said, not angrily, for once, but she did notice that he avoided eye contact with her. To Kessan he said, 'Everyone was present when Fallor made the decision. If you didn't like it you could have spoken up then.'

Artell noted that Fallor had stayed out of the conversation so far. He looked to be chewing his gums, almost stubbornly, as though he were trying hard not to get involved, now that he had stepped down.

That was a shame. He had made sensible decisions as their Leader, for the most part. Artell did not like how Soffus had avoided her question. Nor did she like the way he used the last meeting as a challenge to Kessan. That had clearly not been a meeting for sound debate. This matter should have been discussed more earnestly, in private, and any decision should have been broken more lightly to the village. This was the normal way of things before Fallor had stepped down, rightly or wrongly. She considered voicing these thoughts but, annoyed as she was, she could not necessarily argue against the move. Things *had* been changing in recent years. Tensions had been growing, spurred by depleting food supplies, which had perhaps even led to her son being attacked, and consequently labelled a murderer. She still could not accept that he had been banished from Hillock. *Banished from me.* But in a different village with different laws and leadership, perhaps previous decisions could be challenged. It was worth a chance. So she kept her silence, as Soffus moved on.

'As I said, the decision has been made,' he said, to a mixture of satisfied and sour faces. 'What we now need to discuss is how and when the relocation will happen.' He looked at each of them sternly as though he was dealing with children. 'Talks with Anell, surrounding this, have been in place for some time.'

'I'm sure they have,' Kessan scoffed petulantly.

'By the peaks, let me finish!' Soffus suddenly yelled at him.

Kessan was so startled he simply gaped helplessly at the other Elders, probably hoping for some support. When he didn't get it, he subsided meekly and folded his arms again, looking deflated and defeated.

Artell felt for him. Kessan was not a bad man but neither did he possess the required skills to oppose Soffus for leadership, and his snide remarks were not helpful here.

'Toldir,' Soffus said, referring to his colleague. He kept his eyes on Kessan as though reminding the Elder of his victory.

Toldir took up the lead smoothly. 'We have thirty canoes finished,' he said, 'some for people, some for belongings – just like the ones we use for trading. More are in production. Anell has half as many new homes built and they've promised us enough for everybody. Of course, wood for these we're giving them for free,' he added, needlessly.

'Yes,' Soffus said, retaking charge. 'So we will not be looking to move until after the winter.' There was no argument on this front. 'There's no point wasting our current crops.'

Then he was interrupted by a commotion outside. 'What now?' he said, and the Elders turned their attention to the doorway, where panicked shouts could be heard beyond the *Palakhar's* walls. Before Artell had a chance to process what was happening, Ryll, Karth's youngest son, burst noisily into the *Palakhar*. His bloody state ended the meeting with immediate effect.

'The Grinth!' Ryll gasped in a voice thick with anguish. He winced in pain and his hand moved to where he was bleeding heavily from a long gash in his side.

Artell just stared at him, as dumbstruck as everybody else. The sight was so unexpected, his wound so horrific, that she almost wanted to believe this had been staged somehow by Soffus, to facilitate his plans for them to leave. *Even he wouldn't stoop this low.*

'They're in the forest,' Ryll groaned through the pain. 'We tried to hold them off but when we knew we couldn't they sent me back to warn everyone. There were so many!' His face twisted again in agony. 'You have to leave now!' he shouted at them.

'What are you talking about, boy?' Soffus said gruffly.

'Soffus, look at him!' Artell said. She stood and moved to Ryll's side. 'What can we do?' she asked urgently.

'Nothing!' Ryll said, his face pleading with her. 'You have to leave, now!'

'Ok,' Artell said. 'Tell everybody you can find to get to the canoes,' she told him. 'Everybody!'

He nodded at her, then looked to his father. 'My brothers,' he said desperately, shaking his head. The tears in his eyes told that they were already dead. Karth only stared at him as though he wasn't real.

'Ryll!' Artell said firmly, regaining the young man's attention. 'Tell them now!' He nodded at her, again, and with one final glance at his father, was gone.

'Everybody out,' Soffus commanded, finally unearthing his resolve. His voice rose as he began issuing orders, 'Karth – send as many men as we can spare to hold them off; when everybody else is safe, get them out. Toldir – find Brorn and Arteus and make sure they stay with the council. Artell – I want you to get as many people as you can to the canoes.'

'There aren't enough!' Artell said, suddenly realising. Her head was still reeling from the news and the sight of Ryll's horrendous wound. Soffus looked at her blankly.

Their world had dissolved in an instant and none of them knew what to do. Her head filled with visions of horror. *This can't be happening!* For a second she toyed again with the idea that this was all just some sort of foul trick Soffus had prepared to test them, but his own panicked expression told her otherwise. *This is real. It is happening.* Shock and revulsion swept through her body, threatening to overwhelm her if she didn't keep her calm. *Always calm.* 'There's not enough,' she repeated.

Soffus strode up to her and gripped her arms roughly. 'Then save as many you can,' he growled, and with that he ducked through the doorway and was gone.

Artell's head spun and she thought she might throw up. Meggum was at her side, pleading with her. 'Artell! What should we do?' Her friend was pale with fear. Her comfortable life had been turned upside down.

'Get the council to the boats,' Artell said assertively, into her eyes. 'The Soulslide will take you to Anell. All you have to do is follow the river. You can do this,' she added when Meggum only stared at her. 'Go now.' Meggum nodded but looked no more assured.

Artell left her to it and ran out into the chaos. People were already grabbing up belongings. 'Leave them!' she urged. 'Just get to the river!'

All very well until the canoes run out, she thought. Then again, if everything they knew about the Grinth was true, that may not be an issue.

CHAPTER 9

Kallem returned to consciousness to find the hawk watching him. As he eased himself up onto an elbow, the bird tilted its head, squawked, and then flew to land on the skull that topped the shaman's staff. The hawk rustled its brown feathers briefly and then sat still, resuming its watch.

'I should apologise,' Draneth said. 'You needed rest and I needed time to think.'

Kallem leapt swiftly to his feet, taking in his surroundings. It took a moment for him to register that the hum in the background was the sound of the waterfall and not the throbbing in his head. He wiped his eyes clear. Before him, the fire had long since burned out, leaving a blackened pile of ash on the rock-floor. *It is daytime*, he noted, by the light spilling into the cave mouth. He looked to his left and found the girl sitting, already awake. She smiled at him as though she thought the situation amusing.

'What did you do to us?' he asked the shaman, his right hand reaching instinctively to check for the red sword. It was still sheathed securely at his side. He remembered that he had not yet cleaned the blade since the Grinth, and made a mental note to do so as soon as he could. *I must not let the blade rust.*

'I put something in your food to help you sleep,' the shaman said bluntly, eyeing Kallem from beneath his scowl.

'Do you poison all your guests?' Kallem asked, looking at the girl again. She seemed fine. He tried to recall the nature of the previous evening's conversation, and failed. Physically at least, he had to admit that he did feel refreshed. Protecting the girl had been exhausting and he hadn't slept for many days. But that was irrelevant. If the shaman thought it acceptable to slip something into his food...

What else is he capable of?

Who cares? It was my choice to come here.

This one is trouble, too.

Draneth grinned and for once his frown lines straightened somewhat. 'We don't get many guests,' he said, stroking the hawk's head with the back of his hand. The bird closed its eyes appreciatively. 'Perhaps my manners are a little out of practice.' He looked up at Kallem again. 'Would you have eaten it, if I told you?' He asked, raising an eyebrow.

Kallem chose not to respond. *The girl is ok, that is all that matters.*

Is it? Since when did you care? Why did you help her again? She is doomed anyway.

'You had travelled far,' the shaman continued, ignoring Kallem's silence, 'and we must make that journey again, so it is good you are well rested.'

You expect me to return to Hillock? Kallem wondered. That would go down well with the villagers.

'We must leave at once,' Draneth said, more brusquely. 'There is no time to waste.'

'I'm not going back,' Kallem told him.

No, the village is nothing to you. So the Grinth have returned? They will learn their folly, then, the hard way.

My mother, too?

He picked up his pack and made to leave. 'Are you coming?' he said to Sill over his shoulder. He could feel her hurt without having to see her face. He had already grown accustomed to it. *She wasn't happy there either. Why would she go back?*

'We have to warn them,' Sill said, as if responding to his thoughts.

He turned to look at her, ignoring the shaman's prying eyes and dark frown. 'I can't go back,' he said. 'I have been banished, remember?' He turned and walked from the cave, leaving her to chase after him.

Is that what you wanted?

The roar of the Frosty Falls intensified as he ducked through the low entrance to Draneth's cave. He let the sound wash over him. *Perhaps it will drown out my thoughts.*

'Don't you care?' Sill's shout was barely audible above the din of the Falls.

That's a good question, he thought. 'No,' he said aloud. *Why would I?* He started towards the slippery steps that would take him back down away from the cave – away from her – but the girl continued to follow. *She is stubborn*, he thought.

'Are you scared?' She yelled this time.

Scared? He turned and looked her over. *She* was scared, that was plain to see. She was angry, too. The spray from the waterfall had already wetted her hair. It clung to her face, messy and tangled, but she made no effort to wipe it away.

'It's ok to be scared!' she shouted through the tangles. 'I'm scared all the time.'

No, it isn't, Kallem's memories reminded him. *They screamed whilst you just hid and watched.* 'I'm not scared,' he told her truthfully. *I'm not anything.*

'Then why won't you come?' she pleaded. Her voice was just a squeak above the crashing of the falling ice. 'The Grinth! If they're really back, they could kill everyone! Our friends. Families.'

The Grinth, he thought. *Family*. He had thought killing a Grinth might have stirred more emotion in him, but perhaps there was nothing left to stir. Just like killing Marn, there had been no anger, no sadness, and certainly no remorse. As for family...

Yours are already dead.

My mother is not dead yet. Does she deserve to die like that? Does the girl? That's what will happen if she returns alone.

She is nothing to you. She is not your responsibility.

He turned his back on her and started walking down the icy steps.

The girl continued to follow him, shouting at him as they went.

He reached the bottom of the stairs and moved towards the lake where the heavy ice collided with the water, crushing itself under its own weight. The noise and power was staggering, but he did not waver.

He dropped his pack on the ground and knelt by the water. Ripples hurled themselves at the side of the rock like small, angry waves. Spray from the waterfall soaked his face and clothes but he ignored it. *I will soon dry off in the sun.*

That depended on which way he went. There was little point heading downhill. The Grinth could already be flooding through the Inner Lands for all he knew. *Up then, into the mountains?* It was hardly the comfort of the forest he was used to, but he could survive there. *For what purpose? Is survival enough?*

He pulled his sword from its sheath. The tip of the red iron was still caked in dry black blood, the rest of the blade spattered and stained. He thought about Marn's blood dripping to the ground. *It was dark but not black. More real than this.* He threw the thought from his mind and dipped the sword into the foaming water, wiping the blade clean on a smooth, moss-coated rock.

'What about your mother?' He barely heard the girl shout from behind him. 'Are you going to let her die, too?'

Too? That he heard. He stood and spun, the red sword hanging loosely in his grasp. The last of the black blood slid from the blade to drip down onto the wet rock below. He gripped the hilt more tightly. *I didn't let them die! I didn't! I was just a child, just a boy. Weak and useless. Weak and pathetic.*

But you are not a child anymore. You should show her, like you did Marn.

No, that's not what she meant. She wasn't talking about them.

The girl was soaked through, just as he was. She moved forwards slowly, tentatively. His sword hand tensed and his eyes widened as he watched her wrap her slim, young arms around his waist, hugging herself against him, her head barely reaching his chest.

You could end it for her now. She won't have to suffer like they did.

'Please, Kallem,' she mouthed up at him through the roar. 'I need your help. I can't do this on my own.'

But I don't need you. I don't need anyone. He looked down at her sad eyes, felt her embrace – something he had not experienced since he himself was a child – and yet still he felt nothing. *There is nothing left of me.*

Gently, he removed her arms and sheathed his sword. She took a step back and watched him like a child waiting for a parent's appraisal. *Or a brother's.*

She had no brothers or sisters, he knew. Her father was a cruel, uncaring man and she had not known her mother.

She did it because she needed to, his mind said, *not for you.*

Does that matter?

'Ok,' he said to her, though he did not know why, 'I will come.' *What difference does it make anyway?*

'Promise me,' she said stubbornly, her sodden hair still sticking to her young face. 'Promise you won't leave me.'

Everyone leaves eventually, he thought, *but she already knows that*. 'I promise,' he said for her sake.

Draneth appeared through the spray, looking decidedly drenched and dour. He clenched his teeth into a grimace and shook his staff at them angrily. 'Are we done getting wet?' His coarse voice somehow scratched through the clamour of the falls. 'Can we go now?'

Kallem nodded.

In silence, he followed the girl and the shaman as they snaked their way back through the mountain and eventually emerged out into the bright, white morning. Snow had fallen during the night, covering the previous tracks they had made. The black blood had been hidden, too, as though the Inner Lands sought to hide any evidence of the Grinth's presence within its borders. Two mounds of snow were all that marked the place where they had fought and died, their bodies buried for now, but only until the snow melted again, as it surely would beneath the virgin sun.

Before them, in the mid-distance, the land shone with bronze browns, vivid greens and golden yellows, making a patchwork of the hills leading east. To their right, the Southern Range loomed tall and bare, the furthest peaks reaching up to touch a pale blue sky smeared with wispy puffs of sparse cloud. Ahead, and further east, Kallem could just about make out more mountains, but they were mere grey bumps on a faded horizon. Somewhere in that distant corner of the Inner Lands, Rydan Fort must stand. If the Grinth were really coming, shouldn't they be warned? As far as he knew, no one from the Fort had visited Hillock for many suns, years even. *Does the Fort even still stand?* And, if it did, how much protection could it really provide against their enemy? *Perhaps our time is ended, as it should be.*

But not your time. Not yet.

He thought about asking Draneth if the Fort should know but then decided he didn't really care either way. It was only the girl he had made a promise to, no one else.

The journey back was not so tough as before. Although a sense of urgency remained, Kallem detected no pursuit this time, nor did they encounter any threat or sign of the Grinth along the way. The shaman seemed to be more wary of Kallem than his surroundings, but he did at least keep them well fed and hydrated. Draneth was adept at making fire, and his flask appeared to hold such an endless supply of drinking water that Kallem could almost have believed some of the stories of his supposed magics. He suspected it was more likely, though, that the shaman simply carried several identical flasks beneath those long fur robes that he wore. *What else are you concealing behind there? I would bake beneath so much clothing.* But the shaman did not seem to mind. Kallem was still adapting to enduring the company of others, but neither Draneth nor Sill spoke much and he was thankful for that. He did not yet trust the shaman, but the girl appeared to have accepted him and perhaps she was a better judge than he was. *Then again, she trusts me, too,* he thought. The girl herself looked deep in thought. She stayed close to Kallem when they walked and talked even less than Draneth, certainly less than she had done on the outward journey. Concern had become a constant feature of her young face and it had begun to play on Kallem's mind. His own sister had been full of happy laughs and unhindered smiles, but Sill had little motive for either of those things. *These are cruel times*, he thought as he watched her, *better suited to people like me.*

You're not starting to care about her, are you? She is not your sister. She's nobody to you.

I made her a promise.

Draneth's hawk had not accompanied them on the journey and the shaman cut an even grumpier figure without the distraction of the bird's presence. Every now and then he would scan the skies as though expecting the hawk to reappear, but it never did. *The bird is wiser than we are*, Kallem thought.

After days of endless walking, they finally caught sight of Hillock and at first glance everything looked to be quiet and relatively normal.

'Where are all the people?' Draneth asked Kallem as though he would know the answer.

Kallem gazed up at the slopes. *They can't have left for Anell already?* His eyes drifted back towards the trees. He had surprised himself by feeling something resembling pleasure at the sight of the forest and its familiar *serethen* trees. So much so that he had barely noticed the village or the lack of people. He could not lie to himself that returning so soon did not make him feel...*something. Is this apprehension?* he wondered. Most of the people here still feared him or otherwise wanted him dead. *I should not have come back.*

The girl took off at a run.

'Sill, wait!' Draneth hissed at her, but the girl did not listen. The shaman frowned briefly at Kallem, then started after her, his robes billowing as he moved.

Kallem stared up at the slopes a moment longer. Could he make out somebody at the top? *Something's not right here.*

The girl was already starting to climb the hill, the shaman pursuing her at a surprising pace, even though one hand held the heavy staff out before him.

Kallem began to move, too. He broke into a run, covering the distance to the foot of Hillock's southern slope in no time at all. Then he was sprinting up the hill, his legs moving quickly and powerfully, his arms guiding him forwards until he stood with the others, looking down at the forlorn figure of Fallor, Hillock's former Leader.

The Elder sat, cross-legged and alone, just a short distance from the *Palakhar*. His face stared down towards the forest, but his eyes held a glazed sadness as though his mind was somewhere else.

'Where is everyone?' the girl panted, ignoring all courtesies. 'Where have they gone?'

'Gone...' Fallor repeated softly. 'They've gone.'

'Where?' Sill pleaded.

'Snap out of it, man,' Draneth growled at the Elder. He prodded him with the end of his staff. Fallor grabbed the wooden skull with both hands and eyed the three of them fiercely.

'Where are all your people?' Draneth asked him, wrenching the staff back from the Elder's frail hands. 'What happened?'

Fallor's features softened and his jaw began to tremble. 'Gone...to the river,' he said, his voice as thin as he was. He wheezed out a sad sigh. 'To Anell,' he said wistfully.

'Where is my mother?' Kallem asked him.

'Kallem?' Fallor looked at him with something resembling sympathy.

Spare me your pity, old man. 'My mother?' he repeated.

'She went with the others,' Fallor waved a hand towards the north where the Soulslide River lay. 'To Anell. There weren't enough canoes...' he said and his eyes drifted off again.

'What happened?' Draneth asked again. 'Was it the Grinth?'

'Yes,' Fallor said, a haunted look creeping onto his face. His mouth twitched as he pointed a weak finger down toward the trees. 'In the forest,' he whispered as though they might hear, 'the rest are trying to...hold them back, so people can...escape...but they won't last. Not against *them*.'

The forest, Kallem thought.

'We must head to the river, quickly,' Draneth told them. He reached out a hand to Fallor who ignored it.

'No,' the Elder snapped, 'I'm staying.' He folded his arms resolutely.

They do not belong there, Kallem thought. Not in the forest. *Is this anger I feel?*

Isn't this what you've been waiting for? What you've been preparing for, all these years?

Something was stirring within him. Something long forgotten. Something savage.

'Very well,' Draneth snarled at Fallor, 'stay and die like the old fool that you are.' He stomped the butt of his staff into the ground. 'Will enough not die already?'

It was my forest, not theirs, the child in him remembered. He felt his muscles tense. *I am angry*, he realised. Action spurred him into motion. His sword was released from its sheath and he found himself running downhill, towards the trees. *Not again. I won't let it happen again!*

'Kallem, don't!' Draneth's words chased him down the slope. He might have heard the girl calling, too, but if so, the sound was lost in the haze of returning memories and emotions.

Fear, sorrow, hate. And now more. Horror, anger. *No, not anger...rage!*

Feelings trapped for years seemed to boil up inside him, threatening to overflow. Flashes of claws, teeth, his father's stunned face, his sister's screams, flickered like fire across his mind.

Yes, remember, one of his voices told him, but it was not like he had a choice. The desire for vengeance, for blood, was overwhelming.

I'm already too late, he realised as he entered the trees.

The stench of death corrupted the usually clean air and now he could hear shouts and screams as men fought and died somewhere deeper in the forest. The guttural grunts of the Grinth could be heard, too, tainting the typically tranquil sounds, just as the smell of death polluted the air. A frenzy seemed to spur him faster. It coursed through his veins and ignited his blood until blood was all he could think about.

Black blood. It would flow at his hands, spray across the ground and blot out the sun until everything turned to dark. He passed a reddened body with a severed arm. Its face stared up in surprise, the skin grey and dead.

Ryll.

You played with him as a child, didn't you?

I might have saved him if I'd been here. If I hadn't killed one of my own kind.

Rage led him deeper, his body skipping over roots and ducking under branches until he reached the battle. The Grinth were all around him and so were the bodies, both human and Grinth. These creatures were stronger than the ones he had killed before but that did not stop him. The nearest lost its head in a shower of black that drew the attention of others. They died as quickly, except for one that lost its legs first until its head followed moments later. The men around him were not faring so well but Kallem barely noticed. Blood was what he had come for and blood was what he took. It soaked the ground around his feet, splattered against the trunks of trees, dripped from green leaves, and covered him, too. He did not notice that he was the only man left alive until the Grinth began to back away, leading him after them. Then he found himself in a clearing.

Above, the sky was still blue. *Only I am black*, he realised as he looked down at his arms and clothes. He stood panting in the sunlight, shielding his eyes as he waited for them to come at him. Grinth moved among the trees, grunting and hissing their hate, but they did not advance. Yellow pupils peered at him through otherwise dark, opaque eyes. *Come on, what are you waiting for?*

It was only then that he noticed the voices.

We know you, Kallem, the voices whispered. *We have tasted you before.*

What is this? he thought, looking around him. *Who are you?*

'Who's there?' he shouted at the trees. 'Show yourself!' He turned about, looking for the source but only sharp Grinth teeth grinned and hissed back at him.

You are ours, Kallem, the voices hissed. *You belong to ussss.*

They're inside me, he realised. *Inside my head.*

More Grinth had appeared, crowding around the trees and snarling threats at him through their pointed, lipless teeth and vile, yellow eyes. Some twitched their claws eagerly as though desperate to poke them into him. Others, less patient, scraped them across the bark of the trees. A mist had begun to fog the air around them as though clouds were descending on the clearing.

'Come on, what are you waiting for?' Kallem growled. He began to advance but he knew he was now desperately outnumbered. The mist grew thicker, beginning to hide some of the creatures from sight. Dark shapes moved through the fog. *I'll kill as many as I can*, he thought, bracing himself.

Just as he was about to charge, a man stepped out before him from the other side of the clearing. The man stopped and smiled faintly at him as though they were old friends. A yellow sword hung from his belt, matching the yellow of his eyes.

'What are you doing?' Kallem said, bewildered. 'Get out of here!'

'Why?' the man asked. His smile took on a quizzical edge as though he was the one who was confused.

'They'll kill you!' Kallem said. The mist was clouding everything and he twisted left to right, making sure he wasn't being surrounded.

'They mean me no harm,' the yellow-eyed man said, calmly. 'No more than they do you.' He smiled again, pleasantly.

Kallem stared at him, incredulous. *What is this madness?*

Come with us, Kallem, the voices whispered.

'Stop it!' he shouted at them. He held his hands to his head, trying to block them out. He wondered if his eyes were yellow, too, right now.

'My name is Zyan,' the man before him explained in a friendly tone. His voice was soft, almost gentle. The yellow iron sword remained at his waist as though he had no need for it. 'Why do you fight?' he asked casually.

Why Kallem? The voices asked, too. *Why do you kill ussss?* Guttural calls boomed out from the trees and others responded somewhere deeper in the forest.

The frenzy that had spurred him had vanished, evaporated into the fog that now choked the clearing. He shook his head, trying to shake out the voices and wondering if this strange man who stood before him was real, or just a further reflection of his bruised psyche. Zyan, he had called himself. *Is your blood red or black Zyan?* he wondered.

Zyan tilted his head as though he could hear Kallem's thoughts. 'Is it death you seek?'

We can give it to you, Kallem, the voices hissed. *We can give you anything.*

There was barely a sound as the hawk shot past Kallem's head, its body sweeping away some of the mist in its path. Zyan ducked as the bird opened its wings and clawed at his head.

Run Kallem! A different voice now said.

The bird swooped again and Zyan leaned nimbly to his right, batting a hand at it as though the hawk were no more than an annoying fly. The surrounding Grinth hissed irritably, their eyes fixated on the brown hawk.

Run, Kallem, the voice said again. *You promised her.*

He had not thought about the girl since the frenzy had taken him. Had not thought about anything. Just acted. Now the memory of her and the shaman standing at the top of the hill came back to him with a jolt. *I shouldn't have left her*, he thought. *I made a promise.*

The hawk dived again and this time its wings swept the mist back enough to reveal the purple bodies crowding forward, shining in the sunlight.

Run, Kallem, the voice urged. *Now!*

This time, Kallem took the voice's advice and turned and fled through the mist at a sprint.

Sill waited anxiously at the river's edge as Draneth wrestled the half-cut canoe into the water. She stared into the forest, hoping that at any second more men would appear from the trees, hoping Kallem would appear from the trees. And not *them*. She could hear their noises getting closer. Each grunt seemed to echo from the mountains, driving fear into her heart so deep she could only bury it there and stare dumbly at the trees, waiting for one of her two imagined scenarios to come true. Either the Grinth would skulk from the darkness and make the nightmare real, or men would emerge to wake and save her from this awful dream.

A *keeeeeee* from above turned her eyes upward and she watched in a trance as Draneth's hawk spotted them and swooped gracefully down to land on the prow of the makeshift canoe.

'He's coming!' Draneth called to her.

How do you know? She watched the forest, picturing any number of horrors unfolding before her eyes. Her father's burned, twisted frame, half-man, half-Grinth; Raffin, yellow-eyed and vacant, his head pouring red from the wound she had given him. Had Raffin escaped with the others? He was smart: surely he'd managed to get away? *He must have.*

The shape that did burst from the trees was not any of the things she had imagined but, at first sight, equally horrifying. Human-shaped and black from head to foot, it stopped at the edge of the forest, then spotted them and started running in their direction. *Is that Kallem?* As he neared them she saw that his hair was matted; wet and thick with Grinth blood. His face and clothes were dark, too, and even the sword that flew in his hand was black instead of the red she remembered. But it *was* Kallem. He slowed to a jog as he reached them, the whites of his eyes a bright relief in contrast to all the black. Sill could smell the death on him and she couldn't help but take a step back as the bile hit the back of her throat, making her cough. She swallowed it back and then gasped at the sharp taste. Kallem stopped to watch her briefly, then hurried past and splashed noisily into the river. She turned and watched as he helped Draneth manoeuvre the raft, seemingly unmindful of the stench he bore. The shaman gave Kallem a cold glare but otherwise exchanged no words as the two men readied the canoe in the water.

'Sill, come on,' Draneth said and she began to drift towards them, struggling to draw her eyes from the ghastly sight of Kallem's bloodstained shape.

'Sill, get in!' Draneth shouted and now she obeyed, accepting his hand as he helped her up onto the unfinished wood.

She sat as best she could in the hollow, near to the front, holding the sides as the canoe rocked unsteadily in the flowing water. Draneth clambered up and sat behind her in the centre. Kallem held the canoe steady and then hopped aboard, too, sitting astern at the back-end, perhaps as far away from them as he could. He swivelled his body around so he faced back towards the trees and bowed his head so that his long hair fell about his shoulders, hiding his features. Water from the river had washed some of the blood away and now black liquid dripped and drizzled down his back, no doubt staining the *serethen* wood of the canoe.

'Was it you?' he said softly from behind his hair.

'Was what, who?' Draneth asked moodily as he plunged his staff into the water and pushed off the ground, sending the canoe out and forwards with the current.

'The voice,' Kallem said, still facing the trees.

'Ah,' Draneth chuckled. He withdrew the staff from the murky waters and rested it evenly across the breadth of the boat like a paddle. 'I'm not anywhere near that magical,' he said. 'It was Tamarellin you heard.'

Kallem nodded slightly as if he understood.

Sill didn't know what they were talking about. She looked at the hawk, who had now taken up residence on Draneth's shoulder. It looked back at her, tilting its head quizzically as though it was as interested in her as she was in it.

The canoe was swaying heavily in the water and Sill gripped the sides more tightly, afraid it would tip her out. The water was dark in the oncoming dusk and she could not see through it. She wondered if more horrors lurked below. *A voice? Tamarellin?* She tried to make sense of what she was hearing but nothing seemed to make sense anymore. *Is that you?* she asked the hawk in her head but, if it was, she received no answer. Was it so unbelievable that a bird could talk? Sill knew better than most that there was more to the Inner Lands than people realised. She now recalled the conversation the shaman had seemed to have with himself that night in the cave. He had mentioned the name Tamarellin then. *Was he talking to the hawk?* she wondered, amazed.

'Where will we go?' Kallem asked.

'Anell,' Sill said quickly. 'I have to know if Raffin is ok.'

'Who is Raffin?' the shaman asked, almost suspiciously.

'A friend,' she said. *My only friend.*

'And where then?' Kallem asked quietly.

Sill had not yet brought herself to think beyond Anell and the hope that Raffin had made it out of Hillock safely. She could barely cope with what was happening *right now.*

'Before we left the Moonmirror,' Draneth said, 'I sent Tamarellin to Rydan Fort with a message that the Grinth were here, and that they should be prepared. I also told them to evacuate as many villages as possible to the mountains or the Fort, although something tells me the mountains would be the safer option, even with winter coming.' The shaman's frown darkened as he continued. 'Tamarellin is not sure what their reaction will be. They are led now by a man named Venth. He's as stubborn as the peaks themselves and it's a pity that he was also probably their best choice. He and I don't exactly see eye-to-eye.' The Soulslide had begun to bend slightly and the shaman dipped his staff into the water again, keeping the canoe in line with the current. 'Once we reach Anell, I plan to take a small party to Rydan,' he said, in answer to Kallem's question. 'I would like you both to come with me.'

Sill looked at him in surprise. *He wants me to go to Rydan Fort?* she thought numbly. *What for? What about Artell? What about Raffin?* He would never leave his family. *What about the Grinth?*

'The Inner Lands have a balance,' Draneth explained, perhaps in response to their silence. 'This place creates what it needs to survive. I believe that is the answer you have been seeking Sill.' He raised a knowing eyebrow at her as she turned her head to face him. 'Your power is not a curse, it is a gift. If we are to survive against the Grinth we cannot run forever – the Grinth have proven that – and if there is to be a final stand, I believe it will be here, in the Inner Lands. That is why I am going to Rydan. You both have a part to play in this war, I think, but the choice has to be yours.'

Sill listened to the shaman's words, but could not bring herself to understand or agree with them. If the Inner Lands had such a balance, then where had all the animals gone? *And why did my mother have to die for me to receive this 'gift'?* The thought made her angry. How had he known about her power anyway? She had not even mentioned it and had certainly not attempted to use it since the Grinth had attacked her and Kallem. *I was too scared,* she remembered bitterly. *I'm still too weak.* But whatever strange knowledge Draneth might possess, something about him made her want to trust him, especially since they had spent more time together. She wasn't certain why she felt that way, but just like she had known to trust Raffin, she felt a similar way about the shaman, and Kallem, too. *I hope I can trust my instincts,* she thought. *Maybe I've just been lonely for too long?*

Draneth continued to guide the canoe, apparently in no hurry for a response from either of them, and so Sill did not give him one.

The river flowed softly and steadily, the water jingling below them and lapping gently against the side of the crudely cut canoe. In the background, the forest could still be seen, the front line of *serethen* standing tall and dark in the fading light; the last sentries between the deceptively tranquil world outside and whatever still lurked within. If an Anell trader was paddling upstream at that moment, they would be forgiven for thinking nothing was amiss.

Kallem was the first to speak. 'There is something I need to tell you. Both of you.' His voice was as dispassionate as ever, as though nothing in his world had changed, but Sill knew better. She had seen it in his eyes at the river's edge. *He is different now. We all are.* His head remained bowed, his face still concealed behind the blood-streaked hair. Just like the darkness of the river water, whatever depths he may contain, for now, lay hidden. 'You spoke of men with yellow eyes, like mine,' he said to Draneth.

'I did,' the shaman said. His tone urged Kallem to continue.

'I met someone in the forest,' Kallem said, his voice distant. 'A man. We were surrounded by Grinth but he just stood there amongst them, without fear.' A silence hung over him for a moment as though he were reliving the memory. 'His eyes were yellow. I think he was travelling with them.'

'Tell me about him. What was he like?' Draneth asked. His eyes met briefly with Sill's and she saw that his forehead was again wrinkled with the stern lines of a harsh frown.

'He was not afraid,' Kallem said with a shrug. 'He was cheerful. He said his name was Zyan.'

'Zyan?' the shaman repeated. 'Did he say anything else?'

Kallem paused for a moment. 'He said they mean me no harm.'

'Hah,' Draneth said with a sneer, 'and did you believe him?'

'No,' Kallem said plainly. He seemed unmoved by whatever it was he'd witnessed. *And yet he chose to tell us.*

The shaman went quiet and let the silence grow around them.

Sill wondered if perhaps he was talking again with Tamarellin but the hawk was focussed only on cleaning its wings and, to any unknowing onlooker, was as oblivious to the business of humans as any other bird.

The motion of the canoe was making Sill's head spin and she shut her eyes, allowing the darkness to engulf her. She had tried to close her mind to the memories of the Grinth, but now an ugly, purple face began to creep back through. She squeezed her eyes tighter but white teeth flashed in the dark and narrow yellow slits glowed against the black of her eyelids. The Grinth's hooves shifted in the snow, edging to its right as it circled around her. Its breath steamed the cold air as it grunted through thin nostrils.

'My eyes are yellow when the Grinth are near, aren't they?' Kallem asked suddenly into the stillness. 'Am I like him?'

Sill opened her eyes again to look at what she could make out of Kallem's back. *No,* she wanted to say, *you saved me.*

'No,' Draneth said, sparing her the need. He twisted his body to face Kallem's back. 'You are not like him, like this Zyan. I'll admit I had my doubts when you first came to me. From what I understand, from our history, the Grinth have a way of turning people to their will, using our despair against us. But if you truly didn't care anymore, you would not have come to me. You would not have returned to us from the forest.' Draneth talked gently for once and Sill was glad that he was not cruel to Kallem. *He already hates himself enough.* 'You gave up on yourself a long time ago,' Draneth continued. 'That much is clear, but you are stronger than you think you are. You have *resisted* the Grinth, Kallem, though you do not see it, and that means you are stronger than any of us.' The shaman turned to face the front again, his blue eyes bright and alert in the growing dusk. He reached a hand up to ruffle Tamarellin's feathers. 'Tamarellin is a better judge of people than me, and he seems to trust you.' The hawk squawked as though confirming the shaman's words. 'Therefore, I will, too.'

Sill thought she noticed Kallem's back twitch slightly but other than that he showed no sign that he had been affected by the shaman's words, and quietly resumed his surveillance of the canoe's rear.

As if in response, a booming, cough-like sound echoed loudly from the direction of the forest. Sill watched in horror as dark shapes began to emerge from the fading line of trees. There were dozens of them, more than she could count. She tried to cover her ears from the noises they made but the rocking of the canoe made her tip sideways and she was forced to grip the sides again. She looked at her feet, trying in vain to concentrate on the more pleasant sound of the water.

Outside of the boat, back on dry land, the bad dream she had dreaded now swarmed forth from the depths of the forest, gradually soaking up the shore in a seething mass of dark purple.

Tamarellin squawked once, loudly, as if in response to the rabid booming, and Sill wished he would be quiet. *You'll draw their attention!* Tiny waves lapped against the sides of the canoe, flicking cold water up onto Sill's white knuckles where she gripped the wood so tightly.

The shaman wore a heavy frown as he stroked and soothed his feathered friend, but he did not turn to look back behind them.

Kallem's hand moved gently towards his sword hilt.

Sill closed her eyes to the sights and her ears to the sounds, but she couldn't close her mind to the fear; or to the nightmare, that she now knew was real.

CHAPTER 10

The canoe drifted for what felt like an eternity. Sill's wrists burned from clinging so tightly to the wood so she had loosened her grip, but only a little. The growing distance between themselves and the Grinth was the only thing that kept her hands from letting go, but her forearms hurt so much now they felt like they could cramp at any moment. Once again she was reminded of the quilt she had so painstakingly sewn for Fallor's birth-sun. *The only good thing I ever made and it was burnt to ashes.* Fallor was no doubt dead by now, too.

The grunting calls of the Grinth were already softening, thanks to a still wind, and Sill wondered if the shaman's rowing had dragged them out of sight by now. When the awful sound finally faded beyond hearing and she reopened her eyes, she was greeted by the piercing yellow pupils of Tamarellin. She jumped at the sight of the yellow, but then forced a smile for the bird's sake. The hawk shifted its feet and turned its back on her as though it was either insulted or had simply lost interest. The shaman fondled Tamarellin's head and beckoned silently for Sill to look behind her. As she did so, she was relieved to find they were steering towards land. The river had opened up into what must have been Soul's Rest, the lake that ended the Soulslide's flow and framed the west and north sides of Anell Village. It had grown too dark now to make out much of the village, but the many roving firelights that speckled the shoreline were a welcome sight.

People.

As Draneth steered them closer, she saw now that other canoes already lined the shore. Some were slim, sleek and smooth, evidently fully finished, whereas others were much like their own and still half-covered in bark, more tree than boat.

Someone on the shore had begun to point at them and shout and now others ran to look, perhaps hoping their relatives who had stayed behind to fight had returned after all. Sill turned away, not wanting to face their disappointment when they realised it was only her. Kallem had his back to them, too. *He probably feels the same*, she thought.

'Sill?'

It sounded like someone had called her name, but she could not let herself believe it just yet.

'Sill! Is that you? It is you, isn't it?'

Raffin?

Sill turned to find her friend waiting for her at the water's edge, just as she would have dreamt, had she been able to dream anymore. For a second it crossed her mind that she was still sleeping and this in fact was a crueller nightmare than the one she had left behind; she would probably wake to find the Grinth instead, stalking them along the side of the riverbank. *But it feels real enough*, she thought, *as real as anything now*.

Men rushed into the water to pull the canoe ashore and she heard Draneth thank them curtly and then instantly begin to demand answers. *How many had made it from Hillock? How many were left behind? Had anyone come from Rydan?* But it was all just background noise. She felt herself pulled from the canoe and someone check her for cuts and bruises, not all that gently, before thrusting her forwards to where Raffin stood waiting.

But Raffin's face was a far cry from the excitable boy she had left behind. His eyes were hard and wary; void of the playfulness that had cheered her a thousand times over. His mouth was sombre and straight, and no mischievous grin parted his lips when he looked at her.

'You shouldn't have left,' was all he said. Then he grabbed her and hugged her tightly.

It was so unlike him that she felt her whole body tense and her heart started to race, but, at the same time, she did not want him to let go. Relaxing, perhaps for the first time since she'd first left Hillock, she allowed herself to enjoy the feeling of his warmth against her chilled skin. But she could not bring herself to return the embrace. It was all just too much and she could not bear to think about the fact she might have to leave him again. *How can I even begin to explain,* she thought sadly. *I'm no good at it.*

'Did you see them?' Raffin asked as he released her from the hug.

She nodded.

Raffin hugged her again but then suddenly let go and she saw his eyes narrow as he looked beyond her.

Sill turned to see Kallem crouched at the water's edge, cleaning the dried, black blood from his sword. 'He protected me.' She told Raffin but her friend only frowned uncertainly.

'Seize that man!' a gruff voice called, and Soffus appeared through the night, a flaming torch pointed in the direction of Kallem. Brorn stood by him, the torchlight throwing shadows up under the huge man's square jaw, leaving dark holes where his eyes should have been. People paused, not knowing how to react whilst Soffus strode confidently up to the shore.

'Him! Kallem!' Soffus' voice boomed in the dusk. 'That man has been banned from our lands.' The positive mood that had greeted their arrival began to subside. People looked at each other but did not hasten to act upon Soffus' demands, perhaps not recognising his authority.

Kallem froze, just for a second, and then returned to cleaning his sword as though nothing had happened.

Brorn stepped forward from Soffus' side and found himself barred by Draneth's staff. He raised an eyebrow at the shaman, then looked back at Soffus, awaiting further instructions.

Soffus glowered suspiciously at the newcomer, his dark eyes all but hidden beneath the bushy black eyebrows that lined his brow. 'Get out of the way, stranger,' he said, his voice full of threats.

'Don't be a fool,' Draneth said, not moving an inch. 'Our fight is not with each other.'

'This man is a known murderer!' Soffus called out so that everybody could hear. 'He must be kept under guard.'

'This man has already fought and killed more Grinth than anybody here,' the shaman returned hotly, 'and is likely the only one from your village who lives to speak of it. What authority do you hold here?'

'I am Leader of Hillock's Elders,' Soffus said in a voice that sounded appalled at Draneth's ignorance, as much as his tone. He straightened himself as though trying to appear taller, but the attempt fell flat in the presence of the mighty Brorn.

'Well, Hillock is gone,' the shaman said bluntly. 'I suggest you concentrate on what remains and you can start by getting your people to safety.' He glanced at Kallem. 'All of them.'

Soffus' eyebrows were raised and when he spoke his tone was at least one note higher than usual. 'You deem to tell *me* what to do?' he said, clearly outraged. 'Who, by the peaks, do you think you are? And tell me why I shouldn't have Brorn here take that stick of yours and knock that insolent look off your face.'

Draneth grinned and just for a moment Sill could have sworn the skulled tip of his staff glowed a deep red. 'My name is Draneth,' the shaman said slowly, 'and who I am is not as important as what I know. I must speak to both villages, immediately. To *everybody*. The attack on Hillock was just the start and we must prepare ourselves for what is to come.' He twisted his staff back to vertical and weighed Brorn up with his eyes. 'And the big one is welcome to try,' he said with a scowl, 'but as I said before, our fight is not with each other.'

Soffus' jaw moved in silence as though he was grinding his teeth. His pointy, grey beard twitched a couple of times and he began to stroke his hand through it as though the action calmed his nerves.

Brorn made no move to assault the shaman, but his eyes shone brightly as though he might relish the challenge.

People watched uncomfortably, waiting to see what would happen.

'We will hear what you have to say, shaman, for your name's sake at least,' Soffus said finally, to a noticeably relieved crowd. 'But make no mistake, you have no authority here.'

'So, they do still talk about me in the north?' Draneth said, flashing Soffus a wry grin.

'Not much of it is good, Draneth, believe me,' Soffus said, with a scoff. 'And you are a stranger to these parts, so you must forgive us for exercising more caution than usual, especially in light of recent events.' He began to turn away. 'Follow me, then,' he said, pointing the burning torch at Kallem, 'and bring *him* with you. Brorn and Arteus will keep watch on the both of you.'

Kallem rose slowly and Sill hoped desperately that he wasn't going to put up a fight. He walked towards Draneth but then stopped as he passed her by. He looked down at her.

'I'll be ok,' she said, understanding. She felt Raffin tense beside her.

Kallem glanced briefly at him, then nodded to Sill and walked on after the shaman.

Brorn let them both pass and then followed the two into the dark, until only the flickering of Soffus' torch could be seen, a fiery wisp, floating through the night.

Intrigued by Draneth's words, some of the onlookers began to follow them, whilst others continued to go about their business as though they wanted nothing more to do with this new reality.

'Come with me,' Raffin said at her side. 'There's food and shelter. Most of the others are there. The ones who... got away.'

'No,' she said quickly, 'I have to go with Draneth, too.' When he looked at her, hurt, she said, 'I have to decide.'

'Decide what?' he said angrily. 'What choices do we have left?'

His sudden anger shocked her, as unfamiliar as his face now seemed. *How can I explain it to you? You wouldn't understand why I left in the first place.* She tried to remember what Draneth had said about balance, but it only muddled her thoughts further.

'Don't you understand?' he said to her silence. 'I thought you were dead! I nearly went after you when you left but I didn't know where to look. I waited for you for days! I waited for you at the river, too, for as long as they'd let me and you never came.' Tears started to well in the corners of his eyes, another uncharacteristic sight. It seemed to make him madder. 'What is there to *decide*?'

I'm sorry! Sill thought miserably but the words got stuck in her throat. *I don't want to hurt you. I keep hurting you.*

He glared at her, waiting for an answer, but when it didn't come his eyes softened and the hurt gently subsided from his face. 'I'm sorry, Sill,' he said, a bit of the kind boy she remembered returning. 'What you must have been through....you shouldn't have left,' he repeated. 'I mean, you should've told me.'

'I know,' she said, mustering the last of her courage. 'I'm sorry. I just had to....do this on my own.'

'Why?' he said.

She looked at him, hoping desperately that he would understand her. 'Because you wouldn't have let me go.'

'Would, too,' he said, just for a moment reverting back to childishness. Then he paused as if really considering it. 'I would at least have gone with you,' he said finally.

'Would you? But Hillock's your home.'

'Not anymore,' he said quietly. He gazed out sadly across the still lake, biting his lower lip.

'What about your parents?' she said. He wouldn't have left his family, not even for her.

Raffin shivered suddenly and a few of the mounting tears escaped to slide silently down his cheeks. He sucked in a deep breath through his teeth and hugged his arms together as though cold.

'Raffin?' she asked. 'What's wrong?'

He inhaled again, still shivering. 'They never came either,' he said.

And at last she realised. *Oh Raffin!* She threw her arms around his neck and clung to him, returning the embrace he had so willingly given her. *How could I be so selfish!* she thought, bitterly. She held him until he finally stopped shaking and then gently led him away from Soul's Rest.

By the time they reached the gathering, word had already spread through Anell of the shaman's arrival and the meeting, of both villages, to discuss their imminent future.

On their way they had passed many new people and some that Sill recognised from home. Even if she had not known them, it was obvious to tell who was from Hillock; their faces were still fresh from tragedy. Some visibly cried, mourning their lost loved ones. Others sat alone, still and silent. Parents, husbands, wives; even some children had been out in the forest when the Grinth attacked, Sill learned. At one point, she thought she had seen Telfor, the villager who had taken them on the trade, walking off alone into the night, but she could not be certain it was really him. She kept an eye out for Artell, assuming from Fallor's scant words that the rest of Hillock's Elders had made it out alive. Raffin confirmed that he had seen her helping the other survivors, and that she appeared to be unharmed.

There are so many people, Sill thought. It would not be hard to lose someone in this place. In Hillock, if you were missing someone, you only had to wait at the top of the hill and eventually they were bound to show up. But Anell was flat with many homes and Sill was struggling to get her bearings. *How can people live like this? Everything looks the same.* She assured herself it would be easier in the daylight.

The rest of Hillock's Elders, save Fallor who had stubbornly stayed behind, and Artell, were already present at the gathering when they arrived. Whatever else he may have lost, Raffin's curiosity remained unscathed, and just like at the village meeting in Hillock, he managed to sneak them in close to the front.

Perhaps short of ideas themselves, both villages appeared willing to allow Draneth to occupy the open centre, and the shaman was absorbing the attention with typical impatience, continuously rubbing a bony hand over his bald head as he waited for the formal introductions to finish. Tamarellin sat atop his staff, nervously eyeing the growing crowd.

Despite being the larger village, Anell named only six Elders on their council. Tess, Bray, Lothar, Gully, Rasak and their Leader, Drell, were all in attendance. The Hillock Elders, two short, since Fallor had stayed behind and Artell was still nowhere to be seen, sat sullenly opposite them, each face carrying its own personal visage of grief. It did not look like much of a union.

Drell stood and clapped his hands together, drawing everybody's attention. 'Welcome.' He sighed and looked around as though wanting to express his empathy with each of them personally. He looked to the shaman. 'Draneth, if you'd be patient with us there are a few things to say.'

Draneth raised the hand from his head in assent but his facial expression betrayed his urgency to get on with things.

Drell had a nice way of speaking, Sill thought. The Anell Leader sounded calm and calculated, despite the direness of the situation. Or maybe, for Anell, the reality just hadn't sunk in yet.

'May I begin by welcoming Hillock to our village,' he said, 'I'm so sorry it has not happened as we planned it. Many of you have suffered losses, please accept our deepest condolences. This is your home now as much as it is ours and we will mourn your loved ones as though they were our own.'

'Did you know my sons?' Karth asked, his voice hoarse with emotion.

'No, but...'

'Then how can you mourn them like they were your own?'

'Karth,' Soffus muttered but the scold was half-hearted.

'I'm sorry,' Drell said, with what looked like genuine regret in his eyes, 'I did not mean to offend.'

'It is we who should be offended!' One of his Elders, the one named Tess, said. 'We all know the Grinth will come here next,' she said, looking to the Anell portion of the crowd for support. 'You've led them right to us!'

Drell sighed and began to rub his forehead with his finger and thumb.

'Where were we supposed to go?' Karth rose, fuming.

'Why not to the mountains?' Tess said. 'Or south, to Rydan?'

'The Grinth were between us and the mountains!' Kessan added, also enraged. 'And we would never have made it south.'

'That's not our problem.'

'Tess!' Another Anell Elder said. 'Stop this.' The man was Bray and looked far too young to be called an 'Elder'. He stood to make his point. 'This serves nothing,' he said, imploring his fellow villagers to take heed. 'Imagine what they've been through.' He turned to Drell. 'Drell,' he said softly, 'please continue.'

'I think we've heard enough.' Now Soffus stood, his own patience waning.

'Please,' Bray said but Soffus held up a hand and shook his head, leaving the young Elder to reluctantly sit back down.

'We thank you for your courtesies,' Soffus said with all the authenticity a man like him could muster, 'and for your warm welcome.' For a second his eyes flicked to Tess, but then quickly refocused on Drell. 'But she's right. The Grinth will come here, too, and we must decide what to do next. The shaman has news to share with us. We should hear him first.'

Drell nodded obediently but looked more than a little unhappy that his plans to unite the two villages were already in tatters. 'Very well,' he said. 'What can you tell us, Draneth?'

'It's more what I can't tell you that troubles me,' Draneth said quickly, perhaps taking the opportunity to hasten proceedings whilst he had the chance. 'I have come from the south-westerly corner of the Inner Lands, from the Moonmirror,' he explained, addressing the whole crowd. 'There had been signs of change; animals moving south, a strange scent in the air...'

'This is your news?' the woman named Tess scoffed. 'Animals and scents in the air?'

Draneth glowered at Tess for a moment but then, almost immediately, ignored her remark and continued with his story. 'When two of Hillock's villagers came to me, two Grinth followed them.' There were gasps in the crowd, the news of Grinth already in the south, clearly a surprise. 'They were weak and we were able to kill them. I believe these Grinth had travelled far and were very weary. I believe they were the first to travel so far south; I would have known if there had been more. But the Grinth have not changed from the stories. This is important as they still did not look equipped for scaling the Inner Lands' mountains, so they must have found another way in. Unfortunately, we reached Hillock too late to find out what that was and now it may not matter. Before we reached Hillock, I also sent a message to Rydan Fort. I was hoping someone would have come, but it appears you have had no word from them?' He looked to Drell for confirmation.

Drell shook his head. 'We have not heard from Rydan for many seasons,' he said sadly.

'They are not interested in us,' another Anell Elder, Rasak put in. 'We must deal with this ourselves.'

'Rydan is supposed to protect us from the Grinth,' Karth said, 'and yet where were they when my sons were fighting and dying? Do we even know if the Fort still exists?'

'Yes,' Draneth said. 'The Fort still stands.'

'Then they sent a message back?' Drell asked hopefully.

'No,' the shaman said.

'Then how do we know?' Tess asked.

'*I* know,' Draneth said, sounding vexed. 'Because I have been there. And because Tamarellin was able to deliver my message.'

'Who is this Tamarellin?' Kessan asked dubiously.

Draneth sighed. 'This is Tamarellin,' he said, stroking the hawk's feathers. 'The hawk does as I say. Now can we please move on?'

The crowd began to murmur.

He's losing them, Sill thought worriedly. *He's been away from other people too long. He doesn't know how to talk to people like Artell does.* But Draneth had to make them listen. *Don't they understand? We need to leave, now!*

'You trusted a *bird* with this message?' Soffus said, incredulous.

Tess openly laughed.

'I told you,' the shaman said, his expression growing dark. 'The bird does as I say.'

Tamarellin squawked angrily as though he disagreed.

'This is madness,' Tess said. 'Why are we listening to this man? We do not know him.'

Draneth gave Tess such a glare that Sill thought for a moment the shaman might kill her where she stood. Instead, Draneth turned his attention to the brown hawk who had now hopped up from the staff onto his shoulder. 'Tamarellin,' he said in a low voice and the hawk screeched as it took off, flying directly at the Anell Elder's head.

'What is he doing?' Tess shrieked as she ducked away from the bird's claws. Tamarellin twisted away and flew off above the crowd's heads before disappearing into the night sky. A *keeeeeeee* sounded somewhere overhead and with a rush of air the hawk shot back into view.

'What is this? Stop him!' Tess screeched as Tamarellin swooped past her left ear.

'What makes you think I can?' Draneth grinned, raising a malicious eyebrow.

'Enough of this!' Soffus' voice boomed. 'You've made your point, Draneth, call him off.'

Draneth's grin curled into a snarl. He looked to the sky and, without a word, Tamarellin appeared to open his broad wings and then glide back down until he again sat atop the skulled tip of Draneth's staff. The hawk settled his feet and closed his eyes as the shaman softly stroked the bird's head.

'Heed my words,' Draneth said loudly and slowly, 'and do what you will with them. The Inner Lands has a balance that we humans have not respected. We've taken this place for granted and now we are paying the price for it.

'If Rydan have not responded to our needs we should not rely on their aid but I at least mean to take a group to the Fort to ensure they know the true danger. There are men there who can fight against this enemy, who *live* to fight against them. The rest of you should head for the mountains: you may still stand a chance there.'

It wasn't exactly the rousing speech Sill had hoped for, but perhaps the shaman just wanted to tell them what they needed to hear. *He didn't have to come here,* she thought.

'You do not make decisions here, shaman,' Soffus spoke up.

'Then somebody better had!' Draneth barked at him. 'And quickly! Save yourselves, for peaks sake! Do you think I came here for my own ends?'

Soffus stared at the shaman, his eyes glowering beneath his dark, bushy brow, but he had no answer to Draneth's question.

'I *will* ask for a few men who can fight,' Draneth told them fiercely, ignoring the looks he got. 'Preferably volunteers from both your villages. Rydan will need to hear this from more than just me, and the way will be dangerous. You must be prepared to leave immediately.'

'What about women who can fight?' Sill recognised Hiddelle from the trade. The muscular Hillock woman stepped forward, a determined look etched across on her face.

'Hiddelle!' Her husband, Trew, appeared at her side, anguish straining his voice. He tried to grip her arm to get her attention but she shrugged his hand away, folded her arms, and remained stubbornly facing the shaman.

Draneth nodded. 'You'll do fine,' he said. 'What about you?'

'Appears I have little choice,' Trew said with a rueful shrug. 'I guess you have two.'

'And two more,' Arnak stepped forward, spear in hand. Broll moved to his side and nodded. 'We've always wanted to see Rydan anyway,' Arnak said with a meek grin.

Sill was glad she would at least know some of her companions. *Here goes.* She stepped forward, hoping that she would not look too ridiculous amidst all the strong adults of her kin. 'I'll go,' she said as loudly as she dared.

'Sill, what are you doing?' She heard Raffin whisper behind her.

The shaman eyed her up as though seeing her for the first time.

There were some scoffs from the villagers, but to her surprise nobody spoke up. *Nobody cares*, she realised, dishearteningly. *Nobody wants me.* But then who could blame them? *Who would want an extra child to take care of now?*

The shaman furrowed his brow and she hoped he, too, wasn't going to reject her. *You said I had to make my own decision.*

'Are you sure?' Draneth asked. He looked at her hard.

'You can't be serious?' Soffus interrupted. 'Peaks man, she's just a girl!'

'And yet she's already travelled further than most of you,' Draneth said, not taking his eyes off her. 'And she's survived the Grinth once. The girl is brave,' he told her with a twisted smile.

She could not tell whether he was serious or not but she nodded all the same. *What choice did I really have?* she wondered, as the reality of her decision began to sink in. She looked around for Kallem but he was nowhere to be seen. *Will you still protect me?*

'Good,' Draneth said. 'Who else?'

'Me,' Artell said, appearing suddenly at Sill's side.

She felt Artell's hand rest gently on her shoulder and was glad for the touch. She smiled up at Artell, relieved the Elder was unharmed.

Is this what having a mother would feel like?

'This is madness,' Soffus said. 'I am Hillock's Leader! I will decide the fate of my people.' He took a few steps forward into the centre where Draneth stood, baring his teeth. The shaman's knuckles were white where he gripped the staff. 'No, you will not,' he told Soffus flatly. 'Everyone must now decide their own fates, and we have little time left, and even less choice. Anybody who wants to come with me can.'

'Artell's place is with the council,' Soffus insisted. 'We will need to rebuild.'

'Rebuild what?' Draneth asked. 'This is about survival, man. Now, who else will come with me?'

'I will.' Kallem appeared like a ghost from the dark, the less inconspicuous Brorn tailing him. 'But only if my mother stays.' He turned to face Artell.

Draneth raised a quizzical eyebrow but looked to Artell to make her own decision.

'Yes,' Soffus said, grasping at the opportunity. 'Kallem should go, he shouldn't be here anyway. Artell stays with us where she belongs.'

Sill felt Artell's grip tighten briefly on her shoulder, then the Elder turned and vanished quickly back into the crowd.

How could you do that? Sill stared at Kallem, wanting to yell at him, but she could not bring herself to do so in front of the crowd. She thought about going after Artell but Draneth was right, there was no time. *Everyone must decide their own fate.* But the sinking feeling inside told her that she felt bad about leaving Artell like this. Really bad. *What could I say to her anyway? I can't handle my own emotions, let alone anyone else's.*

Kallem returned her look as though nothing at all had happened. Then he nodded to the shaman before himself slipping back into the night.

Brorn started after him, but Soffus caught his arm and shook his head, seemingly no longer concerned with Kallem's whereabouts. Brorn watched Soffus' hand on his arm until the Elder removed it. Undeterred, Soffus folded his arms as though he had won some small victory.

'Who else?' Draneth asked urgently.

There was a brief silence before Brorn slowly stepped towards Draneth. 'I will come with you,' he said.

Soffus' mouth gaped as he stared at the giant Hillock man. 'No,' he said, visibly rattled, 'you can't. I, *we*, need you.'

'It is not your decision,' Draneth said, stomping the butt of his staff into the ground. Tamarellin fluttered his wings in a panic and then, upon reclaiming his grip on the skull, squawked noisily in Draneth's direction. The shaman ignored him.

'Brorn. You will accompany the Elders up into the mountains,' Soffus ordered.

Brorn shifted his big bulk slowly to face the Elder. 'No,' he said simply.

Soffus' eyes widened and his face grew red. He looked ready to unleash a tirade onto the big man until Brorn held a large, warning finger up to silence him. 'No,' he said again.

Hillock's Leader looked like he didn't know whether to be outraged or terrified. His face remained a dark crimson as Brorn spoke.

'Once you reach the heights of the mountains you will be safe from the Grinth,' the giant villager said to the crowd, 'then what will you need me for?'

Soffus' mouth seemed to twitch behind his poky beard as though he was still trying desperately to devise a way to keep Brorn from leaving him.

'Here, I can fight,' Brorn continued, raising his voice so everybody could hear him. 'Fight for our future.' He slapped a large hand against his muscled chest. 'Fight for our lands, so that one day you can return.' And with that, he went to stand with Trew and Hiddelle, leaving Soffus to stew silently in the background.

'Great. Now the Grinth will really be able to see us coming.' Sill heard Trew say softly to Brorn. The big man frowned down at his friend, then laughed, and patted Trew heavily on the back. Hiddelle rubbed Trew's back, too, more gently, as though concerned Brorn may have inadvertently hurt her husband.

Sill knew Trew was really as relieved as the rest of them to have Brorn coming, even if his size still frightened her a little.

'Good,' Draneth said. 'Is there anyone else?'

It seemed even Brorn's mighty words could not sway anyone else from leaving behind their friends and families for Draneth's sake.

Sill waited, hoping secretly that Raffin would be the next to come forward. She turned to make sure he was still there and found him standing sullenly behind her. He would not meet her eyes. *He's lost everything*, she thought sadly. She couldn't imagine how he must feel. *I never had anything to lose.* It struck her that she had not even thought to worry about her father. She hoped he was safe, despite everything he had done to her. *You're still my father.*

Draneth held up his staff. 'I have my party,' he said with finality, 'we will leave as the new sun rises. I urge you all to enjoy what rest you can.'

'Wait!' Raffin called, suddenly springing to life. He stepped forward to Sill's side. One of his hands was shaking slightly but his face was as determined as ever. 'I want to go, too.'

Sill glanced at him and then felt her eyes welling so she turned her head away, not wanting him to see how weak she was.

When Raffin's hand suddenly held her own she almost gasped, as surprised as she was embarrassed. His touch made her twitch and she nearly let go. She felt him squeeze more tightly so that she couldn't. The whole world seemed to blur around her as she waited for Draneth's answer, and all she could feel was Raffin's hand on hers as though nothing else existed.

Draneth turned to Raffin and waved his staff dismissively. 'We have our party now,' he said harshly. 'This isn't a game.'

'I know that!' Raffin said, letting go of Sill's hand. 'You said we all had to decide for ourselves.'

Sill breathed, only now aware that she had been holding her breath. She could still feel his touch, even though the hand was gone.

'If Sill's going, so am I,' he said, beside her.

The shaman rolled his eyes and looked set to turn his back on them until Tamarellin squawked and hopped onto his shoulder. He eyed the hawk impatiently for a moment as though the two of them were engaged in silent debate. Then his shoulders sagged. 'Very well,' he tutted. 'But no more.' He stomped the butt of the staff into the ground one more time, then turned and marched off.

'How dare you!' Artell was furious as well as hurt. She could not remember the last time she had been this angry with her son. He had not really misbehaved as a child and the only times she had ever yelled at him were to stop him from going into the forest. *That was about as effective as this seems to be!*

Kallem stood with his back to her, hands by his sides, staring out across the lake towards the river. If he was paying attention to her he did not show it, but Artell knew better, and that knowledge only served to increase her wrath.

'Have you ever even thought about how hard it is for me? You only think about yourself! Have you any idea what I've been through for you? What I go through every day just to keep it together?'

Kallem turned his head slightly to the side, indicating that he was in fact listening.

'Kallem, look at me!'

He turned to face her, his eyes a colder version of her own blue-grey.

Does any part of my son remain? 'How dare you tell me what I can and can't do!'

'It is safer for you to stay,' he said as though logic were the only thing that dictated his thoughts.

His lack of compassion infuriated her. *I did not raise you to be like this! I thought you were better than this. I thought you cared about things. I thought you cared about me.* 'It's not up to you!' She tried to make him see. 'It was *my* decision, Kallem. You took it from me, in front of everybody.'

'I gave you a choice,' Kallem said plainly, 'one of us would stay and one of us would go. You made the choice. It was the right one.'

'What are you talking about? Why does there have to be a choice? We could both have gone, Kallem, *together*.'

'No,' he said.

'Why not?' *Just show me something, anything. Give me some indication that you are still my son!*

'I can't...' He paused. 'Can't focus, with you around.'

'What does that mean, you can't focus? Is it so terrible now to be in my presence? We are all each of us has left, Kallem.'

'You care too much.'

'I care too much?' The words hit her like a slap across the face. 'I'm your mother.'

'Yes,' he acknowledged. He sighed and turned back to the lake.

Is that all I get, just a sigh? A sigh is better than nothing, I guess. A sigh means something. She clung to that thought, dismissing his hurtful words into the night air.

'Do you think I'm mad, *Mother*?' Kallem said, staring out across the water.

The question surprised her. *Is that what you want? My reassurance?* If this was her only chance, she did not want to waste it. She had to get through to him somehow. Had to give him a reason to care again. 'No,' she said aloud, 'of course not. I love you. I *trust* in you. You're my son.'

'*Trust*?' Kallem repeated. 'It has never been about *trust*, Mother, not since they died.'

The venom in his voice took her aback. His warm breath steamed the cool air above his concealed face and the breeze brought it toward her, poisoning the gap between them. She had never heard him be angry. Never seen any emotion. Not since he was a boy. But

153

she had always known it was there, always believed in him, despite what everybody else thought. *Perhaps Sill is having an effect on him as I hoped.* 'What do you mean?' she asked, more tenderly. 'Talk to me, Kallem.' *Please don't close up again.*

He laughed but it was not a pleasant sound. The air misted around him again and then dissipated, becoming one with the dark. 'Even now, you still want him back,' he said and his voice sounded suddenly unfamiliar as though somebody else were speaking through him. But there was nobody else around. Kallem bowed his head, the fingers of his left hand tracing the hilt of the red blade at his side. 'When I returned from the forest, alone, you were afraid of me,' he said, sounding more like himself.

'What are you talking about?' *I wasn't. I could never be afraid of you. You're my son.* 'I was afraid *for* you,' she told him, 'of what had happened to you.' *Seeing your own family killed before your very eyes. My poor boy...*

'You were afraid *of* me!' he shouted. He turned his head to the side to direct the sound at her.

His outburst shocked her, but then this was what she had wanted. *He is angry, so he must feel something.* 'That's not true,' she said. *I wasn't. You were bound to be different after what you went through. You said it was the Grinth but the hunters found the bear, and yet you kept going back there. You couldn't face the truth. Couldn't deal with what had happened.*

'Maybe I didn't realise before...' Kallem was saying. He laughed and started to pace slowly along the lake's edge, watching the tiny waves wash over his feet. '... Maybe you thought *I* did it, like some of the others? Is that why you were afraid, Mother?'

'No!' she said. 'I was just afraid of losing you! You're all I have left.' She had to make him understand and this might be the only chance she would get. He had to hear the truth or he would never be whole again. Would never be her son again. 'You kept going back into the forest and I didn't know what to do. I tried everything to keep you safe but you didn't want to be! You just kept going back. Back to where it happened. I couldn't lose you as well, Kallem!' she said. She walked closer to him so she could speak more softly. 'I knew that you wanted to die.'

'Die?' He stopped pacing and finally turned to stare at her. 'Is that what you thought?'

How could that be wrong? Why else would you keep going back? Her eyes begged him to explain what vital clue she had somehow missed. 'Why else would you keep going back?' she asked aloud. 'Didn't you know what it was doing to me?' The memories brought her own anger back. 'Or is that what you wanted? To hurt somebody, because you had been hurt?'

'I wanted revenge!' Kallem yelled.

Revenge? I don't understand! Her usual calm had evaporated and, without it, the words escaped before she could stop them. 'Is that why you killed Marn?'

Kallem stared at her as though she had stabbed him. She watched a tear run down his face. It seemed to take forever to fall.

'Kallem, I'm sorry!' She moved towards him, but he backed away as though he were afraid of her now. *A tear. That was my sign.* But at what cost had it come and was it worth the price?

'Father... sister,' Kallem said, his voice hoarse. He turned his back on her and wiped his face on his dirty sleeve. 'You didn't *see* them,' he said. 'You knew but you didn't *see* them.' His hand moved again to his sword hilt as though the weapon could protect him from his memories.

What have I done? Artell thought. *My poor child.* She wanted desperately to hold him, to share in his suffering

155

but she knew he would never let her, not now. Just as she could never travel with him to Rydan.

'No one believed me,' Kallem said softly, 'not even you. Not even now.'

For a second it was almost like her little boy had returned and she tried desperately to keep him there. 'Tell me,' she said. 'I want to believe you. I *do*.'

'I watched,' the boy said, his voice distant. 'I hid in the trees, and just watched.' Then the man turned and spat at her, 'While it ripped them to pieces!'

'Kallem!' She had asked for the truth but was she really prepared for it?

Kallem seemed to know that she wasn't. 'Is this what you want, Mother?' he yelled at her. 'Shall I tell you how she screamed, when it tore her open?'

'Kallem, stop it!' She covered her ears with her hands but he walked up to her and grabbed them away. 'Kallem, stop!' She pushed herself away from him.

He let go of her hands and stood staring for a moment, his blue-grey eyes wild. Then he swung around and marched back to the side of the lake, exhaling deeply into the air above. 'A bear…' he said, his voice wistful.

'But they found it,' she said and then wished she hadn't. *I said I would believe him.* But what did she really believe? She could not truly say anymore. So much had changed, and so quickly.

'Go to the mountains, Mother,' he said. His voice was flat and hollow and she knew instantly that the boy was gone again.

He has given up on me, she thought, *just as I gave up on him. I don't deserve his love.* The realisation stung her. *He just needed me to believe him and I couldn't even do that. I am no better than the others.* 'Look after Sill,' she said, regaining her own pretence of calm.

His head nodded once in response.

It was something. A deep sense of loss came over her and suddenly she felt very tired. She was glad he couldn't see that her hands were shaking when she spoke. 'Will I see you again?' she asked, her voice as expressionless as his. *He hides it even better than I do,* she realised. *How did I not see that before?*

A lifetime seemed to pass as Kallem stood in silence, the tiny waves of Soul's Rest washing gently over his bare feet. Finally, he spoke. 'Maybe.'

Artell smiled and nodded gratefully, wiping the tears from her face as she walked away. It was the kindest lie she had ever heard.

CHAPTER 11

The way was bleak. The sky remained dull and grey, thick with virulent clouds that seemed to bulge and billow above, but never precipitate or move onwards. Dark were the days and darker still the nights. Without the sun, time stood frozen. The heartening eastern mountains had vanished from sight, cowering beneath the unearthly fog and abandoning the weary travellers in their greatest time of need. Without their perceived protection, the land felt endless, the threat of the Grinth constant. There were no birds and no animals. Only plants and trees kept the land alive but they were wilted and frail, weak with the onset of winter.

Arnak, Trew and the others did their best to keep spirits high but Sill knew it was a lie. They had abandoned their homes, their friends, their families; and some of them no longer had families to leave behind.

Draneth trudged doggedly onwards, the lines of his face contorted into the now familiar frown as he urged his makeshift group forever forwards.

Kallem had taken to drifting some way out at the back, occasionally disappearing into fog and mist, only to reappear unexpectedly at Sill's side as though he had been there all along.

Upon leaving Anell, Hiddelle had chosen to stuff as much in her pack as possible and now bickered constantly, and for the most part playfully, with Trew, about whether or not he should take on some of her load. Broll watched their antics with an air of mild interest, but remained silent and stone-faced as ever.

Whilst the rest of the party laboured to maintain Draneth's gruelling pace, Brorn strolled effortlessly along with his long, tall frame and muscular legs, almost as though he were an adult minding a group of children.

Raffin walked beside Sill, head bowed low and as soundless as the air around them.

Sill herself felt numb, her head clouded as though the weather's reach extended to her physical being. It was all she could do to keep moving and try not to think about what lay ahead; or behind. All the aches and pains of her journey to the Moonmirror had returned, but she had grown used to them now. At least this discomfort was normal, natural. *Not like this fog.* The air felt foul in a way she could not explain; an affront to her senses. She wondered if anyone else had noticed it. Raffin looked too deep still in sorrow to observe anything much. She thought about holding his hand again but could not bring herself to do so. It was too intense, too embarrassing, and now was just not the time. Or perhaps it was the perfect time? *How much time do we have?* Without the sun or any kind of routine it was hard to know how much time had passed. At first, she had tried to at least keep track of the nights but the group only slept in short bursts, sometimes at night, sometimes in the day, and eventually her mind had grown too groggy and confused to remember how many days or nights had passed. At times, she thought about Artell and the rest of the villagers and their own journey up into the mountains. She thought about a life with Artell, Kallem and Raffin, pictured them sitting together like a family, perhaps enjoying one of Artell's hot stews; but she knew it could never be real, it was just a fantasy for a childish girl. *A girl like that won't last long in a world like this*, she told herself. *Life's not like that.* That's what her father would probably say and he'd be right. She could hardly see Kallem making polite chitter-chatter over an evening meal. *I've never even seen him smile*, she realised. *Has he never had a reason to?* Kallem had been particularly quiet since they left Anell, even by his standards. Before they departed, Sill had considered talking to him about his mother but something told her it was not a good idea. *Perhaps she will be safer in the mountains*, she thought. *Where the Grinth can't go*. But then she wondered if that was just an excuse for her not to confront Kallem. Despite what they had already been through together, deep down she was still afraid of him. His blackened, blood-soaked image emerging from the forest still haunted her broken sleep. His yellow eyes, too, when the Grinth had attacked them. *It must mean something?* And his story of the other yellow-eyed man in the forest. Zyan, Kallem had said he was called. Zyan, who walked unharmed among the Grinth. Kallem *was* dangerous, there was no doubt about that, and something about him had changed since Anell. Perhaps he was more dangerous now than ever. And still, in spite of all that and against her better judgement, she was glad he was with them. *I guess I'm different now, too.*

'Draneth, we should rest!' Trew called from behind her.

Draneth turned, up ahead, and glared at Trew through bright blue eyes that contrasted starkly with the dullness of the land.

'We are making good time and there has been no sign of the Grinth,' Trew said, unfazed by the shaman's dark demeanour. 'At this rate, the pace will kill us before they do.' He grinned.

Draneth shot a look to the sky and his eyes narrowed slightly as he scanned the unusual, throbbing clouds. But then he nodded his assent to Trew and whispered something to Tamarellin. The hawk gave a squawk and took off from his shoulder as, Sill had noticed, he tended to do whenever they stopped, acting as a scout for the rest of the party. She watched as the bird's broad, brown wings lifted him effortlessly into the air, rising until he slowly vanished into the fog.

The rest of the party gratefully took their seats on the ground, as Draneth marched back to join them. Sill had to tug on Raffin's sleeve before he realised they had stopped moving.

Brorn alone, remained on his feet, a huge axe strapped to his back that frightened Sill every time she saw it. He began shaking his arms out and she knew he would soon be swinging the axe about again with that terrifying power, and unnerving accuracy. *I suppose I should be grateful*, she thought, as she watched him loosen his muscles. She knew that she had made a promise to herself to be stronger but it had proven much more difficult in practice than she had imagined. *I'll never be that strong,* she thought, watching Brorn, *no matter how hard I try. But I should at least try to be less afraid of everything.* Her father had given her that gift. *Perhaps I will always be afraid of men, no matter how good they seem.*

'Are you not going to sit?' Trew asked Brorn, as though the giant's exhibition of strength made him equally uncomfortable. Trew was no weakling himself.

'Would it make you feel taller if I did?' Brorn asked, unsheathing the mighty axe. Although his voice sounded serious, Sill caught the sly wink that he aimed at his friend. Or was it meant for Hiddelle?

'If you carry on like this, you'll be half the size by the time we reach Rydan,' Trew jested. 'We don't have enough food to feed you and you know I eat more than you do. Aren't you tired?'

'I never tire,' Brorn replied, swinging the axe in a wide arc above his head.

'Your snoring says otherwise,' Trew said, and Sill and the others laughed.

Brorn paused, and for a heartbeat he looked set to take Trew's head off with the axe, but then the big man threw his own head back and laughed heartily. He sheathed the axe and sat down with the rest of them. 'I plan to be ready to battle our enemy,' he explained to Trew. 'But maybe you will talk them to death instead.' He gave Trew a gentle slap on the shoulder and Trew feigned injury, seeking pity from Hiddelle. All he got was a wallop on the other shoulder. 'I won't need to fight,' he told Brorn, rubbing the afflicted arm. 'I have her to protect me.' Hiddelle tutted but Trew grinned at her until he got the smile he craved.

As she watched them, Sill realised for the first time that she was proud of her people. Most of them would likely not have faced any kind of adversity in their lives, let alone the desperate situation they now found themselves in. Yet they remained strong in will and in spirit, despite everything. *Maybe they just haven't accepted it yet?* she wondered. She took some *ether* from her pack, which had survived the return journey from the Moonmirror, broke off a bit and offered it to Raffin who accepted it without a word. *You understand what we're up against, don't you, Raff.* she thought sadly. His world had already been turned upside down. He'd lost two loving parents at once, without warning. *I'm so sorry*, she thought, but sorry wouldn't change anything. The best they could hope for now was revenge, and somehow a way to save the Inner Lands from the clawed clutches of the Grinth, but that could well have been just another childish fantasy. The Grinth had all but wiped out humankind once before, and now there were far fewer of them left to defend themselves. *But they weren't ready*, Sill thought. *We have Rydan Fort.* But where were their soldiers now? For all she knew, Rydan was no longer manned, or worse, had already fallen. In Anell, Draneth had told them he sent word to the Fort with Tamarellin.

So why hadn't they heard anything or seen any of the Fort's warriors? If the shaman really did communicate with the hawk, he kept the bird's knowledge, and his own, largely to himself.

Just as Sill was thinking of him, a *keeeeeeee* brought her eyes to the sky and Tamarellin appeared through the clouds and then plummeted down, until he was suddenly clinging to the shaman's outstretched arm. The hawk hopped from one foot to the other and started squawking frantically as Draneth watched him, his frown narrowing all the while.

'The Grinth,' Draneth announced, without wasting words. 'They are coming.'

Before anyone could respond, their eyes were pulled upwards as the clouds above suddenly changed. As they watched, darker tones swirled amidst the greys, gradually blotting out the sky. Black seeped into any broken gaps until all lingering light from the sun was soon forgotten and the land's last shades of green dimmed and died as everything turned to night. Then a flash of lightning stunned their eyes and the world rumbled as though straining under the weight of the altered clouds. Another rumble muted Draneth's words and the skies erupted, jettisoning water down on them as though Soul's Rest itself had risen to the heavens, only to be flung back down to earth with a violent contempt.

A dim glow lit the shaman's face, as an eerie light began to emanate from the skull that topped his long, wooden staff. 'This way!' he cried against the breaking storm. 'Move!'

They obeyed.

Rain lashed Sill's face so hard it blinded her as she groped for Raffin in the dark. She felt a hand and clung to it, knowing it was him.

'Hold onto me!' he shouted. 'And don't let go, not for anything!' His voice was wild and alert as though the storm had swept away his apathy and brought him back to himself. He dragged Sill forward, following the shaman's lead.

The light from Draneth's staff had expanded and now it enveloped the whole group so Sill could just about make out the others moving around her. They had spread out, encircling her and Raffin but keeping close enough so as not to lose sight of each other in the dark. Arnak and Broll had already drawn their weapons and Brorn wore a face that suggested he was ready to fight the heavens themselves if needed.

Hiddelle and Trew moved together as one, sharing the weight of the packs.

Kallem was nowhere to be seen.

'Where's Kallem?' Sill shouted in Raffin's ear, but either he couldn't hear her or he was just too intent on following Draneth to respond. Sill fought to keep the rain from blurring her vision but it was as much use as trying to see through the Frosty Falls; the water was too dense, and the air too dark.

Don't let go, not for anything! Raffin's words resounded in her head. *But I can't leave him,* she thought. *He promised not to leave* me.

The earth shook again as another band of thunder ripped across the sky.

Sill tried to use her power to still some of the wind that pulled rain into her eyes, but the wind proved too strong, too powerful. *This isn't right,* she thought. If she focussed hard enough she could feel the wind's malevolence, its evil. *This is no ordinary storm.* Thunder rumbled overhead again as though the storm were laughing at her feeble efforts.

'Raffin!' She yanked at his hand until he was forced to look at her. 'We have to stop!'

Raffin shook his head, bewildered. 'We can't!' he called back, pointing forward towards Draneth.

He's right. Sill realised as he tugged her along again. If they stopped for any time at all they would soon slip out of the shaman's light. She wondered if anybody else had realised Kallem was missing. Were they too focussed on the nearness of the Grinth or did they just not care?

I have to get to Draneth, she thought. *Make him stop.*

'I need to speak to Draneth!' she called to Raffin, yanking his hand again.

He looked at her, irritated, but nodded grimly. 'Come on!' he said.

Sill tried to pick up the pace but it had already grown slippery underfoot and she kept losing her hold on the ground, only to be tugged back up by Raffin. He had that determined look on his face she knew so well but had been absent ever since they were reacquainted in Anell. For his size, Raffin had already begun to look sturdier lately and Sill was sure he would mature into as strong a Hillock man as any other. *If we live that long.* She let him tug her onwards again, wiping the rain from her now numb face and scrabbling back to her feet whenever she fell down. Finally, she found herself abreast with the shaman. She grabbed at Draneth's drenched fur cloak until he twisted angrily to face her. His reaction startled her. Water splashed from his bald head as he glared down at her, grimacing as though he were in physical pain. His eyes were ruthless pits beneath the crude wrinkles of his scowl. He had lifted his staff into the air as though he meant to bring it down upon her head. Raffin stepped between them, an arm raised to take the blow that never came. Draneth stared at them for a moment as though he didn't recognise who they were and his jaw seemed to tremble slightly as he slowly lowered the staff. 'What is it?' he asked, his voice hoarse as he squinted at them through the rain. Tamarellin huddled into the shaman's shoulder, a sorry sight, water gushing endlessly from the tips of his tucked wings.

'It's Kallem!' Sill shouted, squeezing around from behind Raffin to stand before him. 'He's gone!' She gripped Raffin's hand even tighter. *Is this what power does to you?* she wondered, seeing the strain on the shaman's face.

Draneth seemed to understand. He gripped the staff in both hands and snarled as the ring of light extended; the creepy, glowing skull growing brighter as he did so.

Seeing the light expand, the others seemed to catch on and Arnak, Broll and Brorn began to scan the edges of the dark for any signs of movement.

'We must keep moving!' Trew called as he and Hiddelle neared them. 'They are close!'

Draneth nodded, another snarl curling his upper lip. His bright blue eyes skimmed the night briefly, then he turned his pained expression on Sill. 'Can you clear it?' he rasped and she knew instantly what he meant.

She shook her head. *I can't,* she thought miserably. *I'm useless, just like my father always said.* The thought made her angry.

'Try, Sill!' Raffin said in her ear.

'I have tried!' she yelled at him. 'It's too strong!' *I can only move the air, and I haven't even been able to do that since I hurt you.*

He let go of her hand and instead grasped her shoulders, pulling her eyes away from the scar on his forehead. 'You can do it!' he shouted. 'I know you can. Just try!'

I can't fight this, she thought, but closed her eyes and tried anyway as he'd asked her to.

The wind howled in her ears. Thunder mocked her from above. *I was born in a storm like this*, she had been told.

I killed my mother.

The wind shrieked as though it knew her thoughts and she let it tug and tear at her, feeling its power, whilst

Raffin held her firm. She could feel its rage – and its sorrow. *This isn't its fault*, she thought, *it doesn't want to be used like this*. She tried to console it, to soothe it, and felt its pull lessen.

She opened her eyes.

Rain still beat hard against her face but it was less savage without the ferocity of the wind.

Arnak looked at her oddly as he approached the shaman. 'There's no sign of Kallem,' he said to all of them. 'I'm sorry, Sill, we have to go.'

Draneth stared down at her for a moment, plainly unimpressed, then spun away, taking the light with him.

'We can't leave him!' Sill yelled but the words were whipped away as the wind returned. She cursed the storm and shot the words back after the shaman. Draneth's head turned slightly up ahead, but if he heard her, he strode on regardless.

She turned back around, hoping Kallem would have reappeared but only found Broll and Brorn retreating towards them as the edge of the light crept ever closer.

A flash of pale blue split the night and Sill gasped as she saw that the empty land they had just trodden was now full of black shapes, dotted with yellow eyes. The shapes disappeared as the dark returned.

Raffin's face confirmed her fears. 'We have to go, Sill,' he said. 'Now.'

Kallem burst so suddenly from the dark that she nearly took him for one of the Grinth. His eyes were afire with the yellow pupils that only confirmed what Sill already knew. His sword was also wet and dark with fresh Grinth blood. He glanced at her as he slowed his pace, and then marched purposefully through the ring of light. 'There are too many,' he said to the others as they stared at him. He looked at Brorn. 'Even for you.'

The giant man bared his teeth unpleasantly as though Kallem had accused him of weakness but then he used his axe to urge the others forward, away from the rear edge of the shaman's circle of light.

At once, Draneth broke into a run and they were forced to stumble after him as best they could, trying desperately not to slip out of the light.

'We must stay together!' Sill heard Arnak call, somewhere behind her.

There were other noises in the air now, besides the wind, rain and thunder, but Sill did not want to hear them. When another flash of pale blue broke the dark, she closed her eyes, not wanting to know what the light revealed. Fear gripped her heart, tighter even than she squeezed on Raffin's hand. Suddenly life had become extremely simple. She must not let go of Raffin, nor stray from the shaman's ring of light. If she did either of those things, she was sure to die, horribly.

'Broll!' Arnak's cry brought the ring of light to a sudden halt. Sill and Raffin tumbled to the muddy ground at the Shaman's feet. Raffin tugged her back up and she turned to see Broll being dragged backwards towards the shadows, a purple, clawed hand wrapped around his ankle.

Lying face down, Broll groped at the muddy ground but it just kept coming away, wet clumps in his hands.

With a roar, Brorn leapt to his aid but three more Grinth crashed from the dark, and he was forced to pivot and swing his axe, slicing clean through two of the creatures whilst the third one hopped back and hissed furiously at him. Water ran from the beast's smooth head, lending its skin a purple gleam in the light of the shaman's staff. After Brorn's next swing the head didn't look so fearsome.

Broll kicked and scrambled against the strength of the Grinth, trying to tug him away from his friends. When Arnak's spear thrummed into the beast's chest, sending it sprawling back into the night, it looked for a moment like Broll might make it, but as he twisted to face his attacker, another Grinth appeared and stuck a long, thick claw through his thigh. Broll cried out and clutched at his leg in horror. Then he was gone, dragged out of sight.

'No!' Arnak raced after him, but Brorn twisted and swung an arm around the trader, holding him back.

The others had drawn their swords but hesitated, perhaps mindful of protecting Sill, Raffin and Draneth in the centre.

'Draneth! Light!' Arnak yelled at the shaman as he fought to free himself from Brorn's grip.

Sill heard the shaman gasp as more power flooded forth from the skull, stretching the circle of light wider until Broll's grounded form seeped back into view.

He was still alive, barely, struggling to fight from the ground, a purple hand dangling from his wounded leg where his sword had severed it from the wrist. Another Grinth lay dead beside him, but more were crowding forward, and he swung his sword frantically at the nearest of them, doing his best to deter their savage intent.

'Kallem!' Sill shouted. 'Help him!' Kallem looked at her briefly as though assessing the need or point but then he flew to Broll's aid as she had requested. Trew made to follow him, but Hiddelle caught his arm and stayed him just as several more Grinth stepped into the light around them.

Brorn had released Arnak and the trader was now dragging his friend back towards the rest of them as Brorn and Kallem fought to keep the incensed Grinth at bay. One lost its head to Brorn's axe whilst Kallem stabbed and slashed in flurries, dropping Grinth bodies left and right in a spray of black fury.

Sill and Raffin watched helplessly as Trew and Hiddelle were embroiled in their own struggle, their

169

breaths coming in short, ragged bursts as they fought for each other, as well as the lives of their companions. The couple were quickly overwhelmed, the desperate whirling of their swords spilling more Grinth blood into the already rain-soaked earth.

The storm raged on, thunder shaking the skies so loudly that it drowned out the sounds of the battle below and the fighting continued in an oddly silent display of wild, innate survival. From where Sill watched, intermittent bursts of lightning seemed to slow time, each flash illuminating the action as though she were viewing still drawings of some war waged in the past.

As more Grinth leered into view, Draneth's light began to ebb and fade. Sill looked on in horror as the edges of the circle crept ever closer whilst the power pulsing from the staff continued to wane. The shaman's face was contorted in anguish as he struggled to keep the light alive. Sill grabbed a handful of Raffin's shirt and saw his eyes dart from one scene to another as though assessing their best chance for survival. *There's nowhere to run,* she thought. *We're not going to make it.*

Then Kallem was there at her side, tearing her away from Raffin. 'We're getting out of here,' he said as he pulled her towards him.

Raffin tried to grab her wrist but Kallem shoved him to the ground, his yellow eyes not wavering from her own. 'I promised to protect you,' he said through the rain, 'not them.'

'Let go of her!' Raffin yelled, clambering back to his feet. 'What are you doing?'

Sill shook her head vigorously. *No! It can't be like this.* But her body refused to fight against his hold, her instinct for survival begging her to submit to him, and let him save her from this terror. *Would I really leave them all?* Her mind said no but the raw fear that encased her heart had brought other impulses to life and every one of them urged escape, over everything else. Over Draneth. Over Trew and Hiddelle. Over Arnak, Broll and Brorn. And even over Raffin. *Oh peaks,* she thought, *don't make me choose, don't do this to me!*

'You don't owe them anything,' Kallem was telling her. 'Where were they when your mother died, or when your father beat you? Did anyone do anything? No. There's no reason for you to stay here. I can save you, I can keep you alive.'

Stop it! she thought, *that's not true. They didn't know, nobody even knew who I was.* But fear seemed to answer back. *Did they really not know what was happening? Could they not see the bruises? Or did they just not care? No one cares about you, you're on your own, you always have been.*

'Tell me,' Kallem said while the others fought madly around them in the diminishing light, 'tell me to save you. You'll die if you stay here.'

'No,' Sill said, her voice a whimper, 'I can't. I can't choose.' The dark was closing in and so were the Grinth. Her eyes filled with tears, making a blur of Kallem's as he stared at her.

'Tell me!' he roared as thunder broke the sky again and his hands gripped her tighter. 'Tell me to save you!'... *and we'll leave them all to die.*

Beside them, Draneth dropped to his knees. He clutched the staff with both hands as he poured the last of his strength into it.

'No!' Sill screamed. 'I won't! I won't do it! Let go of me!' Air rushed to her aid and pushed Kallem back beyond her grasp. His eyes widened momentarily but, absurdly, he grinned at her, then drew his sword and threw himself back into the heart of the battle. The red sword chopped through one of the Grinth, just as it looked sure to sink its claws and teeth into Trew's back. Kallem cut down another and kept fighting, wildly.

'Sill?' she heard Raffin say beside her, but she didn't respond. Something had awoken within her, shattering the fear around her heart. She could feel everything. The baleful wind, the foul rain; the dark menace in the clouds. She stared up in hatred at the black sky and, almost effortlessly, channelled a funnel of air that she hurled upwards, ripping a hole through the dense cloud. The sky rumbled as though pained and a pool of natural light shone down through the gap she had created, replacing Draneth's, just as it slid back into the skulled tip of the staff and vanished.

'I'm sorry,' she heard the shaman croak as though he were unaware they were still alive.

The others were completely outnumbered; the Grinth a ceaseless wave of death and fury. *It's not enough!* Sill realised and now she cried out as she expanded her column of air, tearing further into the retreating clouds.

Her friends continued to fight, against the odds. Brorn was the mightiest of all of them, his axe and body moving in constant flow: an endless dance of blood and dismemberment. But he had been hurt, too. For every Grinth that he slew, a claw would nick him here or there, and his body had become a criss-cross of seeping red lines. It was surely only a matter of time before he fell.

Broll was useless on his maimed leg and Arnak fought like a man possessed to protect him from the Grinth – it was clear the creatures knew who was the weak link.

They don't care, Sill realised as she watched the Grinth bodies pile up, *they don't care how many of them die, so long as they kill us.* Her renewed burst of power was already waning and she could feel the storm regaining its strength, its own power as unrelenting as the swarms of Grinth. There was little more she could do than wait for death. Just like she had at the Moonmirror.

And again it didn't come.

For no apparent reason, the Grinth began to hold back. Just a few at first, until all of a sudden none of them were fighting.

'What are they doing?' Arnak asked, his voiced strained with the pain and fatigue of battle.

No one answered. They were all too exhausted, too weary to contemplate what was happening, too wary to let themselves believe that there was any hope they could survive this.

The rain had ceased as abruptly as the Grinth but its threat remained in the dark grey clouds that hung above. Sill released her column of air and the wind died down until it was just a breeze, flicking, at Kallem's long, bloodstained hair. The sky closed and dark again reigned, though it was not so hard to see, now that the rain had stopped.

Through the retreating Grinth, a man emerged. He moved gracefully, slipping smoothly between the purple bodies as though they were no more than trees to be stepped around. Picking his way carefully, almost politely, through the Grinth, he dodged puddles of black blood and sidestepped twisted purple corpses until he stood before them.

'Well met, strangers,' he said with a smile. Despite the calm in his voice, his black eyes were ablaze with pupils of fiery yellow, each one a smouldering sun burning treacherously in the night, when it should have been day.

They're just like Kallem's, Sill noticed. *Just like the Grinth's.*

As the man spoke, the remaining, surrounding Grinth began to shuffle their hoofed feet and then slowly edge backwards until purple blended into shadow and eventually only the fires of their eyes remained, poking out through the returning mist. Then they were gone.

The storm had dissipated as though the skies themselves had breathed a sigh of relief at the Grinth's sudden departure. Sill watched as the blackness that had weighed upon the clouds swiftly dissolved, bleaching them of the storm's impurity and returning the land to a scene of dullish grey-green, now marred with the blood and bodies of the fallen Grinth. Sill slumped to the ground, relieved but exhausted. The hole she had created in the sky was already a memory, taking with it the final glimpse of shy blue that she had craved more than she realised.

The newcomer surveyed the battleground with a look of vague interest.

Broll groaned where he lay.

Hiddelle was the first to react and rushed to his aid, rummaging in her pack for something to dress the wound with. 'Hold still,' she commanded and Broll's jaw clenched as she eased the claw from his thigh and threw it, severed hand and all, away into the mud. Instantly, blood began to pour from the hole. Hiddelle wrapped the bandage securely around his leg several times until the flow seemed to have stopped. Then she pulled it tight and tied the two ends firmly together. A deeply concerned Arnak knelt over them, a hand on his friend's shoulder, his face as grey as the clouds.

Sill thought she might be sick.

The newcomer watched them patiently through his strange eyes, a slight smile bending his thin lips.

'Thank you,' Trew said, taking the impetus to approach him. 'I don't know what you did but you saved our lives, and you have my gratitude. May I know your name, friend?'

'My name is Zyan, friend,' the man replied in a light voice that hinted at amusement. He turned his fiery eyes on Trew.

'Thank you, then, Zyan,' Trew repeated, though with less conviction now.

Using his staff for support, Draneth raised himself stiffly to his feet. Exhaustion lay heavily on the shaman's weathered face. For the first time since they had met, Sill was saddened to see him look so weak. *How old is he, really?* she wondered. Draneth could well have been as old as Fallor but, if so, looked good for it, or perhaps he was as young as Artell – it was impossible to say – but Sill thought the former was more likely. People had talked of the shaman as though he had been alive for centuries and, although that obviously wasn't true, Draneth did have the air of a man who had lived a long life. In the recent past, a bolder Raffin may have simply asked his age but now her friend seemed defeated in a way she would not have imagined possible just a few weeks earlier. *He's not used to sadness*, she thought. *He's never had to deal with it before*. She wished she could send it away like she could the wind. It pained her to see him like this. *I can't bring his parents back. Nobody can.*

'This is the man you spoke of?' Draneth asked Kallem, pointing rudely at Zyan with his staff.

Kallem nodded. He stood just a short distance from Sill, his hands gripping the hilt of his red iron sword before him. The stained blade curved down until its tip met with the tainted ground at his feet. His blue-grey eyes were fixed on the darker, yellow ones that had mirrored his own until only moments ago. Unlike his, Zyan's eyes had not changed colour with the departure of the Grinth.

'You fought valiantly,' Zyan said, beginning to stroll amongst, and scan his yellow pupils over, the fallen Grinth.

'We had little choice,' Arnak replied bitterly, watching the newcomer's movements with a wary frown.

Brorn was less gracious. 'How is it they did not harm you?' he asked, his manner far blunter than the axe dangling ominously from one large, strong hand.

'Why should they?' Zyan responded pleasantly. 'I mean them no harm.'

'*Why should they*?' Brorn repeated, incredulous. 'Maybe that depends whose side you're on? Do not think we haven't noticed – your eyes are like theirs.'

'I'm not the only one,' Zyan said, his thin lips curving into another playful smile.

Kallem shot Sill a brief look and she shook her head, letting him know his eyes had returned to their natural state.

'It's true, your eyes *were* changed while we fought them,' Arnak said, turning his frown toward Kallem. 'At first I thought it my imagination.'

'At least he fought,' Brorn interrupted, his focus still fully engaged on the newcomer. 'You didn't even have to draw your sword. So I ask again, how is it they did not harm you?'

A yellow, iron sword hung loosely from Zyan's hip, but he made no move to reach for it, presumably unaware, or unafraid of, any posed threat. 'I suppose they did not deem it necessary,' Zyan said in answer to Brorn's question. The response had an air of intrigue as though he had never before considered the question. 'I wonder,' he said to Brorn, 'do *you* mean to harm me?' He looked sideways at Brorn as though genuinely interested in what the answer might be.

He's not afraid of us, Sill realised, to her increased discomfort.

Brorn's impatience had turned to anger. 'Perhaps I do,' he said, raising his axe to hold in both hands. 'If I took that smug head off your shoulders, would your eyes still glow yellow?'

'I have no idea,' Zyan said earnestly. Then he shrugged. 'But I fear my body would be less useful without my head so, for now at least, we shall not find out.'

'I wouldn't be so sure of that,' Brorn said, taking a step forward.

'Brorn!' Draneth snapped, some of his vigour finally returning. 'Enough. This gets us nowhere. Like it or not, this man did save us.' He looked hard at the newcomer, the lines of his forehead contorting into a weary frown. 'Zyan, my name is Draneth. I believe you've already met Kallem, and Tamarellin.'

Zyan smiled pleasantly whilst Tamarellin squawked and shifted his feet anxiously on the shaman's shoulder.

'Well met, *shaman*,' Zyan said coolly and a shiver ran up Sill's spine. Zyan may well have saved them from the Grinth but she was certain this man was not their ally. *He's not like Kallem*, she thought. *He's more like the storm*. But she wasn't sure why.

'This is Trew, and Hiddelle,' the shaman continued. Trew had already moved, perhaps instinctively, to stand by his wife's side. 'That's Arnak, and Broll with the injured leg. The young ones are Sill and Raffin, and that's Brorn with the axe.' Brorn grinned crudely and began to play with the axe, twisting the handle between his palms so that the double-bladed head began to spin.

Sill felt herself grope for Raffin's hand as Zyan's yellow eyes skimmed across her body. Raffin accepted the clasp but his hand did not respond to the squeeze she gave him. Zyan smiled affably at each member of the party, as though they were now all friends.

'Now that we're all *acquainted*,' Draneth said sarcastically. 'For the sake of the peaks, can we get moving?'

'What about Broll?' Arnak asked. 'He cannot go far.'

In response, Broll grunted and placed a firm hand on the ground to lever himself up. With Arnak and Hiddelle's help he managed to stand, but even Sill could see the pain masked behind his stone expression.

The shaman looked gravely at Broll, but before he could give answer, a rumbling sound turned his head swiftly to the south. For a moment, Sill feared the storm had returned but then she saw them appearing through the mist, their brilliant-white manes rippling in the soft breeze.

The riders must have spotted them, too, for they gave cries and spurred their horses in the party's direction.

'Are they from the Fort?' Raffin asked. His voice sounded quiet and detached, rather than hopeful or glad.

What now? Sill wondered, still unwilling to accept that help could be on the way. The stench of death rode thick and intoxicating on the breeze and her legs were wobbly beneath her. She felt dizzy, and her stomach was queasy after staring too long at Broll's injured leg. A dire cold had spread through her veins as though her own personal frost was chilling her bones, sucking at the warmth within. *I'm just in shock*, she thought. It had been the same when she ran to the forest after her hut had caught fire. *I will need to sleep soon.*

'Yes,' Draneth said in answer to Raffin's question, as he watched the galloping horses approach. When Sill glanced up at him, the shaman's eyes seemed sad and distant. 'About time, too,' he growled and the sadness quickly vanished, replaced by a more fitting snarl.

Now that Sill could see the dazzling riders draw nearer, she wondered how it was that the image didn't lift the shaman's spirits. *Perhaps nothing can*, she thought and then she felt guilty for doing so. *I can't blame him for being like that. He's tried his best to help us. He didn't have to.* Even so, the horses *were* a beautiful sight. Mottled-grey coats with flowing, pure-white tails bore the riders ever closer, their hooves splashing lightly through the shallow puddles left by the rain. On each mount, white manes and forelocks lined a speckled-white back as though they had been touched by snow. In stark contrast, the riders wore a deep red, but Sill could not yet make out the detail. As the horses slowed, first to a canter and then into a lighter trot, she saw that the riders were wearing some kind of protective clothing, resembling reddened leather, tough and worn, with red, metal plates somehow stitched into the chest, back, arms and legs. The handiwork put Sill's quilt to shame. *Why don't we know how to do that?* she wondered, crossly. *It might have saved some lives.*

'Blood Riders,' Draneth announced, softly, beside her.

The red riders pulled up just short of the group as though gauging the situation before they dared move any nearer. One man, evidently their Leader, said some words to the others and they all began to trot their horses over to the exhausted travellers. The rider's expressions were steely and uncertain as they assessed the battlefield.

'My name is Captain Ryke,' the man in charge said to nobody in particular. 'I am the Captain of The Guard.' His grey mount snorted and shifted its feet uncomfortably, forcing the Captain to pull on the reins in order to maintain his balance. He steadied the horse and leaned forward to pat its neck. Then he noticed Zyan. 'Surround them!' he cried. He unsheathed a red sword from his side, similar to Kallem's, and held it up in the air.

The Blood Riders obeyed and spurred their mounts to take up positions around the group.

The noticeably unfazed figure of Zyan made no attempt to reach for his own sword.

Each of the riders carried a bright red sword at his side and a long, slim spear, diagonally, across his back.

Zyan smiled up at the man nearest to him. 'This is not necessary,' he said plainly. 'I mean you no harm.'

Sill could tell from the rider's face that the feeling was not mutual. Exhausted as they were, her companion's hands began to reach cautiously for their weapons.

Brorn released one hand from his great axe to let it swing gently at his side. *No!* Sill thought. *This is ridiculous! We're all just people.*

Chapter 12

'Where were you?' Raffin yelled suddenly at the rider nearest to him. He grabbed at the man's leg, trying to tug him from his horse. The Blood Rider gripped his reins tightly and looked at his Captain uncertainly for help or orders. Captain Ryke frowned and only shrugged his shoulders.

'Where were you?' Raffin yelled again and started to hit the man's protected leg with his fists.

Raffin, don't! Sill thought, but nobody moved to stop him.

The Blood Rider swung down from his horse and Raffin beat at his protected chest until the rider was forced to hold his wrists to stop him. 'They killed them!' Raffin yelled up at the man, 'they killed my parents.' The rider released him and he dropped to his knees, and began to shake with sobs. The rider looked again to his Captain, clearly stunned by Raffin's reaction. The Captain of The Guard turned away, his jaw clenched shut. The startled Blood Rider tried to put a hand on Raffin's shoulder to console him, but Raffin slapped it away, glared at the man defiantly, and then scrambled back to his feet and walked back towards Sill and the shaman. Sill moved to comfort him, but he sidestepped around her, wiping his eyes clean, and instead went to stand by Draneth. A pang of pain jolted Sill's heart at the unexpected rejection, and for a second she thought she might cry, too, but she held back the tears for his sake. *This isn't about me*, she scolded herself, *it's his pain. I shouldn't have left the village.* Dejected, she went and stood by him all the same. *I'm here if you need me.*

An awkward silence hung in the air.

'You're a little late,' Draneth's gruff voice cut sardonically through the silence. The bowed heads of the riders suggested they had just realised that themselves. Draneth huffed and strode purposefully towards the Captain of The Guard as though his men posed no threat to the shaman. One of the Blood Riders quickly released the spear from his back and moved to intercept, but Captain Ryke raised a hand and the man was forced to pull on his reins and merely glare a warning at shaman. Draneth ignored him. 'When did it become thus that The Guard threatens its people instead of helping them?' he asked the Captain angrily. 'Can't you see that we need help?'

Captain Ryke's bottom lip quivered slightly as though he were unaccustomed to being talked to in such a manner, and did not know how best to respond. 'My apologies,' he at least had the grace to say, 'but we have heard strange tales from the lands of late, and your companion –'

'Tales?' The shaman cut him off, incensed. 'Is that what they call my messages now?'

'You are Draneth?' the Captain asked, a little too keenly. He turned his horse to face the imposing shaman more squarely.

'I am,' Draneth said, 'and you were just a fresh-faced child when I last saw you, *Captain.* I assume things haven't changed much at the Fort?'

If he grasped the meaning of Draneth's jibe, the Captain of The Guard did not rise to it. 'You can see for yourself,' he said. 'I have orders to escort you back to Rydan.'

'*I* no longer follow orders,' Draneth seethed, 'but since we're headed in that direction anyway, I'm sure my companions and I would welcome your *aid*.' He gave the Captain a moment to contemplate his choice of words.

'Er, yes, of course, sorry,' Captain Ryke said again. He looked about, taking in more of the battle scene and the state of Draneth's companions. They appeared unmoved by the Captain's proclaimed apologies, as was Sill.

Raffin's right, where were you?

'I can see you are weary. And wounded,' Captain Ryke said, noticing Broll. 'You must have fought bravely.'

'So you do see them, then?' Draneth said, pointing his staff in the direction of a headless Grinth.

'I see well enough,' the Captain said gravely. His eyes were distant as he stared down at the Grinth body the shaman had indicated. 'Though my heart wishes it was not true,' he added, sombrely turning away.

'People should pay less attention to their hearts and more to those who have some sense,' Draneth said, still unappeased.

The Captain looked at him evenly and nodded. 'You may share our horses,' he said. 'You are clearly very tired.'

Draneth sucked in a sharp breath and his eyes darkened beneath the scowl but, for once, he seemed to resolve himself to keep quiet. As the riders began to move and the shaman returned to them, Sill could hear the sound of his jaw clicking beside her.

Arnak helped a weak Broll stagger towards one of the horses. 'Fighting for your life will do that to you,' he grumbled, in response to the Captain's remark. Hiddelle had done her best to stem the flow of blood from Broll's wounded leg but already the bandage was soaked red and his face had turned as grey as ash.

The Captain remained outwardly unmoved by Broll's state, or any of the comments he may or may not have overheard. 'Don't worry,' he said assuredly, 'we shall soon have you safe.' He pointed towards Zyan. 'That one remains under guard,' he told his men. Then he turned and began to trot his horse away from the stench of blood.

'Safe,' Draneth muttered, huffing. 'We shall see about that.' But he accepted the hand offered by the rider who had previously glared at him and hoisted himself up to share the back of the man's great, grey-and-white steed. Tamarellin gave an alarmed squawk, presumably not too enthralled by the prospect of riding a horse, and flapped himself up towards the sky.

The rest of the Blood Riders began to help Sill and her companions up onto their respective horses, although Sill and Raffin had to double-up behind a single rider. Sill stroked the horse's back apologetically. 'Sorry,' she said, but if it minded the extra burden, the beast made no fuss.

Sill had only seen a horse once before, when an aging storyteller had come to Hillock to trade news. That one had been much like these, tall and elegant, and the colours of the mountains. That was where they came from, the storyteller had told them. Big as these horses were, she had remembered them to be even larger. *Probably because I was so small*, she realised. She still felt small now, compared to her companions. Hiddelle was the only other girl, except that she was really a woman grown, and as well muscled as most of the men. Even Raffin had got bigger. *Will I never grow up?* she wondered. But it was no good to dwell on such things. *I have to be stronger. I am stronger.* Her use of power had shown that. Now she just needed to work out how to use it when she needed to, and how to control it.

'I am Erran,' their Blood Rider smiled back at them, cheerfully. He had a young face. A kind face. 'Hold on tight,' he said, 'here we go.' He flicked the reins and his mount broke into a trot before accelerating, without warning, into a fierce gallop. Sill did as instructed and gripped Erran tightly around the waist, afraid she would fall at any moment. She could feel Raffin's hands locked around the folds of her clothing, but he refrained from putting his arms around her and, suddenly, she felt an overwhelming sadness, though she could not explain why.

I shouldn't have left him, she thought again, miserably. *He trusted me. He waited for me*. Again, she tried to wrench herself away from such thoughts. *He waited for me*, she reminded herself, more positively. *He waited for me*.

Erran was not what she had expected. Somehow she had imagined the men of The Guard to be older, bigger and more battle-scarred. But all of them looked young, including Captain Ryke, and none of the Blood Riders bore any noticeable injuries. *None of them would have actually even fought a real Grinth*, she realised. *Because there weren't any before*. When they had first ridden up, their expressions had held a mixture of emotions: anger, shock, disgust. And perhaps even fear. Would these men have fared so well as her own companions had, against such an assault? Sill doubted it. And these were the men of The Guard, of Rydan Fort, the only human stronghold; the last defence of the Inner Lands. *They're so young*, she thought, *Why are they all so young?* Perhaps the rest of The Guard would be different, at the Fort itself. Or maybe that would be a disappointment, too. *It's probably made out of sticks*.

She was wrong.

'Up ahead!' Erran called over the rush of wind that whipped at their ears. The Blood Riders turned in unison, and as they did so, Sill got her first glimpse of the magnificence of Rydan Fort. It was the most incredible sight she had ever seen, far surpassing the natural wonder of the Moonmirror. Nestled beneath the tallest of mountains, the Fort seemed to be carved into the rock itself as though it was a part of the land. The walls were huge: two vast, rising, solid blocks of stone, as tall as the *serethen* trees of home, that curved around until they merged with the mountain. In the middle, the walls were divided by mighty gates, which looked to be made from rows of *serethen* trunks, the largest Sill had ever seen, all somehow linked together. The wood of the gates was thick at the bottom, growing into pointier tips as it rose skyward, mirroring the jagged peaks beyond and lending the Fort an air of intimidation. Sill thought the gates resembled a row of Grinth teeth, but whatever they were shaped on, the message was clear: *Keep out*. From this distance, Rydan Fort was a marvel to behold. Both magnificent and foreboding in equal measure. For the first time in her life, Sill felt as though she had made the right decision coming here. *This has to be the safest place in all of the Lands*.

As Erran urged his horse onwards, the walls grew ever taller and the mountains loomed like giants above, protecting the man-made Fort as though it was a younger brother.

Erran reached a hand down to his side and brought forth a painted wooden object, the likes of which Sill had never seen before. The object was circular, with a small hole at one end that curved upwards into a larger hole at the other. The wood had been coloured red with slim, gold rings encircling it that grew in width from the smaller end, stretching up to the larger. Erran put the smaller hole to his lips and blew. A long, low note sounded from the other end and echoed against the Fort's towering walls. Moments later, a matching tone boomed out from the Fort itself, preceded by a mighty groan as the huge, wooden gates began to creak and move. As the Blood Riders sped ever nearer, the gates opened inwards, forming a gaping mouth between the walls as though the Fort would swallow them up upon entry.

Sill blinked, trying to force herself awake so she wouldn't miss any of the spectacle. Her eyes felt glazed-over, as though they no longer held the ability to focus; her mind was active but erratic, constantly flitting from one random thought to another. *I need food and drink,* she thought hazily, *and sleep. Sleep first.* She could feel it coming on like a ripple, slowly spreading over her, until eventually it would consume her entirely. Running from the Grinth, the battle, the bloodshed, her use of power. It was a wonder she was able to function at all.

The horses slowed as they passed through the gates into an open courtyard that spanned the breadth of the walls. Lines of men holding long, thick ropes, dropped them and took up others, pulling on them until the *serethen* gates creaked again and then finally slammed shut, sealing them off from the grim new world outside. *The Inner Lands will never be the same again*, Sill's fleeting thoughts told her. *There's no going back. Not for any of us.* She wondered if Kallem would still have gone with Draneth had it not been for her. He could have gone with Artell to the mountains, left his painful memories behind, and started again. He was already a changed man. But whether that was for better or worse, she could not say. She hadn't had time or energy to digest what he'd done during the Grinth attack. *Did he really mean to take me away and leave everyone else to die, or was he just testing me? Seeing if I was worth saving? I made him promise*, she remembered. But what had that promise cost him? Or her? *I was selfish. I've never asked anyone for anything before. Who would, with a father like mine? I needed him. He's not the monster everyone thought. He's just sad, after what happened to his family.* She wondered why the other villagers couldn't see that.

Erran dismounted to help Sill and Raffin down from his horse and then hopped lightly back onto the beast's grey, mottled back. The other Blood Riders did the same as though they couldn't stand to be apart from their horses for more than a few seconds.

Brorn and Arnak helped Broll to lift his good leg over his mount and then slide gingerly to the ground, aided by his friends.

'Captain Ryke!' someone called.

Sill craned her head to look up towards the towering wall where a man, his head just a small dot, shouted down to the Captain of The Guard. Despite the distance, the man's voice carried well, the authority in his tone unmistakeable.

'Put them in a cell!' the man yelled.

What?

'Riders!' Captain Ryke cried and, instantly, the Blood Riders formed a circle around the group, unsheathed their spears, and pointed them in towards the stunned companions. 'I'm sorry,' he said. 'General Venth's orders.'

CHAPTER 13

'The General will see you now.'

About time. Draneth was almost too tired to be as angry as he wanted to be. Almost. It was enough that Venth had decided to lock them up – and Draneth suspected the act was aimed specifically at him, to demonstrate the General's authority – but what really infuriated him was the fact he knew he would have to keep his calm in front of the man, or risk getting his companions into further trouble.

General, he scoffed. *This is going to be difficult.*

What is he like? Tamarellin asked.

Wait and see, Draneth told him, grumpily.

I want to be outside, Tamarellin complained.

That isn't my fault.

The guard who unlocked the cell door was as young as the rest of them and looked more than a little intimidated as Draneth shouldered past him. *Have some backbone, man, for peak's sake,* Draneth thought. *The fate of the Inner Lands rests on those weak shoulders.* Before leaving, Draneth turned to his companions. 'You shall not remain in here for long, I promise you,' he said. The faces he saw looked worn and dejected. Brorn pushed himself away from the wall and began to loosen his muscles. His great axe had been taken from him, as had all their weapons, and Draneth was relieved that they had given them up without a fight.

Sill gave him a considerate smile, showing that she at least still believed in him, rightly or wrongly. *Don't put your faith in me. You're the one who can give us the edge.*

The rest of them sat resting against the walls of the large cell and didn't trouble themselves to look up.

I don't blame you, Draneth thought. Besides Broll, whom he hoped was receiving better treatment somewhere more comfortable, and Zyan, whom he suspected was anything but comfortable, he had at least managed to keep the rest of their group together. He was no longer annoyed at Ryke; the Captain of The Guard was just following orders and he wasn't a bad man. *Just not a smart one either.*

I should have flown away, Tamarellin said.

I'm glad you didn't, I need you here.

Since their imprisonment, Arnak had spent most of his time pacing back and forth, occasionally and pointlessly shouting at their guard for the lack of news on his friend's condition. Hiddelle and Trew had fallen asleep in each other's arms, perhaps just glad to be alive, and Sill and the boy sat quietly next to each other, consumed by their young thoughts. Kallem sat typically aside from everyone else, legs crossed, eyes closed, and as still as the peaks. To look at him, one might well assume he was sleeping, but Draneth knew better.

He listens, Tamarellin had told him.

Draneth left his companions, vowing that he would keep his word and have them free. *I can't promise what will happen after that.*

The young guard led him along the tight, familiar corridors and up and down the twisting granite steps that Draneth had trodden countless times before. The belly of Rydan Fort was vast and deep and during his time here, The Guard used to joke that the Fort resembled a small boy with a huge appetite, such was the scale of inner-Rydan. The outer walls and courtyard were just a well-guarded entrance. The Fort itself stretched far into the mountain, and over the centuries had been expanded until its different tunnels, rooms and staircases were so numerous that even he didn't know how deep it went. Draneth had spent a good few years exploring the Fort's darker corners, outside of his regular duties as a man of The Guard, and he hoped the current regime would have a similar routine. He had left Rydan for the same reasons everybody did: age. It was a tradition that had lived as long as the Fort itself, that every man, upon reaching the age of physical decline, was forced to leave Rydan. That way, the men of The Guard remained forever young and forever vigilant. *And forever ignorant,* Draneth thought bitterly. He had argued against it during his time here but the tradition would never change. *And neither will they.* Only the General was allowed to remain beyond those years, passing on whatever knowledge he possessed to his successor. *Which is why nothing changes.*

You should calm down, Tamarellin reminded him and he tutted, but awarded the hawk with a gentle stroke.

Tamarellin was right. When Draneth had known him, Venth had been a strict and stubborn man who stuck rigidly to the rules and customs of The Guard. He had always irritated Draneth but the shaman expected the now-General would say the same about him. 'What's your name, boy?' he asked the young guard who led him. *They do not see me as a threat*, he told Tamarellin, amused, *or they would have sent more than just this one.*

The guard did not respond.

He is not sure if he is allowed, Tamarellin explained.

'Have The Guard lost all courtesies?' Draneth growled, preying on the young man's sense of honour. 'I asked you your name.'

'My name is Carsen,' the guard said with a hint of resentment. 'And I am a man, not a boy.'

So you do have a backbone after all? Draneth thought. *Good, you'll be needing it.* 'And do you know who I am, Carsen-the-man?'

'Everybody knows who you are,' Carsen said simply.

That annoyed Draneth. *So they have been talking about me? That means they got my message. Why didn't they act?* That would be the first of many questions he would like to ask the General.

Of course they got the message, Tamarellin said, sulkily.

I never doubted you, Draneth assured him, stroking the bird's head again. *But you couldn't tell me who you gave it to.*

How should I know? Tamarellin complained. *They all wear the same things.*

Draneth grinned. That was true, he supposed, except for the Blood Riders, but it wasn't worth arguing the case. Tamarellin was not obliged to do anything he asked. 'What happened to my companion?' he asked Carsen. 'The one with the injured leg.'

'He is being cared for,' the guard replied curtly.

You will not get much more out of this one, Tamarellin warned. *He belongs to the General.*

You don't like him? Draneth asked.

His head is full of snow.

Draneth grinned. Tamarellin had a funny way of saying things when he was unsure how to express himself to a human.

'And what of my other companion?' he asked the guard sternly.

Carsen did not reply.

I told you, Tamarellin said.

Carsen led them through more lantern-lit tunnels, up and down more granite staircases until Draneth was certain they were back on the same route they had started out on. *He's trying to confuse me*, the shaman realised, entertained by the fact that the General must have thought that would work.

Finally Carsen stopped at the entrance to a room. He turned to face the shaman. 'Through here,' he said.

'Carsen, you have been most diligent,' the shaman told him. 'No doubt you would make a fine Blood Rider.'

Clever, Tamarellin said. *That is what he wants.*

That's what all young men of The Guard want, Draneth told him.

Carsen blinked at the shaman in surprise, evidently unaccustomed to receiving compliments. 'Er, thank you,' he said. 'I like your eagle.'

I am not an eagle, I am a hawk, Tamarellin said, annoyed. He squawked loudly at the boy.

'He likes you, too,' Draneth told the guard.

I do not.

Carsen nodded, not quite committing to a smile, and left them to it.

He is leaving us? Tamarellin asked, surprised.

The General does not see me as a threat, Draneth explained. *Or at least that's what he wants to show me.*

Draneth watched the young guard plod away and then turned to face the entranceway to the room he had been led to. It was more a sculpted cave than a real room, as was the entirety of the inner-Fort, and Draneth remembered the purpose of this room well, although it had never been needed during his time. As he entered, the orange glow of a lantern warmed the granite walls within and made a silhouette of the tall, shadowy figure of General Venth. The General had his back to Draneth and, in turn, stood facing the back of Zyan, who had positioned himself at the far end of the room, well within the locked cell. Draneth noted that no harm seemed to have befallen Zyan, yet.

General Venth sniffed and stiffened as the shaman entered the room. The cell Zyan occupied was much like the one Draneth had just come from, except that instead of one guard, two men were placed either side of the barred door that ran wall-to-wall of the crudely carved room. The metal and granite alone should have been enough to keep Zyan safely locked away. All the same, the shaman approved of the extra precaution.

'What can you tell me of him?' General Venth asked, sparing Draneth any false courtesies.

'I see your men aren't the only ones to have lost their manners, Venth,' Draneth said, the General's tone of voice, alone, enough to make his blood boil.

It does not take much, Tamarellin reminded him, *and it is not like you are any more polite. Calm down, or he will not listen to you.*

'Don't try my patience, Draneth,' the General said tetchily. 'You have come to us keeping some odd company. Did you expect to be greeted with open arms?' He moved his hands behind his back, interlocking his fingers. 'And it's *General* Venth now,' he added. 'You'd do well to remember that.'

This is going to be harder than I thought.

Remember why we are here, Tamarellin urged him.

The shaman took a moment to douse the fires of acrimony before saying, 'Zyan wasn't a part of our group, but he did save us from the Grinth, which is more than you did. Did you not receive my message?'

That is calm? Tamarellin asked.

He will not respect me if he thinks me weak, Draneth told his friend.

'We did,' the General said with a snort. 'You sent a bird to warn us of a Grinth invasion? A bird, Draneth!'

'Tamarellin is more than just a bird,' Draneth told him, trying to thwart the flames that instantly reignited within him.

I am a hawk, Tamarellin repeated, sullenly.

'I did not have time to come myself,' he explained. 'I had other matters to attend to.'

'Other matters?' General Venth snorted, still opting to stare at Zyan's back rather than turn and face the shaman. 'You should have come to us immediately. It is our job to protect the people of these lands, Draneth, not yours, not anymore. Now answer my question, or would you rather go back into your cell?'

Stay calm, Tamarellin told him. *He is upset.*

I can see that for myself, Draneth told the hawk.

'Not much,' he said aloud, 'other than what you see for yourself, but we should not be having this conversation here.' *Not in front of Zyan.*

'He does not concern me,' the General said. 'Speak freely.'

'Very well,' Draneth said to satisfy the General. *On your head be it.* 'He acts strangely, that much is obvious, and his eyes are the colour of theirs. The Grinth also do not seem to harm him. That is all I know.' He was not sure how much more he wanted to share with the General at this point, especially in light of Kallem's own colour-shifting eyes. In any case, Venth would be well-versed in all of the Grinth knowledge possessed by The Guard. So, in essence, Draneth knew little more than the General about men like Zyan. They had only been a myth, a legend. Until now.

We know about Kallem, though, Tamarellin said.

Not entirely, Draneth reminded him, *and we can't share that with anyone. Especially not Kallem.*

'What else?' the General asked impatiently.

'Only that when he appeared, the Grinth halted their attack and retreated,' the shaman said, truthfully. 'Because of this, he saved our lives, but I am not yet sure if his help was intended or just a coincidence.' *Or for some darker purpose.*

'I don't believe in coincidence,' the General stated, 'only good planning, though having said that, the Grinth have never been intelligent creatures. That's why they use humans.'

'I am not so sure,' Draneth countered. 'Tamarellin believes he has found evidence of another kind of Grinth; their Queen, if you like, close to where the Grinth first penetrated our lands.'

'Tamarellin?' the General repeated, turning to look at the hawk for the first time. 'You mean the bird?'

Hawk, Tamarellin said, growing angry himself. *You people know nothing of the world.*

'The point is,' Draneth continued, 'that I believe there is a creature of higher intellect controlling the others.'

'Preposterous.' The General dismissed the idea with a flick of his hand and turned his attention back to Zyan, who had not moved a muscle. 'There is nothing in our records to suggest such a creature exists.'

Draneth had been concerned that the General would not believe him, but he had to try all the same. *We are running out of alternatives.* 'How would we know?' he asked, hoping to keep the conversation alive. 'The records only go back so far.'

The General snorted again. 'I would think our ancestors would not have left out such a vital detail,' he said contemptuously.

'What if they had not known?' Draneth asked. 'Our ancestors weren't prepared for the Grinth. They fought purely for survival, and were defeated. Our knowledge comes only from those few who fled here.'

You are unlikely to convince him, Tamarellin told him. *He has been this way too long.*

He must listen! Draneth thought, exasperated at his kind's ignorance. His hope had been to convince The Guard to send out a unit, on horseback, to search for the existence of the Queen, and kill her, if indeed she did exist. But in order to truly convince the General, he would have to share with Venth knowledge that would put Kallem at risk, and ultimately the gamble was not worth it. As Tamarellin said, Venth was unlikely to change and Kallem may well be their last hope.

What about Sill?

Sill is everything that's good about us. That's why she can't do what needs to be done. It can only be Kallem.

You are too hard on her.

These are hard times.

That is no excuse.

Draneth stroked the hawk's feathers, soothing his friend. Tamarellin was right, as usual, but the hawk did not understand how it was to be human. He had been born a predator and the switch between kindness and killing was natural to him. People were more varied and complex. Some were violent by nature and had to resist their natural urges in order to conform to society, but others were born gentler and forced to harden themselves just to survive.

They would never defeat the Grinth in open battle; there were too many of the beasts and their will to spill human blood was too strong. *It's taken them centuries to breach the Inner Lands*, Draneth knew. *They'd never stopped hunting us and they never will. Not until every last one of us is dead. I must convince him.*

'General –' Draneth urged, thinking the use of the title might help his cause. It didn't.

'Enough of this,' Venth interrupted, waving a hand as though Draneth's words were no more than an irritating fly he could swat away. 'We will get all the answers we need from *him*. If you cannot help, make yourself useful in some other way. We will need all the bodies we can get.'

'Then release my friends,' Draneth said, wasting no more of his breath. *I will find another way.* Inside, he was seething. 'They are all good fighters,' he told the General of The Guard, 'save for the children, but I'm sure your Captain would have told you as much.' *Intolerable fool! Your prejudices overrule your better judgement.*

'Very well,' the General agreed, turning to face him squarely now. 'We could use them, so long as I know they can be trusted.'

'They can. You must at least remember me well enough to know that I would not put us in any danger.'

'Knowingly,' the General granted, 'but who knows where your wits are these days, Draneth? Many years have passed since you left us and we have heard some strange tales of you during that time. I must confess I'm surprised that you appear to be in such good stead, physically, I mean.' The General's eyes gave Draneth a wary assessment before he said, 'Is it true you call yourself a shaman now?'

'Some have called me that,' Draneth said, containing his fury as best he could. 'And I assure you my *wits* are just as sharp as they ever were.' *And peaks sharper than yours.* 'Rest assured, I do not think myself more than a man, Venth. I've just learned a few new tricks along the way.'

'Well then perhaps we can put some of those tricks to good use,' the General said pragmatically. He seemed genuinely unaware of any offence his words might have caused, as though he were immune to the notion that anything existed beyond The Guard's stringent constitution. He nodded towards the stationary figure of Zyan. 'He talks in riddles and refuses to give a straight answer,' he said, with deliberate contempt. 'He irritates me profusely.' General Venth raised his voice to be sure Zyan could hear him. 'Soon, we will try more forceful methods but I wanted to see what you had to say of him first.'

So you do give me some credit? Draneth thought, despite the array of insults. He knew exactly what Venth meant by *forceful* and he had hoped it wouldn't come to that with Zyan. On the other hand...*at least he is willing to do what needs to be done.* There would be many casualties in this war, whatever the outcome, and sometimes saving lives could mean making some unconscionable decisions.

'Zyan,' Draneth said, knowing he was listening to everything. He glanced quickly at Venth whose shrug told him he had leave to address the prisoner, whatever use it might be. 'Are they treating you well?'

'As well as one would expect, shaman.' Zyan's voice sounded softer than ever in the quiet of the cave. 'It is kind of you to ask.'

He talks in riddles, Venth had said, but perhaps he just hadn't asked the right questions. 'Do you believe in fate, Zyan?' he tried.

'Do you?' Zyan responded. There was a hint of amusement in his tone.

'I believe in the balance of nature,' Draneth told him.

'Balance,' Zyan repeated quietly, as though trying out the word in his mouth. 'What is this balance? I am interested to know.'

'The balance between life and death of course; sometimes, one might say, between good and evil. Do you think of such things, Zyan?'

'Yes,' Zyan said, after a pause. 'But they do not like me to.'

'Who are they, Zyan?'

'The Grinth.'

Venth looked sharply at the shaman, urging him with his eyes to pursue this further.

I didn't ask for your approval. 'You talk to the Grinth?' he asked Zyan calmly.

'Sometimes,' Zyan said, almost wistfully, 'although they do not understand me. It can be most lonely, even among so many.' With his back still turned, the acoustics of the cave made his voice sound hollow, almost as though it was not emanating directly from his body.

'Do they talk to you?' Draneth asked.

'No,' Zyan said. 'But *she* does.'

Now the General had taken notice. He narrowed his eyes and leaned in closer to the cell, squeezing two of the bars tightly in his hands.

Perhaps you will take me more seriously now? Draneth thought ruefully, thinking about the note Tamarellin had delivered. How many lives could have been spared if The Guard had acted on his words? 'Zyan?' he asked, straining with all the might of the peaks to appear calm and casual, 'who is she? Does she control the Grinth?'

'She does not like us talking about her,' Zyan said quickly, his voice a whisper.

Draneth met eyes with the General who pursed his lips thoughtfully and leaned in even closer to the bars. *I wouldn't do that if I were you,* Draneth thought. Zyan's yellow sword may be absent from his waist but there was still something dangerous about him that the shaman could not yet fully fathom. *He has no fear,* he thought. But that wasn't true. He did not fear other people, or even the Grinth, but whatever controlled them had him whispering. Perhaps fear was what made him dangerous. *Where did you come from?* he wondered but there were more pressing things to ask. Draneth started with the most important one. 'Where is *she*, Zyan?'

'Nowhere. Everywhere. What does it matter?' Zyan asked.

Draneth tried something else. 'Who are you, Zyan?'

'You already know that, shaman: we have introduced ourselves.' He sounded pleased about this.

'I know your name,' Draneth corrected, 'but I do not know *who* you are. Where did you come from?'

'Who is anyone?' Zyan responded. 'How many of us really know?'

This must have been the kind of answer Venth had been getting. *No wonder he's angry.*

'Then *what* are you, Zyan?'

'I am a man, just like you.'

'But you're not like me, are you?'

'We are different, it's true,' Zyan agreed, 'but then aren't we all different in our own unique ways?'

Draneth was not perturbed. 'And how are *you* different, Zyan? You specifically.'

'Have you not already seen?'

'This is getting us nowhere,' General Venth pushed himself away from the bars with a sigh. Clearly he had grown bored of the questioning.

Draneth glared at him. 'We must be patient,' he hissed in a low voice. 'Has he not already given us evidence of the Queen?'

'He has given us nothing,' Venth stated, refuelling Draneth's ire. 'He is toying with you as he toyed with me.'

Keep calm, Tamarellin urged the shaman. *He now knows that the Queen exists and he has agreed to release the others. He is stubborn but he is listening.*

Draneth hoped the hawk was right. *Did you learn anything from Zyan?* he asked his friend.

No, I cannot read him.

'Is there anything else you'd like to ask me, shaman?' Zyan said suddenly. 'I do enjoy our conversations.'

It was hard to know if there was sarcasm in Zyan's voice, such was the innocence of his visage, but the question sounded almost inviting, as though there was something he wanted Draneth to know but was unable to tell him directly. Draneth exchanged a puzzled look with the General and thought carefully about his next words. *What can I ask that he will answer?* 'Yes,' he said quickly, stalling, 'there is just one more thing.' *What can I ask him that we don't already know?*

Ask him that, Tamarellin suggested.

Draneth smiled. Sometimes the hawk's simplicity was exactly the guidance he needed. 'Zyan, tell us something we don't yet know.' Perhaps it was a desperate attempt and he knew it would sound as much to the General but he didn't care, it was worth a try. To his dismay, Zyan did not answer.

We have already got what we wanted, Tamarellin reassured him, *we should return to free the others.*

Draneth sighed. *Perhaps you are right,* he said.

Wait, the hawk added, *something is happening.*

What is it? Draneth asked but, rather than answer, Tamarellin launched himself from the shaman's shoulder, and in a flurry of wings, flew from the room. 'Tamarellin!' Draneth shouted after him, but he was already gone. *Damn it,* he thought, *where are you going?*

He turned to the General but Venth had barely noticed the disturbance and was staring instead at Zyan, who had finally turned to face them. 'What is it?' the General asked him gruffly. 'Do you have something to tell us or not? This is your last chance.'

Zyan ignored him. He was smiling and his strange eyes now searched the ceiling of the room as though he was looking for something deep within the granite. Perhaps he found it, as the yellow pupils suddenly fixed on the pale blue of the shaman's. 'It has started,' he said.

'Enough of this,' General Venth spat, but before he could make any threats a noise turned his attention away from the prisoner.

It was a deep, low, noise that reverberated ominously through the tunnels and stairwells, crept along the rough granite walls, and echoed around the room they now occupied. It was a noise that Draneth had heard many times in the practice drills he had performed as a younger man. A noise that rumbled the belly of the Fort and sent shivers down the spines of all the men within. This horn meant war. This horn meant the Grinth had arrived.

CHAPTER 14

Draneth shielded his face from the bright daylight, his eyes taking time to adjust from the dimly lit caves below ground. He had never been fond of the darkness. *Another thing I haven't missed about The Guard*, he thought.

You live in a cave, Tamarellin pointed out.

I sleep in a cave, Draneth corrected. *Tell me the whole of the Inner Lands doesn't look like this?*

Tamarellin flew from his shoulder and glided from the Fort's high walls, staying well above the enemy below. The Grinth stretched out as far as the shaman could see: a bobbing purple mass of immeasurable magnitude. Their purple skin gleamed, oily in the sunlight, whilst their strange, booming coughs and the clicks of their claws grated through the stillness of the day. It was worse than Draneth had imagined. Even from this height the Grinth army looked so vast, so endless, that nothing but a dark purple filled the landscape between Rydan Fort and the distant bumps of the Western Range where everything faded into grey. Perhaps at night he might still have caught the twinkle of the Moonmirror's icy, black rock reflecting the light of the moon, but in the sun's blinding stare all he could see was death. *No, you can't think like that*, Draneth told himself. He had been a man of The Guard, trained to live without doubt or hopelessness. The Guard never grew old, never grew careless and never submitted to such petty emotions as fear. *Emotions are what make us human, make us alive: that's why I really left*. Perhaps it was also how men like Zyan came to be. The Guard the shaman had left behind was not the same as the one he had entrusted their future to. He looked around at the faces of the archers who lined the wall, the armoured ranks in the courtyard below and the Blood Riders atop their grey-white steeds. *My generation never had to face the Grinth,* he reminded himself. *It's not a fair comparison.*

'Are we not blessed?' The General's voice rang out over the unsettling quiet of the courtyard.

Draneth had followed him up onto the wall and for a while Venth had merely stared out at the Grinth, a grim frown his only response to the horrifying scene below, whilst his men went frantically about, organising themselves, as they were trained to do at the sound of the war horn.

Now the General turned to look down at those silently lining the courtyard. 'Are we not blessed?' he said again. 'Are we not *honoured* to be faced with such a sight?' One of his hands gestured out beyond the wall, while Captain Ryke's horse whinnied and shifted its feet nervously in the courtyard. 'For centuries,' Venth called out, spreading his arms wide, 'the men of The Guard have lived and died, waiting.' He paused, letting the word hang in the air for a moment. 'Waiting,' he repeated, 'to defend these lands, *our* lands, from our one true enemy. And yet *we* are the ones who will face them!' He drew his sword fiercely and swivelled back to look out beyond the wall, clenching his teeth and curling the fingers of his free hand into a fist. He twisted back to confront his men. 'Men of The Guard,' he urged, 'this is what we have *trained* for. This is what we have *lived* for. And this is what we will *die* for!' He raised his sword in the air and the men of The Guard roared and held their weapons high.

Not a bad effort, Draneth thought, *but I plan to live.* He craned his neck to see Tamarellin circling high above. *Well?* he asked.

205

There are many, was the hawk's answer.

Draneth rolled his eyes but could hardly reprimand his friend for not understanding human numbers.

'Open the gates,' the General commanded. 'Captain Ryke, let us see how black their blood truly is!'

'Open the gates!' the Captain of The Guard echoed below. 'Soldiers, Blood Riders, remember what you have learned and put it to good use!'

He can't mean to gamble everything at the outset? Draneth thought, growing ever more alarmed. He strode quickly along the wall to speak softly to the General who had already sheathed his sword and stood resolutely facing the Grinth, his arms folded.

'Is this wise?' Draneth quizzed him, taking care not to publicly question the General's orders. 'In time, I can give you an idea of how many we face.'

'Settle down, Draneth,' General Venth said without taking his eyes from the enemy, 'we must test their strength, and ours.'

'They have stayed beyond the range of our archers,' Draneth pointed out.

'I know.'

'Well, does that not show some sign of intelligence?'

'Or fear,' the General countered, 'or just basic instinct. We shall see,' he said with something resembling a smile. 'If you're still hoping to convince me of the existence of this *Queen*, you're wasting your time. Look at them, Draneth,' the General said, freeing one of his arms to wave casually at the mass of Grinth at his gates. 'Can I really spare any of my men to run off on some fool's errand? How would you even get past them?'

'We both know there are passages in the Fort that lead out to the Eastern Range,' Draneth urged him. 'Tamarellin believes the Queen is in the north, near Hillock, where the Grinth first emerged. Kallem also ran into Zyan in Hillock's forest – '

'Stop,' Venth said, holding up a warning hand. 'You may be of some use to me in this battle, Draneth, either up here on the wall or down below, fighting with the rest of them, but I will hear no more of "mights" or "maybes". Sometimes wisdom and bravery do not sit well together.'

Exactly what I'm afraid of! Draneth thought, biting his tongue. *I'll have to find another way.*

As the day's sun arced its way across the broad Rydan skies, playing audience to the horrors below, such thoughts consumed Draneth's mind.

As the gates were slammed shut and Captain Ryke slipped from his horse to collapse, exhausted, into the arms of his brothers, Tamarellin finally returned. *There are very many*, he said simply as he settled on the shaman's shoulder. Draneth gave the hawk a stroke and turned to leave the wall, avoiding the sideways look he got from the General as he went. Tamarellin had been gone so long he already knew the news would not be good. The hawk hadn't eaten for some time so Draneth decided not to press him for specifics at this point. *Did you manage to hunt?*

No, the hawk said. *The animals have gone.*

That was not good either. *The balance is tipping in their favour.*

It cannot last. Something will change.

He hoped his friend was right. The hawk's knowledge seemed to run beyond his own experiences and lifespan, though Draneth had never managed to fully understand how that could be. *Instinct*, he put it down to, but Tamarellin was unfamiliar with the term. *I just know*, he would say as though he didn't see the need to explain.

Draneth descended the carved, rock steps with a grim resolve to make a difference in this war, even if it meant taking to the field himself.

That would not be wise, Tamarellin told him as he watched his step on the spiral staircase that wound from the wall all the way down to the open courtyard below. The steps narrowed on the inside where they wrapped themselves around a central column, which was as much a part of the mountain as it was the wall. Although they were well maintained, Draneth was acutely aware that on a wet day the descent could quickly become deadly.

It is not wet today, Tamarellin pointed out.

These steps are not made for legs as old as mine.

The comment frightened Tamarellin enough that he abandoned his shoulder perch to glide away from the stair and land instead on an outcrop of rock overlooking the courtyard.

Can a hawk be scared of heights? Draneth asked him, amused.

I am scared of your legs.

Tamarellin remained on his new perch-point, surveying the bloodied men in the courtyard, as Draneth sought out his friends from the north. He had grown to admire the northerners. Despite their humble beginnings and the sudden attack on one of their villages, they had remained hardy and positive on their journey south and had shown great courage and aptitude in their battle with the Grinth. He could not blame them for losing some of that enthusiasm upon arriving at Rydan. The reality of The Guard was deflating and their treatment had been poor. The men of The Guard were taught to protect the people of the Inner Lands through diligent, unwavering service; taught to be strong, disciplined, courageous and respectful. The only problem with that was that few of them ever came into contact with the outside world and when they had tried in the past, it had often been a disheartening experience, as Draneth had learned for himself. There was ignorance amongst some of the village Leaders, widespread apathy, and worst of all, forgetfulness. Many had forgotten the stories of the past, dismissing history as legend, and rejecting the very necessity of Rydan Fort and The Guard.

During his own time at Rydan, Draneth had argued that they should spend more time with the villages, re-educating and reconnecting with the people of the Inner Lands. But his ideas had been scoffed at and the General at the time, General Rickard, had become more and more disillusioned with the work they did outside of the Fort, until eventually it stopped entirely. Instead, the focus of The Guard shifted to an emphasis on combat and knowledge of the Grinth. General Venth appeared to have adopted a similar philosophy. In theory, the decision was not a bad one, but if their knowledge of the Grinth was wrong...*How quickly can one unlearn something they have spent their whole life training for?*

Draneth found Trew and Hiddelle in the Armoury, equipping themselves as best they could with whatever protective wear they could find to fit them.

'They don't make these for women,' Hiddelle grumbled as she tried to stretch the leather breastplate over her breasts.

'Let me help,' Trew offered but Hiddelle only slapped his hand away and threw the breastplate to the floor in defiance.

'I've always considered myself as strong as any man,' she said, 'and I've never needed armour before. We don't even make it in Hillock. Why should I wear it now?'

'Because there is no Hillock,' Trew reminded her grimly, 'and it would please me if you'd wear this.' He tried to hand the breastplate back to her, but Hiddelle refused it.

'Please *yourself*,' she said. 'And you might as well because I'm not dressing up for you, or anybody else.' She stormed from the Armoury without so much as an acknowledgement of Draneth's presence. *I should not be surprised*, he thought, *I brought them here.*

'I just don't want her to get hurt,' Trew told the shaman glumly, as Draneth approached.

'It is not suited to everybody,' Draneth said. 'She fought admirably against the Grinth before without it.'

'That's what I'm afraid of,' Trew said. 'She is too tough for her own good.' He sighed. 'We have decided to fight,' he said. 'Brorn, too. I'm not sure about Arnak, he has been mostly with Broll.'

'You decided to fight the moment you chose to come here with me,' Draneth reminded him. 'We were lucky to get this far.'

'I know,' Trew said, 'but I wanted revenge for our village and I thought we might at least stand a chance against them. Right now, the cold of the mountains does not sound such a bad prospect.'

'Have you told this to Hiddelle?' Draneth asked. *If I had a woman such as her, perhaps I would not be so hasty to fight either.*

'Whatever we do, we will do together,' Trew said with certainty. He smiled. 'And Hiddelle *will* fight. So I will fight.'

Draneth looked at him sternly. 'There is always a chance you know,' he said. 'Do not lose hope.' Comforting others was not one of his strong points and it had been a while, a long while, since he had even tried.

Trew nodded and smiled all the same.

'Have you seen Kallem,' Draneth asked him, 'and the children?'

'Kallem went straight to the gates as soon as his sword was returned. Did you not see him?'

Peaks, Draneth thought, *is he that eager to die?* This was going to be harder than he'd imagined. 'And Sill?'

'She was with Raffin, exploring the Fort,' Trew said. 'She didn't want Kallem to go, but he wouldn't listen to any of us. He said he would be fine and then just strolled off like he does. I think Brorn went with him.'

Draneth grunted and left Trew to his own dilemmas. *He is a good man,* the shaman thought. *Too good for this world but he will fight to the end to protect his wife, and that's the kind of courage we need for this war.* He wondered if The Guard would benefit from that kind of motivation. The Guard were not allowed to keep wives, although women had occasionally visited from the nearby villages in order to assess the Fort, before letting their own sons join The Guard. *An unwanted but necessary alliance.* That's what he had thought of the practice at the time, but his views had changed since he'd left the Fort. *I was a fool,* he thought, *I knew nothing of the world.* And he imagined the current men of The Guard knew even less.

Dissuading Kallem from fighting may well prove as impossible as convincing a man of The Guard to leave Rydan before his time. *But I still have to try.* Kallem was perhaps the biggest fool of all, fond as the shaman had grown of him. *He thinks he's invincible. If he only knew the truth.* Draneth shook his head, irritated by his own thoughts, and the knowledge Tamarellin had shared with him.

He emerged back out into daylight with the usual shock to his retinas. Squinting through sore eyes, he picked out Tamarellin, still perched on the cliffs above the courtyard. The hawk spotted him, too, and, kicking off from the rocks, spread his broad wings to glide leisurely down in Draneth's direction. *Have you seen him?* he asked as he held the staff still to aid Tamarellin's landing.

Yes, the hawk answered, *over there.*

The hawk's bright eyes focussed on a point of the courtyard and Draneth quickly recognised Kallem through the crowd, standing alongside the colossal figure of Brorn. He marched through the rows of men, ignoring the wary looks he received from The Guard, and the mounted Blood Riders. Tamarellin squawked, startling an injured man who sidestepped painfully out of their way. The man looked too exhausted to even contemplate a complaint. *The real battle hasn't even started yet,* Draneth thought, pitying him.

Draneth was not surprised that neither Kallem nor Brorn had adorned armour, or troubled themselves to try new weapons. The big man grinned broadly at the shaman as he approached. 'Have you come to die in glory, shaman?' Brorn asked him, spinning the mighty axe in his hand.

'We will all die eventually,' Draneth told him. 'I'd rather see the Inner lands cleared of these vermin before I do.' *And you should not be in such a hurry – either of you.* He glanced at Kallem.

'As would I,' Brorn said, 'but don't worry, the going will be quicker with me on the battlefield.'

Draneth did not doubt Brorn's strength. There was no man in The Guard who could match his size, but size and strength alone would not be enough to win this war, and Brorn was not a fighter by occupation. He was a woodcutter, from a small village in the north.

None of these men have trained against the Grinth, Tamarellin pointed out. *He is as good as any and braver than most.*

Indeed, Draneth agreed, *and he'll probably end up in legend like the great warriors of the past. Another dead hero, killed by the Grinth.*

'I do not doubt it,' he said to Brorn aloud. There was no point dimming the man's confidence. A foolish Brorn was better than no Brorn.

His axe will be more use than your light, Tamarellin said, hopping to his shoulder to peck at the shaman's ear.

Draneth flinched at the pain but did not retaliate, knowing he likely merited the hawk's ire. *I must not give up hope, either.*

That is what I keep telling you.

He stroked Tamarellin's head affectionately and turned his frown on Kallem. 'I must have words with you, Kallem,' he said simply, knowing neither of them had the time or patience for small talk.

'I'm busy,' Kallem said, without facing him.

'It's about the girl,' Draneth lied. 'It's important,' he added.

Begrudgingly, Kallem agreed to follow him to a small, quiet room, of which there were many within the carved caves of Rydan Fort, especially now that most of the men were already engaged with war on the surface. Every man of The Guard they did pass along the way glared at Kallem with noticeable distrust, perhaps even hatred. Draneth wondered if Kallem was even aware of the danger he was in. The shaman's word and Brorn's company were likely the only things that had saved him thus far from joining Zyan in a cell; or worse. He was surprised the General had accepted Kallem into his ranks, but then Draneth had fought hard for his cause and Kallem had no doubt proven his worth in the first assault on the Grinth.

He is used to it, Tamarellin reminded him. *This has been his way of life.*

It's his eyes, Draneth told the hawk. *They would have turned as soon as the Grinth arrived, and will likely remain that way. They are not tolerant of yellow eyes here.*

My eyes are yellow.

Then you'd better stay out of the way.

During their descent, Draneth was pleased to note how wary Kallem remained of his surroundings. As he led the young warrior deeper into the Fort, he grew certain that Kallem was studying every turn, tunnel and staircase they had taken since the courtyard, which was just what the shaman wanted.

'No one will hear us here,' Kallem said after a while, evidently aware of that part of Draneth's purpose. 'What did you want to tell me?'

'Just a little further,' Draneth told him hotly, intensifying the light from his staff to remind Kallem he was not some dithering Elder, to be humoured. 'There is another reason I brought you this way. If you continue through there,' he pointed his staff to illuminate a dark corner of the room they had just entered, where a crudely cut hole crouched, almost hidden, in the shadows, 'the way will become wet and brown and you will find yourself deep within the mountain.'

'Why would I want to do that?'

Draneth gritted his teeth, resisting the urge to get angry. 'Because beyond that, you will emerge back into daylight, on the northern side of the Fort.'

'You said this was about Sill.'

'It is, it's about everything and everyone.' The shaman frowned at him, irritated by Kallem's single-mindedness. 'There is more to this than her life or yours.'

'I promised to protect her.'

'And how will you do that? By dying with everybody else?'

'I do not die so easily.'

'Don't be a fool!' Draneth turned his back, trying desperately to calm himself. He normally forgave Kallem his blunt speech, knowing the difficulties the young man had endured and the reasons for being the way he was. But this was too important. *Should I tell him the truth about his family?* he asked Tamarellin.

No, the hawk said, *you should not. Not yet.*

Draneth nodded, somewhat relieved at the hawk's verdict. There was no telling how Kallem would react to the truth. 'Kallem,' he said, turning to face him squarely, 'you came to me for a reason. You could have gone anywhere when your village banished you. But you didn't, you came to me. You wanted to know if you were right about the Grinth, if there was more to the world than Hillock. If there was more to you.'

'I don't care about that anymore.'

'Well, you should! Why do you think your eyes change, Kallem? Because you're weak?'

Kallem paused. 'I thought that before...' Kallem said, his voice faltering for the first time.

'But not anymore,' the shaman finished for him, 'since you fought them?' He didn't wait for an answer. 'Kallem,' he said, looking hard into the impenetrable, glowing eyes that mimicked the Grinth's with such stark precision, 'I need you to do something. It's the only way you can save her.' ...And he told Kallem everything he and Tamarellin knew about the Queen.

'There must be someone else?' was all Kallem could say when he was finished.

'There isn't.'

Kallem paused, perhaps conflicted by the past that so evidently haunted his thoughts. 'Then I'm sorry,' he said, 'but I won't go. I can't leave. I promised her.' And with that, he began to walk back towards the open doorway.

'You promised to protect her,' the shaman growled after him, 'not to die pointlessly for her!' But his words were useless and Draneth knew it. *Peaks!* He stomped the butt of his staff hard into the stone floor and the room grumbled at the impact. Instinctively, he reached a hand up to stroke Tamarellin's velvety feathers and breathed a deep sigh. *If only there were more like him.* Tamarellin gave a small squawk of acquiescence. The shaman loosened his grip on the staff and the lit skull instantly faded. Disheartened but not defeated, he let the light slip away until there was only darkness and the soft yellow glow of Tamarellin's eyes. *You'll tell me if mine turn that colour, won't you?* he asked the hawk.

They will not, Tamarellin said. *It is not you that they want.*

CHAPTER 15

Sill gripped Raffin's arm as they gazed out over the land they'd crossed barely a sun and moon ago. Then, the land had been rich and green with vast grasses, pocketed by small puddles of light that broke apart as the horses' hooves splashed through them on their way to the Fort.

Now, the Grinth filled that land. The mountains that had, for centuries, protected the people of the Inner Lands, had instead become a trap, sealing them in with their eternal enemy until they found themselves cornered with nowhere left to run. *How cruel the world is*, Sill thought sadly. How many had died when the Grinth invaded their lands? How few had escaped? The answers did not bear thinking about.

Far below them, distant shapes, tinged purple and red, fought beyond the range of the archers lining the wall. From this height the battle barely seemed real. But Sill knew Kallem and Brorn were amongst those fighting, and she had watched their small shapes anxiously as they flitted amongst the waves of purple, spraying black spurts out and around them until the battleground had become a patchwork of purples, blacks and reds. For some strange reason it made her think of the quilt she had made for Fallor, although the quilt had been destroyed before she could give it to him. *He never even saw it, and now he's dead.* She squeezed Raffin's arm as another wave of purple swarmed towards Kallem and Brorn, then loosened her grip as more black soon soaked the floor beneath them. One of the Fort's horns sounded and The Guard began to fall back towards the gates. *They're going to get left behind!* Sill thought for an awful moment, but then three Blood Riders went to their aid, cutting lines through the Grinth until the small shapes of Kallem and Brorn started to edge their way backwards with the others. The gates creaked open and swallowed the men up as the Grinth coughed, hissed and snorted at their departure. But the Grinth did not pursue.

'Come on,' she said to Raffin, 'let's go.' And she tugged him away from the parapet to go check on Kallem.

Raffin had watched the battle in an odd state of quiet. Whether he was fascinated or horrified she could not tell, but she was growing increasingly concerned about him. He was not the same boy she had known before, ever since she found him waiting for her at Anell Village. *Of course he's not the same,* she reminded herself. *None of us are.*

'Kallem is fine,' Raffin said as they made their way down the twisting staircase.

Since they'd been released from the cell, nobody seemed to care too much where they went so long as they kept out of the way. When Kallem had gone off to fight, it had been Sill, rather than Raffin, who had insisted on watching from the wall.

'How do you know?' she asked.

'Because he always is,' Raffin said simply. 'And who cares anyway?'

'He's not what you think he is,' she told him. It was not usual for them to disagree and she wished he could see Kallem the way she did.

'I don't trust him,' Raffin said. 'Nobody does.'

'I do.'

'Why? Because he hates the Grinth as much as we do? That doesn't make him trustworthy. Have you seen how easily he kills them?'

'They killed his family. You should understand that.'

Raffin remained silent and Sill knew she had said too much. *I'm sorry*, she thought, but she could not bring herself to say the words aloud. *Maybe I'm the only one who hasn't changed,* she thought. *I'm still weak. I'm still hurting people.* She had made a promise to herself to be stronger but that seemed like a lifetime ago now and she could hardly see that it mattered anymore. *What difference could I make against an army like this?* Raffin deserved a better friend than her. *What is it he even likes about me?* None of the other children had ever taken an interest in her, except when they made fun of her.

As though he could read her thoughts, Raffin took her hand and gave it a light, reassuring squeeze. His touch made her heart race and she had to let go of him, partly out of embarrassment and partly out of shame. He looked at her and she knew she'd hurt him even worse now. *I can't even do that right*, she told herself, disgusted at her own vulnerabilities.

As they reached the courtyard and her eyes successfully sought out Kallem's, they startled her for a moment. *Of course,* she realised, *the Grinth are always near now. He always looks more frightening that way.* Kallem began to stroll towards her and she noticed some of the men pat him on the back as he passed through them. *He doesn't like to be touched,* she thought, slightly worried that he might react badly to the invasion. But Kallem seemed as unfazed as ever in these strange new surroundings. *At least The Guard are coming around to him*, she thought. *Just as I did.*

When he reached her he was not even out of breath but the battle showed on him in other ways. Once again he was coated in a thick layer of Grinth blood and Sill inadvertently turned her head away, holding her breath until her nostrils adjusted to the stench.

'It's ok,' he said in his emotionless way, 'I'm not hurt. I made a promise, remember?'

Without a word, Raffin left her side and marched off back through the crowds of battle-worn men. *Oh no!*

Sill glared up at Kallem's blank face. 'I know,' she said, 'but you can't protect me if you're dead!' It came out more aggressively than she'd intended and she regretted it the instant she left him to chase after Raffin instead. *What if that's the last thing I ever say to him?* she thought for a terrible moment, as she headed towards the entrance to the Fort's caves.

'Sill!' The shaman's imposing voice stopped her in her tracks.

She spun to find his bright blue eyes staring down at her, a familiar frown etched into his forehead. 'Sorry, I can't stop,' she told him, 'I have to find –'

'Leave him be a while,' Draneth interrupted, speaking more softly. Anchoring himself on his staff, he lowered himself to one knee so he was more in-line with her own height. 'Keep an old man company,' he said with a wink. 'I need to talk to you.' The smile he gave her was somewhat unsuited to his harsh features but at least it was genuine. Tamarellin looked tired and nestled his head under the shaman's chin, his eyes closing. 'He's finding it hard to hunt,' Draneth explained grimly, stroking the hawk's feathers.

Sill felt bad for Tamarellin but there was little she could do about it. Raffin, she may at least be able to console. 'I should find him,' Sill said, not wanting to offend the shaman but equally afraid she would lose track of Raffin if he disappeared too deep into the many rooms of the Fort.

'I see,' the shaman said, pursing his lips and rubbing a hand over his bald head. 'In that case I'd better help you. But you have to do something for me first.'

Sill dreaded what he might ask of her, but he did know Rydan well and she stood a better chance of finding Raffin with his help. Besides, she could hardly say no to him after all he'd done for them. 'Haven't you got more important things to do?' she asked, suddenly concerned she was wasting his time.

'Pah! Me?' he said, to her surprise. 'What use am I? And this *is* important, Sill.'

Talking to me is important? she thought. *Or does he mean finding Raffin?* Either way, she found it hard to believe he didn't have something else he should be doing. *I didn't want all this attention*, she thought with a pang of guilt.

But since she had already managed to treat both Raffin and Kallem unfairly, she begrudgingly allowed the shaman to lead her back up the gruelling, twisting stairs of the parapet until she was again standing atop one side of the Fort's massive wall. *I'll find Raffin later*, she told herself. If there was anywhere worth hiding, she supposed they'd all be there.

'It's hard to look at, isn't it?' Draneth said gravely as he rested his free hand on the parapet, looking out over the land.

Sill nodded silently. It was a hopeless view. At least from here the Grinth looked somewhat smaller. *It's better than seeing them up close.*

'I know the odds seem impossible,' the shaman said, his blue eyes scanning the breadth of the land below, 'but you saved us in the last fight, Sill, you must not forget that.' When she didn't speak he turned to look at her, his eyes now narrowing beneath one of his familiar frowns. 'You do not think so?' he asked.

'All I did was move the air,' she said with a shrug, 'I couldn't stop them. The others saved us. And Zyan.'

'Hmmf,' the shaman grunted. 'Move the air, is that all? If you hadn't replaced my light when it ran out, we would all have died. Nobody else could have done that, Sill. Only you.' He knelt before her again and this time used his free hand to gently grasp her shoulder, forcing her to meet his gaze. 'To move the air is no simple feat,' he said earnestly. 'You have great power, Sill. You split the skies and fought back against that foul fog. You should not think yourself so insignificant.'

Insignificant? Draneth had an uncanny way of knowing her thoughts. Amongst all these strong men – warriors – insignificant was exactly how she felt. 'But what can I do now?' she asked. 'I can't do anything to help.'

'Not right now,' the shaman agreed, 'but the time will come. Just try to be ready when it does. You don't even have to be close to them,' he said comfortingly. 'You can help from up here. And try to keep an eye on Kallem, too. Can you do that for me, Sill?'

She nodded and smiled. *I can do that*. But she wasn't sure what good it would do. Maybe she could use the wind to help Kallem fight below? But he was so far away when she was up here. *I could not control the air accurately enough, even if I tried*, she thought...*But I must try*. Anything she could do to help was better than doing nothing at all. *I've done nothing for too much of my life*. The shaman's words were encouraging and she was about to ask him if they could find Raffin now when she saw the Grinth move.

At the same time, one of the Fort's patterned horns sounded from further along the wall. Draneth's expression darkened and he stood up quickly, twisting back around to lean again on the parapet. Sill joined him and peered anxiously over the edge.

Below them, the mass of Grinth swelled as their purple bodies fought against each other to reach the front line. They clambered past and over each other, regardless of any harm caused, in their haste to reach the wall. Sill could see some of them slip on the stains of black blood, but quickly those gaps filled in until the entire land from the wall to the distant horizon was blotted out by the dark army of the Grinth. From this height, their mass looked black as night, until the sun gleamed off a smooth head or shining back and threw vulgar purple across their ranks, revealing their true form.

The Grinth collided against the gates with a thud but to Sill's relief the *serethen* wood held firm, barely budging under the strain. The solid rock walls did not so much as shudder, and soon the thrums and whistles of the archers could be heard all along the width of the wall as the Grinth bodies began to pile up.

Sill watched in mute horror as more Grinth clambered across their dead or dying brethren, mindless of what their hooves crushed or claws stuck into. Whilst the piercing shrieks and guttural calls of the injured fouled the stagnant air, their blood splashed against the grey walls, glazing the natural rock in a gory layer of warm, oozing black. The archers continued to fire down at the nearest of the Grinth and the stacked-up dead continued to rise. Sill stared down at them, baffled and revolted at their mindless, needless violence. No matter how many were killed, more Grinth just kept on coming, their bodies surging up and over the fallen like they were no more than piles of discarded rubbish. The archers rained down their arrows as persistently as the Grinth threw bodies into them, the thrum and whistle of each one a light melody against the raucous noises of the dying Grinth. Each shaft flew about a foot from the wall, creating an odd effect against the grey granite backdrop of their flight. The Grinth were piling up so rapidly that already the dead stretched about a third of the way up the giant walls. 'They're building a wall of their own!' Sill told the shaman to her horror.

The shaman's scowl seemed to grow with the bodies. 'Come with me,' he ordered Sill, moving away from the parapet to stride purposefully off along the wall. Sill scuttled after him, keeping well out of the way of the archers, whose faces were already grimacing from the strain of loosing arrow after countless arrow. She almost bumped straight into a younger member of The Guard who had already dodged around the shaman and was evidently not expecting to find her, smaller body, behind him. The young guard carried several quivers of arrows slung about his shoulders and his eyes widened as he sidestepped past her, veering dangerously close to the inner edge of the wall as he hurried on his way.

At the end of the wall, just before the spiked tips of the gates, General Venth stood still and silent as the mountains as he watched the grisly scene unfold below. Captain Ryke required the aid of a spear to prop himself up beside his superior. His right arm and right leg were both heavily bandaged, and the red breastplate he wore was criss-crossed with scrapes and scratches where Grinth claws must have somehow reached, even though he fought mounted. Sill dreaded to think what shape the poor horses must have been in.

Draneth marched right up to the General, whose slight frown was the only indication he was conscious of the intrusion.

Sill stopped just short of them, not wanting to risk aggravating the General any further than Draneth was already likely to.

'Do you see?' Draneth asked him, pointing down towards the lower half of the wall. 'Do you see what they're doing?'

'I see a pack of wild animals, killing each other over their own frenzied folly,' the General replied with clear disdain. 'What do you see, *shaman*?'

The screams of the Grinth were getting louder. Sill glanced down into the courtyard – partly to avoid what was happening on the other side of the wall – and found the men of The Guard lined up in their organised ranks, watching the gates thump inwards each time they were battered by the frantic Grinth outside. *They're all so quiet*, Sill thought as she tried to pick out Kallem amongst the other men. She couldn't find him. Too many of them were already stained black. Even the horses were spattered with the blood of the Grinth, some worse than others, and Sill was saddened to see their beautiful white coats marred so hideously. Perhaps that's what drove her to speak when she normally wouldn't have. 'They're building a wall,' she said before Draneth even had the chance to respond. Turning back, she met eyes briefly with the General and quickly looked away, startled at the uncharacteristic boldness of her own actions.

'If I needed your council, young lady, I'd ask for it,' General Venth said icily. She could feel his eyes still on her and, although she didn't dare look back at him, his manner had started to annoy her. *It's not my fault if you're too stupid to see it,* she thought, a pang of irritation creeping through her veins. She glanced instead at Draneth and was greeted with what appeared to be an approving half-smile.

'Perhaps you should?' the shaman suggested to the General. 'Even she can see clearly what you cannot.'

'Draneth…' the General hissed softly and the way he said it sent a shiver down Sill's spine.

'General Venth?' Sill was not sure if Captain Ryke did it intentionally, but his interruption was well timed either way. 'Shall I do it now?'

The General paused a moment, his jaw clicking every now and then as Sill had noticed it did when he was most annoyed. Then he nodded curtly and resumed his watch of the marauding Grinth at his walls. 'We're not the fools you think we are, Draneth,' he said softly.

'What will you do?' the shaman asked him.

'We'll burn them.'

'What about the gates?'

The General turned his head to look at Sill. 'You're from Hillock,' he said. 'What happens when you set fire to *serethen* wood?'

Sill couldn't speak at first, afraid that she would give the wrong answer.

'Speak up, girl,' the General insisted. 'You seemed keen enough to council me a moment ago; now I'm asking you – what happens when you set fire to *serethen*?'

'Nothing,' she said faintly. The memory of her father's voice still haunted her at night. *Get back here, you demon!* 'It doesn't burn,' she added, remembering the black smoke seeping from the door of her hut, 'only the sap burns.' *And the leaves...*

The General turned away again, presumably satisfied with her answer.

Tamarellin was watching her more keenly, his neck swivelled around from where he perched on the shaman's shoulder. The hawk tilted his head to the side, something Sill had begun to associate with interest, or perhaps curiosity. *I wish I could understand you*, she thought. A part of her secretly hoped the hawk would answer, but it was Draneth who spoke instead.

'Come on,' he said, signalling that they should leave the General to give his grim orders. 'This is something you don't need to watch.'

Sill was thankful later that he'd led her away. She already had a more-than-ample supply of dreadful images consuming her thoughts and haunting her dreams, and if the sounds of the burning Grinth, alone, were enough to make her sick to her stomach, the smell was even worse. The men on the wall had the misfortune to suffer the full potency of it. It was so bad that the General had been forced to send the archers back down from the wall to seek some fresh air, if they could find it. The top of the wall was now shrouded in a thick, black smoke, infused with the stench of burning Grinth bodies. Below, in the depthless catacombs of Rydan Fort, Sill had wandered lost through the dark, following Draneth's faded form like a ghost, neither alive nor truly dead. They had not managed to find Raffin and, now, as they stood back out in the comparative bright of the courtyard, Sill could only stare dumbly at her shaking hands, trying to understand why she couldn't get them to stop.

Suddenly Draneth was kneeling before her and his spare hand grasped around hers, drawing her eyes away and up into his. 'Sill,' he said with a sigh, 'you have endured so much for one so young. I am sorry that you were born into these times.' She looked at him, thoughtless and wordless until he continued. 'I'm sorry we couldn't find Raffin,' he told her, 'but as long as he is below, he will be safe. Try not to worry about him.' The shaman smiled at her and warmth began to creep into her hands from his and then along her wrists, into her arms. Defensively, she tried to pull her hands away but Draneth wouldn't let them go. 'Just relax,' he said softly. 'You're in shock, we need to warm you up.' Then she noticed that the skull on his staff was glowing again and soon the corner of his upper lip began to twitch slightly as the warmth spread through her body. The heat felt soothing and it was only as conscious thought re-entered her mind that Sill was able to grasp how affected she had been.

She took a deep breath and then exhaled. 'I'm ok,' she said, 'you can stop now. Thank you.' *Don't drain yourself for me.*

Light vanished from the skull and the staff returned to plain wood as though it had never borne such an extraordinary glow. The shaman exhaled once through his nostrils and then refocussed on her. 'Are you sure?' he said, looking her over.

'Yes,' she said, freeing her hands finally to show him the shaking had stopped. 'How do you do that?' she asked.

The shaman smiled slightly. 'I'm still not sure I fully understand it myself,' he told her. 'I just feel…more connected to the world now. Is that how it is for you?'

'I don't know,' she told him truthfully, 'I've just always been like this.'

He nodded and the smile slowly subsided as the glow had done. 'Which is why I need you to come back up to the wall with me,' he said solemnly. 'I'm sorry, Sill, but only you can do something about this smoke.'

Sill looked up at the blurry top of the wall, the black smog clinging to it like a disease. 'I know,' she said, but her chest fluttered again at the pressure he placed on her. *I've always had to do things I didn't want to,* she thought glumly. *I guess growing up is no different. This is what life is like.* But there were still some good things, too. Raffin, Draneth, Kallem, Artell – all people who seemed to care about her. *Which is why I'm so afraid to lose them,* she knew. *I must do this for them. For everybody.*

As Draneth led Sill back through the courtyard, the injured Captain Ryke was rallying his Blood Riders, preparing them for another assault on the crippled front-line of the Grinth army.

'Fools!' Draneth muttered crossly and quickened his step. 'Come on, Sill.'

The shaman led her towards, and then up, the winding steps build into the far northern corner of the courtyard that twisted up and out onto the towering wall. Her legs already ached fiercely from the last two climbs but if the shaman felt the strain, he didn't show it. *He's too strong to be so old*, Sill grumbled to herself, more irritated by her own weakness than the shaman's enduring strength. Her head was giddy when she reached the top of the steps and the reek that greeted her was so intense that she almost tumbled back down. *Oh, peaks!* Fortunately, Draneth was there to steady her and then guide her gently to safety.

'Careful, Sill,' he cautioned and the glow of his staff suddenly cut through the black smoke before her, revealing the way ahead.

Without his light, the wall had become as treacherous as the battlefield below, the viscid smoke blocking any sight of the granite beneath their feet, let alone any view of the Grinth army below. Up here, day had become night, a night imbued with the hot stench of death. It was so utterly overwhelming it sent shock waves through Sill's body and she dropped to her knees, retching, as the rank odour and thick smoke clogged her lungs. She could feel the smoke entering her as she breathed, like thin, black fingers stretching into her nose and throat, reaching down towards her chest and squeezing her lungs. She felt her heart begin to race, pulsing as though it was labouring to push the smoke back out but couldn't, and with every ragged breath she inhaled more and more of it. Thick and hot and putrid, the smoke poured into her lungs, slowly and painfully suffocating her. She felt her head go light and dizzy and her heart suddenly thudded as though in that instant she thought she may slip from the edge of the wall or tumble back down the spiral staircase.

But she could also feel the shaman's hands gripping her shoulders, his fingers pressing into her skin. 'The air, Sill,' she heard him say. 'Control it.'

In blind panic, rather than controlled thought, she managed to summon a small vortex around herself and the shaman, clearing the surrounding smoke in an instant. She gasped and then coughed as the fresher air rushed into her lungs and chased out the last of the foul smoke, banishing it from her body. The shaman tugged her gently to her feet and began to march her forward.

With his light and her wind, they cut a path through the black until they emerged before the General.

General Venth stared at them as though two ghosts had sprung from the darkness. The smoke was thinner this close to the gates, but still his eyes were red and sore and his breathing hard and loud. He watched the air clear around him and then, in a hoarse voice, called, 'Open the gates!' Ignoring them, he turned his head back to the Grinth. Sill noticed that one of his hands had involuntarily moved to his sword hilt, but now he removed it and folded his arms.

She heard Captain Ryke's weary voice echo the General's words with as much vigour as he could probably muster, somewhere far below. The gates began to creak slowly open.

'Is this wise?' Draneth asked.

'Wisdom only goes so far in a fight,' General Venth said, turning to look at them now. 'We must hit them while they're weak.'

'Every time you send them out, they come back less,' Draneth said anxiously. 'Why not let the men rest? You killed many Grinth with the fire and without suffering any losses of your own. But their army is vast. They can afford to test you.'

'Then let them test,' the General said, sounding agitated. 'We've killed far more of them than they have of us. You are no longer a man of The Guard, so leave the fighting to me, Draneth. If you want to help, you can practise your new *tricks* on our prisoner. So far, you have not proved much use to me.' The two men glared at each other while the black smoke swirled around them. 'How *are* you doing that?' General Venth asked, as Sill watched his jaw begin to click.

'*I* am not,' Draneth replied and the General's eyes widened.

'The girl?' he asked.

'The *girl* is called Sill,' Draneth said, 'and yes, it is her who controls the air around us.'

'Blood Riders, on me!' Captain Ryke's small voice called out.

As the General frowned awkwardly at her, Sill heard the rumble of horses' hooves thundering out through the open gates. 'Sill,' the General said as though testing the name in his mouth. 'Perhaps I do have a use for *you*. Can you make it do more than that?'

'I...I'm not sure...sometimes,' she said, worried what the General might ask her to do.

'Show me,' he said.

Sill looked up at Draneth who nodded gravely. Steeling herself, she took a deep breath and concentrated on all of the smoke, using its wrongness to guide the wind and sweep it all away until daylight flooded back to the wall. The warmth of the fires below pushed up at her, but she kept them at bay, rotating the air in a cooling system, a technique she had used many times before, on her own, against the searing heat of the sun.

General Venth stepped forward to the parapet and leaned out, inspecting the scene below. 'Incredible,' he said quietly. 'How did you do that?'

Draneth stepped forward, too, and Sill followed his lead. 'I don't know how,' she said. 'I just...do. But not always,' she added quickly. She peered over the parapet to see if Kallem had left the Fort, but only the red and white shapes of the Blood Riders and their mounts had so far ridden out. A trail of dust had kicked up, blurring the distance between them and the open gates.

The Grinth army had dropped back again, beyond the range of the archers, even though the archers had, for now, abandoned the wall. As the Riders charged out to engage the dormant enemy, Sill watched as other men of The Guard emerged to busy themselves with clearing bodies away from the gates and nearest edges of the wall. Along the stretch of granite below her, the Grinth were still burning and she forced herself to concentrate a little harder, clearing away more of the smoke, before it rose up to claw at her again. *They're evil,* she told herself as the charred remains of Grinth-like forms began to show. *They deserve this.* But it didn't help to settle her stomach, or ease her nagging conscience. As she continued to whip away more and more of the spiralling smoke she thought she saw something move within the remains. *It's just the movement of the smoke,* she thought. *Please don't tell me anything's still alive down there.* But the more smoke she cleared, the more she became certain that something was moving amongst the burning dead.

'Sill?' Draneth asked her cautiously. 'What is it?'

She strained her eyes, trying to make out what it was she was looking at so far below. Exasperated with the black smoke, she closed her eyes and concentrated fully on the burning bodies, then discovered that if she moved the air completely from them, they stopped burning. She extinguished the remaining smoke as though it had never existed. *Oh, peaks!* As she opened her eyes again, she realised what was happening. 'Call them back!' she said but she knew it was probably too late, the Blood Riders had already reached the main Grinth army.

'Why?' The General glanced quickly at her, then both he and Draneth leaned out further over the parapet. Tamarellin squawked and took off from the shaman's shoulder to glide out over the land.

A man screamed by the gates and Sill knew exactly why.

'They used the smoke!' Draneth hissed, straightening himself to turn and face the General. 'Call them back.'

'Peaks!' General Venth cursed quietly. His face had turned grey as he pulled himself away from the edge. He took a step backwards as though he couldn't bear to look anymore. Then his expression grew dark. 'Close the gates,' he called loudly. When there was no response from below he turned and strode angrily to the other side of the wall. 'I said close the gates!' he yelled furiously to those staring up at him from the courtyard.

'What in the peaks are you doing?' Draneth asked him. 'Call them back!'

'It's too late,' the General said.

Draneth stared at him a moment longer, then cursed and took off towards the steps, leaving Sill to wonder whether she should follow him. Not knowing what to do, she watched in silent dread as numerous Grinth emerged from somewhere amongst the piles of dead lining the sides of the wall and began to congregate in the middle. The gates had only just begun to creak shut but the Grinth did not seem interested in the Fort. Instead, they gathered together as one small army and then began to run back towards their main force, trapping the Blood Riders between them. 'They're going to surround them!' Sill told the General.

'I know.'

'So? Can't you do something?'

'It's too late,' he said, his voice edged with bitterness. 'I underestimated them,' he admitted. 'And now I have to protect the Fort.'

'But they'll die!' she said, horrified that he could even consider leaving the Blood Riders to fend for themselves against the entire Grinth army. 'You have to try. Please!'

'Look!' The General pointed as Grinth from the outer edges of the main force began to pour forward to meet with the smaller, onrushing wedge. 'You see,' he said, 'it's too late.'

Sill watched in utter dismay as the tiny figure of Captain Ryke swung his horse around to face the mobile Grinth force closing in on them from behind. His white horse reared up in obvious panic at the realisation they were being surrounded.

We were never testing them, Sill realised suddenly, *they were testing us*. The air coursed angrily through her hair and she had to fight to control it. 'There must be something we can do?' she asked the General. 'Call the archers back up? Send some more men out? *Something*?'

'Do you not think I have considered every option?' the General snapped. 'It is too late!' He walked right up to her and stood, glaring down through his sore, red eyes. 'You could have cleared it at any time,' he said in a voice as black as the acrid smoke. 'This is on you.' Then he walked past her, leaving his words to hang in the air that she controlled.

She let them hang. *This is on you…*

The statement cut into her like a knife. *He's right,* she thought, *I should have done something sooner.*

Whilst her mind struggled to mitigate the impact of the General's words, her eyes could see that the Blood Riders were fighting for their lives. They spun their spears and slashed their swords wildly, cutting down as many of the Grinth as they could. But every time they cleared an opening, more Grinth just rushed in to fill it. For all Captain Ryke's timidity off the battlefield, on it he had come to life. Discernible by his bandaged right side, Sill watched him dispatch Grinth after Grinth, his great white steed wheeling around and sending more bodies flying with its hindquarters as they fought together, as one. She tried to make out which of the men was Erran, the young Rider who had borne Raffin and her back to the Fort, but the chaos and distance made it impossible to tell. To her left, the heavy gates were heaving shut, but just before they closed two riders shot out, one after the other, through the remaining gap. Sill gasped as she saw who they were. It was Brorn and Kallem. *No!* she thought. *Not you, too!* The gates slammed shut ominously behind them, but they paid no heed. The white horses they must have taken charged bravely forward towards their struggling kin. But there were far too many Grinth between them and the Blood Riders.

This is on you.

The General's words still stuck in her mind, and now her misery turned to anger as she realised that this was just how her father had treated her. *It's always my fault.* She had promised Draneth she would try to help and she owed it to her friends to do whatever she could. *I owe it to Kallem,* she thought. *Concentrate!*

She watched Kallem charge towards the army of Grinth and tried to calm herself enough to accurately manipulate the air. She thought back, many suns ago, to when she was in Hillock, using the wind to cool herself on a muggy day, or to swirl leaves around in the forest, making them dance. *This is just like that,* she told herself, *only bigger.* She turned her attention back to Kallem and closed her eyes. She could feel the rush of air created by his surging horse as it raced forward, feel his long, dark hair swaying behind him in the wind.

Brorn's axe was cutting through the currents as he swung it above his head in broad circles. He yelled a war cry and Sill felt his breath reverberate across the currents. A scream disturbed her focus and she opened her eyes to see one of the Blood Riders slashing his sword at a Grinth who had got close enough to sink its claws deep within his leg. The Grinth's arms fell away under the man's sword but others quickly closed in and the Rider was soon dragged from his horse and into the crowd. The dead Rider's horse kicked out in panic, scattering the Grinth around her, but without any aid, the mountain horse was quickly overcome. Sill gasped and squeezed her eyes shut, unable to watch. It was all happening so fast it hardly felt real. When she opened her eyes again, she could see Captain Ryke rallying his remaining Blood Riders. They came together, trying to form a protective ring within the Grinth that they could defend, but when another man slipped from his saddle and disappeared without a sound it became clear they would not last long.

The Grinth had worked themselves into such a frenzy that their back line didn't even notice as Kallem and Brorn crashed through them. Climbing up onto his horse's saddle, Brorn leapt through the air with startling agility and crashed his axe straight down the middle of a Grinth, cutting the beast into two halves before it even knew what had hit it. A spray of black spurted into the air, a tiny puff from where Sill stood watching. Brorn gave his horse a quick pat on the rear and the animal flew off back towards the gates, only to wheel around and whinny when it found them closed. Unaccustomed to fighting on horseback, Kallem dismounted, too, and the two Hillock men were soon fighting back-to-back, sending more sprays of black blood into the air as they fought violently through the rear of the Grinth army. The outer edges of the Grinth force were still pouring forwards to meet each other, and from Sill's vantage point she could see that the two edges would eventually close off everything from the gates and walls, right through to where the Blood Riders fought for their lives. *They're all going to die!* she thought. With a pang of rage, she sent a wave of air down from the wall that rushed through the ranks of the charging Grinth. *Maybe the smell of your dead will slow you down!*

Kallem and Brorn had managed to cut a small circle around themselves and when the Grinth on Kallem's side charged in to fill it, Sill sent a jolt of air that sent them flying back into their brethren. Then she used the space she had created to muster up a protective vortex around them, forcing the wind to spin and twist up and around itself, leaving Kallem and Brorn free to lower their weapons and gape in surprise at the currents swirling around them. Sill hoped that Kallem would realise this was her doing, rather than some new trick of the Grinth. As the Grinth around the two warriors hissed in frustration, she guided the vortex carefully towards the Blood Riders. *If I can keep them together I might be able to protect all of them.* It sounded a ludicrous plan, even in her head, and she did not know if she possessed the strength to sustain the vortex that long. But at least it was something and doing something was certainly better than doing nothing. *Hurry*, she urged Kallem and Brorn as another Blood Rider fell to the Grinth. Already she could feel her power waning. The Grinth were testing the vortex now, throwing their bodies at it whilst she flung them away again. Each attack felt like a direct blow on her being, her soul; wherever it was that her power stemmed from. *Don't panic,* she told herself, trying to stay calm and maintain her focus. *Don't give up. Or they die.*

Kallem and Brorn had reached the Blood Riders and Sill groaned at the effort it took to expand the circle of air until it enclosed them all. She leaned against the parapet, trying to draw strength from the cold stone. Now she needed to guide them back towards the gates but the gates were closed, and between the safety of the Fort and the remaining Blood Riders was a growing number of aggravated, merciless Grinth. *Don't give up,* she reminded herself. *Or they die.*

The parapet was now the only thing keeping her up. Her body had begun to shake under the effort of maintaining the vortex and she could feel sweat trickling down her face and forehead, stinging her eyes. She began to move the vortex back through the mass of Grinth, ignoring the magnitude of their number, their irate hisses and barks, and concentrating everything she had left on commanding the air. Her power was waning fast. *Please, don't abandon me! Not now! I'm the only one who can save them!*

The Blood Riders' horses seemed just as unnerved as the Grinth, whinnying and bucking as their Riders tried to calm and coax them into moving with the air. One Grinth managed to break through the vortex and Sill barely made out the flash of red, as Kallem's sword cut the creature down. Another made it through, then another. *I'm weakening.* No matter how hard she strained, Sill knew her strength was fading. More and more Grinth were breaking through her wall of air but she kept moving it all the same. *Even if it's just unbalancing them, it's still something.* Her head was growing dizzy and her body was shaking so hard she could feel her arms scratching against the rough rock supporting her weight. Tears began to mix in with the sweat as she felt her hold on the wind ebb away. *No!* She told the air. *You won't abandon me! You won't!* As the last of her strength trickled away she watched through blurred vision – horror-stricken – as her vortex shrank woefully small, until it protected only Kallem. Then it vanished completely and the air dropped away as though it had never been coerced at all.

Barely conscious, Sill watched as men fought and died below. She was hardly even aware that the gates had creaked open, but she heard Tamarellin's desperate *keeeeeeee* ring out above; saw his brown wings glide out before her and plunge down somewhere into the midst of the carnage. Through her blurred eyes she could see that the men below were still fighting but it did not matter – the General was right: it was all far too late. *Everything always happens too late,* she thought hazily, as her eyes opened and closed intermittently, fighting against her body's will to lose consciousness.

The last things her mind registered were just flashes – a solitary, bald figure walking from the gates; Captain

Ryke's horse dropping to its knees; Brorn's body pinned to the ground; a black Kallem atop a black horse.

Moments later, a white flash of light ended it all.

Through the gaps in her eyelashes, Sill saw the black horse lying still on the ground, only a short distance from the closing gates. Huddled together, Kallem and Draneth staggered through the gap as a sea of dark purple swept in behind them.

As the *serethen* gates slammed shut, so did Sill's eyes, sealing away the horrors of the outside world. But the dead would not be forgotten so easily and they crept into her head as she slipped from consciousness, following her down into the black. *I'm sorry I couldn't save you*, she told them. But the dead did not care for her apologies and so she sank deeper into darkness, escaping their vengeful glares.

One of the dead watched her fall and with the eyes of her father, screamed at her...*Get back here, you demon!* But Sill was already gone, and even the dead couldn't follow her here.

CHAPTER 16

All was bleak. Draneth strode purposefully through the fog, the glow of his staff signalling his arrival as he buoyed the men of The Guard throughout their vigil. A word of encouragement here, a nod of approval there, but deep down he knew he was just as lost as the rest of them. As lost as Kallem, locked in his perpetual inner-battle. As lost as Sill, who had still not awoken. And as lost as Rydan Fort itself, surrounded as it was in this unnatural fog that seemed to stem from the Grinth. *What grim purpose are they conjuring now?* he wondered, as he gazed at the great gates. Parts of himself remained whole – he had not lost his will, his resolve, his desire to fight – but Draneth had been a man of The Guard and losing the Blood Riders had changed him in ways he could not fully fathom. It was as though the fabric of his being had been torn, and could not be stitched back together.

You are still alive, Tamarellin told him. *You should be thankful for that.*

But I don't know what to do, anymore. How can we win this battle? The Blood Riders and their horses were gone. Brorn had died trying to save them. General Venth had slipped away somewhere inside the belly of the Fort, and Sill had slipped inside herself, trapped in some endless sleep to which there seemed no end and Draneth knew no cure. If he had been able, he would have concocted something that might help to rouse her, but the Fort lacked the required ingredients.

Can I help? Tamarellin asked. But Draneth was loath to let the hawk go; he needed his friend's voice even more than the men of The Guard needed his to keep going, keep motivated. To survive. *I could leave?* He could still sneak out through the dark, secret passages within the Fort, where he had shown Kallem the way. But there was work to be done here, especially now Venth had disappeared.

The men of The Guard treated Draneth differently now. They had, after all, disobeyed the General to let him through the gates.

They respect you, Tamarellin told him.

Hmmf, Draneth grumbled. *They shouldn't. I was too late, too slow. I couldn't save any of them.*

You saved Kallem, the hawk reminded him. *All is not lost.*

Maybe, Draneth allowed but he was not so sure. *I failed to persuade Kallem the first time. What chance do I have now? He has not left Sill's side.*

Three suns had risen and settled since the Blood Riders fell and Kallem had sat with Sill ever since. Raffin had stayed by her, too, providing what comfort they could to her lifeless body. Draneth approved of the sentiment, at least, even if they were wasting their time. *She will need all the help she can get if she is to return,* he told the hawk. *Her eyes are too young to have witnessed all that they have. You were right to bring the boy.*

He is good, Tamarellin said simply. *And she* will *return.* But even the hawk lacked his usual certainty. *Should we visit* him *again?*

Yes, Draneth said but he was not looking forward to it.

Together they left the men of The Guard to their blind watch, and wound their way down into the depths of Rydan Fort, where Zyan was likely already anticipating them, in his cell of granite and iron. Tamarellin shifted his feet uncomfortably on the shaman's shoulder. The hawk could not read Zyan as he could other men, and Draneth knew he was not fond of the narrow passageways and ragged stone staircases, which were far from natural habitat for a bird of prey. He would have been far happier outside, perched on the cliffs or the wall. But on these particular visits Draneth insisted on his company. The hawk's senses were so much sharper than his own that, despite the fact his friend could not *hear* Zyan, he could still perceive other things about his body language that proved useful to the shaman.

I do not like it here, Tamarellin said, confirming Draneth's thoughts. *I do not like him.*

There are mice throughout the lower caves, Draneth tried to encourage him. *Perhaps when we're finished…?*

How am I supposed to catch mice in these stupid, small rooms? I am a hawk, not a wildcat.

Draneth chuckled. Tamarellin had a point. *I will catch you some myself.*

When they reached Zyan's cell, Draneth was dismayed to find that General Venth was already there. Even more so, when he realised what kind of a visit the General was paying. *Taking your frustrations out, are you?* he thought. *We could be learning something useful from him.* The General had clearly reached desperation. Judging from the state of Zyan, and Venth's fists, it had not done either of them much good.

Venth stood within the cell itself, his shoulders rising and falling from the effort, as he snarled down at a bruised and bloodied Zyan.

'You will not get the information you seek this way,' Draneth told him sternly. *And now neither will I,* he thought bitterly.

'Wise words, as ever, Shaman,' Zyan agreed from the floor. Then he coughed as the General's boot connected with his abdomen.

'Perhaps not,' General Venth said with a grin, 'but at least I can make him suffer; as we are.'

'I imagine he has suffered a great deal already,' Draneth responded. *Have you lost your mind?*

No, Tamarellin said, *he's lost his hope.*

That could be just as dangerous in these times.

'*He* has suffered?' the General asked, his body tensing as he turned to glare at Draneth. 'You're worried about *him*?' Draneth watched as the General began to massage his red, raw knuckles, bruised from connecting with Zyan's face. 'What about us?' Venth asked. 'They chased us from our lands, our homes. Slaughtered our families. Controlled us, toyed with us and for what?' He spun to deliver another kick and Zyan coughed again and curled up into a ball. 'We don't even know why!' the General continued, yanking Zyan to his feet so he could stare into the young man's dark eyes. 'My Blood Riders are dead! And this...thing...knows why, I know he does. We must have it out of him, Draneth, one way or another.'

'You're right,' Draneth said, hoping to pacify the General's aggression. 'But *this* is not the right way.' *Your pride is bruised more than your fists.*

'Then what is?' the General asked, releasing his grip on Zyan to let him fall loosely back to the floor. He strode up to the cell door and grasped the bars, leaning in close enough that Draneth could smell the sweat on him. 'Where has your talking got us so far, Draneth? Isn't there some medicine you can concoct, something, that will loosen his tongue?'

'I could mix something that may relax his mind, if I had the right ingredients. I may also be able to help the girl but –'

'Forget the girl!' the General yelled, slamming the palms of his hands against the iron bars. The sound echoed from the thick granite, ringing in the shaman's ears. 'You and her kept things from me,' the General said, looking hurt, 'important things. I should lock the pair of you up for your lies.'

'And what if we had told you?' Draneth shot back, his own frustrations bubbling to the surface. 'Were you ready to hear such truths? It was your ego and ignorance that killed the Blood Riders, not Zyan, and certainly not us!'

General Venth stared at him as though Draneth had just stabbed a knife straight through his heart. Then he twisted away, his hands coming to his hips and his jaw starting to click as he pondered his response. Or perhaps he was just considering another kick at the helpless Zyan.

I knew I should have stayed outside, Tamarellin said glumly.

Draneth sighed. 'The Grinth are to blame for this,' he said, offering his rival some chance of reconciliation. 'Not you or I, or even Zyan.'

'That they are,' the General agreed, his voice softening as his eyes scanned the prone Zyan, who'd remained still and quiet on the ground beneath him. 'But you are right, I underestimated them.' He turned back around and left the cell, closing the metal door firmly behind him and locking the iron bars shut. 'But Draneth,' he said in a low voice, 'there is nothing in the Writings about this intelligence you speak of! Not in any of our knowledge.' He tested the cell door, making sure Zyan remained securely sealed away and then handed the key to the young guard, Carsen, as he led Draneth from the room. 'Walk with me,' he said. Then, part way down the corridor, he stopped and faced Draneth with an earnestness that surprised the shaman. 'How do you know such a thing truly exists?' he asked.

This is the man who became General, Draneth thought more positively. *A man keen to learn about his enemy.*

He has been alone here, Tamarellin said, once again perceiving things Draneth could not.

Of course he has, the shaman realised. *Nobody else is even his age. He has dedicated his life to studying the Writings, preparing for the Grinth, and then we show up and tell him everything he knows is wrong. How did I expect him to react?* A sliver of shame crept into his heart but Draneth dismissed it. *There is no time for that.* To answer the General's question, he said, 'By reading between the lines.' When the General frowned, he expanded on his answer. 'There are signs that indicate the Grinth are more than simple, savage beasts. They are that, too, of course, but there are also men such as Zyan who appear among them. Who is controlling these men? Where do they come from? What is it that really turns their eyes dark, so that they resemble the Grinth's? These are the questions we should have been asking ourselves. There are also questions about our extinction from the Outer Lands. Our intelligence far surpasses that of the Grinth, or any other creature we have encountered here – so how was it that we were so easily overwhelmed? Was it simply a case of numbers, or something more? Many of our so-called *heroes* of old were also men who lost everything, and the Writings suggest that some of them even ended up walking with the Grinth, like Zyan. How was this so? These are the questions that have occupied my mind. When I chanced upon Tamarellin, he opened up so many new thoughts and possibilities that I'd never considered before. I had no idea, for instance, that I could communicate with another creature of this land.'

It was a surprise to both of us, Tamarellin said.

'How is it that you do?' the General asked with genuine intrigue. 'I must confess I did not believe it at first but now that I have seen how the hawk obeys you.'

I do not obey, Tamarellin corrected grumpily, inside the shaman's head.

Draneth ran his fingers through the hawk's feathers, soothing him. 'I am not even sure myself,' he explained, 'but he does not obey. Rather, we are companions. Tamarellin shares our purpose and so he chooses to journey with me. Together we have learned many things.'

General Venth studied the hawk with his eyes, another frown creasing the deep lines of his forehead.

Why is he staring at me like that? Tamarellin asked. *I have been here the whole time.*

Then you should be pleased someone's noticed you, the shaman teased.

'And your staff?' Venth asked, turning his attention to the wooden, skull-tipped shaft. 'How do you create the light?'

'It is hard to explain,' Draneth confessed, relieved that the General had finally started to ask the right questions, instead of simply dismissing things he did not understand. 'I am just more...aware of things now, of the Inner Lands. I *feel* what I can do, I'm still unsure about the *how*. It's like my eyes are only just opening.'

'When all of this is over, you must teach me,' the General said, flashing an ironic smile that forced Draneth to warm to him slightly. *You were wrong,* he told the hawk, *he still has hope.*

Because of us, Tamarellin replied tetchily. *And he is still a fool, just not so much as he was before.*

'Come,' the General said, beckoning for Draneth to follow. 'We must form a plan.'

Draneth gazed uneasily back towards Zyan's cell before turning to follow the General. *I'm not sure I like this,* he said to Tamarellin, of Zyan. *Are you still not getting anything from him?*

I cannot read him, Tamarellin confirmed, *but I do not trust him. He is not like Kallem, he is like the fog.*

What do you mean? Draneth asked but the hawk did not answer and Draneth took that to mean that he either couldn't explain, or perhaps he thought a human incapable of fully understanding the answer. *We will have to speak to Zyan another time,* he decided. Right now, Venth's fragile sanity was more urgent.

'I am lacking a Captain,' the General said with difficulty, as they followed him down another tight, dimly lit corridor deep within the mountain. 'Would you stand beside me, Draneth? Help me fight this war?'

Draneth noted that the General used the word *fight*, rather than *win*. 'I am too old to be a man of The Guard again,' he said. 'You know this.'

'I was thinking it's about time we made some changes to our laws,' the General said, unswayed by Draneth's rebuttal. 'There is a lot that needs changing, don't you think?'

Draneth smiled. If there was any possibility at all that they survived this, things may well be different at last. 'Then yes,' he said, 'I will stand with you until the end. I cannot speak for Tamarellin.'

I go where you go, the hawk said and Draneth stroked his friend's feathers gratefully. He knew he did not have to thank the hawk but he did nonetheless.

I have learned things, too, Tamarellin said in response.

Will he heed us now? Draneth asked, wary of approaching the subject of the Queen again, too soon.

Perhaps, but he needs rest, Tamarellin told him as they walked behind the General. *He has not slept for days. You need rest, too.*

There is no time for rest.

What if you are needed again? Do you have the strength to draw from the Lands?

That was how Tamarellin referred to Draneth's use of power. The hawk was right, as usual. *I suppose I should sleep, just for a while.* In truth, his body was desperate for it, but his mind had been so frantic with the urgency of the Grinth that he hadn't thought sleep possible. Perhaps Venth's apparent transformation had gone some way to relaxing him. *Sometimes it takes big events to truly change things,* he thought sadly. In this case, Brorn and the Blood Riders had been the price.

He is regretful, Tamarellin agreed, as he evidently listened in on the General's thoughts. *He also said something to Sill that troubles him.*

'What did you say to her?' Draneth asked, stopping suddenly.

'What?' General Venth turned sharply around, blinking his eyes in the dim light as though it was a battle just to keep them open.

'What did you say to Sill, up on the wall?'

The General pursed his lips and frowned disapprovingly at Tamarellin. 'I told her it was her fault,' he said. 'I know,' he held up a hand, acknowledging his mistake. 'It was foolish. I was not thinking clearly.'

'Peaks,' Draneth said involuntarily, slamming the butt of his staff into the ground. 'She's just a girl, and her confidence in herself is so fragile. She needs kindness, trust!'

'I understand,' the General said, 'but just as you would treat each man of The Guard differently, I treat everyone the same. I have no experience with children, Draneth, and I did not know how much it took from her, to do what she does. I will make things right if I get the chance. I have learned much these past few days.'

'And what about Zyan?'

'Zyan is our enemy.' The General refused to move on that point. 'And I was trying to get information. We have tried talking to him and look where it got us? At best he is a spy, at worst....who knows what his purpose is?'

'Ok,' Draneth conceded, trying desperately not to provoke another argument. 'Let's not dispute this now.

We both need rest. Let us get some sleep before discussing our next steps. The Grinth aren't going anywhere and Tamarellin will wake me if anything changes.'

I will watch them, Tamarellin agreed.

The General seemed to struggle over the idea for a moment before finally consenting. 'You are right,' he admitted. 'I have not slept at all and don't know if I am able. But I should try. We will speak later.' He turned and began to march away, then stopped suddenly. 'Draneth,' he said, without turning around.

'Yes?' The shaman could feel his weariness growing with each breath, now that he had been made aware of it.

'It should have been you,' Venth said softly.

The statement surprised Draneth so much that a pang of sympathy stung his gut. He searched for something to ease the man's conscience. 'I never had the stomach for it,' he said truthfully. 'The war isn't over yet, General Venth.'

The General paused a second, turned his head just enough for Draneth to see him nod, then strolled purposefully away.

That was kind, Tamarellin told him as Venth's form melded into the shadows.

It was true, Draneth said. *It's not an easy thing to be responsible for so many lives.*

Rest, Tamarellin instructed. *I do not like these caves. I can barely stand the Moonmirror.*

Draneth grinned. More and more often the hawk was choosing to use the human names for things, and the general way that he spoke was becoming increasingly *human. Ok,* the shaman assented, *keep an eye on things. I'll see you in the courtyard and hopefully not before.*

Tamarellin took off, his silhouette flapping awkwardly along the tunnel and then disappearing around a corner. He was bound to give someone a fright on his way out.

Draneth sighed wearily. *I should check in on Kallem and Sill before I rest.* If he could not convince Kallem to travel north, perhaps the stubborn young warrior would at least leave Rydan to collect some of the herbs the shaman required, to help rouse Sill from her lasting sleep. *If she can be roused.* Draneth hoped she had not already sunk too deeply within herself. The use of his own power was draining. He couldn't begin to imagine the effect it had on such a young girl. *The things she can do...*

He wound his way along a network of twisting tunnels and up and down short, craggy stairwells until he arrived at the room where Sill slept. It was no coincidence that this was the same place he had led Kallem, where an innocuous gap in one wall provided an unlikely escape from Rydan Fort. The back entrance led to a narrow pass, higher up on the reverse side of the mountain. If the Fort fell, there would still be a chance for Kallem to save Sill.

Kallem sat cross-legged on the far side of the room, his back close to the crude hole in the wall that led deeper into the uncut caves, and eventually out into daylight.

Raffin lay on the ground, mirroring Sill's prone position on the bed. Only he was awake, and sat straight up when the shaman entered the room.

'The fog still lingers,' Draneth told them before anyone asked. 'How is she?'

'Still sleeping,' Raffin said solemnly. 'Is it night or day? I can't tell anymore.'

'It's day,' Draneth told the boy, 'although it barely matters right now. I must sleep soon and regain my strength, perhaps you should do the same?' He spared a glance for Kallem, suspecting the warrior had barely moved from that spot since they had first escaped the awful fall of Rydan's brave Riders. He was pleased to note that Kallem had at least taken the time to wash, although his clothes would be forever stained with the Grinth's black blood. *I must bring him some new ones,* he thought, making a mental note.

'I've rested enough,' Raffin said, clearly irritable. 'Is there anything we can *do*?'

'There may be,' Draneth said, approaching him. Sill's face looked as peaceful as he had ever seen it, lying still as she was on the bed. *I hope you are somewhere safe,* he thought. *This is the way children are supposed to look. But not under these circumstances.* 'There are some herbs,' he said to Raffin, 'that, when mixed together correctly, may be able to help bring her back.'

'Back from where?' Raffin asked, his face mildly alarmed.

'From sleep,' Draneth calmly reassured him. 'It will give her strength. But I have not had the time to seek them out. If I tell you where to go and what to look for, would you find them for me?'

'Of course,' Raffin said, hopping to his feet, 'why didn't you tell me sooner?' Then he faltered. 'Wait. How can I *go* anywhere with them out there?'

Draneth exchanged a quick look with Kallem who had remained typically silent throughout. 'There is a way,' he explained, 'out of the mountain –'

'What?' Raffin looked dumbfounded. 'You mean there is another way out? Then what are we still doing here? Why are we fighting? Why are they dying out there if we could all have escaped?'

Draneth had expected this anger although he half-wished Tamarellin was here to help him choose his words more carefully. 'And where would we escape to?' he asked the boy. 'Would we flee to the mountains with the others and abandon the Inner Lands once and for all? You chose to come with us and I allowed it. I did not ask for your help.' The boy's mouth moved but no words came out. *I am too cruel,* the shaman cursed himself, as he again thumped the butt of his staff against the rock floor. The sound echoed loudly in the small space. *I'm too tired for this.* He took a deep breath and knelt before Raffin. 'I am sorry,' he said, as gently as he was able. 'Tamarellin urged me to take you with us and he was right to do so. Your loyalty is as unwavering as any of The Guard.'

'So what?' the boy answered, clearly hurt. 'What use have I been? I can't fight, I can't do what Sill or you can do. I can't do anything.'

'Do not underestimate the power of friendship,' Draneth told him. 'You are likely helping her just by being here, even though you would not know it. And you can help her more, by fetching the herbs for me.'

Raffin inhaled deeply through his nostrils and nodded but it was obvious that he was trying hard to control his emotions before the shaman. Draneth wished he had better words to console the boy but that had never been a particular skill of his, nor many others in The Guard. The boy needed to get back to his parents. *They died at Hillock you old fool*, he then remembered, thinking back to Raffin's first encounter with the Blood Riders. He sighed and stood. *This war has no time for tears.* Steeling himself, he explained to Raffin the way out, and what to search for when he got there. The boy listened intently and didn't hesitate as he disappeared through the gap in the wall.

When Draneth was sure that Raffin was out of earshot, he turned to Kallem. 'I was going to ask you to go,' he said, 'but you are not one to take instructions, are you? Do you still hope to win this battle through fighting, alone?'

'What makes you think I ever hoped to win?' Kallem said, closing his eyes and leaning the back of his head against the rock.

Stubborn fool, Draneth thought, quickly angering. *You may deceive everyone else but you don't deceive me.* 'Look at me,' he ordered. 'I didn't drag you through the gates so you could disrespect me.'

'No,' Kallem said without apparent feeling. 'You did it because you believe I'm something I'm not.'

'What do you know about belief? You don't even know who you are yourself, you're still just a boy.'

'Yet a boy lives when many men have fallen,' Kallem countered.

'And many more will fall if we don't *do* something,' Draneth said. 'If you value your life so little, then why shouldn't it be you?'

Kallem did not answer. Perhaps he couldn't argue against the shaman's logic, or perhaps he just couldn't be bothered; it was hard to tell.

'You *are* still alive,' Draneth told him, 'so don't waste it.' *Maybe he needs to rest as much as I do?* the shaman wondered.

Kallem opened his eyes again and looked at Sill. 'Is she…?' He asked softly. 'Alive, I mean.'

'Can't you tell?' the shaman said but then he added, 'I think she is just resting. She exhausted herself saving you.'

'I did not need saving,' Kallem said. He sounded regretful, as though he blamed himself for the girl's condition.

'It was her choice,' the shaman told him. 'She would have saved you all if she could.' Kallem continued to look at her, his dark Grinth eyes giving nothing away. 'What about you, Kallem?' Draneth asked him. 'Would you save us if you could?'

'Have I not fought bravely?'

'That isn't in question. You know what it is I ask.'

Kallem looked to the floor. 'The Queen,' he said.

Draneth nodded. 'Yes, the Queen. Do you doubt her existence, too?'

Kallem glanced at him, then looked away, his bright yellow pupils staring into space. 'No,' he said. His eyes searched the room briefly and then closed again as though the answers he was looking for could only be found within. His right hand moved to clasp around the hilt of his red sword. 'They talk to me, you know,' he said quietly, his Grinth eyes opening again to fix on the shaman.

'I know,' Draneth answered slowly. *I must be careful here.*

'I think it is really her, though,' Kallem said. 'It's like she knows me.'

Draneth bowed his head in acknowledgement. Kallem's was a sad plight and one that could only end in more misery. *He has endured so much already*, the shaman thought, *and I am asking him for more still.* Tamarellin no doubt would have told him that Kallem was destined to suffer either way, but that was not the point. At first he had dismissed Kallem as broken and vulnerable, a man ripe for manipulation, if not by him, then by the Grinth. *Because you judged him too quickly,* he told himself. And that was exactly the reason Kallem was who he was. *Because everybody has treated him the same way.* Or at least that was part of it. The rest Kallem needed to discover for himself and that could well shape the very future of the Inner Lands. *Tamarellin believes in you, so I will believe in you.* 'You must go to her,' he told Kallem forcefully, 'destroy her. If not for us, then at least for Sill, for your mother, and for the man you killed in Hillock. They deserve it, even if we do not.'

As he left the cave, the weight of his words almost overcame him and he had to lean on his staff as he walked, just to stay upright. It was cruel, he knew, to play on Kallem's guilt but if that's what was required, then that's what he'd do. He did not know how Kallem would respond to sympathy, but the wall he'd built around himself was spawned from doubt, distrust and unkindness, as much as it defended him from his own delusions. More of the same was the most likely way to strengthen it. Kallem's indifference was what set him apart. That, and his link to the Grinth. The Draneth who had been a man of The Guard would not have found it so difficult to be hard with a man like Kallem. But the older, wiser shaman felt every part of the pain he inflicted on others, as though they were all just different versions of himself. *This is who I am to others,* he thought. *But it is not who I am. Comfort can also be treacherous, suffering can also lead to great strength. Just like the mountains.* This was a lesson he'd learned long ago, when he had braved the Western Range to gaze out over the Outer Lands; perhaps the first man to do so in centuries. *And still I wish I hadn't*, he remembered painfully. There was no hope to be found in the west.

Draneth reached the room in which he slept and lay down on the hard, wooden bed. He did not bother with a mattress, since he'd got used to sleeping on firmer surfaces. The floors of the Fort's rooms were actually an improvement on the rough rock of his cave in the Moonmirror. *And I have slept in worse places than that*, he reminded himself. He sighed and tried to clear his mind but it proved as fruitless as attempting to dispel the Grinth's malicious fog. He closed his eyes. *I am too tired, even for sleep.*

That must have been why he missed it. As the cold iron bit through him and stuck in the wood below, pinning him to the bed, Draneth groped uselessly for his staff. *Tamarellin!* he cried out in his mind as the blood started to leak from his body onto the rock below. He tried to move but it was hopeless. The pain was unbearable, even for him. 'Why?' he coughed at Zyan, too predictably, as the yellow-eyed man withdrew the no-longer yellow sword. The lines of the effort it took contrasted with the otherwise youthful features of his face. Zyan smiled slightly at Draneth's question, like a parent smiling at something amusing a child had said. He leaned in closer, to whisper in Draneth's ear, and the single word stuck in the shaman's mind before pain and blood engulfed everything, and his life slipped tamely away.

Balance.

CHAPTER 17

He is dead!

Tamarellin shot through the entrance to Sill's cave so fast that Kallem thought the hawk would plough straight into the wall. Instead, he swivelled about, squawking wildly, and landed on the end of the bed, flapping his wings and continuing to squawk until Kallem was compelled to stand and grimace at all the commotion.

'Be quiet,' he said. 'What has happened?'

He is dead! He is dead! Tamarellin appeared too panicked to quieten and for a second Kallem worried he would disturb Sill, until he remembered that was what they wanted.

'Who is dead?' It took Kallem a moment to separate the hawk's voice from the other imposing thoughts, already taking up space in his head. *Tamarellin,* he said, more calmly, in his mind. *Who is dead?* He held out his arm and Tamarellin instantly hopped over, clutching Kallem's forearm so tightly that the bird's talons dug painfully into his skin. Kallem ignored the pain.

The shaman, Tamarellin said, his eyes boring into Kallem's as though the act could force him to understand, *Draneth is dead!* The distress of the hawk's voice inside his head affected him strangely, as though he could feel Tamarellin's pain more tangibly than even his own.

How? he asked. Conflicting emotions began to tug at his insides, sparking feelings that could have resembled shock, loss and pity. Even so, Kallem had trouble believing the shaman could really be dead. *I spoke to him just moments ago.*

Zyan! Tamarellin told him, *Zyan has killed him! We must leave, Kallem. We must kill the queen. We must kill Zyan!*

Just for a second, Kallem entertained the thought that this was no more than a desperate ploy to coax him into acting on the shaman's will. But he quickly dismissed the idea. *Disbelief,* he thought. *It's always the first reaction to someone's death. Just another weakness.*

You would know, one of the voices taunted.

So Draneth truly is dead? Kallem pondered, ignoring the other voice. *Then so is all hope of victory.* He was not ignorant of the affect the shaman had on people. *He trusted me, even though I didn't deserve it. I don't even trust myself. That was his weakness. What will we do now?*

We? the Grinth voice inside him mocked. *Not I? So you care about them now?*

No. Only her.

Then this is of no consequence to you. Are these people your friends? They never did anything for you. Not one of them defended you.

Maybe not, but they are my *people. I know who you are now. Get out of my head!*

I've been here from the start. I'm the only one who trusts in you, Kallem. Without me, you wouldn't be alive. You owe me.

Kallem! Tamarellin interrupted, still frantic. *You must listen to me. We must kill the Queen! We must kill Zyan!*

What about Sill?

You cannot do anything for her, not here. That is why you have to go. Only you can do this. Kill her Kallem, kill the Queen. Kill Zyan!

Tamarellin was right. He could not let Zyan get away with this. Zyan must have had a choice, just as he did, and Zyan had chosen evil. *I chose something else,* he thought, glancing at Sill. *I am not all bad. But can I really leave her? Just when she needs me most?*

You must, Tamarellin insisted, *you cannot help her here. You know this.*

I am sorry for the shaman, Kallem told the hawk, unsure how much conviction his words held. Even though he accepted he'd changed, that he was capable of emotion again, it was still more of a memory than an actual feeling. *A memory of a boy who was once like others. Who was good.*

Tamarellin's presence reminded Kallem of what Draneth had said to him, just a short while ago. *You know what it is I ask,* the shaman had said. *Yes,* Kallem thought, *that's why only I can do this. Because I can resist her. My eyes change but I am still myself.* How could Draneth be dead? *Is Zyan still here?* he asked Tamarellin.

He is no longer in the Fort, the hawk answered. *I am not capable of hearing him, but the feeling of him is gone. I do not understand how he escaped. We must find him.*

The shaman had told Kallem he owed the people he'd hurt. *He told me that before he died,* Kallem realised. *He deserved better. A better end. He was a better man than me. I'm no hero. I'm a murderer, just like Zyan.*

You are not like him, Tamarellin said. *You must be strong: only you can do this.*

Strong? That is all I have ever been and where did it get me?

It does not matter, Tamarellin told him. The hawk hopped to his shoulder. *Time to go.*

He is right, Kallem told himself. *I must act, as I always have. It doesn't help to think about it.* He walked slowly to the gap in the wall, ducked his head low enough so that neither he, nor Tamarellin, would hurt themselves on the unforgiving rock, and squeezed through into the rough passage beyond.

Will you not say goodbye to her? Tamarellin asked him.

What's the point? She can't hear me. He had not said goodbye to his mother either. *Go to the mountains,* he'd told her. *I never really gave her a choice.*

In silence, he felt his way along narrow, unshaped passageways and through small, low caves. It was dark here so he closed his eyes and used his hands to guide him, trusting Tamarellin's keener vision to warn him of any dangers. A soft breeze ran through the passageways, leading him ever closer to the prospect of daylight and clear skies. Even night would be a welcome sight after the thick, fog-filled air of the Fort. He thought about the men and women he was leaving behind. People who'd learned to trust him, believe in him. *And I leave them all to their own fates, so easily.* It had never been about them anyway. It was only about the Grinth. About what *they* deserved. *And they deserve only death*, he thought hatefully. *The Queen especially.* The thought of her made him sick to his stomach. Somewhere out there she cowered, letting others do her bidding. *The Grinth. Zyan. But not me. You will not control me. I will be your end.* Or perhaps she would be his. In the past, it wouldn't have mattered to him, but for some reason it did now. *I will not let Sill die that way. Not the way my sister did. Not if I have a choice.*

A rustling up ahead distracted him and he opened his eyes and drew his sword, half-expecting to meet Zyan in the dark. But it was only the boy.

'Who's that?' Raffin said, sounding alarmed.

'It's me,' he answered, 'and Tamarellin.' Although the hawk's squawk made that pretty obvious.

'What are you doing here?' the boy asked suspiciously. 'Why aren't you with Sill? And where's Draneth?'

'Draneth is dead,' Kallem told him plainly.

Raffin held up the herbs he'd collected to show Kallem. 'But he told me to get these,' he said quietly. 'He said he could make Sill better.'

Another memory of emotion flickered across Kallem's mind. '*You* will have to do that now,' was all he could think to say.

'What happened?' the boy asked. His voice was plain, almost reminding Kallem of a younger version of himself. *He is getting used to the pain now.*

'It was Zyan,' Kallem told him.

'Zyan is free?' the boy asked. 'And you left Sill alone?'

'Zyan has gone. He is not a threat to her.'

Raffin shoved past him moodily, heading back towards the Fort. But then he stopped and turned back. 'How was she?' he asked.

Kallem turned slowly. He was surprised to find he could make out the boy fairly well in the dim passageway. The tears on his young face seemed to glow in the dark. 'The same,' he told him truthfully.

Raffin nodded. 'What about you?' he asked, 'Where are you going?'

'To finish this.' Kallem turned to leave but Raffin's next question stopped him.

'What should I tell her?' the boy asked.

Kallem thought about it. There were so many things he would like to say; so many things he *wished* he could say. *But I never do and I never could.*

This might be your last chance, Tamarellin reminded him.

I know. 'Tell her,' he said with difficulty, 'tell her I promised to protect her.' He looked at Raffin to make sure the boy was paying attention. 'Tell her she never promised to protect me.'

Raffin paused a moment as though digesting the words, then he nodded again, before twisting away into the dark. *He has grown up a bit at least,* Kallem thought. Not so long ago, the boy was nothing more than an overexcitable, rumour-spreading nuisance. Another banal product of the village that had spawned him.

You judge him unfairly, Tamarellin told him. *He has always been both kind and loyal. Can you not see that?*

Will he tell her?

He will tell her.

Kallem turned and resumed his path along the narrow tunnel. *I am not used to having my thoughts listened to,* he told Tamarellin, still mildly troubled by the hawk's prying conscience.

I am not the only one who hears you, Tamarellin replied. *You will need to be prepared.*

He didn't ask what Tamarellin meant by that for he knew well enough by now. The hawk was right. He was not the first voice to intrude on Kallem's mind. Back in the forest, it was the Grinth who had spoken to him, before Tamarellin had come to his aid. And that was not the last time he had heard them. Throughout the storm, with the rain hammering down and the wind tearing across the land, he had heard them. When he fought, with Brorn by his side and the Blood Riders dying, too far from Rydan's safe gates, he had heard them. And whilst he sat on the cold, stone floor, waiting in vain for Sill to awaken, he had heard them again. *And they hear me, too.* The Grinth spoke almost as one, as though they had the same voice, which was why Kallem accepted Draneth's theory about the Queen. In fact, he now believed that all the Grinth voices were really her voice. Their eyes were her eyes and their claws were her claws. Everything the Grinth did began with her. She was to blame for the death of his father and sister. She was to blame for everything.

We know you, Kallem, the Grinth had said, and perhaps it was true.

Then you should know to fear me, he told the Queen, if she was listening. *Tamarellin is right,* he thought. *I must be ready.*

Learning to shut me out may help you, Tamarellin suggested, once again unsettling Kallem with the invasion. *Draneth could choose which thoughts I heard but sometimes he forgot. Zyan can close his mind to me completely. It may be harder with her.*

What if I can't shut her out? he asked the hawk.

Then do not listen to her.

Kallem knew how to ready himself. And so he did. He had spent his life preparing for this – in isolation, in his emotional void; in limbo – waiting for his chance to avenge what had been taken from him. *My father. My sister...my sanity.* As he walked the Inner Lands, he became a shadow, an apparition. The lands were dead and so was he. He left Rydan Fort and his new friends behind, heading north along a steep, ascending, mountain pass known to few humans and certainly no Grinth. Perhaps if he continued far enough he would meet his mother again and the others who'd fled into the high Eastern Range; but there was no time for that.

When he reached the top, he stopped to stare out over the Inner Lands. The view to the west was staggering, stretching leagues out into the distance. From this vantage point, Rydan itself was obscured by the very mountain it had been dug into, but it was evident that the Grinth fog did not extend to stain the rest of the land. When Kallem shielded his eyes from the returning sun he found he could even make out the lonely shape of the Moonmirror; its black tip thrusting out from beneath a shroud of mist, as though the mountain was trying to conceal itself from the sight of the Grinth. That was impossible, since the Grinth were everywhere. Scattered about the lands, their tiny dots wandered, either alone or in packs, all headed slowly in the same direction; south-east, towards Rydan. Being careful with his thoughts, Kallem wondered if the Queen was smart enough to keep any of them back for her defence. *She is not afraid of me,* he knew. Indeed she seemed to welcome his coming, as though she had been expecting or waiting for it his whole life; a notion that nagged at the fringes of his confidence but Kallem refused to let it in. *What is it you think you're going to get from me?*

Not far, Tamarellin said, suddenly coming into view. *I think you will be able to descend but you will need to climb.*

Climb? It was not something Kallem had any experience of, and yet he knew just as well as anybody else that the skill had been humanity's one advantage over the Grinth, whose fingerless hands had prevented them from following those who first fled to the Inner Lands. Kallem thought it likely that the cold had played as much of a part, if not more, in ending the Grinth's pursuit. Whatever halted them, ultimately, had not been forever.

He continued to the point Tamarellin had identified and began to scramble over the jagged, dark rock, until he was faced with an almost vertical drop. The mountainside fell about half the length of Rydan's enormous walls.

It is the quickest way, Tamarellin said, almost apologetically.

Snarling to himself, Kallem turned his back on the Inner Lands and started to climb down, methodically searching out each hand and foothold, and relishing the danger of the drop below. Any mistake would be fatal and Kallem acknowledged the risk as punishment for the wrongs he had committed; for those he'd harmed, and those he'd failed to save. *I should have died when they did.* But he hadn't. And now he had a chance for vengeance.

By the time he reached the bottom, Kallem was ready. As he walked, he shut off his emotions once more. Ignored the rotting corpses of a family huddled together; the songless trees where birds once lived; a severed hand, still clutching the hilt of a rusty sword; a pack of growlers, thin and starved, lying down to die. Everywhere there were Grinth. They stalked around, still searching for any lingering signs of life to extinguish on their way to Rydan. As he passed them, they peered at him through cold, dark eyes. Grinned at him with lipless rows of teeth. Clicked their claws and barked their strange guttural grunts. But never did they move towards him, nor threaten to attack.

They think you are one of them, Tamarellin told him, *like Zyan.*

But Kallem did not need telling. He could hear them, whispering to him, guiding him: the Queen beckoning him on.

He walked throughout the days and the nights alike, never sleeping, never resting. *I'll rest when it's over,* he told himself, trying to shut Tamarellin out of certain thoughts, as the hawk had suggested. *She must not know my thoughts.* But try as he might to hide them, Kallem knew that the Queen was already acutely aware of his intentions. He'd killed many Grinth. How many, he did not know, but it could hardly have gone unnoticed. *Why do you not attack me now?* he wondered. *You've been trying to kill me the whole time and here I am, alone, right among you. Don't you want me dead?* The possibility that they didn't was somehow more chilling. *Whatever you expect of me, you're going to be disappointed. I am not like Zyan, you can't control me.*

But what did he really know of Zyan? Nothing of his past. Only the killing of Draneth had confirmed his allegiance to the Queen. *Then why did you save us? The Grinth could have killed us all before we reached the*

Fort. How did you escape your cell? Was everything that had happened, of the Queen's design? For all Kallem knew, Zyan may well have taken the exact same path as he had. *Made all the same mistakes.* Was shutting off his emotions really the only way he could bring himself to face the Queen? Kallem had always believed emotions were a person's greatest weakness: a common source of both arrogance and ignorance. But since he had spent more time around others, he saw that, for some, emotions were what gave them strength. Loyalty, friendship, love...*Did I choose the easy path after all?* And what path did Zyan take that led him to betray his own people? *Did you despair? Or did you just want to be on the winning side?*

Is that so bad? The other voice asked. It was the voice of doubt; the voice he had come to associate with the Queen.

You made a promise, Tamarellin reminded him. *To Sill. And you owe the shaman, too. He trusted you.* The hawk sounded angry.

I must try harder to hide my thoughts, Kallem said, doing just that.

We are nearly there, Tamarellin told him and Kallem roused himself enough from contemplation to find he had reached the edge of Hillock's forest.

This is where it all began, he said, as much to himself as to Tamarellin.

We must keep going, Tamarellin told him, resolutely.

Where are *we going?* he asked the hawk.

You know where. To the mountain.

Is that where they got through?

Yes.

So that's where she is.

It was so close to home. All this time he had spent waiting, practising his sword amongst the trees. And this had been the place where the Grinth had finally managed to pierce through the Inner Land's natural borders. *Whilst I was away,* Kallem thought. *Was it just a coincidence?*

I do not understand coincidence, Tamarellin said. *She does not either.*

She is getting louder, he told Tamarellin. The voices in his head had risen from a whisper to match the volume of Tamarellin's. They clamoured around in his head as though they were trapped there, forever echoing off the inside of his skull.

Yesss, the voices said, if he chose to listen, *we remember you, Kallem and you remember usss.*

Do not listen, Tamarellin instructed. *Listen to me. I will guide you.*

'I'm tired,' Kallem said aloud. 'I may find it hard to shut her out.' His feet walked automatically, just as it had been before, when Marn had threatened him in the forest; he had moved simply out of action over inaction, nothing more. *Just keep moving.*

I will guide you, Tamarellin repeated. *Listen to my voice.*

At least he thought it was Tamarellin.

Following the voice's instructions, he continued to pass through the trees. The dim light of the forest was a familiar and welcome relief from the relentless, raging sun, although Kallem had preferred that to the claustrophobic caves of Rydan Fort. The tall *serethen* stretched up above him, standing like giant sentinels in his path, guarding the way to the mountain where Tamarellin claimed the Queen dwelt. For all the strength and vitality of these great trees, they had done little to affect the Grinth invasion, and every so often Kallem's shadow slid past a scratched or scraped trunk, now forever marred by the memory of Grinth claws. The men of The Guard had shown what could be achieved with *serethen,* by the astounding gates they had built. But Kallem's people had not been so progressive.

Hillock had been a simple and peaceful village, overall, and after centuries of warring with the Grinth, these descendants of the Outer Lands had never fought against each other. But that did not mean there was no evil within the Inner Lands. *Our demise began before the Grinth came,* Kallem thought, as he walked. *The evil was already among us. In people like Sill's father. In people like me.*

Yessss, the voices said, *we knew. We have always known.*

Kallem drifted through his forest-dream, only semi-aware that the other ghosts he passed were really the shapes of the Grinth, standing dark and still in the shaded light. They watched him keenly now, speaking to him in their one voice as they had done so often before. *We know you, Kallem,* they said. *We remember.*

What is wrong? Tamarellin's gentler voice asked as he swooped down from a high branch to land softly on Kallem's shoulder.

Kallem felt the hawk's talons tighten on his flesh as the bird shifted his head around, surveying his new surroundings uneasily.

They still speak to me, he told the hawk.

She still speaks to you, Tamarellin corrected.

What's the difference? Kallem could sense the hawk's discomfort at the close proximity of the Grinth. He had taken to gliding high above the ground when the Grinth were present, but for once he must have deemed it necessary to endure them. *Because he doesn't trust me?*

There is no difference whilst she is alive, Tamarellin said in answer to his question. *That is why we must kill her. We must kill the Queen.* Tamarellin sounded scared for the first time since Draneth's death.

Kallem could not blame the hawk for that. Anyone in their right mind would be afraid in this place. *Anyone in their right mind...but not a ghost like me.*

You are not dead yet, Tamarellin reminded him. *Try to shut her out.*

You can't hide from usss, Kallem, the other voice insisted. *We are always with you, we are inssside you.*

Try as he might, Kallem couldn't shut her out so he tried instead to just ignore her. Was it the voice itself that unhinged him? Or more the truth in the words? The Grinth *were* a part of him, ever since that fateful day of his doomed youth. A youth so tragically and abruptly ended that his decayed innocence was as lost now as that young boy had been, all alone in the forest. That boy had crumbled and broken. Any morals he may have possessed had scattered like dust on the wind, as though a power like Sill's had simply picked them up and blown them away, taking the boy's future with it. *I was scared once, too,* he told the hawk, vague memories returning in flashes.

But not now, Tamarellin said, *because you have grown strong.*

Yes, Kallem agreed, *I am strong.* But what else was he? *Am I kind? Am I good? No.* He blocked out those thoughts before they spilled out onto Tamarellin. But still he couldn't block the Queen from hearing.

Yesss Kallem, you are ssstrong, the Grinth voices hissed. *Like usss, you are strong.*

I am not like you.

As Kallem the shadow, the ghost, pressed onwards, the voices continued to fight for space in his mind, and he continued to let them. Tamarellin had told him not to listen to the Queen but Kallem thought otherwise. The Queen spoke to him through her disciples whilst she cowered in some dark, forgotten part of the world. Her army spread across the land, bringing death and destruction to everything they touched, and yet she was nowhere to be seen. The Queen was afraid to show herself. *She is afraid of me.* And she was foolish, too, if she thought she could bend him to her will. *You can't change me,* he told her, the shape of a grin parting his parched lips. *I'm coming for you.*

Yesss, come, the surrounding shapes whispered, *we've been waiting for you, Kallem. A long time, we've been waiting.*

They would not have to wait long.

This is it, Tamarellin said as they emerged from the trees to find a steep, muddy cliff face rising out from the ground before them. It stretched vertically up for what must have been about a hundred feet and was criss-crossed with pale, dry roots from some unseen *serethen* at the top. The roots bulged and twisted down through the dry mud like exposed veins of the underworld.

Kallem could only think that the land must have shifted significantly at some point in the distant past, to create such a stark change in the ground level. He'd never come this far through the forest before and now he wondered why. *I wasted my time waiting, when I should have been searching.*

Somewhere above and beyond the dirty wall before him, more mountains loomed, although he could not see them from here. Were it not for the gaping hole in the earthy cliff face, this could well have been the end of the world. *The end of my world.* Kallem could see right away that this hole was not natural. It had been gouged out from somewhere deeper within, carved through rock and earth, scraped and scratched and clawed through who knew how many years. *Centuries,* Kallem thought. *They had never stopped hunting us.*

The hole stretched off into darkness and Kallem felt himself drawn into it, deeper and deeper, until his shadow faded and then vanished altogether, along with the last of the light. Only Kallem the ghost remained. Tamarellin pecked nervously at his ear, reminding Kallem of his presence. To Kallem's surprise, he found again that he could see reasonably well in the dark.

It is your eyes, Tamarellin said.

Of course, Kallem realised. *I am already part-Grinth.*

I can see, too, Tamarellin said, as though that were supposed to comfort him.

The ground underfoot had become unstable and Kallem looked down to find he was standing on bones. They were everywhere, thousands of them. And they were unmistakably non-human. *They died here, carving this hole.* He knew the realisation should petrify him, send shivers down his spine, but Kallem had long since lost the necessity, the will, for fear and Kallem the ghost had even less use for it. So he navigated his way stoically along the graveyard tunnel, knowing that each skeleton represented another dead Grinth; another Grinth that would never again taint the fragile beauty of this already broken world. As he went deeper, mud became rock and the tunnel grew damper until water trickled from the wet walls as though the mountain was weeping. Grotesque shapes boiled and bulged from the slimy, grey-brown rock. Thin tendrils barred his way where softer rock seemed to have bled down from the ceiling to the floor, and occasional pools of water hid unknown secrets or fears within their murky depths. These were natural caves. Not the carved, defiled tunnels of the Grinth, or the sculpted man-made halls of Rydan Fort. As he travelled further into the heart of the mountain, his surroundings constantly shifted. In places, dark, slim gaps barely wide enough for a man to pass through, opened into huge chambers with glowing, moss-like ceilings. Stumps of rock reached up from the ground, trying to touch the spikes above like giant teeth threatening to clamp together and crush him. At other times, gaping chasms ate away the ground completely, sinking so deep into black that even Kallem did not care to look at them for too long. As he edged around one such chasm he almost slipped on another of the many bones that littered the caves. He kicked it into the hole, pausing a moment to hear the sound when it hit the bottom. The sound never came. *We're wasting time,* Tamarellin said and so he pressed on. The bones of the Grinth were far fewer where they had not needed to dig but every now and then he would come across a patch of them, indicating that he was still on the right path. Some of the skeletons he found, resembled neither Grinth nor human, as though they belonged to some creature that must have shared a semblance with both species. Perhaps he should have been troubled by this, but were it not for such signs, he would long since have been lost down here in the dark.

The network of caverns and caves was so staggeringly vast that it dwarfed even Rydan Fort by an immeasurable margin. *Were they lost, too?* Kallem wondered. *Is that why they died here? Ether* had kept him moving for how long he dared not wonder, but there was no food for Tamarellin this deep underground and the hawk had remained still and silent for much of their journey, perhaps conserving what small amount of strength and stamina he had left for what lay ahead. The Queen had grown quiet, too, and the silence felt strange to Kallem, especially with the empty space that surrounded him. Drippings from the ceiling, his own footsteps, and Tamarellin's breathing were the only sounds he had heard for some time. And all he could do was to keep moving, drifting through the cold, dark caves, like the ghost that he was. *Perhaps I really am dead?* he wondered for a time, although, if that were the case, he could not recall when it had happened. This was certainly as fitting a place as any for the dead to roam. Tamarellin's feathers against his face felt real enough, and when the hawk suddenly roused himself, Kallem knew he was still alive.

We are here, Tamarellin said.

The hawk's voice sounded weak and distant in Kallem's head and he stroked the bird's soft feathers, as he'd witnessed Draneth do so often. *How do you know?* he asked. *Does she speak to you, too?*

No, Tamarellin said, *I can feel her, like I feel my prey. Only it is the opposite. He is here, too.*

Zyan?

Yes.

Good. Kallem had been prepared for that possibility. And yet now faced with it, he was unsure if it was truly better or worse to meet Zyan down here with the Queen. At the very least he had come expecting the Queen, and however many Grinth she had held back to defend herself. In his dreamlike state he'd sometimes imagined fighting them, killing them, until he either reached the Queen, or died trying. Zyan was another complication and, even though he deserved death, Kallem could not say that he relished the prospect of killing another human. An image of Marn's stricken face passed through the dark. *One, is enough for a lifetime.* And Zyan could well prove to be a challenge, even for him. *He killed the shaman.* Who knew how long Zyan had walked with the Grinth?

He is not human anymore, Tamarellin said. *And yes, he killed the shaman. That is why he must die.*

I know, Kallem said. *Do not worry, I know what I have to do.* He ducked his head under a low part of the ceiling and emerged from the current tunnel to find himself in a huge, spacious cave with a high ceiling and tall, angular walls. More openings, no doubt leading to more, vast networks of caves pocked the moist walls; some big, some small, some high, some low. At the far end of the cave, the Queen sat in all her monstrous glory;

a fat, faded lump of purple, as unlike the Grinth as he could have imagined. She towered above the standing figure of Zyan. And a smaller, equally ugly shape squatted beside him.

The Queen resembled her Grinth brethren in colour but little else. Her lipless grin bore no teeth as far as Kallem could see, and her shorter, stubbier arms had no claws. She was at least three times the height of a regular Grinth, but she was hugely fat in comparison and Kallem could not begin to contemplate how she'd managed to navigate her way so deeply into the mountain. *Unless she was here already?* To Kallem's disgust the smaller, more brightly coloured lump was a similar shape to that of the Queen and must have been her baby, perhaps lending some credence to his theory that the Queen had matured down here. As Zyan rubbed the smaller creature's enlarged head with his hand, the baby Queen opened its mouth in a sort of stupid grin that oozed a thick flow of drool onto the cave floor.

Zyan raised his own happy face to look at Kallem, and three sets of golden pupils now gazed at him from across the cave. The Queen's were by far the brightest. And the most piercing. Even in the dark and from this distance, he could tell that she was pleased to see him.

Welcome, Kallem, her voice said in his head, and it was like a thousand voices spoke at once, drowning out all but his most base thoughts.

Remember, Tamarellin said as Kallem moved towards them. *Do not listen to her. Or to him.*

'Isn't she beautiful?' Zyan said, his voice loud and light in the echoey expanse of the cave.

Kallem stopped halfway, assessing the level of threat that either Zyan or the Queen might pose. He scanned the other openings for signs of Grinth but did not find any.

We are busy, the Queen said, her golden eyes mimicking the movement of his before turning back to bore into his soul. *Always busy. You will not find any more of usss here.*

'They do not fear us,' Zyan said informatively. 'That is not why they kill us. It's just what they do.' He turned his head and smiled as the baby Queen closed its eyes for a moment in response to his stroking its head.

'Why?' Kallem asked. 'Why do they want to kill us so badly?'

'Does it matter?' Zyan asked. 'We humans are but a speck in time, a blot on the pages of history. But they will live forever. Their memories are passed on, from Queen to Queen, so they never forget. Not like us,' he sighed and looked at Kallem. 'We forget so easily. Forgive so hard.'

You remember Kallem, don't you? You are just like usss. The fuzz of the Queen's voice was so intense, her eyes so penetrating that Kallem dropped to his knees and clutched his skull as though he had to keep his head from exploding under the pressure. 'Get out of my head!' he cried.

Do not listen! Tamarellin urged, flapping from his shoulder to perch on a craggy ledge nearer to the roof of the cave. *Shut her out!*

Snarling, Kallem tried to do as Tamarellin said but the Queen's dazzling eyes continued to pierce into him, cut through to his thoughts as though he had no thoughts but hers. He could not even look away.

Kallem, do not listen. Tamarellin began to squawk and beat his wings noisily from his perch. *You must kill the Queen.*

Why would you hurt usss, Kallem? the Queen asked. *We would not harm you. We want you, Kallem. They never wanted you, but we do.*

'Why do you think you made it this far?' Zyan said chirpily, abandoning the baby Queen to walk towards him. As he did so, he bent to pick up a small rock and then set about studying it, rolling it over and over in his hands. 'Because you're so different from everyone else?'

Do not listen to him, Kallem, Tamarellin urged, still squawking wildly. *Get up, you must get up!*

'Because you're such a fearless warrior?' Zyan continued. 'Because you're special?' He laughed. 'Maybe it's because of the bird?' Without warning, he flung the rock violently into the air and suddenly Tamarellin went quiet.

Through the chaos in his head, Kallem heard a flap of wings and then a thud. A speckled, brown feather drifted past his face, briefly obstructing his view of the Queen.

'You're alive because they wanted it that way,' Zyan said, approaching him. 'Nothing more.'

'You're wrong,' Kallem said. *You're both wrong*, he told the Queen. He tried to stand. His legs held him up but the pressure in his head made him dizzy and unstable. 'I chose to go on living. I chose to fight.'

Why fight usss? The Queen asked. *We do not fight you, Kallem.*

'Yes you do,' he said, confused. 'You've been trying to kill me from the start!'

'Who are you really fighting?' Zyan asked, tilting his head. 'The Grinth never harmed you, just as they have never harmed me. We are much the same, Kallem, you and I. You will see. You will join with them, just as I did. My time is almost done. It is your turn now.'

'What are you talking about?' Kallem growled, slowly lowering his hands from his head to concentrate on Zyan. 'The Grinth killed my father, my sister! I fought them in the forest, at the Moonmirror, outside of Rydan –'

Why do you hurt ussss, Kallem? the Queen's voice surged through him.

I must not listen, he told himself. *I must make it stop!*

'Oh yes, you fought very bravely,' Zyan said, 'and you will be stronger still when you let her in. An unbeatable warrior, that no man can match. You will kill thousands of them. Their swords will be but whispers in the wind, their faces echoes of the humanity who abandoned you, banished you, led you to us. They will rue the day they tried to kill you, the day they outcast you; all the times they put their pain, their weakness, onto you. But don't worry, she will take it away. She will make it stop. All you need to do is let her in.'

Why do you still fight ussss, Kallem? We would never hurt you.

Lies! he told the Queen. *All you have done is try to hurt me. But you failed. I, I was too strong.* A flicker of self-doubt crept into his crowded mind.

'Did you really think they couldn't kill you if they wanted to?' Zyan asked, sounding amused. 'When do you think they tried?'

When?

A vivid memory lurched suddenly into Kallem's head.

Hillock. He was in the forest. In a clearing. The sky above was blue but all else was stained black. The Grinth were there, moving softly through the mist. But they did not attack. *I fought them, they were killing the villagers.*

Yesss, you killed usss. But we did not hurt you, Kallem.

He watched as the skies closed and the tall *serethen* shrank into the ground. Another memory shot up, taking their place.

It was cold. Kallem looked around. A thin veil of snow coated the ground and a dark mountain loomed behind him, glimmering in the twilight. *The Moonmirror.* Two worn Grinth, one with a damaged arm, circled him, trying to get at Sill.

But not you, Kallem, the Queen hissed, *never you.*

No, Kallem thought, *it isn't true! They would have killed us both.*

The Moonmirror melted into the ground and the land became flat. A great battle raged around him. The Grinth were everywhere and Kallem slashed and chopped at them with his red sword, killing more and more until their blood soaked the ground black. But not a drop of his was spilled. Not a scratch lined his body.

I was never harmed, he realised. *Not even in the fight before Rydan, when there were only a few of us. They never attacked me.* He dropped back down to his knees and laughed. *What a worthless fool I am!* He thought bitterly. *I thought I was tough! I thought I was invincible! But I'm nothing. Just another stupid boy, playing warrior.* That thought led him to his childhood and he remembered his father and sister. 'I don't care!' he yelled at Zyan and the Queen. 'You still killed my father and my sister!'

Did we? The Queen's hot, yellow eyes penetrated his again and another memory flashed through his head. He was in the forest again but this time it was different from before. He watched a young boy play with his father, testing out the red sword he had been given as a present. It was too big for him. *That's me,* Kallem thought, *so then who am I?* He looked down and saw the yellow sword at his waist. *I'm Zyan,* he realised, *this is Zyan's memory.*

Zyan smiled down at him in the centre of the cave. 'Keep watching,' he said quietly.

'No, make it stop!' Kallem groaned, clutching at his head again. 'I know what happened here.' *I don't want to see it again!*

'Do you?' Zyan asked. 'Do you really?'

The Queen's hold was too strong and he found himself watching anyway. His sister giggled as he sparred with his father. He tried to hit at the bigger man's legs, but his father parried the attempt easily.

Please! Make it stop! Through Zyan's eyes, Kallem tried to look around for the Grinth that had killed them, but his head would no longer move. He tried to reach for the yellow sword at his waist but his hand wouldn't move either. He could only watch.

Suddenly his father stopped playing.

'Kallem, what's wrong with your eyes?' he heard his sister say. *I don't remember that,* he thought. His father bent down to look at him and Kallem watched through Zyan's memory as the younger Kallem drove the red sword straight through his father's stomach. *No!* Kallem tried to yell. He tried to run to his father, but Zyan's body held him in place. He fought against it and for a moment managed to return to the cave.

'That's not how it happened!' he screamed at Zyan. 'It wasn't me. A Grinth killed them! I saw it! I remember!'

'Are you sure?' Zyan asked.

Are you sssure? The Queen repeated and her gaze plunged him back into the forest.

His father stared at the younger him, a mix of surprise and sadness haunting his eyes. Blood was dripping from one of his hands where he gripped the blade. The other hand reached out to his son in pity.

Please, Kallem begged the Queen, *no more! This can't be real. It isn't real!*

The young Kallem grinned and pulled the sword slowly back through his father's body while his sister stood in stunned silence. The body slumped to the ground and the boy started walking towards his sister. 'Kallem?' Her voice was a whimper.

No!

The trees around him uprooted, tearing apart the earth, and then shot up into the blue sky. Then the blue merged into brown, until it again became the roof of the Queen's cave.

'No.' Kallem bowed his head to the moist rock floor and wept. 'I couldn't have,' he said. 'It wasn't me.' But even as he said it, the memories came flooding back to him, drowning out even the Queen's voice. 'No!' he cried, shaking his head. He beat a fist defiantly against the rock, making his hand bleed. He looked up at Zyan, who met his eyes with that same infuriating smile. 'Why didn't you do anything?' he growled through his tears. 'If you were really there, why didn't you stop me?'

'I could not have stopped you any more than you could yourself,' Zyan said and, just for a second, the smile faded. 'I have done many things,' he said sadly. 'And you will, too, in time.'

You're wrong, Kallem thought, but self-doubt was all he was now. *It's all I've ever been. She was controlling me from the start. My people were right,* he realised, *I am mad. I did it. I killed my own father. Slashed my sister to shreds!* He winced at the memory, gasped at the blood, the horror on his sister's face. *How could I do such a thing? I truly am a monster.* His whole life had been a lie.

'And Marn?' He realised, looking up at Zyan as the barriers in his mind continued to fracture, letting the bitter truth spill through into his consciousness. 'He didn't really attack me, did he?'

Marn knew the truth, the Queen told him. *He tried to help poor little Kallem. But only I can help you. He thought he could change you, but when he threatened you with the truth, the real you killed him. You are mine, Kallem, you always have been.*

The baby Queen made a whining sound as though it still wanted to be stroked. 'It's hard at first,' Zyan said softly, placing a hand on Kallem's shoulder. 'But she will take the pain away, you will see. It's much easier once she's inside you. Don't worry,' he said reassuringly. 'All you have to do is not fight it.'

A flurry of feathers sent Zyan sprawling to the ground. Tamarellin squawked in rage and pecked at his face whilst Zyan fought to keep the hawk at arm's length. Calmly, Zyan moved his head left and right, somehow avoiding the bird's beak, before he finally managed to toss the hawk aside. He rolled swiftly to his feet and drew his yellow sword.

Flailing around on the ground, Tamarellin tried to right himself but his damaged wing wouldn't allow it. *It was never your fault, Kallem!* the hawk's voice insisted in his head. *Remember that. Remember who you were before. Remember who you are now.*

Zyan grinned down at the wounded hawk, his eyes burning as savagely as the summer sun.

'I am a monster,' Kallem confessed, staring up at Zyan. 'And so are you!' He leapt at the young warrior, tackling him to the floor with a thud. Growling, he grabbed Zyan's head and smashed it against the hard rock. The baby Queen hissed furiously but her mother just watched silently, urging him on. *Yesss,* she said, *kill him, Kallem. Kill him and take his place.*

Kallem pulled the red sword from its sheath, ready to plunge straight through Zyan's tainted heart, but when he looked down at the young man's face, he faltered. Blood leaked out from beneath Zyan's head, trickling along the grooves in the rock. The grin was gone, and his searching eyes were no longer yellow but a soft brown that contained such a sorrow, that the red sword slipped from Kallem's grip and clattered uselessly to the floor. He clutched at Zyan's chest, curling his fingers into the dying man's garments. 'Why? he asked desperately. 'Why did you make me do this?' He reached to grab up his sword again, and this time gripped the hilt in both hands. He held it steady above Zyan's chest. *Just do it!* he thought. *It's what he deserves.* But the man beneath him was no longer the same one who'd caused so much harm. Without his yellow eyes, Zyan's face looked only gentle and haunted. He might have been younger than Kallem when the Queen first took him. *It doesn't matter*, Kallem told himself, *he has to die.* Zyan blinked and reached a hand slowly up to touch the back of his bleeding head. 'Is it black?' He asked quietly.

'No,' Kallem told him. 'It's red, like a human's.'

'Good,' Zyan said, 'that's good.' His brown eyes scanned the cave ceiling momentarily as though searching for something that wasn't to be found. 'The things I've done,' he whispered. Tears slipped from the corners of his eyes and ran swiftly down his cheeks to mingle with the blood below. 'Please,' he whispered, groping with his hands until he had hold of Kallem's clenched fists. 'It has to stop.' He squeezed Kallem's bloodied hands around the hilt of the sword and Kallem knew what he wanted. He leaned forward to whisper in Zyan's ear. 'It's ok,' he said softly, 'you can rest now.' Zyan nodded but his mouth twitched and his eyes continued to leak tears. 'I lived so long,' he gasped, 'so very long.'

Kallem roared and plunged the sword down, ending it quickly. Shivering, he watched the last of Zyan's life trickle away. Then he stood slowly to face the Queen.

Yesss, she hissed gleefully, *yessss! You are mine now, Kallem. You will take his place.*

Kallem wiped the sword clean on the side of his thigh. Zyan's blood was fresh and human, and the smell of it made him sick to his stomach. *You became a ghost long before me,* he thought, sparing one final look for the dead man. Then he strode purposefully towards the baby Queen.

What are you doing? The adult Queen tracked his movement with her bulging head and piercing eyes. Then she screeched as she must have realised he was not under her control.

The sound was like daggers in Kallem's head, and he hesitated just briefly before breaking into a run. The Queen began to scuttle towards her baby but she was too slow and too late.

Kallem faced her, snarling, as the baby Queen's head fell to the ground, its thick neck spurting black blood like a fountain.

The Queen screamed with such raw, ragged rage that Kallem was forced to cover his ears. Immediately, Grinth began to appear at the darker corners of the cave, emerging through hidden openings and pouring in through the main entrance in a wave of purple fury. They hissed and barked in panic at the sight of their dead young Queen.

I thought they weren't here? he mocked the Queen. He pointed his sword at her headless baby and grinned. *I bet now you want to hurt me, don't you?*

Before she could answer, the mountain began to rumble. The rock beneath Kallem's feet trembled and he was forced to crouch, putting a hand to the ground to steady himself. A crack ripped its way violently through the ceiling of the cave and a chunk of rock broke from it, shattering when it hit the ground just a few paces from the Queen. The Queen swung her mighty head around, watching her cave start to collapse. She screamed one last time at Kallem and then scuttled off towards one of the larger openings, crushing or flinging any Grinth that got in her way. Kallem started after her, but another piece of rock fell before him and he was forced to dive and roll to safety. Crazed and panicked, the Grinth continued to flood into the cave and Kallem cursed, knowing it was already too late to pursue her. As the mountain shook again, he braced himself for the onrushing Grinth. The front-runner lost its balance and tumbled clumsily to the ground, scraping its claws uselessly against the rock before meeting the sharper end of Kallem's sword. Several others were crushed as a huge tooth of rock flattened them suddenly from above.

Kallem stepped back as large cracks began to weave their way across the cave floor and a giant hole formed, swallowing more Grinth.

The mountain shook again and the tunnel the Queen had escaped through vanished under another pile of rubble. *I hope your death is painful,* Kallem told her as he leapt aside, just in time, as another length of rock smashed to the ground, making a further mess of the baby Queen's already limp body.

Kallem, help...

Kallem looked around to find that, somehow, poor Tamarellin was still alive. He ran to the hawk, helping him onto his shoulder, and then snatched up Zyan's yellow sword as the mass of Grinth closed in on them. Holding the red sword in his right hand and the yellow in his left, he prepared himself for the death he deserved. The mountain rumbled angrily, shedding more loose rocks from the cave ceiling that exploded on impact with the ground, spitting small fragments of stone painfully into Kallem's legs. He knew it was only a matter of time before the cave collapsed in on him completely, or he fell into one of the deep crevices opening up around him. *Can you fly?* he asked Tamarellin.

No, the hawk said sadly, *I think my wing is broken.*

I'm sorry, Kallem said. *I'll kill as many of them as I can.*

CHAPTER 18

Wake up! Sill opened her eyes.

She had spent so long in the dark that even the dully lit cave was initially too bright for her unpractised eyes. She rolled over on her side, expecting to find leaves and tree trunks but instead found only granite and firelight. *Did I dream of the bear again?* Neither Raffin nor Kallem were there, but she knew they had both been waiting for her. Even locked so deep within herself she had felt their presence, their compassion; their love. But it was something more unsettling that had awoken her, dragged her back from the dark before she was ready, before her strength had fully recovered. *I should find Draneth*, she thought. *Something bad is going to happen.* Or perhaps it already had?

The room she was in gave no clues as to how long she had slept for. It could have been an eternity for all she knew, such was the timelessness of the Fort's caves. *Somebody must have replaced the saplights*, Sill thought, so she knew she was not completely alone. She swung her legs over the side of the bed and tried to stand. Her feet felt cold on the rock floor but her legs held her up, despite the wobbling of her knees. Then she gasped. *Not you!*

His shadow entered first, stretching out into the room until it almost touched Sill's toes. Then his strong, spindly body was in the doorway, his hands pressing against either side of the carved, rock frame, barring the way to the passages behind.

'Father!' Sill breathed.

The malice in his crooked smile was mirrored by the bright yellow orbs that shone in his eyes, like two radiant glowbugs, hovering ominously in the dark. The glint of metal as it touched the saplight brought Sill's eyes to her father's waist, where a long, sharp knife sat snuggly in his belt. Half the length of the knife was already dark with blood.

'What have you done?' she asked him, backing slowly away until she bumped into the bed.

'What have *I* done?' her father hissed, taking his first step into the room. 'That's so typical of you, always blaming someone else.'

'What did they tell you to do?' Sill asked instead. She thought about making for the hole she had noticed in the cave wall behind her, but she knew her legs could not yet manage to run. *Running never helped anyway*, she remembered.

'No one tells me to do anything!' her father snarled at her. 'They *asked* me to let him out and I obliged. It wasn't right what they did to him. And now that he's killed that meddling shaman, you should be thanking me.'

'Draneth's dead? No!' Sill shook her head, not wanting to believe it was true. *Not the shaman. Not Draneth! Father, what have you done?* 'You freed Zyan, didn't you?' she realised, horror-stricken.

'Yes,' her father said, taking a step closer. 'It was you he really wanted but you were always protected, weren't you? Always getting people to do what you want. He killed the shaman to lure your precious Kallem away. She has special plans for *him*. She chose me to deal with you instead. She liked that idea.' He laughed. 'That shaman deserved what he got. Always running around, sticking his nose where it's not wanted and acting like everyone's father. But he's not *your* father Sill, *I'm* your father!' He took another step closer.

'No, you're not,' Sill said, as clearly as her dry mouth could manage. 'She's controlling you.' *How did I not realise you were here?* It made sense that he would be. It might be the one place in the Inner Lands that would take him in. Or maybe the Queen had wanted it that way?

'Those things he could do. It's not right,' he was saying, 'it's not natural. Only brings death and sorrow. Just like my daughter.'

That wasn't my fault! She wanted to yell at him, but did she really believe that was true? They said a great storm had raged, the night of her birth – the night her mother had died. *No, it wasn't my fault*, she told herself. *I was just a baby. I don't even have that much power* now. *I loved my mother, even though I never met her. I love her still. I miss her.* Her father took another step forward and she backed weakly around the bed, using it for support until she reached the corner of the cave, where she sat down against the rock to weep hopelessly for her dead mother. *And now Draneth is dead, too, when Zyan really meant to kill me! Does nothing I try to do matter?*

Her father looked at her oddly as though he didn't understand why she might be upset.

That's because it's not really him, she thought. Maybe he had been under their control all along? *All my life.* 'You're wrong,' she told him. 'They're controlling you! You mustn't listen to them, they're evil.'

'*They're* evil?' He threw his head back and laughed. When he looked at her again, the crooked smile was gone and his yellow pupils blazed with such hatred that Sill could barely breathe. 'Are they any worse than *you*?' he rasped, his voice so coarse it felt as though it could bring the cave down around them. 'They understand, you know,' he said, his vulgar head nodding vigorously.

'They're not that different to you. She told me what you did. How you tore your own mother –'

'Stop it!' Sill shrieked, covering her ears. She tried to push herself further into the wall but it was solid rock and there was nowhere to go. 'I was just a baby,' she said, 'it wasn't my fault.' *It wasn't my fault. It wasn't!* 'I loved her, too!'

'You didn't even know her!' her father roared. 'She was my wife! She was everything!' He grasped his head with his hands and groaned as though he was in pain. Then he pulled the knife from his belt.

Sill froze. All that she had survived, when others had not. Like the Blood Riders and Raffin's parents. Like Draneth and Brorn. The Grinth must have killed thousands. And yet it would be her own father who would finally kill her. Perhaps it was more fitting this way? *I was lucky to survive this long. I should have died when I was born, instead of her.*

And yet she still wasn't ready to let it happen. Wasn't strong enough to accept it. The thought of the knife cutting into her, of leaving Raffin alone, of letting Kallem think he'd failed her. *I wanted to be stronger but I'm not strong at all,* she realised. *I never could be.* A numbness filled her belly, eating her resolve from the inside out. *Only the strong get to live. That's why they've survived so long.* Tears continued to flood her eyes and her father became nothing but a blur before her. The blur crept closer.

'It wasn't my fault,' she told him again, feebly.

Her father knelt before her and she wiped her eyes until she could see the grin playing upon his lips. 'But it was your fault,' he whispered hatefully. 'You brought the storm.' The darks of his eyes accentuated the radiant, yellow pupils that captivated her like the last dying embers of a fire; blazing impudently, in the hollows of night.

It isn't even him, Sill told herself, staring into the Grinth eyes. *He's just their tool, their weapon.* She wiped some more of the tears away to search the eyes for any lingering trace of a father who cared about his daughter. 'Did you *ever* love me?' she asked softly.

His face contorted as though the question pained him, and he groaned again. The malicious grin faded for a second but then returned even stronger. 'How could I ever love you?' he hissed at her. 'You brought the storm!' He gripped the knife tightly and drew back his arm.

It wasn't my fault! Anger rushed in to fill the void inside her and Sill gasped as power and emotion surged through her small body. Without her even willing it, a rush of air swept in to stay her father's arm as he tried to plunge the knife inside her. His arm swept back behind him, but he kept his grip on the knife, fighting against the force of the wind. He snarled at her in frustration.

Using the wall for support, Sill slowly pushed herself back to her feet. *You would really kill your own daughter?* The anger inside turned to hate, rage, disgust. 'How could you do it to me?' she yelled at him; all the cruelty, all the beatings coming back to her now like a powerful tide that was impossible to push against. 'I loved you and you *hated* me! That wasn't the Grinth, that was just you! You're as evil as they are!'

'You brought the storm!' he rasped again, as though the air staying his hand justified his words.

Sill screamed in anguish, her body shaking. 'I'll give you a storm!' she yelled. Glaring into his hateful yellow eyes, she concentrated harder, letting the power swell within her until it became so great that it seeped out into the world. Wind whistled through the tunnels of Rydan Fort, kicking up dust and flying to her aid; blocking the space between her and her father.

'Sill!' Then Raffin burst into the room, losing his footing as he met with the force of the air. The wind rolled him some way across the floor until Sill eased the flow around him.

Impossibly strong, her father writhed before her, every sinew in his wiry body straining against the barrier of air as he sought desperately to bury the knife deep into his daughter's flesh. The air she threw at him pressed against his face, distorting his already ugly features, and widening his grotesque grin.

A rumbling sound shook through the room as dust and fragments of rock began to fall from the ceiling. *Am I doing that?* Sill could feel her power growing still, a limitless supply born of the treachery of her father's absent love. It wasn't hate that fuelled her, but more injustice. The injustice of her mother's death, of her father's cruelty, of the Grinth's senseless and irrational evil. More dust and debris shook from the ceiling. *I could bring it all down if I wanted.* But that would kill all three of them. Instead, she directed the full might of the air at her father, finally dislodging his footing to send his body flying backwards to collide with the far wall. The impact made him drop the knife and as Sill freed her grip on the wind, Raffin grabbed up the knife from the floor and, with both hands, pushed it deep into her father's chest, just below the sternum. Raffin yanked the knife back out and backed slowly away until he reached Sill. Then he sank to the floor as her father laughed and coughed horribly.

Sill sat down beside her friend.

'What did I do?' he breathed.

She put her hand on his. 'He wouldn't have stopped,' she said.

They watched as her father tried to walk but instead fell heavily on his side. Then he managed to roll to his front, chuckling again as he tried to pull himself forward along the ground. Finally, he gave up and started to gurgle and gasp for air, blood leaking from his mouth.

He looked at them through his yellow eyes as though he couldn't understand what was happening to him.

Sill watched with a strange sense of pity as the yellow pupils gradually darkened to brown and the black surrounding them faded back to white. And her father was gone. She pressed her head into Raffin's shoulder and took a moment to contemplate the man who had tried to kill her. *Why do I still feel sorry for you?* The man who had hated her, beaten her, punished her all her life, for the woman they had both lost.

'Don't you dare cry for him, Sill,' Raffin said as he wrapped his arm around her, hugging her close to him. 'Don't you dare. I'm so glad you're awake.'

'Me, too,' she said, exchanging a brief smile. There was no time for mourning anyway. 'Help me up,' she said, 'there's something I need to do.'

Raffin gave her a quizzical look but obeyed, helping her to her feet and watching her closely as though trying to assess whether she was really fit to be standing.

Taking his hand, Sill led him from the room and along the passageways of Rydan Fort, heading back towards the surface. 'Kallem's gone, hasn't he?' she said as they emerged into the dingy sub-light, still saturated with the putrid stench of the Grinth fog.

'Yes,' Raffin said sombrely. 'He gave me a message for you. He said to tell you that he promised to protect you, but you never promised to protect him. I think I know what he meant now.' He gave her hand a light squeeze, which sent tendrils of warmth along her arm and through her body: alive and awake as it had ever been. 'Tamarellin was with him, too,' Raffin continued. 'I think they've gone to fight the Queen.'

Sill nodded. *You're still protecting me somewhere, aren't you?* She thought, knowing that he was alive at least for now. *I can feel you now,* she realised. *I can feel everything.*

She led Raffin up the winding steps and along the wall to where she had watched the Blood Riders die their awful deaths. *Nobody else will die like that,* she vowed, *if there's something I can do to stop it.* She could feel the weight of the wall beneath her bare feet, feel its strength. But there were also cracks, weaknesses, running throughout the rock. *I could collapse it all if I wanted to,* she knew. Power still surged through her as though it was desperate to get out. If she didn't do something with it soon, she felt like it might overwhelm her, explode uncontrollably. And take the whole Fort down with it.

The Grinth fog seemed to cling to the air surrounding the wall and courtyard. At the end of the wall, General Venth stood alone. His dark silhouette was hazy in the thick fog, another lost soul waiting to be freed from its torment, one way or another. Although he stood tall and upright, when they reached him, his face looked gaunt and defeated.

Sill peered over the parapet to see what he was staring at, but there was nothing to be seen through the thickness of the fog.

'It was my fault,' he said to her. 'I made the decision. I gave the order. It was wrong of me to blame you. We were supposed to protect the people of these Lands: that was our duty, *my* duty. But I failed.'

'I just killed my own father,' Sill said and the General turned his head slowly to stare at her, the creases in his forehead scrunching together.

'You mean I killed him,' Raffin said absently.

The General's stare fixed upon the bloody knife in Raffin's hand, his mouth opening as though he meant to say something but had lost the means to do so. Then he turned his frown away and leaned forward, placing his hands on the parapet and bowing his head sombrely.

'It wasn't your fault,' Sill told him gently. 'It was the Grinth. They're to blame for your men.'

'It was me,' General Venth replied bitterly. 'I made the decision. The shaman...' He exhaled into the fog. '...Draneth, he tried to tell me, but I wouldn't listen. I suppose you know he's dead?'

'Yes,' Sill said, 'but we're not. Not yet. We mustn't give up,' she told him firmly. 'Not ever. That's when they really win.'

The General snorted. 'I would have given my life for them, you know,' he said. 'For all of you. That's what it really means to be a man of The Guard.'

'You shouldn't have to,' Sill said. 'None of you should have to.'

'You care.' Raffin put in. 'That's enough. Let Sill help *you* now.'

'What do you mean?' the General asked, turning to look at them again.

'Watch,' Sill said and a heavy gust of wind whooshed in to sweep away the fog around the wall. Then, she sent it down into the courtyard, forcing the fog up and away, over the mountain Rydan Fort was built into. The men in the courtyard moved around as though readying themselves for another battle. *They probably think that was the Grinth,* Sill thought.

No sooner than the fog had cleared, the Grinth below began to hurl themselves against the *serethen* gates, their guttural barks booming so loudly that the sound travelled straight into Sill's body, reverberating through her inner organs.

'Prepare for a breach!' General Venth shouted down at his men below.

'I need to concentrate now,' Sill told them. 'Please don't disturb me, no matter what. Not until I'm finished. They will try to come for me.' She knew now that she was as much of a threat to the Queen as Draneth or

Kallem. Perhaps more so. *That's why you want me dead, isn't it?* she said to the Grinth below.

The General walked past her and drew his sword. 'This sword was made for the Generals of The Guard, to wield against the Grinth,' he said, eyeing the long blade, 'and yet it's never even seen battle. Finally, today it will.' He looked at Sill. 'Do what you need to do,' he told her. 'No Grinth will stand upon this wall whilst I yet live.'

'What do you want me to do?' Raffin asked.

'Just hold my hand,' Sill said, 'and don't talk.'

Raffin gave her a knowing smile as if to say, *You should know that's harder than it sounds,* but he was no longer the boy she had grown up with and he did as instructed, leaving the words unsaid.

When his hand entered hers, Sill felt another surge of power run through her, as though she was bolstered by his touch. She could feel everything now: the rough stone of the age-old wall and Fort; the cold of the snow on the tips of the mountains; the fury of the Grinth, and the fortitude of the men of The Guard. She could feel Raffin's deep hurt and General Venth's fearlessness, as he descended the spiral steps that led to his fate, whatever it may be. She could also feel the *serethen* gates begin to crack and splinter as the Grinth continued to break their bodies against it. *They're not going to hold*, she thought, *I need to hurry.* Going deeper within herself, she let her power spread further across the land, until it touched the icy cascade of the Frosty Falls. *No, that's not the way. I need to find Kallem.* She concentrated on the feeling that was Kallem. On his protectiveness, his loneliness. *There you are!* But he was not alone. Tamarellin was with him, too. And so was the Grinth Queen. Her presence caused a knot in Sill's stomach that made her wince; in sickness and in pain. She felt Raffin's grasp tighten but still he did not speak or disturb her from her purpose. She wished she could affect the Queen directly, but her connection was with the land and for the land the harm had been far more grievous. The Queen was like a wound, cut deep into the heart of the mountain that had suffered her evil for far too long. It was as though the mountain itself was corroding away, bleeding from the inside; hollowed and harrowed and starving. Conversely, the sensation she felt from Kallem and Tamarellin was much fainter. They were both alive but only barely. And there was another human there, too: *Zyan*. But not as she had known him. *Sill, is that you?* The little voice inside her head startled her until she realised it was Tamarellin's.

Yes, she said, *it's me.*

Where are you?

I'm still at the Fort. Upon mentioning the Fort she became absently aware that the Grinth had already managed to breach the gates below and were spilling through into the courtyard to clash with the swords of The Guard. But that wasn't her focus. Her focus was on Kallem, the Queen, and the faint voice of Tamarellin.

Can you help us?

There was a desperation in Tamarellin's voice that made the knot inside her twist and tighten. *Not without hurting you,* she told him truthfully.

Then you must, he said quickly. *You must kill the Queen.*

Sill knew he was right. This had been her plan, after all: to kill the Queen before any more lives were lost. But not like this, not whilst harming her friends. *I can't,* she thought. *I can't kill them.* After all Kallem had done for her, was this how she would repay him? *Is that what you meant? When you said I never promised to protect you?* Had Kallem somehow known it would come to this?

Please, Sill, Tamarellin pleaded weakly. *You must.*

A surge of power pulsed angrily through her. *Why?* she thought. *Why does it always have to be like this!* People were already dying around her and she knew she could not delay any longer. The knot inside her tightened again, squeezing fresh tears from her eyes. *I'm sorry!* she said bitterly. *I'm sorry for everything!* When she focussed her power on the mountain it rumbled, almost involuntarily, as though it was crying out for her to end its long suffering. She concentrated harder, finally letting the power escape her, pouring everything she had into the brittle heart of the mountain. The mountain shook, its ageless rock crumbling at her touch. With its foundation broken, it was only a matter of time now before it would collapse, crushing everything within.

Please get out if you can, Sill told Tamarellin, but there was no response from the hawk and just like that her power was spent. There was no telling whether any of them were even alive anymore.

'Whatever you did, it worked.' The General's voice forced her eyes open and she looked up to find him kneeling beside her. She felt Raffin's hand beneath her head and realised she must have fallen.

'Did I collapse again?' she asked the General, confused, but he only grinned.

'You did it, Sill, look!' Raffin said, and as they helped her to stand, she let them lead her to the parapet, so she could look out over the land. The sight was astonishing. Everywhere, Grinth lay dead. Men of The Guard were busy slaying those that still yet lived but the remaining Grinth were few and running about, almost aimlessly, as though they had lost the means or the motivation to fight.

I did all this? Sill turned away, clung to Raffin, and cried for the world that had suffered so much. Nothing would ever be the same again. And neither would she.

Epilogue

Artell stood atop the precipice, looking down on the world. Gone was the weariness of the climb, replaced instead by a numbness, an emptiness, so deep, it could fill up the Inner Lands several times over.

It's killing me, she thought. *I have to let go.* But she could not. Even up here, where life still thrived.

Below the place she now stood, red, rocky earth gave way to broad stretches of fertile land, rich with green grasses and yellow, sun-touched flowers that rose up proudly towards the vast, open skies. Through one of the grasslands, a large family of mammals moved slowly and gracefully, occasionally stopping and stooping to graze on the abundant food at their feet.

Artell sighed. *Why could I not have been born one of them?* she thought. *Life would have been much simpler.*

It was not the wildlife she came here for, though. Beyond their forests and grasslands, beyond the hills of sand and the winding rivers, lay the biggest body of water she could ever have imagined. From this distance, the colour of the water was a deeper shade of blue than that of the sky and shone with a radiance borrowed from the sun. The water stretched beyond what her vision was capable of seeing.

Is this the edge of the world? she wondered. *No*, she told herself, *it's just a very big lake.* She wondered if somewhere, leagues away, somebody like her was staring out over the other side. *No*, she thought again. *There is nobody else*, and she brushed aside the white lock that had again fallen to cover her eyes. She no longer minded the white hair and had stopped tying it back. Instead of being a reminder of her pain, she now used it to remember a happier time. *When things were simpler... when I wasn't so alone.*

It seemed like such a long time ago. *If we'd only been braver*, she thought, looking out over the Outer Lands. *We might have come here long ago, before it was too late.*

Her people had made themselves comfortable enough on this side of the mountain, already beginning to construct homes from felled trees that the men had somehow endeavoured to haul up from the surrounding vales. *If only we were as good at travelling as we are at settling. Must we always live in fear?* There was no sign of the Grinth here and surely their reach couldn't stretch beyond the water. *Not yet*, she reminded herself. They had thought themselves safe in the Inner Lands, too.

Artell had kept herself busy, trying to re-create the vegetable and herb gardens she had nurtured in Hillock, and teach the youngsters how to tend to all the different plants. 'It won't be easy to maintain here,' she had told them. 'It doesn't rain enough.' But nobody really cared so long as they were safe. That was all that mattered to most of them. *Why should I want more?* she thought. *I'm one of the lucky ones.*

As she was about to turn away, a high-pitched *keeeeeeee* caught her attention, and a brown hawk swept over above, for a second blotting out the sun. The hawk glided down and, with some heavy flapping of its wings, landed awkwardly on a nearby rock. It shifted its feet to look at her, tilting its head to the side as though curious at what she might be.

'Even you haven't survived unscathed, have you?' Artell said, looking at the hawk's missing feathers.

You are his mother, a voice said suddenly.

'What?' Artell spun around, not expecting anyone else to be here. But there was nobody else around. Just the brown hawk, staring at her.

You do not remember, the voice said.

Except it wasn't a *voice* as such, more like a sound inside her head. *I'm going mad*, she thought. *I have to stop this, I have to let him go.*

No, you do not, the voice said.

She looked at the hawk. 'Is that you?' she asked, incredulous. *What is happening to me?*

Yes, the hawk said in her head. *Why is everybody always so surprised? You do not remember,* it said again and she wondered if it was referring to *her* or just *people*.

'I'm sorry,' Artell said, though she knew it sounded ridiculous. 'What do you mean, *I don't*? I don't have to let go?' *Am I just hearing what I want to hear?*

No, the hawk said. *My name is Tamarellin. I came to tell you: he lives.*

The End

THE INNER LANDS BOOK 2

Dark Tidings

Five years have passed and tensions are mounting as the people of the Inner Lands grow tired of being cooped up in the claustrophobic caves of Rydan Fort. The Guard's stoic service is also beginning to strain, and incidents of violence are breaking out. Kallem has returned but his injuries, both physical and psychological, have left him scarred and broken. Artell is making plans to leave the Inner Lands in search of new homes, and General Venth seems to be hiding something from them all. Only Sill is truly happy in this new life; her relationship with Raffin and others providing her with the closest semblance she's ever had of a real family.

But something's still not right, and as everything starts to unravel, the people of the Inner Lands, their relationships and their lives, will be pushed to new limits, even more unbearable than before. Will anyone survive the hardships of the Inner Lands?

Review this book!

If you enjoyed this book, please review it on Amazon.
New authors rely heavily on positive reviews
for their books to be seen. After all,
a writer is nothing without a reader.

You can follow A. J. Austin,
or even connect with him on:
Twitter: @author_austin
Facebook: theinnerlands
Website: www.theinnerlands.wordpress.com

Printed in Great Britain
by Amazon